"A New Queen of Er
—*Romantic*

Praise for **BLO(**

2007 National Readers' Choice Award Winner for Erotic Romance

"A blazing path into forbidden dreams . . ."
—*Romantic Times BOOKreviews*

"Ms. Page weaves an erotic and suspenseful tale that . . . puts you on a sexual roller coaster and doesn't let you off . . . If you're a lover of vampire romance, curl up on a cold winter night with *Blood Red* to warm your heart!" —*Just Erotic Romance Reviews* (Gold Star Award)

"An erotically charged tale . . . a wonderful action-packed story that combines suspense, intrigue, horror, bondage and yes, a whole lot of sex."
—*Coffee Time Romance*

Praise for **BLOOD ROSE**

"Page's *Blood Rose* has scorching love scenes to make you sweat and an intriguing plot to hold it all together."
—*New York Times* best-selling author Hannah Howell

"*Blood Rose* is an action-packed, sexy paranormal over-flowing with suspense, horror and romance. Sharon Page is a master of the ménage—prepare to be seduced!"
—Kathryn Smith, *USA Today* best-selling author

"The female protagonist is completely believable, and the two vampire-slaying heroes . . . are simply hot! This is a thoroughly entertaining read."
—*Romantic Times*

"Buffy the Vampire Slayer meets Regency England! Two sexy, to-die-for heroes, a courageous heroine, and a luscious ménage make *Blood Rose* a sinful treat."
—Jennifer Ashley, *USA Today* best-selling author

"A chilling tale of vampires with loads of suspense and intrigue combined with searing erotic heat . . . the magic of pure sexual steam that can only mean one thing—it's another winner from Sharon Page!"
—Renee Bernard, *USA Today* best-selling author

"Intriguing paranormal romance along the same lines of Laurell K. Hamilton's early work . . . magic, mischief, and ménages."
—Fresh Fiction

Praise for **SIN**

2006 National Readers' Choice Award Winner for Erotic Romance

"How do you have an orgasm without sex? Read *Sin* by Sharon Page! . . . Thoroughly wicked, totally wild, utterly wanton and very witty in its execution, *Sin* is the ultimate indulgence."
—*Just Erotic Romance Reviews* (Gold Star Award)

"Strong, character-driven romance . . . extremely sensual and erotic."
—*Romantic Times BOOKreviews*

"Sinfully delicious. Sharon Page is a pure pleasure to read."
—Sunny, *New York Times* best-selling author of *Over the Moon* (anthology) and *Mona Lisa Awakening*

"Sharon Page blends history, emotion, and hot, hot, hot sex within an amazing love story. Blazing erotica!"
—Kathryn Smith, *USA Today* best-selling author

"An erotic page turner that must be read only in an air conditioned room as the book is hot hot hot . . . Sharon Page is now on my 'must be read' list."
—*Romance Junkies*

Praise for **BLACK SILK**

RT TOP PICK 4 ½ Stars: "This wonderful, well-written Regency has emotion, blindingly hot sex, complicated characters, and a surprise ending."
—*Romantic Times BOOKreviews*

"I can sum this novel up in one word: wow! . . . Not only were the encounters burn-your-fingers-hot but also emotional and romantic." Gold Star Award!
—*Just Erotic Romance Reviews*

Praise for **HOT SILK**

"With an interesting plot, likable characters, suspense, sexual adventure, and romance, this story satisfies."
—*Romantic Times BOOKreviews*

"A delightfully sensual story of love . . . Outstanding read!"
—*Coffee Time Romance*

Blood Deep

SHARON PAGE

APHRODISIA

KENSINGTON PUBLISHING CORP.

http://www.kensingtonbooks.com

APHRODISIA BOOKS are published by

Kensington Publishing Corp.
119 West 40th Street
New York, NY 10018

ISBN-13: 978-0-7582-2879-6
ISBN-10: 0-7582-2879-1

First Trade Paperback Printing: June 2009

10 9 8 7 6 5 4 3 2 1

Printed in the United States of America

Blood Deep

Prologue

Magic

London
April 1807

Lord Sebastien de Wynter was bound to the bed, his arms and legs spread wide. A white sheet lay over the ridge of his erection. Four dark-haired courtesans smothered him with kisses— one hungrily mashed her lips to his, one licked circles around the root of his cock, a third leaned over his chest and suckled his nipples. The last flicked her tongue around the toes of Sebastien's right foot.

Zayan smiled at his friend's long, fierce moans. He saw Sebastien thrash in pleasure against the ropes binding him. Good. It was what Zayan needed tonight. It let him forget . . .

"Master?" The woman's soft questioning voice floated to Zayan. She was tied up as Sebastien was, but her ropes held her up against a wall. Weights of beaten gold dangled from clamps at her nipples. He had hung small globes of black iron from hooks he threaded through piercings in her labia. She waited, submissively, for him to take her on the next step.

"I wish to learn, Master. I wish to be trained to serve ye."

2 / Sharon Page

Soft, throaty, hers was an exquisite voice marred only by her country accent.

She expected to be whipped, but he did not want to do that.

He had waited two thousand years for this night.

Slowly, everything in the brothel's large salon—every being, living and undead—took on a red glow. The red shadow crept around them all, perfectly matching each form in the act of writhing, jiggling, and driving toward sexual ecstasy. No one else saw the caressing mantel of red. He did. Brilliant crimson, it was the exotic, vivid color of blood.

It began faintly at first, a light outline. On his courtesan, the glow traced the full curve of her bare breasts, the flare of her wide hips. It burned brighter at the points of her nipples, partly hidden by the metal clamps. It glowed fiercely at the junction of her thighs where the weights dragged at her nether lips.

Zayan dropped his head back and let his hands rest on his thighs, palms up. He lay on a mound of silk cushions, surrounded by courtesans waiting to attend him.

The spoils of war . . .

This had once been his life, two thousand years ago, when he had been a mortal man. To return from battle and be treated like a god. To feast on the most delectable treats—plump grapes, luscious figs, roast meats. And the orgies. Women to feed him succulent food, pour his wine, and pleasure him with their tongues and their scented bodies.

He closed his eyes.

Blood. In his mind, sightless eyes stared at him from pale faces surrounded by a halo of blood. He had seen thousands of blank, lifeless eyes. He had joined in the games his men played with skulls, artfully kicking them back and forth.

He had never thought he would see blind, unseeing eyes on the people he loved.

Do you remember their faces?

A woman's voice. It came from the haze of red that now

filled the room, and gave him the peace and serenity that other men sought from opiates.

This had been the voice that had sung to him as he had surveyed his battlefield and saw his army mowed down as though smote by the gods. Lush and alluring, it had called to him. It had promised him everything he needed to be victorious, and its price had not seemed like a price at the time. . . .

His soul. Immortality. To become undead.

Do you remember the sound of their laughter? Do you even remember their smells as you held them close?

No. He fought every day to remember, but the faces of his children drifted farther away.

Embrace me and I can return them to you. Embrace me and I can give you what you truly need.

A woman waggled her bare bottom in his face. She had a thick ivory wand pushed up inside, and long, luxurious peacock feathers flowed from its base like an exotic tail. Another approached and presented her derriere to his view. She had two candles in her bottom, tied with a white satin ribbon. Another series of ribbons were wound around that one and affixed her candles to her thighs and her waist. The wicks were lit and the molten wax dripped. Some droplets hit her stockings and she squealed. The last courtesan whispered, "I have nothing inside, Master. Won't you fill me?"

The woman with the peacock's tail was toying with her own swollen clit, lazily teasing and playing, obviously highly aroused. But her strokes quickly became more deliberate.

"Patience," he barked. "No climax yet."

"I wish to be stuffed with your magnificent cock," simpered the courtesan who had begged to be filled.

"No, slave. Candles for you."

He grabbed one thick one and slathered it with molten oil. At his command, the other girls gently eased it into the moaning tart's quim.

"Light her candle from yours, my sweet."

And they amused him by trying to transfer the light from one of the two wicks to the long one on the thick white candle, without using their hands. They cheered their success, their faces flushed and strained from prolonging their arousal.

But he would not free them.

He needed them like this.

The red power fed on this heightened sexual need, and it gave him blissful freedom from the agony that now racked his body, the shrieking pain that ripped through his head. Opium hadn't worked for him, but feeding this mystical power did.

"Pleasure me," he commanded the bevy of women. Panting, they kneeled before him. The red mist swirled around him. But before the first prostitute could touch him, her irises turned red. Red fluid poured from her eye and she screamed in horror.

She clawed at her face. The others tried to pull her arms away. Zayan jolted up, grasped her wrists, and dragged her to him. He sent a rush of healing magic through her, but she still screamed and thrashed.

She slumped in his arms. Spittle bubbled at the corner of her mouth.

The red fluid no longer poured from her eyes, and it slowly vanished as though it had never existed.

By the gods, what had happened? He was supposed to take the power into him tonight. It had been promised. For two thousand years he had waited to take the full magnitude of the power the red mist could bestow.

Thank you, a voice mocked him from somewhere inside his mind, and blissfully, the pounding, searing pain lightened in his head.

He felt a sigh rush through his body. When the mist came, it seemed to possess him. It spoke inside him in the way he was able to do with mortals. *Her soul is too scarred to satisfy me long.*

The power had never taken a soul before, but it did not surprise him. He took the blood, and through him the red power consumed the victim's life and soul.

But he felt an odd tightening of his heart as he laid the limp girl gently to the floor. The other courtesans were whimpering, and a crowd was beginning to surround them—other patrons and whores must have heard or sensed the disturbance and were coming to see.

"She just collapsed."

A woman sobbed.

"Was she sick?"

Sebastien, obviously now freed from his bonds, pushed his way through the crowd, his face stricken. He was wild, sensual, but softhearted; he had almost torn one abusive customer limb from limb. Pain touched his silvery green reflective eyes—eyes that fiercely snapped up. "What in blazes happened to her? Did you kill her?"

"He didn't touch her!" one of the courtesans cried.

"She just collapsed."

She had been a favorite of Sebastien's and he lifted her in his arms.

No one spoke of the red fluid.

"Take her to one of the bedchambers," he demanded. Servants rushed to do his bidding, but Sebastien was the one to carry her away.

Zayan straightened. Why this ache around his heart?

Remorse, Zayan, whispered the voice. *If you help me, I can give you what you desire most. You cannot have my power—I cannot give that to you. You did not understand. But I will give you your children and your soul. I will return them both to you as though two thousand years never passed. I can give you heaven on earth. I can give you both peace and love, and you remember, I know, how sweet they were. But you must serve me. The price is your service—for a few more years, until you find the ultimate prize.*

Of course she could not give him the power—he'd been betrayed again by a woman. *I have served you, damn it, when I vowed to serve no one,* he roared in his head. *For that, return my children to me.*

He had been the most feared Roman general. He had carved a brutal swath through the Gauls. He had been legendary—struck a hundred times by killing blows, only to rise again. Then his emperor, his closest friend, and his *wife* had all betrayed him. He had vowed never to serve again—but for the chance at immortality he had broken that vow.

In answer, pain sliced through his skull. Excruciating. He sank to his knees, pain slashing at his body. By the gods, he would drive a stake in his own heart to be free of this.

But he never would be.

He knew it meant the answer was no. The red power would not give him his children back unless he continued to serve. To see his children again, to give them another chance at life, he would have to be a slave.

Mayfair, London
May 1807

She was quite certain she was dying.

To take on the vampire Zayan had been foolish. The impetuous choice of a woman determined to prove she was as tough, resourceful, and fearless as any man. And she had been, Eugenia Bond thought. The vampire had just been stronger.

Zayan had not even been the one to wound her. She had been completely foolhardly. When Zayan had retreated from her, she'd triumphantly believed she could destroy him. She'd surged forward with her stake and another vampire, one named Guillaime, had come out of the shadows of Hyde Park, had wrenched her sharpened bit of wood from her hand, and had attacked her with it.

Just remembering the pain made her weak.

Eugenia stumbled along the streets of Mayfair, keeping to the shadows, seeking one house alone for refuge. Her brother would understand what had happened to her. He would be angry, but he would accept her into his home. She did not know how she could keep moving forward, given her wounds. But she had to. To stop would be to die.

Blood had soaked her gown and was dripping down her arms and legs. She was pulling herself along, clinging to wrought-iron gates and lampposts when she needed support.

Her brother's house was so close. Only another block.

But there must be footpads in the shadows waiting for drunken gentlemen to rob. Would they come out for her?

Coaches clattered by, and several were stopped outside other mansions to unload passengers. Voices milled everywhere. Horses whinnied and shied. Coachlamps and lights at gateposts threw a brilliant flickering glow onto the street. It was a public, crowded place for a vampire to pursue her.

It was not Zayan who was following her, but some younger, lesser vampire who might be stupid enough to let himself be seen.

There. She heard them—stealthy footsteps behind her. She didn't have the strength to turn. All she could do was throw her fear into a headlong plunge forward. The steps sped up behind her into a run.

Thank heaven for the crowd. Even though the dimwitted members of the ton merely gasped in shock at her and stepped back to give her room, it meant her vampire attacker would not spring in front of so many witnesses.

Number 16. Just the sight of the front door and its lion's head knocker made her want to cry in relief. She stumbled up the steps.

"Madam!" cried a young footman in shock as he opened the door, and she promptly fell against him.

"Footpads," she gasped, for his benefit, and that of the servants hurrying forth. Her pompous brother Edward would not want it to be made public that his sister was a vampire hunter. Edward thought her mad. It was only because he knew that vampires were not myth but reality that he had not already locked her into Bedlam.

Boots thundered across the tile floor. She had sagged on her back against the wall, clutching her side. Icy cold swept over her, and her fingers were numb. Dimly, she saw Edward's face. Instead of being livid with fury, he was anguished with fear. "Eugenia. Dear God, what have you done?"

Engineered my own death. She thought the words but couldn't say them. Her strength evaporated then, and the cold claimed her.

She slithered to the ground.

A brilliant light shone upon her, welcoming her, embracing her. In her mind, Eugenia reached out to it. It promised refuge from the cold. It was beautiful to behold, flooding out fear and uncertainty.

"Aunt Eugenia?"

She heard a child's voice from far away.

"Don't die, Aunt!" the girl cried.

Eugenia felt a pressure on her chest. The weight of a young girl's head. *I have no choice,* she wanted to say. *It is my time to go. This battle, I've lost.*

But warmth flooded through her, a heat that took on a greater strength and made the bright, beckoning light fade away. Eugenia was pulled backward, pulled down to the bed on which her body lay, and she slammed back into herself with a jolt.

She forced her eyelids up and saw a girl standing at her bedside.

Miranda. The child was twelve, her golden hair still caught up in braids that did not tame the tempestuous curl. Her skirts skimmed below her knee. The child blinked rapidly, her blue eyes glistening, and tears streaked her cheeks. "Are you . . . all right, Aunt Eugenia? I felt the heat. You aren't going to die now, are you?"

Good heavens, the girl had brought her back to life. She was weak still and could not sit up, but Eugenia felt the beat of her heart grow stronger and faster.

Her niece had pulled her back from the afterlife, and had, well, resurrected her.

She had encountered such strong magic only once before—in the vampire Zayan.

Exhausted by the ordeal of saving her aunt's life, Miranda collapsed at Eugenia's side. Weakly, Eugenia embraced the slim, shaking girl, and she whispered soothing words until Miranda stopped trembling.

"I don't know what I did," Miranda whispered against Eugenia's bosom.

"You saved my life," Eugenia answered softly. "You were a brave and wonderful girl. You are very special, my dear."

She tried to make it sound simple and matter-of-fact for the child, but Eugenia knew it was anything but. Her niece possessed magic that made demons and vampires look like fumbling amateur mesmerists.

Now she knew what her mission must be. What would happen to Miranda as her dear niece grew up with this astonishing magical power? She might belong to the Royal Society for the Investigation of Mysterious Phenomena, but Eugenia knew exactly what the *men* of the Royal Society would want to do—either destroy Miranda or hold her captive to study her. The girl needed to be protected from that. Miranda would need a great deal of help. She must learn to fit into society while keeping this power a secret. And Eugenia knew how great and dangerous a task that was.

"Dear sweet girl," Eugenia whispered, stroking her niece's slender back, "I will take care of you. Always."

1

Captured

From the diary of Miss Miranda Bond
1 March, 1819

There is nothing more exasperating than the sound of a woman in pleasure if that woman is not you and there is very little hope that the woman will ever be you.

It is said, I think, that momentous journeys begin with the smallest impetus. . . . Well, perhaps it has been said only by me, but it sounds very well, so I shall use it as my motto, my mantra, my slogan for the campaign I am about to embark upon.
That cry of pleasure was my impetus.
To save my debt-ridden family, I will race to the windswept moors—to the estate of the mysterious and notorious Lord Blackthorne. Rumors of his strange, erotic tastes abound, but I believe not one of those salacious tales is true. Blackthorne saved my brother's life on the bloody battlefield of Waterloo, and I know him to be a true hero.
It is more than the necessity of saving my family. From

the letters we have exchanged for a precious, glorious year now, I know I love him.

So I must go to him, seduce him, and marry him.

Assuming I do not get lost, robbed, or murdered on the way . . . .

15 March, 1819

"I want to plunge deep inside you, angel. I want to make you scream."

Miranda shut her eyes and felt a shiver of anticipation tumble from her bare nape to her low back. He was here, again, hidden in the shadows behind her. His voice was purely erotic—the sound of it low and deep, rich and sexual. Completely male—both lusty and unapologetic.

It isn't real. It is a dream, Miranda, her inner thoughts warned.

How could she know that? She was part of the dream—lost in it—but somehow she knew it was just a fantasy, and that if she forced her eyes to open, this exquisite moment would disappear.

His large hand settled on her neck. Skin-to-skin. No gloves. She was feeling a slightly roughened, long-fingered gentleman's palm caressing her nape.

To have a man's bare hand touch her flesh? It was exotic. Forbidden. Fire sizzled down her spine.

Miranda arched her back and daringly pressed her derriere against the man standing behind her.

Proper ladies did not do such things.

But the whole point was she could not be a proper lady anymore.

Tall. She knew he was tall. She couldn't see him, but she could sense his head above hers. His long hair hung loose, and silky strands teased her skin above her bodice. She couldn't hear him breathe, and when he didn't speak, there was no sound at all.

She was staring into a cheval mirror, seeing nothing but her own reflection and the darkness surrounding her. She could never see him at first. Slowly, her dream world would reveal him to her.

His finger lazily drew circles on the back of her neck. "Do you want me deep in you, angel?" His voice held a wry, teasing note. "I can't enter you—unless you tell me 'yes.' "

Something hard—and thick—poked against her rump.

She knew what it was. Each night her dreams had become more daring. Last night, her last night spent in her own bed before leaving her home, she'd lost her virginity in her dream.

Not in reality, though. And in her dream world she had never seen the face of the man to whom she'd surrendered.

Was he Lord Blackthorne? Did she never see the man in her dreams because she had never seen Blackthorne?

Yet the scandalous, shocking, carnal things he did to her in her dreams felt so real.

Suddenly, her clothes fell away. The weight of gown and skirts simply dropped to the floor, though no hand had unfastened them. Her corset unlaced by itself, compelled by the magic in her dream.

"Y-yes." She spoke on a tremble, her voice filled with passion, nerves, and frustration. "I want you inside."

His hand skimmed along the round curve of her rump to cup the underside of her thigh. He coaxed her to raise her leg and perch her foot on a silk-cushioned stool. It opened her nether regions to his hands, and his fingers invaded.

She was so wet, drenched with juices.

"This is how I like you, angel. Slick and wet and open for me."

He never used her name. But she was certain she knew his—

that her fantasy was indeed Lawrence Adrian Phillip South-wick, the Earl of Blackthorne.

Miranda tensed, then moaned with delight as he opened her wider. All she could think of was his fingers: two inside her, spreading her open; then three—impossibly, he slid three fingers deep into her core, and flicked his thumb back and forth over the most sensitive spot at the junction of her nether lips.

"You belong to me, love."

She did. From the moment she had opened his first letter, she had.

"You belong to me," she said in return; though in her dreams, she took action more than she spoke. She did things like saucily turn to try to see him while she licked her lips. "And I want you deep."

She couldn't see him. Darkness slanted over his face. All she could see was his wide chest—all ridged muscle and hard nipples and rippling skin. Then he gripped her hair, yanked it free from her pins, wound the length of it around his wrist. Holding her like his captive, he surged into her.

It felt so good. Good enough to melt her like chocolate in the sun.

How she did scream. And, oh, but he did go deep. Right to her womb, and delicious agony spiraled through her. How could it feel so good when it made her sob and whimper and howl?

But the very exquisite agony of it was so . . . addictive.

He'd vowed to make her scream, and he did. With his hard thrusts, with the ruthless lunge of his groin against hers, with his low, ragged growls and the harsh rush of his breath against her ear. Her bottom slapped against him, her cheeks shimmering with each bounce. Her breasts danced in front of her—until he clasped them and tugged on her nipples, twisting them until she begged him to stop . . .

Then begged for more.

"Come." He said it as a command. She was at the precipice, wound up like a spring, like a keg of gunpowder awaiting the sizzle of the fuse. And on that word, she burst.

Sheer pleasure took command, and all she could do was surrender her body to the intense, wonderful wash of it. She cried out, cried out to heaven above, let her head fall forward and back, until she was dizzy with the ecstasy.

He held her through her wild dance, chuckling gently by her ear. Then the pulses of her wet quim began to ease and she could finally drag in a desperate breath. Sweat drenched her.

Something cold touched her skin.

Cool and sharp, something that felt like a knife's blade ran along the side of her neck, from her jaw to the lobe of her ear.

Miranda froze in horror. It was not a knife. The flash of white in the mirror stole her breath.

Fangs lapped over Blackthorne's lips. She could not see his mouth—it was too dark, but moonlight glimmered on his two long, curved teeth, like those on a wolf. It wasn't possible.

But on some nights she had dreamed of demons chasing her; she'd imagined pounding feet and animal-like growls, and powerful hands reaching for her.

Oh God, she was sliding into one of those dreams. She shook helplessly. She didn't want to dream of demons now. She wanted this luxurious erotic dream. For one night, she wanted to be free of fear.

She blinked and his fangs were gone.

"Not tonight, my love," he murmured. "It is not the night to make you mine. Not yet."

Make you mine. But what did he mean about biting? The shadows seemed to be swallowing the air around her. She wanted to wake up. It wasn't real—it was just a dream. But she could smell her sweat and his. The tangy aroma of his seed rose from between her thighs. She felt damp, sticky, and sore. All those sensations seemed more real than a pinch to her arm.

How could it feel so real when she was asleep?

The window flew wide on a clatter of glass panes and creaking wooden frame. "Goodness!" She almost jumped out of her skin. Darkness rushed inside as though the night air was pouring into the room.

No, not darkness. In her dream, everything she saw seemed distorted and confused. She didn't even know what room she was in. She now saw the walls surrounding her were stone. Embroidered tapestries hung upon them. Could she be dreaming of Blackthorne's castle?

A man now stood in front of the window, inside the room. Another naked man with golden hair that fell past his shoulders. He was erect, ready to take her.

Her dream lover held her shoulders and turned her to face the man who had—who had just flown in through the window.

His golden hair flew around him, shielding his face. His voice seemed to thrum in her blood. "Until you learn about the power of three, you are in mortal danger, Miss Bond."

She was afraid now. *Wake up. Wake up!* Miranda shouted it in her head, but she was trapped in the shadowed room, imprisoned by the hands on her shoulders.

"What is the power of three?" she demanded. She yelled it, hoping it would snap her free of her dream. Dreamers never died, did they? They fell but never reached the ground. They might be struck, or shot, or be drowning, but they woke before the end.

Didn't they?

A sharp, sudden pain ripped into her neck. Screams filled the room and flew out into the night. The screams belonged to her. She could see her body and realized she was floating in the top of the room, just below the ceiling. Her arms and legs were stretched wide, her hair streamed back like a cape, and she coasted on the cool air wafting in through the window.

But she was looking down on herself below, as though she

were soaring over her body. The golden-haired man prowled toward her below. Her mouth was wide open in a shriek, but she could hear no sound. His erection wobbled in front of him, reflecting moonlight. Naked, defined by the hard bulges and curves of solid muscle, his body seemed to glow blue-white within the shadows.

He tipped his head up and fangs shot out of his mouth.

He bent to her neck and she felt a dull ripple of pain as she saw his canines penetrate her neck below. Air currents began to spin her. She slowly circled and watched as two demons drank the blood from her body, gulping hungrily, making low moans of appreciation.

Wake up. Wake up.

She was sinking back to her body now, losing blood and growing weak. If she didn't wake up, she would die—

The golden-haired man lifted from her neck. "Now, angel, we take your power. And make you ours for eternity."

"We know what you are, Miranda," the other man murmured behind her. "A witch."

On a fierce scream, she bolted upright. A heavy fur throw slid down her lap, and the world lurched drastically to the left. Miranda pitched against the side of a moving room but struck softness. A clattering sound, rhythmic but jarring, hammered into her brain. Somewhere, horses gave muffled whinnies.

She was in her carriage, or rather, one of her brother's carriages. Her corset clamped her lungs, dug into her ribs, and prevented her from taking a deep breath. Lace along her neckline itched, her skirts were tangled around her legs, and her feet throbbed hotly in her tightly laced half boots.

She was alive. Alive and alone. And safe.

It had all been a dream. Thank heaven.

"I am not a witch," she shouted aloud to the empty carriage. But she was shaking, despite the fierce way she was hugging herself.

Two weeks ago, she had written down her plan to save her impoverished brother and his wife by racing to Lord Blackthorne and convincing him to marry her. How trivial poverty seemed now.

The day after she'd made her plans, a vampire slayer named James Ryder had come to her brother's house. Like her Aunt Eugenia, Ryder was a member of the Royal Society for the Investigation of Mysterious Phenomena. And once he began to ask her questions, she realized he knew of her special power.

Aunt Eugenia had warned her never to tell anyone—not even the Royal Society. So she had pretended not to understand him and had played a vapor-brained twit until he'd left in frustration.

But Ryder had come upon her in the park.

You are a demon. Or a witch, he'd said. *Only an evil, otherworldly being can possess the power of magic. And as a slayer, it is my sworn duty to destroy you.*

The intense, almost fanatical fire in his blue eyes had terrified her. It certainly proved she wasn't a woman to swoon—she'd never had a better reason to faint. But she'd stayed on her feet, determined to fight for her life. She had blustered that he must be mad, that she knew nothing of magic, and was certainly no witch. And inside, she had been thinking, *I've saved lives. That's all I've ever done.* But after all, how many innocent women had been burned at stakes through history?

The Royal Society believes you must be removed, he'd said coolly. He'd stroked her cheek, and she'd been too horrified to pull away from his touch. *You'll never know when it will happen, love. But I promise it will hurt.* Then he'd slipped away and disappeared in the crowd of the ton that filled the park. Simon and Caroline had caught up with her, and though she'd lied about what happened, she knew they'd sensed her terror.

The Royal Society wanted her dead. She couldn't put her

family at risk. And by staying, she was putting Aunt Eugenia in danger.

Lord Blackthorne was the only one she could turn to. He'd told her—in letters—that he was falling in love with her. She prayed it was true. She prayed that she could go to him and find safety. And through his power and wealth, she could also protect her family.

"Hold hard!"

The coachman was shouting. That was no dream; his furious shout was real. Suddenly, the carriage skidded on the road and the horses screamed in terror.

"What is it?" Miranda cried, clinging to the seat. But over the clatter of the traces, the frightening creaking of the carriage, she did not think anyone would hear.

The wheels seemed to catch in the road and tipped to the right, then swung back over to the left. Men—the coachman, the outriders who thought they were escorting her on her brother's orders—shouted and hollered. A lot of colorful cursing filled the air. But they were going to overturn . . .

There was no way to stop it. Miranda grabbed the seat, but the force of the spill threw her. The other side of the carriage slammed her back and she tumbled around as the carriage went over. Her face hit the frame of the window, stunning her. Had she lost all her teeth? Broken her cheek? Pain shot through her and her stomach churned.

The side of the carriage scraped across the rutted ground as the horses tried to run, dragging the heavy carriage behind them.

Then it stopped.

Miranda let her head fall to rest against the wall. Oh dear God.

She wanted to be sick.

Women were supposed to swoon over far less. But she was going to stay conscious, even if it killed her. Her lower lip stung and she wiped her hand across it. Of course, blood instantly streaked her white muslin glove. She tasted the coppery tang on her tongue.

Someone wrenched open the door that was now above her. Brilliant sunlight and cool air poured in.

"Miss? Are you all right, miss?"

"Yes." And she was. Though she was lying on her back and her feet stuck up in the air. Her skirts had tangled around her legs, her pelisse had wrapped itself around her arms. It was a most undignified situation, and her head ached like blazes.

The coachman flushed red. "Would you allow me to help you out, Miss Bond?"

"I don't see how else I'll get out." Blasted clothes. "What happened?"

His hand came down—he tried to grasp her wrist without actually looking at her. Apparently, he didn't want to be accused of behaving improperly. She sighed, then grasped his hand.

"The horses went mad," he said. "And then, out of nowhere, some sort of creature appeared in front of us. We tried to rein in, but the horses were wild with fear. Then the carriage went over."

"A creature? Do you mean a wolf? A wild dog?"

"No, my lady, it wasn't that." He pulled her upward, and she struggled to gain purchase against a wall or the seat, something to lift her out.

This was certainly an adventure. When had she ever had to hike up her skirts to climb out of an upturned carriage, then slide off the wall, which was now up in the air like the roof?

Her brother's coachman looked mortally embarrassed as he helped her scramble through the door opening. He was a handsome man with coal black hair and flashing eyes, but he was not supposed to be clasping arms around a lady's waist to set her on the ground.

"Thank you," she breathed, to let him know that she didn't care one whit about propriety in the situation.

She and the coachman shared an awkward moment while he gruffly acknowledged her appreciation. The sunlight promised a beautiful day, but the air she sucked in was crisp with the newness of spring, and her shoes were sinking into the muddy road. Fading gold light picked out a scene of madness: of the poor horses, one was on its side and screaming, and the other was fighting the constraint of the traces. Outriders were struggling to free them. The carriage was a battered wreck.

She was lucky to have survived.

That made her more determined to know what had happened. "If it wasn't a wolf or a dog, what was it?"

"It was a massive beast with fangs," the coachman said at the same instant one of the outriders shouted, "It was a vampire!"

"Oh, surely not," she discounted. Had the servants been drinking? She hoped not. And they had not stopped long enough at an inn for the men to have a drink.

It would be expected that she would say such a thing was a foolish superstition. But she knew there really were creatures with fangs that drank human blood and who hunted the English countryside. When she had been very little and Aunt Eugenia told her vampire stories, she had not believed such monsters were real. She'd loved Aunt Eugenia but always had thought her eccentric. She'd thought her aunt just liked to scare her.

Now she knew monsters and demons existed.

"It was a man," one of the outriders insisted. "A giant of a man, with fangs."

"Blow it," growled the coachman. "I doubt we can set this thing to rights. What are we to do?"

Miranda wrapped her arms around herself. A cold wind cut through her pelisse, and she still throbbed with pain all over.

"The village of Little Darkling is yonder." Her coachman

pointed. Through the budding trees of a small forest she could see muddy fields, a few stone farmhouses and stables, then a huddle of buildings. Sunlight glinted on paned windows and smoke curled from chimneys—the little cottages looked rather enticing.

"Let us walk, then," she suggested. It would be a slog in the mud and would take hours. Clouds rolled swiftly over the sun. A few snowflakes wafted down, and the dampness seemed to rush through her skin. Her beautiful day was vanishing. But what choice did the have?

Before any of the men could answer, a low growl rolled out of the stretch of dark woods that separated them from the warm, inviting homes. Branches cracked, leaves twitched, but Miranda could not see a thing. Snowflakes thickened and swirled in wild spirals. Miranda gasped as the coachman drew out his pistol. "Get back, my lady," he cried.

A silvery shape exploded out of the shadows—a wolf with dark fur and long legs that swallowed up the ground as he tore toward them. The animal's jaws parted. Arm rock steady, the coachman took aim, but Miranda cried, "No!"

Like a streak of lightning, the wolf shot past.

"Heavens," she gasped. "Something frightened it. It was not running to attack us, it was running for its life!"

The coachman looked at her as though she was mad. But she ignored that; it was not uncommon for a man to roll his eyes at any woman who voiced an opinion.

But what had spooked the wolf?

Her outriders, two staunch men who had served her family for years, crossed themselves. "I told yer," said one, who held the horses by the reins, "I'm not going that way. Not through those woods."

But the other, holding a pistol of his own, had crept ahead a few yards along the narrow road. "It's likely another wolf. A bigger one," he shouted back.

"It makes no sense," Miranda muttered. "Wolves are nocturnal." Aunt Eugenia had told her of the eerie sounds of them in the Carpathians, and she knew their howls from her family's country home.

Before her eyes, the dark shadows of the forest seemed to surge out of the trees and rush down the road. Thick blackness swarmed around the man and he turned to run. He howled in sheer terror. It was as though the gloom of the forest had swallowed him whole. Miranda cried out, and the men stood transfixed in shock. A shot exploded. Her coachman had fired, and the flare of powder blinded her.

Blinking, she focused again on the road.

It was empty. The man had vanished.

"No, that's not possible." She swung around on the coachman. "We must find him. He must have been dragged off the road—"

"We can't kill a vampire with a pistol shot."

"It's not a vampire. This is daylight, for heaven's sake! Vampires cannot come out in sunlight." Or so Aunt Eugenia had told her.

The horses reared, tossed their heads, and hooves flailed. The other outrider had to release the reins; the horses were almost berserk. Then, hooves pounding and throwing up muck, the animals ran.

"They sense it!" The coachman grabbed her arm and pushed her ahead of him. "Run, miss!"

Run? If it was a wolf or a wild dog, she couldn't outrun an animal like that. And an animal would scent her . . .

A growl sounded right behind her. Behind her, in the grass, when she had seen nothing go past. Miranda hauled up her hems and stumbled through the mud, away from the forest.

Wasn't running the worst possible thing to do? Wasn't it madness to run?

Wind rushed in her ears, but she didn't think it really was

the wind—it was her fear, the race of her blood. She knew something was running behind her. She just . . . knew.

Was it her coachman with his weapon, or something else?

Black clouds slid across the sun like fingers clutching at the light, and then she was plunged into complete darkness. All light had been extinguished like a candle blown out with a puff of air. There was no sunlight at all—in the middle of the day.

She stopped, stunned, her chest heaving.

All her landmarks were gone. The line of trees, the dip of the fields, the waving heather—it was all just a sea of formless shadow.

Miranda turned in a helpless circle, afraid to take a step.

The ground crunched, and she knew that whatever was chasing her had made the sound deliberately. It was playing with her.

And it was working. She was paralyzed with terror as she heard a soft crack, then the relentless thud of footsteps. She spun around but could see nothing but shadowed trees and rippling grass.

There had to be a way out, or some weapon she could use. Even her reticule would be something, but it lay in the overturned carriage.

Where were her coachman and the other outrider? Had they fled for their lives and left her? When the coachman had pushed her to run, he looked as if the very devil himself was about the drag them to a fiery hell.

Another growl, closer now.

She didn't understand why the animal didn't spring. It could take her to the ground and tear her apart. Why did it wait? She wished she had food in her hand, something to throw as far away from her as she could.

"But that would not help, my love," a deep masculine voice growled. "For you are the only delectable treat that tempts me."

A man! Where? But not a savior. She knew that from the

hungry, predatory sound of his voice, from the words he'd chosen. Had he been the thing chasing her?

Realization froze her to the spot. She had not spoken aloud. He had answered words she'd uttered only in her head.

The shadows stirred and he stepped forward; her eyes had grown accustomed to the dark, so she could see him.

He was *huge*. He stood far taller than her—far, far taller— and he was surrounded by a dark cape that whipped in the wind. She realized that his hair was waist length and it danced around his chiseled face. Something white glinted at her—

Long, evil-looking fangs, just like in her dream.

Suddenly, strong hands wrapped around her wrists. A guttural laugh echoed by her ear.

He'd been several feet away from her and now he was gripping her, and she hadn't seen him move.

Any sensible woman would faint. Why go to death conscious? But Miranda realized she couldn't let herself take that way out.

Powerful arms swept her up, and she kicked and scratched and screamed. A scent enveloped her along with the strong arms. Sweet and rich, as alluring as chocolate. Primal and musky and unbearably mesmerizing too. Somehow the man's smell made her relax and tense at the same time.

"Quiet. I won't hurt you. In fact, it's my need, pretty little lass, to do the opposite." His husky, baritone voice spoke English in a sensual accent.

He pulled her closer to him, squashing her breasts against his wide, hard chest. She'd never been so close to a man, except in her dream world. She'd never been held like this. A bit of cloud slid away from the sun and light slanted over his face.

His cheek glowed as though it had caught fire. Smoke spiraled off his skin.

She almost gagged on the smell of burning flesh.

A man with fangs, one who burned in sunlight. A vampire.

His full, seductive mouth curved into a grimace of pain, then the faint bit of light disappeared.

"What are you?" she managed. But her traitorous body did not want to struggle in his arms. His scent made her . . . weak. Her skin felt warm, and her head felt too dizzy. But she had to break free, and she forced her legs to thrash wildly.

"Stop. I am Zayan," he growled by her ear. That rumble of sound was not like an animal, but like the way she'd heard her brother Simon growl to his new wife, Caroline. Lustful. Hot. Aroused.

She should be afraid. But her nipples hardened, and her breasts lifted against the soft brush of her chemise. Between her thighs, she ached and got hot and sticky, the way she did when she had her dreams.

She must be going mad. Or she was trapped in another dream. In the last dream, she'd been dying!

She would break free of this nightmare. This was enough. Miranda lashed out. Her boot flailed wildly and made contact with his hip with a thud that she felt through her shin. She hammered her fists against his arms, writhed, and twisted against his grip.

And nothing worked. He gazed down at her with amusement, those terrifying fangs exposed by his smile. His eyes were the dark silvery gray of the snowy sky. They held her like a hypnotist's twirling silver watch.

A thunderous roar exploded from the woods, and a brilliant red light exploded outward from inside it. The light scattered into winking stars and disappeared, but out of its core, another man appeared. As large as the one who still held her. His hair was as long and black but bore a brilliant silvery white streak within it. He, too, had fangs.

"Bloody hell, it's daylight." This man's hands were bare, and smoke plumed from the backs of them. "Your brilliant plan was to escape our prison into the bloody middle of the day?"

Wake up. Wake up, Miranda! But she was awake.

"I've cast darkness around the sun, but it will fade soon—" Zayan broke off and muttered a curse. A particularly coarse one.

Clamped to his body, Miranda twisted to look.

A mass of snowflakes swirled over the grass to the side, and they looked as red as blood. Then the fluttering flakes joined, forming a shape. It grew legs, a thick body, a long neck, and a giant head. A dragon.

Impossible.

Whatever it was, it ran toward her and the . . . the vampires.

Stay.

She heard Zayan's voice in her head, and though she tried to force her limbs to move, they would not.

The ground shook as the red dragon charged at them, and though she blinked a dozen times, the monster did not vanish. Wide blood-red wings seemed to hang in the air. Giant legs swallowed up the ground as it half-ran, half-flew at them. An enormous, serpent-like head leaned forward, leading the massive body.

Flames tore out of the dragon's mouth. Bracken caught fire, flared, and became instant ash. Miranda meant to scream, but it caught in her throat, choking her.

The other vampire muttered, "Bloody Christ Jesus." He stalked toward the beast and held up his hand. Flames launched from the slavering jaws and hit the vampire's hand. Then disappeared.

The dragon gave an unearthly shriek and it sounded like a cry of frustration. Calmly, wearing a glare of impatience, the vampire formed a ball of pale blue light between his hands.

That was most definitely not possible. But Miranda was watching it happen.

The vampire shot his whirling ball of blue light at the snowflake dragon. An explosion shook the ground and the dragon fell. The beast's body disappeared as it hit the waving fronds of heather.

It was gone.

That, she heard Zayan say, *proved far too easy.*

Too easy?

We must return to your carriage. And with that, he released her.

"How ridiculous." Suddenly, her arms were free and she waved them in fury. For anger was better than giving in to shock and fainting dead away in the road. "I am not taking you within my carriage. And I cannot—it's lying broken on the road and the horses are gone."

Intriguing. You are not begging for your life. You are not crying or quivering in fear.

Could Zayan not hear the fevered beat of her heart? Aunt Eugenia said vampires could hear heartbeats. And could smell blood. "I doubt either would do me any good," she exclaimed. "You'd laugh if I begged and hurt me even if I cried."

Zayan grinned at the other vampire. *A courageous woman. I have met so few truly brave women. Most will fight for their lives with every weapon they possess.* Then he looked her over in the most . . . lecherous, scandalous, audacious way.

She did not want to hear his voice in her head. "Speak in words! Speak out loud! I do not even think you really exist. I'm dreaming!"

Hold out your arm, Zayan commanded. Her arm, entirely against her will, extended at his wish. The other vampire cocked his head, as though laughing at her. Zayan bent over her wrist.

He *licked* her.

Flicked his tongue along her skin.

He *bit* her.

She wrenched her arm, fearing that his teeth would rip her skin open, but he let her go.

Dreams might bite, angel, but that little jolt of pain would awaken a dreamer. Now, my dear, we need refuge or the sun-light will burn us to ash.

"Then take the carriage, for all the good it will do you." She pointed toward where her carriage was. She could see the wounds on her wrist. Two puncture marks showed just below her veins. A vampire's bite, exactly as Eugenia had described.

"And what do you intend to do, angel?" The other vampire asked.

She wouldn't answer that.

"Ah, you plan to walk to the village." Zayan tilted his head and the wind threw his hair behind him. Long, wavy, it looked like the style of the rakish and handsome Charles II. "I would not advise it. There are wolves out, and they are excited by the scent of magic in the air."

The scent of *magic*? But she shivered—he was correct. She smelled something in the air—an exotic richness, a breathtaking scent that was alluring and indescribable.

The other vampire, the one with the streak of silver in his hair, strode forward. "You are to come with us, sweeting."

"I won't."

"I can force you to come with me. I can control your mind, and you will obediently place one foot before the other and follow me."

"Then do that," she snapped, "because I won't go willingly."

"I am glad, fair lady, that yours is the first carriage we've encountered. But I have not the time to do battles with words."

This vampire also wore a cape, one of black velvet, trimmed in a thick, luxurious fur of gray and white. Wolf fur. A jeweled clasp held it.

He tossed her over his shoulder, his hand clamped on her bottom to hold her in place. He squeezed her rump through her skirts.

"Put me down!"

"Let us take a look at your carriage first."

They strode over, and though she kicked and struggled, she could not break free. She could not even see the wreck of the carriage, though she felt a perverse sense of satisfaction when the vampires paused, and the one holding her groaned.

She remembered what it had looked like. Jagged shards of once gleaming wood had jutted up into the air. The door had been hanging off. Bits of one wheel were strewn about.

She could also smell the vampires' burning skin.

The vampire who held her snapped his fingers. At once, she heard the horses neigh, then the sloppy sound of hooves fighting through the mud. Within moments, the horses had returned, tossing their heads.

"Gentle," the vampire murmured, holding up his hand. Manes waved in the snow-laden air, but the animals stopped prancing and fussing, then lowered their heads.

Docile fools, she thought.

Zayan waved his hand in a graceful circle. He conjured a vivid purple light that twined around his arm like a snake.

The light spun through the air and hit the carriage, where it seemed to rain down like soft rose petals. All she could see was a lovely violet glow.

As in the fairy tale *Cinderella,* a carriage materialized before her eyes—but not from a pumpkin and mice, from the wreckage of Simon's best traveling coach. She blinked hard. As her lids lifted, she discovered the horses in their traces.

She twisted in the grasp of the vampire in the wolf's cloak. "What did you do?"

"It would be much better for you to travel in comfort," Zayan answered.

"That's not what I mean. You can't just wave your hand and have a broken carriage leap back onto its wheels, fixed and perfect! It's not possible."

"That is the power of magic."

The vampire holding her began to stride to the magically repaired carriage. "Enough talk. We need refuge from the light." The hand massaged her derriere in the most scandalous way. Unwanted heat rushed through her.

She should be terrified, not growing hot. Not breathing in this . . . aroused way.

Vampires, Aunt Eugenia had warned, could control a woman's mind. With ease, apparently. And they possessed an allure no woman had to resist, a "glamour" that drew women to them and made them willing victims, a power that was supposed to be the work of the devil.

Miranda had to find every ounce of strength to fight.

The vampire patted her derriere. "I hunger, sweeting. I have appetites that have been denied too long."

"Yes, angel." Zayan laughed. He gave the same naughty chuckle as the unseen man in her dreams. "We both hunger."

2

Labyrinth

The Chamber of the Scholomance
875 A.D.

Impossible to believe he was here, that he now stood inside the labyrinth that led to the Chamber of the Scholomance. As his father had wished, he had been selected to be an apprentice to Lucifer. He would learn the timeless magic. He would learn to control the winds, the rain, to summon powerful bolts of lightning or baking heat. He would know all the mysteries of nature, alchemy, and death.

Candles burned in a ring on the dirt floor. He dropped to his knees and let his head fall forward in the pose of a penitent man. Feminine laughter rippled over him in response.

The woman who waited in the shadows stepped out. She carried a beautifully wrought axe with a sharpened blade, and she was nude. Stars were painted over her nipples. She was entirely shaved of her nether hair. Where the thick bush of her pubic hair should be, a circle had been painted in red blood. Her hair was a rich red—almost the color of flame—and it spilled over her shoulders and down her back in soft, fragrant-smelling curls. When he breathed deeply, all he smelled was the sweet promise of new grass, fresh wildflowers, sun, and birth.

He could not believe, when he smelled her, that she was a demoness.

"Very good," she murmured. "But I wonder if you will remain obedient for long."

"I will," he promised. But rebellion sparked deep in his soul. He was twenty-one—the age when a man is fool enough to grab up a sword and launch a single-handed attack on an army. The demoness laughed again, as though genuinely amused.

She paced gracefully in front of him. Just breathing in her smell made his cock rigid and thick. Already his juices gathered at the tip and leaked down the head. He was also nude, and she could see the response of his body. Her full, dark red lips curved in a smile. "You are very young."

"I am not."

"Your youth is an asset. Do not despair. For it means you will be forever as beautiful as you are now." Humming, she laid her hand on top of his head. She stroked his hair.

His hair was long. It had never been cut. That had been the first clue in his realization that his father had always intended to offer him as an apprentice. He had realized his father had lied. He was not being sent to Lucifer to ensure the Vikings did not capture Wessex and destroy the last English king—the last king who embraced God. His father had plotted his destiny for much longer than that.

His father believed in the God of the Catholic religion, and so he had believed in Lucifer. The devil, his father had said, was the true path to power. Their bloody battles with the Vikings could be won only if they harnessed the powers of darkness—

The demoness moved to him, her breasts swaying. He licked his lips as he watched them bounce from side to side. What did the paint taste like on her nipples? Would she let him put his lips there? He wanted to. Her breasts were heavy and full. They hung lower than those of the young maidens he had bedded, and they entranced him. Through the thick cape of his hair, he watched them move.

She began to hack at his long hair, sawing through it with the blade. It fell in yard-long piles around him. "It is my duty to name you."

He told her his name, but she shook her head. "You are not that young man anymore." Her lashes were very long and ebony black. She smiled. "You are well endowed."

"I hope that pleases you."

"It does, but I will not be allowed to sample you. Once your head is shaved, you will never be allowed to have sex again."

He jerked and the blade nicked his scalp. Pain shot through him, but he didn't care. "What do you mean? I was told my seed would be precious."

"It will be. But it will not be permitted for you to spill your seed in a woman."

By all that was holy, what did that mean?

The demoness smiled. "Surely, you did not think that you would be accepted without a price?"

"I did not think the price was so high."

Her laughter was throaty and rich. "Only a man would say that." She cocked her head, considering. "I could be persuaded to wait before cutting your hair."

He rose up from his knees until he was standing. She was voluptuous and petite, and she had to tip back her head to meet his eyes.

"What will persuade you?" he asked. He reached out and pinched one of her nipples. The greasy paint let his fingers slide around the hardening tip.

"Would this?" Emboldened, he slid his hand between her hot thighs. Already, her nether lips were slick with her juices. They were like exotic silk to his touch. His cock bucked, and he knew it was dripping with its lust.

He took her hand to his shaft. "Do you like this?"

"Young men. Obsessed only with their cocks." She scraped her nails along his rigid shaft and he moaned at the pleasure and pain. She stroked his hipbone. He had to admit the caress was an arousing sensation. "I would like to touch you, to stroke and savor you, but I know you are thinking only of shoving your erect cock inside me as quickly as you can."

Her words had made it only more important that he bury himself inside. Every breath was bringing him close to release. There was something about the erotic smell of her cunny, of scents he could not describe, but that were feminine and lush and appealing, and that had him on the brink of orgasm.

He threw aside the pretense at being submissive, and he pulled her into his embrace. Fighting and warrior exercises had made him strong. Standing, he could lift her to straddle his cock, and he impaled her on his rigid spike.

She laughed. Her eyes changed to a vivid red, and she rode him until she tore at his neck with her teeth and ravaged his back with her nails. Climax after climax took her, then he surrendered to his orgasm. Laughing, she pulsed her cunny around him, sucking him dry with her muscles. His legs collapsed beneath him and he let them both fall to the ground.

She leapt up to her feet while he was still gasping for breath.

"I will name you Lukos, and your beast shall be the wolf. You shall be a predator, sleek and swift, without mercy. You shall be a beautiful beast, my pet. And you will put behind you your mortal name, your mortal ties. You will give everything up—"

"Including pleasure," he grumbled.

She smiled, eyes narrowed, her thick black lashes batting playfully. "A small price."

"After that bout I know it is a great sacrifice."

"Do not flatter." She waved away his words, then went to a table in the corner of the vaulted chamber. She dipped her blade into a gold dish of hot water. She stroked it along his head. He felt the scrape, the awareness of pain, of sensation. She worked, shearing his hair from his scalp.

"You will lead me there?" he asked. "Through the labyrinth."

"Ah, there is so much you do not know. That is not the way you meet Lucifer."

"How then?"

"You will find out very soon. Now, let me finish."

After his head was shaved to his scalp, she bade him to stand. He lifted his arms as she commanded, and she drew the blade on the skin beneath his arms. She pricked him several times.

He caught his breath as she shaved his chest, then took off the downy line of hair that ran down his abdomen.

"Stay very still," the demoness murmured.

He stood like a statue as she drew the blade along the plane of his pubis to reach the root of his cock. She cooed and stroked his soft member until it swelled again, and his blood rushed into it. The scrape of blade over his skin aroused him, and made him harder than he'd ever been. He held his breath, afraid the slightest twitch would send the sharp edge into his flesh.

He'd always been proud of his thick, rigid organ. The maidens of Wessex all loved it. He wasn't ready to lose it.

She gave him a wicked glance, then licked the head, running her tongue around and around as her hands deftly shaved his nether curls. He watched the hair fall to the ground.

Then he shuddered as she drew the shaving blade over his ballocks. She pulled the skin tight to shave and the pressure chased his balls around in their sac.

With a tap on his buttocks, she urged him to bend over, and she swept the sharp edge around his anus to take away the hair there. She cleaned the blade in the water and even shaved his legs, then finally, his arms. She took off the long golden hairs on his forearms.

"There, you are finished."

She stroked his hard shaft. "And now, your poor sweet organ will no longer be able to play."

He did not believe that. He refused to. He reached for her breast, but she slapped his hand away. She still held the blade, so he jerked back quickly.

"Now you will take me to Lucifer."

She gave him a robe of fine scarlet fabric, sensually soft. "Put this on and get down upon your knees."

His scalp prickled where it had been shaved. His ballocks itched. But he forced himself to ignore the nagging desire to scratch his testicles, to ignore the stinging places where the blade had drawn blood.

"Close your eyes and tip your head back."

A shudder passed over him. A shadow of wariness. But he had lived for this moment, the moment he became one of Lucifer's ten apprentices, and he had to trust.

But his lids opened and he relinquished faith—

He saw the countess's arm move in a smooth arc. The blade penetrated his throat, and her strength drove it through his skin to the bone beneath. He felt a pass of cold, then a spurt of warmth.

Panic flew up like frightened grouse. Blackness swirled in on his vision. He spluttered. He fought to breathe.

She had sliced his throat open.

Her voice sang by his ear. "This, Lukos, is how you meet Lucifer."

Her hands were held together and a strip of her own petticoat was being wound around her wrists to bind her.

Miranda bit her lip, fighting to stay calm, but her chest heaved on a fit of panicked sniffles. The vampire with the white streak in his hair was tying her up. His breath whispered softly over her neck as he meticulously wrapped the cloth around and around her crossed wrists. His breath was surprisingly . . . warm.

The shades were drawn, the carriage lamps were not lit. She sat in the gloom, a prisoner of two otherworldly beasts, trapped in shadow. Trapped in fear. To think she'd been terrified of poverty and the workhouse.

Miranda didn't understand. Why tie her up? They were so strong. Wouldn't they just plunge in their fangs, drain her blood, and leave her dead?

"Not too tight, Lukos. We don't wish to harm her pretty hands."

So the vampire with the white streak in his hair was called Lukos. She had seen her brother's schoolbooks—*Lukos* was the Greek word for "wolf." There were tales she'd heard of men who could transform themselves into wolves. Between the vampire and the werewolf, she would be torn limb from limb.

Wouldn't she?

"Where were you traveling?"

The mesmerizing, silky baritone of the vampire Zayan compelled her to turn to him. Against her will, she drew in a sharp breath at his stunningly handsome face. She could not fight against the need to stare into his silvery, reflective eyes.

Could she break free, throw herself at the carriage door, and fall out? She ran the risk of being run over by the wheels. But wouldn't it be better to die that way than by a vampire's bite? And if she forced the door open, she'd burn the vampires inside.

Zayan's compulsion was pushed aside and another took hold. Lukos. She sensed anger between them—it was like sparks of lightning in the carriage. Fire shot from their glittering eyes at each other. She had seen gentlemen before a duel, struggling to keep rage beneath a restrained and refined exterior. She could sense things about people—their darkest fears, their most primitive emotions, the things they did not say but that they felt deeply. And she could almost taste the hatred between these demons.

"Good plan, but it won't work, sweeting," Lukos growled. "You'd never get the door open. Tell us where you were going."

It was like a command, and inexplicably the words came to her lips. She couldn't understand why they wished to know. "To Lord B—" She stopped, battling the compulsion to speak.

She looked at Zayan again, was drawn to him.

He undid his cloak and let it fall from his shoulders. The thick cape was lined with dark, rich fur—an animal's pelt that was as black as his long, untied hair. His burned skin had now repaired itself. Within moments of being inside the carriage, with the shades drawn, he had healed. "Are you going to your husband?"

"No!" She cried it out, afraid that these beasts would hurt Blackthorne if they thought him precious to her.

"Why does a proper lady travel to an English peer alone?" Even in the shadows, his eyes glinted silver at her. "You do not look like a mistress."

What did it matter to them? They were only going to kill her. She wriggled her hands; she pulled, but the cloth would not tear. Even though it had been ripped so easily from her skirts, it would not give now. Her chest felt as if it would burst out of her corset.

Lukos bent to her ear. "Relax, sweet lass. We mean you no harm."

Her heart slowed, as though Lukos could control it. Fear slithered through her, but her body did not behave as if she were as terrified as she was. Her cheeks burned hot. Her body felt tight, but in a pleasurable way. And all she could think of was the pressure of the bonds at her hands.

"You are obviously innocent," Zayan murmured. "And very sweet." But he stared so deeply into her eyes, she felt he was searching for more.

"Tempting," Lukos agreed. And he actually leaned to her

neck and sniffed. Like a *wolf*. "This man you are traveling to see, you are in love with him. You intend to marry him."

Sheer horror raced through her blood. Lukos had read all of that in her thoughts. Would he see the rest—that it was her intention to marry Blackthorne because she had no other choice? "No, none of that is true," she lied in a desperate, blurted rush of words.

Zayan shook his head. "So you are traveling to your fiancé, but unprotected."

"No, I had the servants, of course." Servants who had been somehow compelled or hypnotized by these vampires to do their bidding and drive the carriage. They were traveling in this direction only because she had foolishly looked this way along the road when Zayan had first asked where she was going. She had revealed the truth even as she refused to speak.

Lukos lifted his hand. A swirl of red light flowed from his palm. It danced through the air toward her. She screamed and pulled at her bonds, but the twinkling light encircled her neck. It touched her like a caress. Pleasure, terrifying pleasure, shot through her every nerve. She moaned with it.

Lukos grinned, his white fangs flashing. He bent to her neck. *Dear God, no.* But the red lights were delighting her, as he pressed his warm lips to her throat. His touch made her skin ignite with sensation.

He lifted. "Just a kiss. Nothing more." The magical light disappeared. She was weak with relief, even as her body was heightened and aware. Heaven help her, she wanted another touch.

Stop, Miranda. You must *fight.*

The mad thought struck her that Lukos was also astonishingly handsome. His silvery eyes, almost violet in the soft light, compelled her to watch him. He looked so young, perhaps younger than she was, but he seemed ancient at the same time.

Behind his wicked smile, she could sense his emotion—pain so acute she winced with it.

"I would not hurt you," he promised softly. "Nor will I drink from you until you ask me to."

Miranda pushed aside her connection with his emotions. "I would never ask you," she cried. "No matter what you do. And I won't kiss either of you willingly. I-I'll spit on you if you try to kiss me."

Lukos's deep, rusty laugh rang in her ears.

"My turn." Zayan stood, and despite the swaying of the carriage, he wrapped an arm around her waist. She squirmed but to no avail. He scooped her up and carried her across to his side.

God, this was so . . . humiliating and awful. They were taking *turns* with her.

Zayan's touch reminded her of how strong these men were. Lukos had carried her over his shoulder as though she weighed nothing. And Zayan's hand spanned her waist, nipped in by corset and snug pelisse.

The shades rattled at the window; Miranda could see the light fading beyond. The sun was setting. Soon it would be nightfall, which meant her best chance of escape was now. They could not chase after her in the sunlight.

Though they'd lasted in the sunlight for long enough before.

Zayan's hand neared her face.

She shook. "Tell me who you are. When did you become a vampire?" She thought of every tale Aunt Eugenia had told her about vampires. Her aunt wanted to know the entire story of a vampire's background. That, she claimed, was what gave a slayer power over a vampire. Not weaponry, but understanding. Most slayers did not bother to know their prey, which was why many died. "Who made you?" Miranda asked, trying to look at the clasp of Zayan's cloak and not his magnetic eyes. "When were you turned?"

If she could make him talk, she could keep his mouth off hers, couldn't she? She could play for time.

"I have been Nosferatu for many centuries, love. I have lived an eternity." He spoke with a touch of weariness. She had the sense that he really had no interest in her. If this was a game to him, it bored him.

"But what happened to you? Who were you as a mortal? You didn't choose to be a vampire, did you?" She fired her questions out in a tumble, one atop the other. Anything to keep him talking to her. To postpone the moment he would bite her or ravish her. "I want to know. I know I won't survive this night. But I need to . . . to think of things. All I have left is curiosity."

Zayan's black straight brows jerked up at that. He laughed. The sound was as smooth as the deep velvety night, like the ripple of a nighttime breeze through the trees. The other vampire, Lukos, had a lusty throaty laugh, one that implied he was thinking very rude thoughts.

Miranda shook her head. Why did she think these things?

"I have lived for almost two thousand years," Zayan said dispassionately. "I was a Roman general. My name, in my mortal world, was Marius Praetonius. I took most of Europe in the name of Rome. I was celebrated, worshipped. Your fiancé might have read about me in his schoolbooks." Lines were suddenly carved at the side of his mouth as he smiled more deeply.

I sense a great power about you. . . . You intrigue me. . . .

Miranda heard his deep voice in her head, felt it in her entire body, the way music would vibrate through her. She heard it and went ice-cold. Could he guess that she had special powers—a power she couldn't even understand? That she possessed some kind of magic? She shivered. What would that mean? Would it spare her life? Was any of what he had told her true?

"Of course it is true," he said in answer to her thoughts. "What do you think—I'm some insignificant slave who concocted a fancy tale?"

She recoiled from the sudden anger in his voice. His lower lip thrust out, in the way her brother would do when she had caught him making some foolish mistake, such as gambling.

Vampires were once mortal men. That is the critical thing to remember when hunting them. Aunt Eugenia had told her that over and over again.

She remembered her response to Aunt Eugenia: *I am a gentlewoman. I am supposed to even fear the power of mortal men.*

But Aunt Eugenia scoffed at that. *A woman is as powerful as she believes she can be.* The words had almost made Miranda laugh—she painted watercolors, diligently perfected her embroidery, strolled the gardens with a dainty parasol. How could she be powerful? But she had wanted to believe her aunt. And Eugenia's words had a strange power attached to them. As though, by thinking them, they could give her greater strength.

Zayan stretched his arm along the back of the seat. It was such a masculine gesture—such a normal, human one—that it caught Miranda by surprise. "Does knowing who I once was make you more willing to kiss me?" he asked, amusement heightening the allure of his looks.

She fought the instinctive tug of feminine admiration at his chiseled jaw, full lips, at even the crinkles at the sides of his mirror-like eyes.

"Of course not!"

"Wise girl." Across from them, Lukos had propped one booted foot on the velvet seat of the coach. "He's a vampire. He's taken the blood of thousands of innocent women and children."

She froze, horrified.

"As have you," Zayan growled. He was watching her, his gaze hot and intense. "I would like to know what you are. Not a normal, flighty, empty-headed woman of society, are you?"

Miranda twisted her bound hands. Her entire body tensed,

but she tried to look rather stupidly at Zayan. "Of course I am just an empty-headed, ordinary woman."

But he held her gaze, seeing through her, she was certain, with his mirror-like eyes.

She had slid along the seat to put as much space between them as she could. But he reached out and caught hold of the bindings at her wrist. With two fingers, he tore the cloth. She wrenched her arms apart, fighting at the fabric, even as he unwound it.

Oh. Her hands tingled as feeling returned.

Zayan reached for her hand. "Isn't a kiss on the hand the way a proper English gentleman begins his seduction of a lady?"

His hand clasped hers; his fingers threaded through hers. Like a perfect gentleman, like a man she might have dreamed about, he raised her hand to his lips.

"No, don't do this." She could not bear a mockery of courtship before she was killed and her blood taken. "No, I know nothing of magic. I didn't even really believe in vampires!"

Soft and full, Zayan's lower lip touched the back of her bare hand. A jolt of warm pleasure ignited there at the brush of his mouth. He kissed her hand as no man had ever done before—a tantalizing play of mouth and tongue. She'd had no idea a kiss to her hand could make her blood rush madly through her. Could make her nipples lift against her shift.

But Lukos was not going to simply watch, she realized. He had moved to their side—he was on his knees. It startled her that a vampire, a demonic creature, would be on his knees for her. "I do not share," he growled, looking like a defiant boy. "We could have her choose—"

"Choose!" she cried. "I'd never—"

"But we can both compel her thoughts," Lukos continued, ignoring her outrage. "I propose a competition. An amusement for a long journey."

The fiends were speaking as though she were not even there. And butterflies took flight in her belly at the word *competition.*

"No magic?" Zayan asked.

"Magic is allowed, but only for seduction, which will begin like this . . ."

Miranda held her breath. Lukos bent to her neck. She felt him approach. Her skin seemed to anticipate him, tingling before he touched her.

His lips brushed her, and she moaned with desire. What was wrong with her? Zayan suckled her fingers one by one, and the sensations left her dizzy. She could not fight the . . . the heated desire rising in her. They were competing for her, like she was a prize.

What if she touched them? What if she touched them as she did to others who had died? Could she bring them back? Could this mysterious power she possessed do that—to men who had been vampires for centuries?

Did she dare try? If she could change them, they couldn't kill her.

The shade rattled away from the carriage window. Barely any light filtered in.

The sun had set. She had to try now. She did not have any more time, and this might be her only hope to live.

London, at that moment

"An innocent from a good family will cost you, sirrah."

James Ryder drew out a handful of gold sovereigns and dropped them, one by one, into the greasy silk glove on the madam's outstretched hand. "Gentlemen pay at least five hundred pounds for my virgins, sir." She reached out to return his money.

Five hundred. He had it, but he hadn't wanted to part with so much. There were houses where that handful of coins would buy him the use of every cunny in the house. That amount of money would let him do whatever he wanted to the girls.

But he wanted to dip his wick here. In this place that was the exclusive domain of earls and dukes. In this place where he could take the maidenhead of a woman he would not be allowed to address on the street.

Tonight, Miss Miranda Bond had evaded him. To ease his frustration, he had destroyed a vampire, and the excitement of battle now sang in his veins.

He wanted the best. And he could pay for it.

He caught the madam's wrist. "That is a small gift for you, madam. I am willing to pay the price for quality."

"Who are you, then, sir? You are not known to me." She sniffed and looked down her beak of a nose at him.

How in bloody hell did she dare look down at him?

"I am a son of the Marquess of Hiltshire." The truth, though he was a bastard son. He pulled out a wad of notes and pushed those into her hand, forcing her to drop the sovereigns on the gleaming parquet floor.

The coins clinked. Her hand squeezed around the money. She stared down, her hand-drawn eyebrows arched in surprise.

He made a move to pick up his hat and start for the door.

"Wait!"

He turned to see her stuffing the money between her large, plumped-up tits, wadding the notes down below the scooped neck of her bodice, between the sweaty lumps of her flesh.

"I have a girl available. A vicar's daughter, left homeless. She is most definitely a virgin. A true innocent, quite frightened and apprehensive, even though she goes willing to her fate for the welfare of her younger siblings. She was promised to the Earl of Huntingdon. She could, however, be yours, for one thousand pounds."

Christ, it was a bloody fortune. But to steal the virgin who would have spread her thighs for the Earl of Huntingdon? It would be worth it. He wrote a vowel for the rest, and to his surprise, the madam accepted it.

No doubt, she thought he would return after he'd sampled the vicar's daughter. He'd crave another virgin, just as her noble clients did. With a snap of her fingers, she sent a brawny footman to lead him to the bedroom. He found it empty. He sat on the edge of the bed but would not begin to undress until the girl was brought to him.

He'd trusted once—bought a virgin and stripped down in preparation, only to find the brothel was more interested in stealing his money, beating him blind, then throwing him out. But the stupid madam and her brutes had not understood what a vampire slayer was capable of doing with a weapon.

Ryder drew out a cheroot. He moved to the fireplace and lit the smoke from the licking flames. The room was opulent, a sign that it did cater to refined tastes.

God, he was hard with anticipation. His John Thomas strained against his linens. His arousal made him restless, angry. He should be in pursuit of Miss Miranda Bond tonight.

But he knew where she was headed. He would be on the road after he'd had his little treat, and he would travel faster than her.

With a click, the door opened. He swiveled on the bed as the footman brought in a tall, slender girl who wore a ghastly gray dress. A dress she'd worn from her home, or a costume? Her face was plain—freckled nose, pink cheeks, ivory skin. Her lashes were as mousy brown as her hair, but her skin and hair promised to be peach soft.

No seasoned whore could clean up like that. This girl was genuine. Her spine was stiff, her fists clenched. "Do you want me to take off my dress, sir?"

She was doing this to save her family. That sent a rush of

blood to his rod. She thought she was going to nobly sacrifice herself.

"Let me undress you, love," he said. "I'm very good and I'll be gentle. This will be enjoyable for you."

Her back twitched.

She looked nothing like Miranda Bond—who was blonde, with large blue eyes. Miss Bond was stunningly beautiful. But she was flawed. She was a creature of evil. Something he had to destroy.

This poor sweet angel was someone he would nurture for an hour. He could barely afford the money, but he would be giving her a wonderful experience—a night with him would be far better than being thrust into by a drunken earl.

He undid his cravat and tossed it aside. She was standing at the doorway, kneading her skirts in her fists. "Let's undress you, love. That changes everything."

She frowned at that. "I don't want to be . . . undressed."

"It seems strange to you now, but you'll enjoy it. This is what you were meant to do—give yourself to a deserving man."

The vicar's daughter gave a half-laugh, half-sob at that.

She had no idea what he was saving her from.

The wench smelled of a heavily flower scented soap, the soap the whores of this place must use. On one of them it would be sickening—on her it was poignant.

He would rescue her in this small way. He had the money. Why shouldn't vampire slayers be as inventive as Bow Street Runners? He took private commissions, and for some vampires, he took payment to leave them alive. And to protect them, up to a point. Many vampires had amassed fortunes, using their power, strength, and the advantage of time, endless time, to become wealthy men.

What else would they do with their money than use it to keep cheating death?

Ryder stripped to his shirt. She was watching him, with her plain bodice rising and falling. "Take down your hair for me." He wanted to watch the tresses fall as he kicked off his boots and took off his trousers.

She bent her head slowly, obediently. She pulled at the pins. In a waft of sweet fragrance, her long brown hair fell down her back.

He sprawled back on the bed, but she didn't join him. "Don't make me impatient," he warned. "I've paid good money for you. I know you won't see it—no matter what that bitch of a madam told you. Please me well and I'll give you something special. Something for you to keep to yourself."

She looked horror-struck, but she began to unfasten her dress. This was how he wanted Miss Miranda Bond to be for him. Taking her clothes off with shaking fingers. If he narrowed his eyes, he could imagine this pasty-faced wench was Miss Bond.

The Royal Society would not disbar him, or destroy him, if he went about killing Miss Bond in his own way. They needed him too much, needed him to do the dirty work. To carry out the secret assassinations, like this one. They needed him to do things like hunt down the seemingly innocent sisters of gentlemen and make their deaths look like accidents.

But he had seen what Miss Bond could do.

Two weeks ago, she had laid her hand on the chest of a child who had been run down by a carriage. The body had been mangled. The thing was dead.

But beneath her touch, the body healed. The lifeless eyes took in light once more. The child had been resurrected by just the *touch* of Miss Bond's hand.

He hadn't believed it.

But the gentlemen of the Society had assured him it was true. The damned woman could raise the dead.

His mission was to kill her. Ryder understood what the old

men of the Society wanted to do—destroy that which they couldn't understand.

And in return for murdering a lovely, twenty-three-year-old woman, he would have a mansion in the country. He would live better than his father, Hiltshire, whose estates were impoverished.

Hell, he would enjoy that.

All that stood between him and everything he'd always planned for was one little gently bred lady. One simple death and he would have it all.

His cock lurched against his belly at the thought. He reached out and clasped the hand of his vicar's daughter, who now stood trembling in her shift. "Now, love," he leered, "I'll teach you how to suck me." But first he pulled her to him, stuck his hand beneath her chemise, and gently worked his index finger up her tight, hot ass.

3

Touched

Chamber of the Scholomance
875 A.D.

Lukos awoke to find that he lay on a smooth stone floor in a lake of his own blood. It was encrusted on his neck, smeared on his freshly shaved scalp. The great gaping wound in his throat had somehow knitted together. It was still spongy and painful, but as he gingerly explored with his fingers, there was no longer a wide, open, bleeding gash.

Was he dead now?

His strength almost faded again as he struggled up to his knees, and he fought the lure of unconsciousness. Darkness surrounded him. It clung to him like grasping hands. Raw and cold, panic swept over him. Ever since he'd been a child, he has always awoken in the dark like this—sweating, frightened, terrified enough to run. He had hid these fears because it was his destiny to be a great warrior, but they rose up now, and made him whimper.

He was too old to make such sounds, like a child. And in the blackness, he looked around for the demoness. Had she left him for dead?

Slowly, he grew accustomed to the dark. And he saw her, curled up on a shelf of stone, watching him. A robe of dark crimson swathed her, and she stared at him with sorrowful eyes. "I am sorry, Lukos. But your eyes are next."

He threw up his hands, but a sharp, searing-hot point slammed into his right palm. Instinctively, he pulled his hand away. This time the red-hot poker went into his eye. As he screamed in pain, something grabbed his arms and restrained him. He howled. He tried to fight. Some monster in the shadows had hold of him. He was raging against the grip, throwing his head wildly. The pain. God above, the pain—

But despite his wild struggles, the poker drove into his left eye, completely blinding him.

This would kill him.

Unless he was already dead.

Did the dead still feel pain?

He would have cried, but the searing heat had taken away his tear ducts along with his eye.

He smelled her. Over the stench of his own flesh, over the excruciating agony, he knew she had come to his side. She knelt by him. Her hands went around his bare shoulders, and in her sultry voice, she chanted. The soft, lovely sound flowed around him like a vivid light and took away the pain.

"You cannot see him, Lukos. It is not for you to see him until you have completed your apprenticeship."

He laughed in anger and bitterness. "I'm blinded. I'll never see."

"You will. Lukos, he can give you ultimate power. He can easily give you sight."

"What do you do now? Cut off my cock so I can't fuck?"

"No." The demoness's voice was soft and soothing. "You have endured all that you must for now. I will take you to the chamber, and you will rest there. Tomorrow, you will begin to learn."

Learn. With his eyes gouged out? His throat slit? Each breath was a torture, and he was rasping and wheezing like an old man. He'd run over corpses on the battlefield less wounded than this. "Am I dead?"

"You will be reborn, Lukos."

She had opened his robe then and had taken hold of his cock. He had lost his eyes; he'd had his throat cut, but somehow she made his organ stand up. She straddled him, took him inside, and rode him. He could feel her slick heat engulfing his cock. He could smell her, smell the ripeness of their joining. He could feel her full buttocks slamming his groin. God, yes . . .

"You're having sex with me—"

"No, I'm not. You are dreaming this, Lukos." She slapped him. The sudden jolt of pain made his fantasy disappear. Instead of her creamy juices, he smelled the dankness of wet stone. Instead of warmth and pleasure, he felt sharp rocks beneath his knees.

"Sometimes men go mad from the fear and the pain, Lukos. They lose themselves in a world of darkly erotic fantasy. They believe they are always having sex, but they are trapped in the fantasy. They starve to death because they no longer know to eat. They are sometimes killed. Those who go among the mortals are killed or committed to asylums. But in their own minds, they are in a world of constant orgy." Her laugh was wry and cold.

"But you are too strong to seek that kind of escape, Lukos. I would not have chosen to be the one to guide you if I did not believe so." She took his arm. "Come with me now. For you are soon to be a demon born. And I know that you will be the strongest yet. You will make me proud, Lukos. You will give me the world."

As she led him, he clung to her, the only thing he could trust in his newly dark world.

He would have given her anything she asked for. If she'd wanted to cut out his heart, he would have let her.

He could taste the magic through her skin.

Zayan pressed his mouth to the Englishwoman's delicate hand. Magic thrummed through her, snapping within her, raging inside her. He could sense she was resisting it. She was not willing to accept the unearthly power within her. It frightened her.

Through the contact between his lips and her silky skin, he could sense all these things. He'd had one glimpse into her thoughts before she had somehow shuttered them to him. He had seen a lavish bedroom, filled with white silks and fluttering lace curtains. Another young woman, a brunette, lay in the bed, pale and drawn, smiling a weak smile. *Miranda,* the fragile inhabitant of the bed had whispered, *I feel so much better today, and I think it is because of you.*

He felt in Miranda, the woman whose hand he was kissing, a love he had almost forgotten—a feeling of tenderness heightened by the need to nurture.

In an instant, the image had vanished. But now he knew the name of the dainty innocent-looking woman who possessed the strongest magic power he had felt in decades—in centuries. *Miranda.*

He turned her hand and kissed her palm. Miss Miranda rewarded him with an unwilling shiver of pleasure. Now he understood what had intrigued Sebastien de Wynter about Althea Yates, the vampire slayer—it was all that sensuality trapped behind such rigid propriety.

As much as he hated Lukos, he had agreed to the game of seduction as an amusement, something to pass the time with their pretty captive. Something to distract him from the urge to kill the vampire who had once tried to destroy him.

Now he knew Miranda was much more to him than just a game. All that magic in her could be his last hope.

He needed it.

Which meant he had to dominate her. And now that he knew she was no an ordinary mortal, he would have to find a different way to do that. Even now, she was staring at him with narrowed blue eyes, and he felt her resistance to his seduction. She was fighting him with everything she had. And at the moment, she was winning.

Zayan admired her strength, though strong women could not be trusted. If they chose to be deceitful, they were more destructive than any army. More vicious. By the gods, he had seen women cut down their own men with axes when the males had retreated from battle.

If he wanted to control this woman and her magic, he would have to try harder.

Expertly, he dabbed his tongue in the center of her palm and made her whimper. Slowly, teasingly, he flicked his tongue over her wrist. He sucked her skin and felt the magic throb beneath his lips, along with her pulse.

Miranda moaned. He felt a surge in her power as she struggled against the desire he ignited. Suddenly, he realized how incredible she would be in his bed, in a bout of resistance and magic and surrender.

Years ago, he made a bargain with the red power. To bring his children back to life, it had demanded magic—it devoured every kind of power. It wanted the magic of youth. The energy released in sex. It had demanded the power of other magical beings. In that decade, before he had been banished into imprisonment by Elizabeth, one of the vampire queens, he had drained the energy of some foolish angels and a few demons, and like a slave, he had turned that energy over and waited obediently for his dream to be realized.

What a damned fool he'd been.

He had quickly understood what the red power intended to do. It would always hold his children as a prize, as a lure to make him serve it. But it would never give him what it had promised.

But now he knew a way to take control of the red power. He could take Miranda's magic and use it to first tempt the red power, then blackmail the red power into giving him what he longed for—his children.

He ached to see them. He yearned to hold them again.

But to claim her power, he had to bring three words to her lips: *I love you.* It would open her heart and break through her defenses. In that moment, he could take her magic force and make it his own.

This was more than just a physical seduction, more than a game. He had to break through to her heart.

Miranda kicked out wildly. "Y-you can force me to feel pleasure, but you will never seduce me!"

Zayan jerked his attention upward to see Lukos stroking his fingers along the neckline of her pelisse. Miranda opened her eyes wide. They locked with his. Hers were vivid blue—the brilliant shining blue of the waves that lapped at the southern shores of Italy.

She didn't look frightened. She looked . . . hopeful. It shocked Zayan so much, he straightened from her wrist. Strangely, he could not draw away from her steady, determined gaze.

"You *won't* seduce me," she said again. "No matter what you do. But I want to touch you. I believe I can return your soul, Zayan."

Did she really think she could save him, the naïve child? His answer was harsh. "You can't, angel."

"Let me touch you," she said.

He had not expected this. She spoke to him as his wife used to. He was the general, but his wife had spoken sharply to him, had expected him to obey her command.

Zayan jerked back as the woman's hand struck his chest, her fingers splayed wide. Heat surged through his pectorals, a hot spear through his muscles, a fiery grip around his heart. Her power held him transfixed. He couldn't move.

By the gods, she was strong with magic.

Far more than he'd guessed.

His temperature soared; heat raced through his veins as though he were being consumed by fire. Could she make him burst into flame? Could her touch make him explode, burn to ash?

"Oh! Oh!" she cried. Her body was convulsing. She moaned. She moved her hips in the fierce bounce of a woman caught in the throes of a powerful orgasm. Her lips opened wide as she rode out the pleasure.

Zayan's nostrils flared at the tang of her juices. He could scent her cunny becoming wet and creamy. Lukos could scent her, too, he knew. Lukos could shift shape and become a wolf, which made the demon even more primal about sex than Zayan was.

"What in hell is she?" Lukos growled.

Still enduring the blasting heat, Zayan could barely speak. "Not a demon," he managed. "Not a vampire." He drew in a deep breath as the heat began to ebb. He wasn't going to go up in a ball of flame. "An avenging angel?" But he didn't think so.

Miss Miranda slumped back against the seat. Her chest rose and fell. Zayan saw the horror in her eyes. The stark fear. She stared down at her own shaking hands.

She didn't understand her own power. He read it in her thoughts before her intense emotions became a blur that he couldn't understand. He'd never had that happen before. The only minds that could shutter themselves from him were those of vampire queens, and demons who had been Lucifer's apprentices. But he had glimpsed the most powerful emotion Miranda felt—she was afraid of herself.

You don't know what you are, do you? he asked softly in her thoughts. He tried to shield them from Lukos but doubted he was successful. Zayan was the older vampire—and stronger, he believed. But not quite strong enough.

Helplessly, Miranda looked at him. "It's never felt like that before. That's never . . . never happened. I don't know if I did anything."

Sweetheart . . . Zayan had only ever spoken so softly and gently to his children. *What exactly were you trying to do? You can't believe your touch could return my soul.*

Miranda couldn't let them find out the truth. "I-I thought you could be saved," she lied, "by a good soul."

Lukos chuckled. "You thought what? The touch of a virtuous woman would drive his demons out?"

Mute, Miranda nodded her head. She prayed they thought she was just some impetuous do-gooder. What a fool she'd been to reveal herself. But she'd thought it would work. She had saved Aunt Eugenia, her brother, Simon, her sister-in-law, Caroline, the young boy in the park, and others over the last twelve years. She'd thought she could save a vampire.

Miranda rubbed her hand. It felt as though it had been burnt. She'd felt the heat and even thought it had gone into the vampire. It had seemed to bounce back into her.

That scorching heat had turned into desire—desire and arousal she didn't want and couldn't control. It had grown so strong. She'd ached and throbbed, and had needed to rub between her thighs. She had squeezed them together, unable to fight the yearning. Then she'd burst—she couldn't explain it any other way.

She hugged herself. That explosive feeling must be what drove her brother and his new wife to their bedroom so often and was responsible for those agonized moans Caroline made that could be heard through the bedchamber walls.

It had to be. Her pleasure had been so intense she'd feared her heart might stop, or burst.

Her cheeks still burned. She couldn't catch her breath.

Miranda stared at Zayan. He smiled at her. He still had fangs. So it hadn't worked. And she didn't believe she had returned his soul.

Why not? What had gone wrong?

Was it because he was not dead but undead?

She remembered the terror she'd felt when Simon had drowned, when she had been eleven and he had been thirteen. It had been like her heart had stopped along with his. She'd been almost physically sick, her stomach leaping upward, bile in her throat. Tears had been streaming down her face. She'd begged him to live. She'd touched his heart. Then he'd coughed and sputtered and had thrown up a lot of horrid, slimy water.

It had been the same when she had saved Aunt Eugenia—she had desperately wanted her aunt to be alive again. With her parents, she'd never had the chance. Her mother had died when she was very young; her father just over three years ago, but on shipboard while crossing from Calais during the heady newness of peace. His body had been lost.

She thought of the child in Hyde Park. Even though she hadn't known the little boy, it had shattered her heart to think he would die. That he was dead. Each time, her heart had been broken and she had been determined to bring life back. Each time, she had truly cared.

She could never care enough about these vampires to give them their lives back. That avenue of escape was lost to her.

The carriage began to slow its breakneck pace. In the space between the window and the shade covering it, Miranda saw hints of light. They were in a village now. This—this would be her chance to get free.

She turned beseeching eyes to Zayan. "Please . . . I am so hungry. I need . . ." She blushed, as a respectable lady should while discussing the privy. "I need to relieve myself. Please?"

It was Lukos who answered. "We'll stop. I need to feed."

* * *

Coaches clattered into the yard beside the inn. Twilight had settled in, and only a strip of soft violet remained along the horizon. Lamps burned, and Miranda noticed both Zayan and Lukos hid their faces to ensure the light did not glint on their reflective eyes.

Lukos held her wrist and she could not break free of his hold. Could she scream to the surrounding crowd—the families and gentlemen and elderly ladies leaving coaches or approaching others?

There were children in the crowd.

And she remembered the magic that Zayan had done. He could possibly kill dozens of people with his power if he threw a bolt of it into the crowd to stop her.

She had no choice but to go along with the vampires. And then find a chance to escape.

"We'll go to the dining room and you may have a meal."

It was on the tip of her tongue to sarcastically thank Zayan for being so kind. But she bit down. Best to let them think she was so frightened she would obey them.

Lukos shook his head. His long hair fluttered in the breeze, and his eyes gave a betraying flash of silver. "I need to hunt."

Miranda caught her breath. He meant he was going to hunt down an innocent person and take their blood.

"No, you can't." She pointed to her own throat. "If you need to feed, take the blood from me. I don't care. But I won't let you hurt anyone else."

"You have no choice, love. And I can't feed from you. But if you wish, you may choose the person I'll feed from." Lukos waved his arm to encompass the crowd of innocent people.

She stared. A mother embraced a child. A woman urged four young boys toward a stage that was preparing to leave. A couple gazed lovingly at each other in a tender good-bye. An elderly man patted the hand of his elderly wife. She couldn't select anyone. Each person was loved and cherished by someone. They all deserved to live.

"You're evil!" she spat.

"Yes, angel, I am. I served Lucifer. I was born to be evil."

"If you must feed, why not bite Zayan! Or bite a pig!"

Lukos merely inclined his head. "I need a mortal's fresh, rich blood, angel."

Was there anyone there who deserved a vampire's bite? A man who abused his wife? A vicious man who preyed on children? A woman who snared innocents for brothels? A murderer? A thief?

She could not do this.

But she couldn't let him just select anyone. "Who would you choose?" she asked softly.

"When you eat, sweetheart, do you select the dish that tempts you most? Would you choose mutton over lamb? Or tough beef over a succulent roast?"

She shuddered. "You'd chose someone young and pretty, you mean."

"Sometimes I choose children."

Miranda clapped her hand to her mouth. "That's unspeakably evil!"

Should she scream? Perhaps the vampires' magic couldn't hurt all these people—but what if her horror led to one death?

"I would choose children who had little hope, angel, and then I would change them. I would give them unimaginable strength and speed. I would give them the chance to turn the world upon its ear."

She shuddered. "Can you not feed without hurting someone?"

Lukos winked. "For you, pet, I'll try."

She didn't believe him. But Zayan had hold of her arm and Lukos strode away. He was so tall, so striking with his long hair and cloak that he did not vanish in the milling crowd—he stood out. Men watched him warily; women stared with obvious desire. He prowled toward the shadows.

She could not swallow over the lump in her throat.

Zayan's arm slid around her waist. There were men walking with women this way. Those women wore low-cut gowns, had rouged lips, and were obviously doxies. People would think that of her.

She choked on a laugh. They would think her a whore. They would have no idea she was going to be a vampire's victim.

"Aren't you going to feed?" she whispered.

Zayan cocked his head. "I do not need to yet, my dear."

Blast, she'd hoped he would want to leave her to feed. Of course, he wouldn't let her go. She was likely to be his meal.

"But I expect you are hungry," he said. "Let us get you some dinner."

"What do you plan to do to me? If you intend to kill me, why feed me?"

A stage arrived, rushing into the yard before Zayan answered. He watched it in a pensive silence. The grooms jumped down, the doors opened. Boxes were thrown down as the people began to spill out. Other grooms hurried forward to unhitch the horses.

And others rushed forward to greet friends and to make ready to take their journey.

Was he watching to choose his victim? She had to act. She turned and pointed across the yard. "Look! Our carriage is leaving! It must be Lukos!"

As Zayan spun around, she pulled away from him as hard as she could. His surprise—and anger—had loosened his grip. Her pelisse tore, but she was free!

She yanked up her hems and plunged into the crowd.

" 'Ere miss, have a care!"

Someone elbowed her in the back. She tripped, almost fell, but grabbed a man's coat to stop herself. She stumbled forward.

She heard a roar behind her. That must be Zayan and she cringed, waiting for a bolt of his magical power to strike her.

A man shouted. Out of the corner of her eye, she saw the man sail backward off his feet and land hard in the mud.

Zayan wasn't using magic.

She squeezed and pushed her way between bodies.

Someone shoved her forward and she slammed against the side of the stage. Her wind flew out of her chest. Gasping, she raced around the large vehicle.

What was she going to do? She couldn't outrun a vampire. Could she leap into a passing carriage? Three were leaving and she raced blindly toward them.

"There's been a boy trampled!" someone shouted. "My god!"

Standing still amidst the cries of shock and horror, Miranda slowly turned toward the gathering crowd. She could not just run away now. She had to do something. Shivering, glancing around for Zayan, she made her way to the circle of people who were all trying to crush forward, to see. She had to elbow her way between these heartless people. They weren't doing anything, they were feeding on horror and disaster like a vampire fed on blood. And it was like trying to fight a raging current.

"Move," she commanded one man. She had to kick another to get him to jump aside. Through the gap between bodies, she saw a tiny form sprawled in the dirt and a woman leaning over him, screaming, tears streaking down her face.

She had to act now. She didn't have much time.

From behind her, a hand clamped down on her right wrist, holding her captive. "Got you, you witch," a man growled.

That voice. She recognized it. Her heart threatened to leap out of her chest. Miranda twisted to meet the hard gaze of James Ryder—the vampire slayer who wanted to kill her.

4

Rescued

"It's no use. She will not take my milk anymore. She doesn't even want blood."

Althea Yates, Lady Brookshire, heard the frantic desperation in her voice. How could she be so helpless? So useless? She did not know what to do. Her child wouldn't eat, no matter what she tried. She had consulted with midwives, wet nurses, experienced women, and vampires, too, and nothing worked.

Her maid hurried away. Althea heard Nan's rapid footsteps on the stone floor of the ancient castle's corridor. The frightened girl would be fetching Yannick and Bastien, Althea guessed.

If her daughter didn't eat, surely she would waste away.

Althea licked away the tear that dripped to her lip. She could cry. She may be a vampire, but she could cry. But what would tears solve?

She gazed down at baby Serena, known as Serry, so as not to be confused with Serena, Lady Sommersby, Althea's very best friend. Althea smiled at soft, puckered lips that blew tiny bubbles, and at the fragile, translucent lids, and the dark lashes that lay along small cheeks. One thick lock of downy blond hair lay along her daughter's cheek. She guessed Serry must look as both her husbands had when they were infants—since both men were blonde.

Was Serry immortal, as she, Yannick, and Bastien were? Althea didn't know. No one could tell her that. But now that her little daughter was nearly three months, she would not eat.

"Please, little one, please take some food," Althea whispered.

She clasped the tiny hand. Her daughter's fingers curled around Althea's baby finger and clutched her tight. Serry had been so strong when she was first born. So healthy. For the first few days, her daughter had drunk from her breast with gusto, had always wanted to feed. Her breasts had swelled large with milk, and she'd known the most intense pain as the milk flooded in.

Right now, her breasts were beginning to ache again. Just the *thought* of feeding set them off. The pain would get more and more excruciating because Serry would not take her nipple and would not take her milk. Her breasts would become engorged and rock hard, and then, even though pain shot through her when she just touched her bosom, she'd have to ruthlessly massage the fluid out herself.

And soon it would stop coming in altogether, she'd been told.

Althea stroked the soft cheek. "Please, Serry, you must eat." But the tiny fingers released their grip. "You are going to waste away. Please, please, please."

Althea, the maid came in a panic. Bastien's worried tone reached her through her thoughts. Within a heartbeat, he strode into her bedchamber. His golden hair was loose and drifted over his shoulders. Even in darkness, she saw the stark fear in his eyes. He glanced to her bared bosom, her breasts huge and full, her hands working painfully to make the milk pour down her chest, where it soaked into a linen towel.

It gave her strength to share the burden. "I don't know what to do, Bastien! I don't know how to make her eat. I don't even know what to feed her."

"Yannick has sent for Lady Draycott."

"Serena's mother, Eve?" One of the oldest vampires—the first Eve created by God for Adam, but Eve had then been rejected by Adam and had long harbored hurt and pain.

"She bore a vampire child," Bastien reminded her.

"But her daughter Serena was not fully vampire at birth. And Eve has already refused to help me. Yannick forbid her to come to this house because of her cold refusal."

"If she can help you now, he's willing to forgive."

"She won't help now. She will not change her mind. There's nothing we can do. We are going to have to watch our child die. I can't stand it!"

"No! It won't be like that. I vow that it won't."

She knew Bastien—one of her two husbands—possessed great strength and bravery, but in this he was as powerless as she. "The truth is, Bastien, no child of two vampires has survived before! The vampire queens finally admitted this to me after letting me think I could bear a child. They believe we can't breed." Her daughter was a warm bundle in her arms. Was she condemned to watch her just fade away? Was Serry condemned to die? Was this payment for the fact that she, Bastien, and Yannick had defied death?

She had come from Italy to the Carpathians for answers, had forced them all to travel into these remote mountains in search of hope, and had found . . . nothing.

Bastien was on his knees in front of her. He laid his large, strong hand on his daughter's stomach. Even though they could not be certain whether Yannick or Bastien had actually been Serry's father, both men considered themselves to be. And she considered them both to be. It didn't matter who had actually given her Serry. She belonged to both men. And they were both loving and devoted to their child.

"She is so innocent and so beautiful. I can't bear to lose her," Althea whispered.

He looked to her in shock. Perhaps he believed a mother never gave up hope. "We won't."

"Unless we can find someone who can perform miracles—"

"We will."

"Who would perform a miracle for us, Bastien? We're vampires."

Warm and comforting, his hand stroked her cheek. His thumb brushed away her tears. "Sweetheart, that does not make us unworthy of miracles. I promise you that."

Mr. Ryder gripped her arms tight and dragged her away from the boy and his sobbing, frantic mother. Miranda sank her heels into the dirt and clawed at his arm. "Stop! Don't you see the boy is dying?"

Ryder wore a long greatcoat of deep burgundy, and a tall beaver hat was tipped over his pale blond hair. "Indeed," he drawled, "I saw him fall in front of the carriage."

Good god. Miranda stared up into the slayer's deep blue eyes. There was no compassion in them, only triumph because he'd captured her. She remembered again the words he'd spoken to her in the park the day before she'd run away. . . .

You are a demon. Or a witch. Only an evil, otherworldly being can possess the power of magic. And as a slayer, it is my sworn duty to destroy you.

She'd fought fear of this insane slayer then and she could do it now. "You have to let me go to the boy, Mr. Ryder. I can save his life, and he is only a child."

He hauled her another step away and her boots skidded. She didn't have the strength to resist. His breath, scented with the smoke of a cheroot, washed over her. "It's too late. Bringing him back to life will only ensure that these simpletons will tear you apart."

"But you only want to kill me. What do I care how I die, if I can give that child a chance to live?"

"It is my duty to ensure that these people do not know what they have amongst them."

She didn't even know what she was. Ryder spoke as though he knew, but all she could think of was the dying boy. And something Ryder said sliced through her fear. "You said you saw him fall," she accused. "Couldn't you have stopped it? Or saved him?"

"The little wretch had tried to pick my pocket."

He'd let the child fall beneath a carriage. "And that meant you wouldn't raise a hand to stop a death?"

"It brought you to a halt, didn't it?"

Horror hit her like ice water. "You let an innocent child be crushed just to capture me."

Who was worse—the vampires or the vampire slayer? She was caught in a nightmare, where every man around her was a villain.

Mr. Ryder pulled her to him, grinning, and she stumbled against him. Her knee flew up, for she'd seen maids protect themselves from arrogant, lecherous men this way. She slammed right between his thighs.

"Christ Jesus!" Mr. Ryder let go of her arm. His face distorted and he howled in pain. His hand clamped between his legs and he sank to his knees.

Thank heaven! Miranda darted away, almost falling over the uneven ground. She should run for her life, but she couldn't do that. Instead, she shoved aside a curious man who stood holding his tankard of ale and raced toward the fallen little boy.

Heat. Overbearing heat. Ironic that he had once served Lucifer, but he found this taproom, with its roaring fire and tightly packed human bodies, as hot as an oven. Lukos's enhanced senses choked on the stench of human sweat, foul breath, stale ale, and even urine, which implied that some of the drunken crowd either relieved themselves in a corner or let it dribble down their legs.

But he also heard the thrumming of blood and the pounding of strong, healthy hearts. God, he hungered. He hated taking blood—he had seen so much spilled on Wessex battlefields a thousand years ago, that it had sickened him to be like a scavenger searching for stupid prey. His father had told him that power was what elevated men above beasts. For him, it was what had made him into one.

Lukos moved into the shadowy corner of the taproom. Here the patrons were slouched over tankards. Here were those seeking to drink their way to oblivion.

He offered another way to escape the mortal world—

A hand grabbed his buttocks.

He turned slowly, aware of heavy breathing behind him, aware of the smell of sex, cloying perfume, onions, and beer.

A woman sidled close to him, shoving her bosom beneath his nose, and her hand boldly caressed his arse beneath his cloak. Fear, need, and sexual hunger burned in her small black eyes. Her mouth was thin and deep lines bracketed it. Wrinkles surrounded her eyes, and her skin was dark and puffy beneath. Broken blood vessels covered her nose.

Her life had aged her. She was perhaps in her middle thirties, but she had been used up by mortal life. Lukos heard the labored beat of her heart. He could smell the sickness around her. Drink, disease, hopelessness—this woman was dying. She was selling her body for a little comfort, a little money, a little warmth and contact.

His lip curled. He would take her. "Come, love. Do you have a room?"

The prostitute shook her head. "I don't rate one anymore. But I don't charge much; you can take me in the corner outside. Or in the stable. It's warm there."

Lukos glanced around. The young barmaid cast him a saucy glance. All the women in the room were beginning to look at him. To want him.

But Lukos wrapped his arm around the waist of the woman cooing beside him. "Come, love, let's find a place."

She led him out of the low door and they left the heat for the cool air of the spring evening. He could feel the effort it took her to breathe. Her fist went to her mouth to smother a cough. He stopped her and drew her back in the shadows that had gathered here, at this corner of the building.

She tugged her bodice down so her full, white left breast jumped up over the tight fabric and her nipple puckered in the brisk air, long and chocolate brown. She was hauling up her skirts when he leaned in and blew his breath gently by her ear.

"You're dying, love," he said softly.

Her skirts stopped at the top of her stockings. Fearful eyes met his. "What on earth do you mean, sir?"

"Would you like to be strong again? Stronger than you've ever been? Strong enough to take any man that hits you and break his neck?"

She tried to pull away. He pushed her back against the wall. Scarlet cream smeared her lips and sat in circles on her wrinkled cheeks. Henna-dyed curls fell around her face.

He used to transform dying street urchins into the undead. He would do it with this woman. It amused him to save the damned, to give them strength in a world that left them powerless.

"Do you want revenge on those who've hurt you?" he asked. "Couldn't you have had more than this, my love?"

She shook, staring at him. Captured by his gaze. But there was a core of strength in her, a yearning to survive—he felt it.

"I can give you a gift of everlasting life. . . ." He licked her neck. His tongue almost curled at the taste of sweat, at the gritty feel of her skin.

"N-no, sir," she managed, but she had no choice.

Lucifer had held him captive in a cell buried underground in rock for a thousand years, and then the earth had rumbled and shook and had split open before his eyes. He'd been free—free to feed, to search for his destined mate, to prepare for his revenge. It had been short lived. Within days he had been captured by Eve, the oldest vampire queen, and imprisoned again. This time with damned Zayan, the bloody ruthless vampire who had captured his sister Ara for Lucifer. Unfortunately, they'd been trapped in a sort of paradise, where it had been impossible for him to kill Zayan. He'd had no choice but to work with Zayan and combine their power to escape.

In the brief time he'd been free on the earth, Lukos had fed from mortal necks. Each time, he'd felt an intense rush of sexual arousal.

This time he felt nothing. Only an anger at the hunger that needed to be sated. Had imprisonment changed him? His slow heartbeat sped up slightly. *Feed. You must feed or die.*

Not die. He had too much to do first. He had a thousand-year-old prophecy to fulfill.

He wound his fingers in his prey's dirty hair, jerked her head to the side, and sank his fangs into her flesh.

"Help me! Please help me! Help my son!"

Miranda sank to her knees at the side of the motionless boy. His anguished mother was crouched on the other side of him. She had her arms wrapped around her boy and was sobbing against his chest. People crowded in closer and closer, forming a tight circle of mud-splattered skirts and boots, but no one did anything to help.

It angered her that people would do nothing but gawk, but the packed crowd gave her a few seconds before Mr. Ryder could capture her again.

"Oh, Will. Open yer eyes, please, me wee lovey." The mother's sobs echoed in Miranda's head.

She could not ignore a plea for help. She could not.

"Please move away from him for a moment. Let me see what is wrong," she urged the mother, but the woman would not budge, and Miranda had to grasp the back of the woman's rough gown and pull her away.

Bleary, tear-stained eyes looked up into hers. "He's dying. Please . . ."

Miranda touched the boy's throat. She felt no pulse. She slid her hand down to his small chest. She felt that sucking, hollow sense she got when someone had died.

"It's too late, miss."

She barely spared a glance at the morose-looking gentleman who'd made the pronouncement. Quickly, she babbled, "Oh, no. Children can deceive you. This happened to my wee brother—" As she let the words flow, she put her hand on the boy's chest. She had to clench her teeth as the warmth of her power rushed through her, but she found her tongue again. "He'd fallen in the pond and we thought he was gone. We'd thought there was no hope, but then one of the grooms hit him on his back—" She pressed harder. The heat roared down her arm and her muscles jerked with the power. It shot into the boy's body through her fingers.

"All this water rushed out of him, and suddenly he started sputtering and his eyes opened wide." She kept lying. She had to make this not look like a miracle. "Before our eyes he had come right back to life—" Her hand hummed on top of the boy. This story was the true story of what had happened to Simon.

Miranda could feel this boy's heartbeat—not through her fingertips, but in her soul. His pulse sped, then slowed, working erratically as the power surged through her.

What did everyone around her see? Could they guess what she was doing? Could they sense that she had a power that no one, not even she, could understand?

The boy's heartbeat began to settle in the steady, fast patter of a small child's. He would live. She was certain of it—so certain that the heat began to fade in her. The thrumming that filled her senses and screamed in her ears began to blissfully subside.

She saw the boy's lashes flicker. His eyes were going to open.

Gulping in a breath—it felt as though she didn't breathe while the power surged through her—she turned to Will's mother.

"Did you send this boy to pick a gentleman's pocket?" she asked softly.

The mother flushed. Beneath her tattered straw hat, she gave a surly, sly look. "We've got to eat."

"But he's just a child, and that thievery almost cost him his life."

Resentment simmered behind the woman's eyes.

Will's eyes opened. Wide, clear blue, and darting about in fear and confusion.

"Oh, me wee lad." His mother gathered him up and held him tight, and her straw hat tipped to the side. Tears ran down her pale cheeks.

Miranda didn't doubt that Will willingly did his thieving. He probably felt the responsibility already for his family. She dug out some coins she'd slipped into a small pocket in her pelisse. She had only moments. She heard angry protests behind her. Mr. Ryder must be pushing his way through the crowd, and within moments he'd have her. Panicked, she looked around, but the circle had tightened as she performed her miracle, and already the story was spreading from mouth to eager ear—a boy had been dead and some unknown woman had brought him back to life.

Will was crying along with his mother now; he'd have pain, but that would fade soon. She put the money in his hand.

Strong arms grasped her shoulders and pulled her back. She cried out, but the sound was swallowed by the crowd, and the firm hand dragged her into the crush of people.

"Got you, you soft-hearted twit," Mr. Ryder growled by her ear.

"Better that than a monster," she gasped.

He was dragging her through the crowd again. She realized he held a pistol, which was making the sea of bodies open for him.

"That pistol is drawing more attention than my miracle," she snapped at him.

The look of raw fury he gave her made her quiver. He yanked her along and she could see the gleam of lamps now, between the people, which meant he'd have her free of the crowd in an instant.

She could try to run. Would he shoot her? Or worse, would he try to kill her and hit someone else?

Roughly, he shoved her through the sparser grouping of people, toward the carriages that still flowed in and out of the yard. The story was spreading like wildfire. She heard the word *witch* muttered, then laughter and denials.

"You see," Ryder snarled. "I'll be more merciful than they will."

"I doubt that." How infuriating to have magic power yet be so powerless now. At least she'd saved Will. If that was her last act in life, it was worth it.

The pistol drove into her side. "Hurry toward the stables, Miss Bond."

Miss Bond. He was going to blow her away with his pistol, but he still adhered to good manners. She choked on the hysterical laugh that bubbled up.

The hum was behind them now. Then she heard a man shout, "Where did she go?"

And the babble rose again.

Mr. Ryder shoved her forward and she stumbled against the stone wall of the stable. The tang of manure came to her nose, making her gag. The low whinny of horses filled her ears, and she filled her lungs and screamed.

No one came. No one shouted or called out to find out what was wrong. A woman's screams weren't unusual, weren't enough to bring the stablehands out to the rescue.

Ryder's hand clamped over her mouth. The leather tasted of dirt and sweat, and was smooth from holding reins. The pressure crushed her lips against her teeth and she tasted the coppery warmth of her own blood.

He spun on his heel. She felt weightless for a moment, then the stone wall of the stable slammed hard into her back. Tears sprang instantly. Her breath exhaled into his hand. More blood. She had to swallow hard to take it down, it welled so fast.

"You think you saved that boy, don't you?" he rasped by her ear. "You brought him back from the dead. That's what you think, isn't it? That's not what you're doing. You don't have any bloody idea how you're cursing the people you think you save."

Cursing? She stared at him. Could it be true? She'd just thought they would live—she'd never thought beyond that. But Ryder belonged to the Royal Society, and they must know more about her than she did.

Ryder leaned closer, until she could see the silvery sheen of moonlight cross his blue eyes. "You're a virgin, aren't you? A baron's daughter and a treasure in your world. A shame to kill you. But you've got to be stopped."

The pistol was underneath her heart, and his hand was still clamped over her mouth. He'd shoot her, tear her apart, splatter most of her against the stone wall, and steal her final scream with his hand.

A black shape materialized behind Mr. Ryder. Moonlight rippled over dark fur, flashed on teeth as a jaw opened wide.

Long, curved fangs drove into Mr. Ryder's throat, and the wolf pulled back, dragging the vampire slayer off her. Ryder clawed at the animal's snout and punched it with the pistol.

Wild panic was in his eyes. The wolf was a huge beast, as black as night.

She should run back to the inn's yard. She should cry for help. She should cry for the magistrate. She should save Mr. Ryder's life—

Bang!

With a burst of smoke, a deafening roar, the pistol fired. She gasped. The pistol's muzzle was right against the wolf's throat. Blood spurted, but the animal did not drop. It did not even loosen its grip. It reared up, dragging Mr. Ryder, then flung him to the side. He screamed as he flew, then landed with a thud in a muddy puddle.

A flash of light dazzled her—it was like watching small diamonds being thrown in the air. Then Lukos stood there, fangs long and red with blood, his eyes ablaze, reflecting light like silver coins.

Lukos caught her in his arms and she didn't fight. His chest was broad and solid as he drew her to him and held her tight. His hands were big, his splayed fingers a shield for her back. She didn't even care that he had his other huge hand under her bottom.

His embrace felt so protective. She'd rather be with Lukos than with Mr. Ryder.

Lukos swept her into his arms, balanced her there easily, and began to run. "Where are we going?" she demanded. He'd returned because he'd fed. She guessed that. She didn't want to know. Her stomach turned somersaults inside her.

"The carriage," he growled. "Then the hell away from here." His long strides were taking them around the inn on the side away from the yard, through the black shadows cast by the trees.

"Who in hell was he?" Lukos demanded.

"A vampire slayer."

They were nearing the yard. The clop of hooves grew louder, along with the babble of voices. Had people forgotten about her and the man with the pistol?

"Most slayers don't attack innocent maidens." He lowered her to her feet. "Can you walk?"

"Y-yes," she said shakily. "I saved a child's life. I brought him back from the dead. He saw me do it and thinks I'm a demon he should destroy."

She heard voices—a group of women gossiping about the fallen child and the mysterious lady who had helped, who had been dragged away by some gentleman with a pistol.

They certainly hadn't forgotten.

"That's what you did when you touched Zayan—you tried to return mortal life to him?" He flashed a brief grin. "A naïve hope, love." His arm on her elbow urged her forward.

The carriage was rumbling toward her. Where was Zayan? Already inside?

"Why naïve?" she argued. Why was she trying to cross swords with Lukos? Why did she feel such a need to understand that she was willing to fight with a being who had transformed from wolf to man in front of her eyes? "You are without souls; you are the undead. I thought—"

"Our souls are not lost. They are not in limbo; they cannot be returned. Lucifer owns my soul, and I sold it willingly."

Why? But men were willing to sell their souls—for power, for wealth, for sex, for revenge. . . . Miranda raced after Lukos and realized that he wasn't holding her arm anymore, yet she was willingly pursuing him. "Am I a demon? You are one, so you should know, shouldn't you?" Why was she doing this? How could she trust his answer? But she couldn't stop herself. "Do you feel it in me? Am I evil?"

The wind snapped his long black hair around his face, and his cloak whipped about like large wings. "You are powerful, my lady. That is all I can sense about you."

My lady. "Is that the truth? I can't trust what you say."

"Then why ask?" he growled. He took a long, loping stride, leaving her as the carriage rumbled to a stop. He sent magic to fling the door open wide. He turned back to her.

Should she run?

To what? She glanced back toward the stable and saw the gleam of golden hair—Mr. Ryder had hauled himself out of the mud and was in pursuit.

She bit her lip, hard, and tasted a wash of blood. A foolish thing to do in front of a vampire.

Lukos held out his hand. She took it. He had saved her life. He had faced a slayer to do it. She was safest with him. Or was she? Or did she just not care what happened to her anymore?

And if what Ryder had said was true—she was damning those she saved—she was no different from a vampire.

She chose Lukos.

But as she jumped up into the carriage. Lukos threw in a powerful ball of purple light and suddenly the interior transformed before her eyes; it changed from a simple carriage into a lavishly sinful space. The seats became larger, and covered in white silk, mounded with ivory pillows. As she stared in astonishment, the purple lights suddenly raced under her skirts. They rushed up her legs as she shrieked in shock, then danced in wild circles between her thighs. Suddenly, the energy surrounded both her wet cunny and the astonishingly sensitive entrance to her derriere.

Lukos jumped into the carriage and slammed the door behind him.

"Stop this—" *Oh goodness,* it felt so incredibly good. She stood there, her hands braced against one of the seats as the magic lights beneath her skirts whirled and spiraled and teased her. Her legs were melting. She had to resist . . . she had to . . . "Stop—"

But her voice died away. Why stop? She couldn't remember

why. There was Blackthorne ... whom she had fallen in love with, but she couldn't have him. She couldn't marry him when she might be a demon, when her power might truly mean she was cursed—

Lukos was on his knees in front of her. "I saved your life, love, because I've felt a desire for you I've never felt for anyone before. I realized you were the reason I felt no sexual need when I fed—desire came in the instant I saw you."

He began to lift her skirts, and she couldn't stop him. Not with the magic teasing both her throbbing clitoris and her tingling bottom. She was rocking, feeling that same intense pleasure as she had when she'd tried to save Zayan.

"Let me make love to you, my angel," Lukos growled.

Oh heavens. Heavens. Heavens. She couldn't answer. She cried out. The lights had delved inside both her cunny and her rump, filling her and stretching her, and she'd burst—simply exploded—in pleasure.

"Good, sweet angel." Lukos's voice was hoarse with approval. "You're coming."

5

Punishment

Translation of the Prophecy of Lukos
From a manuscript held in the archives of the Royal Society for
the Investigation of Mysterious Phenomena

A rend in the earth shall set him free. Signs shall be sent to his disciples, to those who serve him nobly. They will feast in blood in preparation of his rise, until the seventh day before Samhain, when they will fast in honor of the final ascension. And once he steps upon the earth, he shall summon those disciples and they shall stand at his side, an army of unthinkable power and infinite evil.

He shall find the woman bred to be his mate. Vampyre, mortal, and descendent of a god. His mate has been created to destroy God's creation: man. But as he prepares to launch his army and subject the earth to eternal darkness, the mate of his soul will bear him a son, and that son shall bring him to his knees and take his very life.

His army will continue and much blood will be spilled, and the earth will be plunged into two hundred years of darkness, doom, and strife, and then the world will come to an end—

Something unexpected happened as the woman—Miranda—came for him. Lukos felt it in his mind. It was as though he had thrown open a large door and had let blinding light fall upon him. He'd opened himself to her. He could feel his thoughts racing into her mind, and hers flooded into his.

He had Miranda's skirts in his hands—a bunched swath of silk that carried her rosy, innocent, and alluringly feminine scent. This had never happened to him before. Since the first night he had gone into Lucifer's labyrinth, he had been able to keep his mind closed to anyone and anything.

He had not even experienced this with Serena Lark, the half-vampire woman who he'd believed was his intended mate.

Another smell came to him—the earthy, rich perfume of Miranda's juices as she rocked in her climax. It called to him. His desire surged. He yanked up her gown and put his mouth to her damp nether curls, letting her skirts and lacy petticoats fall around his shoulders.

Thrusting his tongue out, he licked her creamy cunny, tasting the pleasure he'd given her. With one hand, he freed his cock. He moaned as it sprang from his trousers, standing up to the heavens and pointing to Miranda's slick passage. The purple lights whirled around her, brighter now. The energy of her orgasm was combining with his magic, lighting the carriage with a beautiful, unearthly purple glow.

It reminded him of a sunset, and that made him bury his face between her thighs and lick her harder.

"Lukos." She spoke his name breathily. She clutched his shoulders. This was his world—the darkness of a bedroom, the gloom of a carriage, the crisp, cool dark of the forest, where leaves crunched underneath a woman's arse as she fucked. His world was night, and he could glimpse in Miranda's mind and

see her thoughts were always about sunshine. His only pleasures were erotic ones, and he saw in her heart a great love for
family. Dimly, he remembered that—what it was like to be part
of family. To love others.

She opened up too much in him, this woman. So he clasped
her firm bottom and pulled her quim tight to his face. So he
wouldn't have to think.

You are magical, Miranda. And she was. Her cunny was still
pulsing, the walls clutching his tongue as he thrust it in. She
tasted of ripe, earthy juices.

Touch yourself, she whispered in thought.

He saw her hands at her breasts, kneading and squeezing.
Her climax had shattered her defenses, and the magic was igniting her natural wanton urges.

I don't need to, he answered in her thoughts, and he held her
hips as she began rocking against his mouth.

She looked down, her now disheveled hair falling free of her
pins. It hung in spun-gold waves around her face. He knew his
cock was standing proud, bobbing in rhythm to her gyrations
on his face.

He still sensed a hesitation inside her, a ripple of fear. He
wanted to free her completely. And he knew how to do it. He
added another spell to the magic already swirling around
the carriage. This one would control them both; it would tap into
Miranda's most private, darkest fantasies and bring one to life.

"What do you mean—my most private fantasies?" Miranda
asked sharply.

She realized she was clutching her breasts, her skirts were
bunched up on Lukos's broad shoulders, and he was licking her
silly. But she'd glimpsed his thoughts.

And they were extremely naughty.

Since the moment he'd saved her from Ryder, she'd felt a
kind of connection with him. Energy crackled when he'd touched
her like tiny bolts of lightning.

"Now," Lukos growled.

Suddenly, the blue lights lifted her, and a stream of blue stars forced Lukos to the floor of the carriage. He was lying on his back. She actually saw surprise—and fear—in his reflective eyes. She was hovering twelve inches above the floor.

Lukos's arms were outstretched above his head, and the blue light spun around his wrists, locking them together. The lights transformed into blue velvet—a band tied neatly to bind his hands together. Another band of velvet appeared at his ankles to secure them. And one, to her shock, wrapped around the very base of his . . . his erection, and magically tied a bow.

You dream of being in control. Dominating a man. His deep voice vibrated in her mind.

Blushing hotly, she protested, "No, of course not. What madness."

Deny it all you want, he chuckled. *Why else are my hands bound? I'm enjoying this, my love, and want to share this with you.*

She had to admit she liked having him this way. Though she suspected he could use magic to break those bonds whenever he wanted.

The blue lights suddenly rushed around *her.* Her dress opened by itself, buttons popping free of their loops, one after another, like tiny fireworks. Her bodice fell and was dragged down her arms as though by invisible hands. Her corset laces undid themselves— she twisted to watch—and the ends whirled through the air as they loosened by magic. Her corset dropped just below her bosom; her shift disappeared. Simply vanished, leaving her bared breasts propped on the firm shelf of her corset rim. It made them stick right out, made them look huge, the nipples dark and hard.

The sight was unbearable exciting. It felt wanton and delicious.

Lukos licked his lips.

He grinned. "I can control myself, my dear. Even when faced with the two most perfect tits in existence."

Even that word in his husky voice—tits—felt deliciously naughty. She wriggled on him, making her breasts sway. Blue lights appeared at the tips of her breasts. "Oh," she moaned, as the tingling sensation struck her nipples. Then she felt a jolt of agony. A thrilling, shocking pain. She could barely breathe. Then saw. The lights had vanished, leaving two metal devices that were hanging off her nipples, pinching them. They were lined with velvet, but the pressure was so intense.

The lights swirled again, and her hands were pulled back. Ropes wound around her wrists, just as they had done to Lukos; then they whirled up her arms and wrapped around her breasts, making a tight figure eight. The ends suddenly threaded through rings on the clamps on her tits. And when she wriggled her hands, she tugged those vicelike clamps, and sent pleasure and pain rushing from her nipples to her quim.

Dominating him, indeed. She liked the feel of the ropes.

Surely this couldn't be *her* doing? Her fantasy? How she realized, in that moment, she was not a normal proper woman at all.

More ropes materialized, looped around the one binding her hands, and these wrapped in an intricate pattern of knots around her thighs, then encircled her ankles. She was bound, and each time she moved, the roughness of the rope teased her skin.

Her quim ached. She was fluttering the muscles herself. She wanted, wanted, wanted to come again.

"Then put me in your fantasy, love." He laughed. "I'll be happy to oblige."

"Hush, I'm in charge," she admonished. To her shock, a gag of silk appeared over his mouth, tied so tight she could see the curves of his smile through the fabric. Had she summoned that?

She was lifted by the blue lights and set down on Lukos's

face. Underneath her gown, she wore snug drawers with a lace-trimmed slit. She straddled Lukos's chest, and he lifted his head, his eyes drinking in the sight of the drawers, pulled taut against her pubic curls. His hips gyrated slightly.

Instead of moving back down toward his groin, she pinned his biceps with her knees, and pushed her hips forward so her now damp and aching quim brushed his chin. She wriggled again, so her sex and its lips—exposed just at the tips—sank down against his gagged mouth. Her drawers and the pretty lace edging were growing wetter and she could smell her potent arousal.

Lukos breathed deeply. She felt his tongue push the silk into her. His mouth worked against her, trying to suck the lips of her sex but unable to capture them. As the blue lights rushed around them, Miranda danced her hips on him, twisting and grinding her mound into his mouth. She rocked ahead to bury his nose into fragrant silk and wet curls through the slit in her undergarments.

Ah, love, I think your fantasy is to torment me.

She heard a rhythmic pounding, turned, and saw his hips lifting and his bottom bouncing against the floor. It was thrilling to be in control—to have her wet, aroused, ripe sex on his face. Feeling naughty, Miranda turned herself around, her cunny still against his mouth, but her silk-clad bottom pushing against his nose.

The swaying of the carriage sent her rocking against his face.

"You are not to climax," she admonished, in a deep and threatening voice.

As you wish. I'm your prisoner, and this, my love, is your fantasy.

The erotic smell of her excitement was becoming too much to bear. His silk gag was soaking wet from her leaking fluids and his saliva as he tried to manipulate her with his mouth.

Even bound, he was trying to pleasure her.

She was so excited she could barely think. He thought she

wanted to torment him? She could think of no better torture than reaching orgasm on his handsome face while he was destined to remain unsatisfied. The ties at her hands released.

Dipping a finger between her curls, she found her throbbing, aching clitoris—Caroline had told her about *that*—and rocked on him while rubbing herself. He let out a muffled groan. She wriggled to and fro, engulfing him with her generous bottom and growing closer and closer to an explosion.

His arms and wrists and hands strained at the bonds as she worked faster and faster. His hips began to thrust up in a rhythm to match hers, and she realized he was going to please himself.

"No," she cried. In a desperate action—without thinking—she bent forward and slapped her hand down on his thick shaft to stop him from moving.

He came. His whole body went tense and arched up from the floor of the carriage. His face lifted, burrowing right into her sopping, melting, eager sex.

There were no more magic lights. Suddenly, Miranda saw that the twinkling blue and purple stars had vanished. Lukos's magic wasn't controlling her—she was doing this because she was wild and wanton and she wanted it.

The shocking realization hit her just as she climaxed.

She writhed with the powerful explosion. Lights burst before her eyes—not magic lights, ones triggered in her own head by the wonderful pleasure streaking through her. She was crying out, loud enough to be heard in London.

As it died away, she fell back and hit the carriage wall. Miranda didn't care. She clutched the two seats to keep upright and greedily sucked in breaths of air.

She had just flown. She had whirled and soared. And now she was damp with sweat and barely able to breathe.

Lukos sat up beside her and she impulsively reached out to him. She put her hand against his broad chest, right above his heart—

Blackness. It enveloped her, and she suddenly couldn't see anything, even with her eyes wide open. She heard a distant crackle and roar—the sound of flames. She smelled a sharp, acrid odor that made her stomach churn. Footsteps. Shuffling ones. And rasping breathing. The sounds came from all around her. She was twisting, trying to see in the heavy, hot darkness. Panic rose. Her limbs were shaking, and they felt numb, unable to move. Something was coming for her and she was trapped.

An image suddenly appeared before her. It was a young man without hair. A woman grasped his jaw and wrenched his head back. A red light glowed. Suddenly that glowing tip plunged forward and Miranda saw it pierce Lukos's eye.

She screamed. The vision vanished and another came. She felt pain through her entire body, and she saw Lukos strapped to a smooth rock surface. He was being whipped, punished because he had failed to learn the magic he was being taught that day. Blood ran freely on his back. His brain was swimming with the pain, but some magic prevented him from finding the escape of unconsciousness. She heard a deep, angry voice: *I will whip all the rebellion out of you, Lukos. You are my servant. An apprentice of Lucifer. Defy me one more time and I will destroy you. I will have your body torn apart inch by precious inch . . .*

The blackness and the images whirled away before Miranda. They sucked into a glowing point of light, then vanished.

"You were tortured," she gasped to Lukos. "I—I saw it." She shivered and realized she was perched on the carriage seat, her wrinkled skirts spilling out around her. She was shaking. The blue ropes had vanished, but Lukos was sitting on the floor, staring at her with his brows slanted down over his glittering eyes.

He leapt up to her side and drew her into his embrace. He was the undead, but he was warm, and the fear and icy darkness inside began to fade away. "I saw you being whipped. I saw your eyes—" She had to stop. Just thinking of it made bile rise. "I felt your pain."

"Angel." He crooned it, rocking her.

She could not believe she felt such comfort in the arms of a vampire. But he had been tortured. "Who?" she gasped. "Who did that to you?"

His hands stroked gently. "What did you mean you saw it?"

Halting, she described the vision of him being whipped. Miranda knew it was dangerous, but as she stared into his handsome face, her heart lurched in sympathy.

Lukos wrapped his arms tight around Miranda. He had not embraced a woman to comfort her for a thousand years, not since he had last hugged his sister and had promised her that he would be fine, that his apprenticeship with Lucifer would bring peace and security to his home.

"Are you an empath?" he asked her softly. He had thought her only a mortal woman when he had first seen her on the road; now he realized she was a unique being, one he had never encountered before. If she was an empath—

She had to stay away from the likes of him. His memories of his time serving Lucifer could steal an empath's mind, could send one into permanent madness. The devil wove magic to block some of the torture and fear, to help his apprentices survive, but an empath would feel it all, without any relief from Lucifer's shields.

"I don't know. All I know is that when I touched your heart, I saw images—dark, horrible, nightmarish ones."

"Don't touch me there again," he warned. He did not want her to release his memories. If she could see them in her own head, experience them herself, she risked condemning herself to insanity.

"I felt something. A deep sort of tug in my soul, and I thought I could help you—"

"Don't," he snarled. "You can't dare." He had to push her

away. He had to stop her, and to do that he had to make her see him as an evil demon again. Which was what he was. He brusquely released her and pointed to her dress. "Straighten your skirts or everyone will guess you've let a vampire beneath them."

She jerked back. She moved down the seat away from him, smoothing her clothes. The surprise and betrayal in her eyes lanced his heart. It had been almost a millennium since he'd felt pain there. He remembered now why he had turned that kind of pain into hatred and thirst for revenge. He, who had known torture at Lucifer's hands, found the hurt in this woman's eyes crippling. He couldn't understand it.

She had captivated him with her arousing fantasy. She had not wanted just to dominate him. She'd fantasized of bringing him to his knees with her sensuality. He'd learned what English ladies were like in the nineteenth century. Even though he'd been imprisoned for a thousand years by Lucifer for his act of rebellion, he had been allowed, on each solstice and each equinox, to cast himself into the body of a mortal man.

For one night each season, he had been able to experience life. It was meant to be a torture as much as a reprieve. One night gave him a hunger to live again, but he would be banished from the mortal body with the dawn. As the sun rose, he would find he was once more in his rock prison.

Nearly four thousand nights he'd been free of his prison—almost eleven mortal years. For the first decades, he had spent those nights in search of his younger sister, Ara. Lucifer had taken her prisoner to make him obedient. Had the devil released her as he'd promised?

But he had not found Ara. And after one hundred years of searching on those four nights of freedom, he had known there was no reason to hunt anymore. If she had been freed, she would have been dead. She would have gone on to the after-life—an innocent, good woman—which meant he, the demon, had lost her forever.

For Ara, he wanted to rip Satan apart with his own hands. But he needed power to do it—the power of the mate described in his prophecy. He'd thought he could find that power with Serena Lark, the woman who had been the child of the union between Eve, the first vampiress, and a fallen angel. He had thought she was the woman of the prophecy. But Serena had never glowed with the power that radiated off Miranda like a golden halo.

Could he take Miranda's power and use it to find the vengeance he craved, once and for all?

And he, who lusted for revenge above all else, wanted now to get on his knees before Miranda, kiss her hands, make her forgive him for his sudden cold cruelty, and speak to her heart—

He couldn't let himself do it.

The carriage door flew open, and Zayan leaped inside, cape flowing around him, eyes silver and wild with feral excitement. "They are on the hunt for the woman they believe is a witch. We must—" He broke off, and Lukos saw the vampire's gaze lock on Miranda's crumpled skirts. No doubt the vampire could scent the smell of sex in the carriage. Even a mortal man would be able to do it.

Zayan's eyes turned vivid red with rage.

Lukos tensed, ready to fight to the death—or for them, since they were undead, the ultimate destruction.

It took a great deal of trust for him to let himself be tied up.

Drake Swift pulled at the ropes that bound his wrists and secured him to the posts of the enormous bed. Had he not done exactly the same thing to Serena, long ago, while trying to seduce her and capture her heart? She'd trusted him, and that meant he could not refuse her wish to be the dominant in this erotic game now.

He did trust her. After a lifetime of trusting no one, he would trust his wife Serena and Jonathon, the Earl of Sommersby, with his life. Or rather his existence, not his life, since he was a vampire.

He glanced up now to see his lovely wife. She was pacing at the end of the bed. Her hair hung in loose black waves to the small of her back. Her wrapper was open, revealing her larger breasts and the taut curve of her ripened, pregnant belly. She tapped her chin, letting her gaze slowly slide up his body from bound ankles to secured wrists. Heat rushed over his skin in the wake of her blatantly aroused look. "Now that I have you bound, I am not certain what I should do with you."

"Leave him there," urged a masculine voice from the door. "Leave him and come to *my* bed."

"Don't even think of it, Sommersby," Drake called out. He craned his neck to see Serena's other husband—and his former partner when he had been a vampire slayer—lounging in the doorway. "I'd shift shape to a bat and reach your bed before you did."

Jonathon chuckled.

Serena placed her hand on her hips. "I thought you had both agreed not to argue while I am enceinte. I do not wish my twins to be learning these habits."

"We're not arguing," Drake and Jonathon protested together.

Serena, though married to both he and Jonathon, had taken Jonathon's name. Drake had insisted on it. She should be a countess, he had decided. English society would not have accepted a love affair between an unmarried woman and an earl, so it had to be marriage. And Jonathon and Serena were obviously so much in love that society would have noticed. Of course, Drake and Serena were deeply in love too. But no one cared who Drake Swift was married to. Only their closest friends knew they lived in a ménage à trois. And those friends were those who knew they were also vampires.

Drake grinned. "I think you should be fair, little lark, and tie

Jonathon up too." His cock lifted from his groin as she crooked her finger to bid Sommersby to come for a little punishment. . . .

Serena sighed. They had fallen to the mattress in a tangle of heaving chests and sweaty limbs. "A bath," Drake suggested. "I've ordered one to be prepared.

"Ooh, lovely," Serena gasped. But she rolled away from him, cradling her heavy stomach. She was a lucky woman to have two such delicious men. Drake would be the leader in bondage games, and she and Jonathon would follow. Then Jonathon would lay her down afterward and lick her cunny for an hour, as he'd done tonight, until she was weak from orgasms and wondering if she could melt away to nothing in sheer sexual exhaustion.

Tonight, she had tortured her two bound men by sucking each one in turn but stopping as they came close to climax. She was certain they could break their bonds, but each played the game. And then, to add to their exquisite torture, she'd slid two ivory wands inside their tight derrieres and one up her own. She'd ridden them both and climaxed hard for each one, before they had exploded in their own ecstasies.

But now, glancing up, she saw the strain in both men's eyes. She knew the men, just as she was, were terrified to face the truth that their twins might not survive. She knew both were working to find a solution in their own ways. Drake through using his charm to coax all the knowledge he could from the vampire queens. Jonathon had been forcing himself to work in his laboratory even during daylight hours.

They were men and believed they must be stoic—unflappable, unemotional, rational, and strong. They must be the strength on which she could rely.

In silence, she took both men's hands and led them to the bath.

* * *

Serena's belly floated, buoyant in the water. It took some of the weight and pain away, and soothed her back. Her breasts were large and full, her nipples dark, and they bobbed as the water sloshed.

She finished washing Jonathon, soaping her hands and rubbing them over his solid, well-muscled chest. Each man possessed shoulders as wide as the huge bathtub, and because of their large, long-limbed frames, Drake and Jonathon sat at each end of the tub, and she nestled in the middle, between them.

Serena hated to spoil the erotic pleasure of the moment, but knew she could not avoid it any longer. "There is something we must speak about," she said. "I know you men will not. You are afraid to worry me."

She stepped up out of the water, and the rivulets ran down her body. Drips gathered around her protruding navel. Instantly, both Jonathon and Drake were on their feet to help her from the tub. With each of her men's hands clamped securely on her wrists, she clambered to the step, then stepped down to the thick mat beside the tub. She reached for a towel that hung by the fireplace.

The men were waiting and she had to speak of it. "Althea's baby is not thriving," she said softly.

Jonathon swung out of the bath and grabbed a white towel to wrap around his waist—actually below his waist, just at the line of his hipbones. He picked up another and rubbed at his hair with one hand, but wrapped the other around her and drew her close. "We'll find the answer, Serena. Your mother has agreed to help us."

She clutched the towel to her heavy breasts. "I don't think she knows how, Jonathon. I have searched through the library here, and the one at the monastery—" That one was a famed library of the Royal Society, tended by the monks for several centuries. She and Althea had been the first women permitted to enter.

And that had been only at the insistence of Lord Denby, the Head of the Society. He was the only member of the society who knew that she and Althea were here. He was too afraid that rogue members would try to destroy Althea's child—a vampire child—and would try to kill Serena before she could give birth to her twins.

"There is an answer, Serena. The books talk of born vampires."

"But we've never found any. And no book speaks of how the vampire children survived. If we cannot figure out how to feed them—"

"We will." Drake's deep voice cut through her rising panic.

She trusted both Jonathon and Drake, but she knew there were some disasters that even the deepest love could not prevent.

"I don't believe my mother can help. She barely remembers how I survived. She surrendered me to a mortal wet nurse. And that has not worked for Serry."

Jonathon tossed aside the damp towel he'd used on his dark brown hair. Wild and tangled, it hung rakishly around his dark eyes. "I just received a letter from Denby. I just read it before our . . . session."

She had to smile at his choice of words. They had all just done the most erotic things. And she heard the uplift of his voice. The hope.

"Has he found an answer? A way to save our children?"

Jonathon kissed to top of her wet hair, then turned her and began gently drying her hair with a towel. "The Society has discovered a young woman living in London with a power they have never seen before. Apparently, she has the power to resurrect the dead."

She jerked around, which meant he tugged her hair.

"What?" cried Drake from the tub. Sloshing water told her he was getting out.

"Miss Eugenia Bond claims that her niece has this power. She finally revealed this to Lord Denby. She was attacked by a vampire with her own stake, and the lady in question—Miranda Bond—brought her back to life. Just by laying her hand on the victim's chest, Miss Miranda Bond is capable of returning life. Either by bringing back the soul or imparting some sort of force into the body that jolts the heart back to life." He paused, thoughtfully. "I would like to study her."

"Jonathon . . ." But she knew his methods of study would not be like his father's. His father cut vampires open to try to understand how they worked. The late Earl of Sommersby had dissected dead vampires and "live" ones.

Serena bit her lip. "Do you mean that you think this woman could bring our children back to life if they . . . die?"

Drake was at her side. He stroked her shoulder and faced Jonathon. "Or return their souls to them and make them mortal before that happens?"

Jonathon nodded. "This may be the only answer."

"But we don't know. And this lady is in London."

"We would have to travel. With Althea's young baby and you—"

"Ready to pop out two babies at any moment," she added ruefully. "But it's March and some of the passes are still filled with snow."

"Denby says the Society is trying to protect her. Eugenia has been keeping the girl's power a secret, but a slayer named James Ryder has found her."

"Ryder," Drake spat.

Serena swallowed hard. "I've never heard of a slayer named Ryder."

"He's rogue. For years he's worked for himself—he offers vampires protection for a price. He's even killed some of the demons that the Society has been protecting because he was paid to do it by other vampires. He's driven by greed."

"So someone wants to kill this woman?" Serena asked.

"If she can revert vampires to mortals, there are a lot of the undead who would want to see her destroyed," Drake answered.

She shivered. She knew what it was to have both demons and the Society in pursuit of her.

"So we must go to London." There was no other choice. She looked up at Jonathon and Drake. "But could I be made mortal? Could our children? If we are born of the undead, do we even have souls?" She looked from Drake's silvery green eyes to Jonathon's, as dark and reflective as jet in the low light of the fire. "Would you both choose to be mortal again?"

"I would choose to be whatever you wish to be and can be, Serena," Drake vowed.

"As would I," Jonathon added.

But Drake had been made by Lukos—he had never had a choice. And Jonathon had chosen to be made a vampire by Drake to save his life.

What right did she have to keep them from making the choice that was really in their hearts?

Drake waited until Serena was asleep. She lay on their large bed, turned on her side. A pillow was caught between her legs, and one partly supported her rounded belly, for this made her more comfortable when she slept.

Drake lit a cheroot and walked out to the balcony. Clouds raced past the half moon, and the peaks of the Carpathians were lost in a haziness that meant a snowstorm approached. Jonathon was leaning on the carved balustrade, also smoking.

Drake joined him. Jonathon acknowledged him with a brief nod, while not turning his gaze from the turbulent sky.

"I felt an awareness of Lukos today. Since he was my sire, I am connected to him."

Jonathon nodded. Drake had sired Jonathon.

"For a few moments, my heartbeat changed. It slowed," Drake sighed. "And I think it did so to match the rhythm of Lukos's heart."

Jonathon rubbed his jaw, withdrew his cheroot. "That would mean he's freed."

Six and Nine

"I'm looking for a whore—one who does not object to a good whipping." Fury crackled in him, and James Ryder needed a release. He also needed information, so he would engage in two business transactions with the innkeeper.

The burly, balding innkeeper rubbed the side of his nose. "I don't usually send any of my lasses to men who like such things."

Once again, it all came down to money. He threw a pile of notes in front of the man. "Did you see a blond woman traveling with two unusually tall, dark-haired men? The men had long black hair and were wearing fur-lined cloaks."

The man hesitated. Ryder added another note to the pile, then made to remove them all.

At once the innkeeper held up his thick hand. "I did, indeed, see a dark-haired gent in such a cloak. He needed direction, but asked for my discretion."

Paid for it, Ryder knew. He left the stack and threw on another note.

The innkeeper looked anguished. "The problem is, I can't remember where he wanted to go. It's as familiar to me as my own name, but I can't remember."

"Blackthorne Castle," Ryder offered, and the truth was enough to break through the vampire's compulsion for a moment. The innkeeper's eyes brightened, but almost immediately the glow faded. He looked wistfully at the money. "I'm afraid I can't bring it to mind."

"Well, I want to go to Blackthorne Castle. Which road would I take?"

But the man could not help him there—claimed he knew the way, but again could not remember it. Bloody vampires. So Ryder bought a woman, a seasoned whore with large breasts who liked to be spanked and tied to the bed.

She glowed with life and was moaning the instant he began to undo her dress. He wanted her naked, wanted those lush breasts to smother him as he wrestled her on the bed. "I want to tie you up but fight you to do it."

She shrugged at that.

"Take your blinkin' bonnet off," he muttered. He didn't intend to undress. "What of Blackthorne Castle, do you know it?"

She shook her head. "No, but there's those who work for Mrs. Coventry that do. She's got a place in the next village along the road—Witherby on the Marsh."

Ryder tackled her then, shoving her onto the sagging bed. She laughed as though she'd never been so carefree and excited. Women who'd done this for a while, who were used to haste and indifference, were the most eager to play.

He had her wrists pinned to the mattress when she asked, "You a friend of Lord Blackthorne's? Is that why you want to play this game? 'E holds the wildest orgies. Dozens of girls are brought in for 'is pleasures. Some girls have never come back. Are ye one of them, then?"

So Miss Miranda Bond was racing to a pervert who murdered some of the tarts he slept with?

"I'm no friend of his," he snapped.

"Oh." Her strength flowed surprisingly and she flipped him

onto the bed. Her large breasts covered his nose and mouth, and he coughed for breath. Her flesh was hot, her nipples large and hard. He was reaching for one plump teat with his lips when moonlight caught them both and he saw it—the sharp tips of newly made fangs. She was laughing wildly, her eyes gleaming, the light flying off their reflective surface. "You are young and beautiful," she cooed. Though lined with dark paint and wrinkles, her eyes glittered.

Vampire eyes.

He would have to stake her after their bout.

She suddenly reared back. "You mean me harm," she gasped. She scrambled off him and the bed. Her dress gaped open, hanging off her shoulders, but she ran for the door.

He was up and in pursuit, but she reached the door first and wrenched it so hard the hinges gave out. She tossed it back toward him and leapt through the opening.

He let the door hit the bed and followed his fleeing vampire. She was newly made. Had she been made by the damned vampire who had attacked him to save Miranda Bond?

He could run as quickly as a vampire—he'd made a pact with one of the queens once to spare her life and in return she'd given him the speed of a demon.

But his vampiress had vanished in the hallway. A door swung sharply, caught by a gust of wind. Stake at the ready, Ryder went to the room. The curtains blew in from the open window. He was at the sill in an instant.

A red cloud swirled below him. He glanced around, perplexed. He couldn't see the vampire. She wasn't in the red haze roiling below. And there wasn't any red light that could cast that hellish colored glow on the fog.

Damnation, she couldn't have gone this way.

He had to let her go. He had to go on to the next village and find his route to Blackthorne Castle. Once he'd destroyed Miranda, he could return for this vampire.

Miranda was his ticket to wealth, to power, to the realization of his dream to crush his damned father.

The pleasure of staking a heart through a set of plump tits wasn't worth losing everything.

She was trapped again.

Miranda sat at Zayan's side and moonlight flickered into the carriage as the wheels raced beneath the trees. Branches reached across the road and clacked together in the crisp spring wind. The horses drove hell-bent for leather, and they overtook other carriages, rocking and jostling on the uneven road.

Miranda's heart was in her throat. She sat opposite Zayan and Lukos—and of course could not help a quickening of her heart as she looked on Lukos. But her breath also came hurriedly as she glanced to Zayan. Moonlight turned both into men of unearthly beauty. The bluish light painted their rugged faces, highlighting the sharp lines of cheekbones, the full curves of their sensual mouths. Their eyes glowed like silver. And when each man looked at her, he did so with a possessiveness that made her shiver.

She had just stopped them from tearing each other apart. She had, entirely by accident, used their magic against them to stop the fight. And once again the magic had dipped into dark fantasies she had no idea she even had.

What it had forced the vampires to do had stunned her . . .

Even now their chests were still heaving. Vampires, it appeared, also became short of breath when they had intense climaxes. And what she had done had left the vampires speechless.

She shivered. They sat across from her. She had insisted she wanted to sit alone, and after what she'd done to them, they allowed it.

Watching her beneath his dark brows, Zayan undid the jeweled clasp at the neck of his cloak. He offered it to her, but she shook her head. She would rather be cold than accept a gift and provoke the two men again.

They might be vampires, but they were also posturing men. Impossible to deal with.

She turned nervously to the window. As they had hurtled out of the inn's yard, she'd given them the wrong directions to Blackthorne's castle. She had no idea where they were headed and at what point the men would guess that she'd lied. She could not take them to Blackthorne and put him at risk. And she could not go to him herself, not after what she had done with Lukos and Zayan. . . .

How could two enormous males brawl in a carriage without tearing it apart? Zayan had jumped into the carriage and, after taking one look at her and one deep breath of the erotic scents hanging in the air, he had slammed his fist into Lukos's face. He accused Lukos of seducing her with magic against her will.

Lukos's fists had collided with Zayan's strong jaw and his gut, and he fell back against the carriage wall. "I wasn't using magic at the end," Lukos said. "She was putting me into a most wicked fantasy, and doing it willingly." His grin was mocking, making him look more like a young man of barely twenty-one. "I've seduced her first," he goaded. "She's mine."

What had she done by being so wanton? Miranda couldn't even escape—she'd likely be crushed by the two fighting men if she tried to get to the door. *Or perhaps,* whispered a voice, *she didn't want to escape.*

Fists flew as the men pounded each other and paced in a tight circle, looking for a chance to plunge fangs. One body, then another, would fly into the opposite seat or smash against the wall. The carriage rocked with each slam.

"Stop this!" she shouted at them. Her brother Simon had fought like this when he was a child—stubbornly, stupidly, without thought to safety or sanity. These vampires were like two thirteen-year-old boys throwing punches while tumbling down a hill together, heedless of the cliff they'd fly off at the bottom.

"People are going to notice this carriage is rocking on its wheels and is about to tip over," she cried.

And then, amidst the mad fighting, they began to undress. Zayan's fur-lined cape flew off first and landed on top of her. Then Lukos tossed his and pulled off his shirt. Zayan did the same, so they were now grappling on the floor, bare-chested. Apparently they'd stripped, as it made it easier to swing punches.

The fight became more of a scramble, the men wrestling and shouting curses.

"Roman bastard," Lukos snarled.

"Saxon garbage," Zayan spit.

Miranda almost began to laugh. Then she saw Lukos's firm buttocks sticking up in the air, and his back muscles bunching as he struggled to pin Zayan. Her heart hammered. The blue light began to zip about in the carriage again.

Had she summoned it?

Her hand strayed to her throat. Zayan threw Lukos off, then jumped on top of him. His crotch ground against Lukos's breeches-clad thigh as they struggled. His back was beautiful, a broad-shouldered sculpture of muscle, each exquisitely defined.

And this fighting looked almost like what she and Lukos had done together. . . .

"Christ Jesus, what happened?"

Zayan was sprawled on the floor, with Lukos on top. But Zayan's head was in line with Lukos's crotch, which meant Lukos was in the same position on Zayan.

Lukos's head jerked up. His gleaming eyes caught hers. "This is your fantasy, angel?"

She knew her eyes had gone saucer wide. "What do you mean?"

"You want us sucking each other's cocks. Just as I made you come with my mouth."

She was stunned but could picture it perfectly.

Her face flamed. "I—I don't know what you mean. I just wanted you to stop fighting."

But Lukos grinned. He had already seen a side to her she hadn't even known about. Just looking at his full, delectable mouth made her grow hot and molten. And after what she had shared with him, she should be . . . be willing to pledge fidelity, shouldn't she? She was confused. She was supposed to be intimate only with a husband.

Zayan stared at her in amazement, from between Lukos's thighs. Both men looked not . . . angry, but intrigued. Almost amused. And their eyes seemed to be glowing gold. But she *hadn't* thought of anything sexual between the men—

No, she had. She'd thought the fighting looked sensual, and next thing she'd known they'd been thrown into this position. And heaven help her, she was . . . worked up by the idea that Lukos would put his mouth to Zayan's crotch. And Zayan would do the same.

Somehow the magic had put the thought into her head. It created fantasies that excited her, but that she would never think of on her own. Or was it the men? They were vampires—she was being drawn under their spell, and she, fool that she was, didn't even want to fight.

The most erotic thoughts surged through her—of being able to command both men to do what she wished.

She had to escape. But as she forced her shaky, desire-weakened legs to straighten, an invisible force pushed her abruptly down to the seat. Was this part of the magic of the blue lights? They were almost acting on their own.

Join us. Zayan held out his hand.

She stared. This was madness.

Women love to be shared by two men. I have delighted many women by taking them with another man. Don't deny yourself the fun, my angel.

"No!"

Laughing, Lukos ran his fangs along the bulge in Zayan's breeches. His gaze held her the entire time, and she was certain her face had colored from merely pink to flaming red. Zayan ripped open the falls of Lukos's trousers. Lukos's long, heavy member dropped free, and she almost melted on the spot as Zayan's mouth slowly approached the head.

She'd only ever seen male equipage on statues. Soft ones tucked demurely against male bodies. Lukos's was long, straight as a sword, and topped with a thick, bulbous head that looked just like a plum. A big, ripe, succulent one, tempting her to put her mouth there and taste—

But Lukos had ground his crotch into Zayan's face, and she had lost her breath at the sight of one man's lips pressed to the other's shaft. She should be stunned. Shocked.

But she was caught up in the heated magic of it. They made such an exquisite picture, two pairs of long legs stretched out to touch the carriage walls, two muscled abdomens curved, mirroring each other. Biceps bulged as each man leaned toward the other's cock. Her heart stuttered as Lukos stuck his tongue out and laved the head of Zayan's member. A growl came from deep in his chest. He grazed his teeth over the taut flesh, as though preparing to bite. Then Zayan sucked Lukos's ballocks into his mouth, and Lukos retreated to moan harshly, to shudder at the sensation.

Miranda found her fingers had crept down and were pressing her skirts into the vee between her legs. She ached there, ached for relief.

Men, it appeared, knew how to please each other. Obviously they knew how those things—their cocks—worked and knew where the most sensitive places were. She gaped in fascination as Lukos opened his mouth wide and took Zayan's large, thick shaft in deeply. The entire thing disappeared inside. It amazed her how hard and fast their hips moved, how fiercely they thrust their cocks into each other's mouths.

Steam seemed to fill the carriage. It even beaded on the glass windows. The men panted fiercely between fevered sucking. Miranda had to pull up her skirts to bare her legs, because it became too intensely hot. She saw how fast they moved their hips now.

They were straining for climax, racing toward them.

You'll die first, Zayan growled.

She heard his thoughts as though he'd shouted them.

No, damn you, it'll be you who surrenders first, Lukos threw back.

There was anger behind the passion. And Miranda feared what she'd done. But Zayan bucked suddenly and she glimpsed his thoughts for one moment—

She felt a burst of pleasure that shot through every nerve, that sang through every muscle, that blanked his brain and took away his control. She felt the way it sapped his strength, and the burst of sheer, intense delight it gave him. She flopped limply back on the seat as he had to sink to the floor of the carriage.

Then Lukos came, and she shared his remarkable pleasure. But felt the edge beneath it, the anger he had over surrendering. Anger that made the final explosion so intense she feared she'd melt into the velvet-cushioned seat.

Lukos retreated off Zayan's cock as Zayan did the same. At once, after his body had stopped jerking, Lukos pulled away and flung himself into the seat. He snarled like an angered wolf, retreating in the shadows in the corner.

Miranda's heart pounded so hard, she was surprised it didn't rattle the windows. What had she done . . . ?

The carriage stopped. Miranda felt the lurch. Felt her head bounce gently against the velvet seat.

"Where are we?" She'd murmured it before she'd remembered who she was asking. For one bleary minute she thought she was traveling with Simon and Caroline. She must have gone to sleep while remembering the fight between the men and the carnal aftermath.

Using her power always left her weakened and tired. After the night she had saved Aunt Eugenia, when she had been twelve, she'd slept for two days. Her father had been in a panic, believing her ill. And Eugenia had forbidden her to tell the truth—for her own good.

She realized Lukos was still sprawled on the seat opposite. He'd allowed Zayan to stay at her side, but he was glaring like a chaperone. He was talking of the attack by James Ryder, the vampire slayer. She realized, after he'd saved her, and had made love to her with his wicked tongue, she'd almost forgotten what he was—a vampire.

"When she touched you," Lukos was remarking conversationally to Zayan, "she was trying to return your soul."

The anger she'd seen before was hidden now. He appeared nonchalant, like a jaded gentleman using his practiced ennui as a shield.

"I saw what she did in the inn's yard." Zayan stared at her. "Alas, love, that's not possible. I didn't lose my soul—I gave it away. It can't be retrieved."

Why would you want to save me? She heard his thoughts as he rubbed his strong, graceful hand over his jaw.

"The power to resurrect life? I didn't know that power existed."

So that is why she felt so strong—

She heard the snippet of Zayan's thought. Then Lukos's thoughts entered her head. *I want her.* Simple and direct. But because of her power? Or for carnal pleasure? She felt the intensity of both men.

"This was to be a competition," Zayan said, watching Lukos.

"But the prize is much sweeter than just an innocent lass." He reached out and lightly traced the neckline of her pelisse, gently brushing her heated skin. "The prize is unique magic and a pure, powerful soul."

Horror raced through her—a cold, frightening contrast to the pleasure she'd felt just a few hours before. "You can't fight over me," she cried. "I'm not the spoils of war. And I promise I won't simply go with the man who wins. I might be nothing more than a prize, but I'll fight to my last breath."

She saw pain in Lukos's eyes, in the harsh lines around his mouth. "Miranda, I don't mean to hurt you. I never would. For a woman as powerful as you—I would give my love."

Zayan snorted. He leaned back elegantly against the seat. "Don't believe the lying demon. It was his plan to take a mate and breed a race of demons that would rule mankind."

Slowly, she took in Zayan's words. She had not believed Lukos was pledging love to her. It had to be a lie, and it irritated her he thought she would be so easily tricked. What he wanted, she realized, was to use her power for some reason.

But it meant they were not going to kill her. With her power, she was more valuable alive.

Lukos's face took on a dark rage. He looked like a demon then, and she retreated instinctively against her seat.

"I told you he has taken the lives of many innocents—women and children," he snarled. "Zayan took my sister's soul. He gave her to Lucifer so the devil could control me."

"Damnation, Saxon, that's a lie. I've vowed to you it was a lie. Stop being such a damned stubborn fool and listen to the truth when it's told to you." But after growling at Lukos, Zayan turned gently to her. The carriage began a slow ascent suddenly, creaking on its springs.

"I asked for direction to Blackthorne's castle at the inn," Zayan said.

She swallowed hard. "You mean, we are heading there now?"

"Why did you lie about it?" Zayan asked. "Don't you think your fiancé will save you?"

"I—I was trying to save him." Not just from the vampires. *From her.*

This was to be her fate—to either survive this night with the two vampires or end up dead. But she couldn't force Blackthorne, an innocent man, to take on her battles. And she could not lie to him about her power. In his letters, he'd told her he loved her.

She'd come racing to him because she had nowhere else to go. But now she had seen what she was—not a proper English lady at all, but some sort of wanton being. It was because of her power. She could not go to a decent man and pretend to be a decent woman.

Zayan stroked her cheek and she stiffened. "This is where you belong. With us."

"You weren't made to live in the mortal world, by confining moral rules," Lukos murmured.

"I was," she protested, but she now believed it wasn't true.

None of the things you've done with us has ruined you, angel, Lukos argued in her thoughts. *You've celebrated your sensual nature. Love, I understand why you do not want to go to Blackthorne. You fear now that you don't belong with him. And that's the truth. You do belong with us, with demons, yes, but also men who understand you and accept you. Who would never hurt you.*

Miranda froze. She didn't belong anywhere. Mr. Ryder wanted her dead, and he claimed the Royal Society did too. Aunt Eugenia had warned her to hide her gift, even if she had to let someone die rather than help them. But she had never been able to do that. She would save someone even if it exposed her.

And even if she could go to Blackthorne, he would never accept her. He wouldn't have married her. He might have had her locked away, believing she was mad.

Lukos crossed over to sit beside her. He lifted her skirts, his fingers lazily teasing her calves through her thick stockings. She let him. She wasn't normal. Perhaps she wasn't even human.

Both men bent to her nipples, suckling them through the bodice of her dress. And she couldn't help but savor the sensation as they pulled at her nipples. Jolt after jolt of pure pleasure rocketed through her, like Vauxhall fireworks.

This was not magic controlling her. This was what *she* wanted.

But Zayan jerked back and his nose flared. He cocked his head toward the window. "By the Gods, do you smell smoke?"

Lukos lifted from her breasts, pressed a quick kiss to the tip of her nose, then lifted the shade from the glass. "Torches. It appears we've encountered a torch-bearing mob. And that blasted vampire slayer is their leader."

Earlier

A rap sounded from the closed bedchamber door. From beyond came a maid's voice, "My lady? Lady Draycott has arrived."

Serena had only just awoken with nightfall. She swiftly sat up in bed, clasping her tight, rounded stomach, which she had to move about with her hands so she could get out of bed. "I must go and speak with her," she said to Jonathon and Drake. But she already believed that going to London was their only hope.

The thought of traveling so close to her time filled Serena with fear. But if her babies' lives were at stake, if this was the only choice, she would do it.

She pulled on a negligee of fine ivory silk, then drew on a thick robe of velvet and tied it at her waist. Drake groaned and rubbed his eyes, while Jonathon slid out of bed and snatched up his trousers.

Serena smiled, though she knew the smile did not reach her eyes. She knew her fear still showed. "I will go ahead." Slipping her feet into her slippers, she hurried out into the corridor.

The hallways were lit with torches, and tapestries of rich embroidery hung on the stone walls. This fortress was ancient and had been held by the Royal Society for five hundred years. It had once been one of the houses of the Countess of Moravia, who had worked for Lucifer and who was, in fact, a demoness. She had brought him apprentices for the Scholomance. Serena had unearthed the countess's journals. She described her encounter in 875 A.D. with a new disciple—who was to be called *Lukos*.

It was said that the tunnels and dungeons below led to the Chambers of the Scholomance. And through there, one could enter the Underworld and find Lucifer himself. But for five centuries the Royal Society had tried to find the secret to enter the chambers. They had never succeeded.

Serena heard footsteps behind her and knew that her men followed. They did not catch her, though they easily could, perhaps understanding she needed to walk alone for a few moments, needed time to reflect on her own. She walked with her hand on her tummy, and beneath her palm she felt the twins struggling for room or perhaps wrestling.

Even though brilliant minds had struggled with the secret of the entrance to the Underworld for so long and failed, she and Althea had tried. It had kept Althea's mind—and her own—from the constant fear for their children. The worry sapped their strengths and made them wooly-headed so they could barely think rationally. They needed something—anything—to take their minds away from fear.

"Now we might have hope," she breathed aloud. "I know Althea will be afraid to travel with her baby. She hated having to make the journey here. But we have to try this."

A maid passed, who must think her mad for talking to herself.

The scent of coffee came from the drawing room. This chamber had been changed from a spartan room of cold stone into a luxurious retreat. Two fireplaces blazed and the warmth wrapped around Serena as she hurried inside.

Her mother rose to her feet. Eve, the dowager Lady Draycott, the oldest and first vampiress, had Althea's daugther Serry in her arms.

Serena moved forward and embraced her mother. She felt the reserve in her hug and was certain her mother had. Eve had refused to provide more help when Althea's daughter began to lose strength.

Drake and Jonathon stepped into the drawing room behind Serena and stayed at her side until she settled on a large comfortable chair. Jonathon provided a pillow for her to rest against, Drake a footrest. She saw Yannick and Bastien, Althea's men, were already there. Bastien wore an open shirt, leather breeches, and tall boots. His hair was loose. Yannick was formally dressed—after all, he was the Earl of Brookshire.

Jonathon asked Eve permission to speak first—showing deference to a vampire queen. He quickly told them all about Denby's letter and about Lady Miranda Bond, who might be able to save their children. Or change them all back to mortals. Serena bit her lip at that. All, perhaps, except for her. Born of a vampire and a fallen angel, she had never been exactly human.

Eve nodded. She returned the sleeping baby to Althea. "It is true. The queens have told me about this woman. Her power came in slowly, beginning when she reached puberty, early at the age of twelve. She has no idea how to control it. Nor do the queens know exactly what her power is or what it means. We do not know what the power to bring a mortal back to life will do to the . . . correctness of the world."

"Correctness of the world?" Bastien de Wynter was the one to speak. "We're supposed to be dead."

Eve shrugged. "But you have not easily cheated death, have you? You pay a price. Do you ever wish to walk into sunlight?"

The question hung in the air. Serena loved the night, she loved to wake and throw open the windows of her room and breathe in the cool, sweet air of the night. Sunlight enriched the body, but the night, she believed, made the heart stronger. But there had been many times, more and more often, she dreamed of playing on a sun-drenched meadow with her children.

"Do the queens intend to destroy Miranda Bond?" Jonathon asked.

Eve shook her head. "The queens want to understand her."

Serena saw Yannick and Bastien exchange glances. She knew that none of the men trusted the vampire queens. The women—all ancient vampiresses—plotted to preserve their power and maintain their superiority over the demons and other magical beings that aspired to take their place. But they also worked to protect mortals from demons that would otherwise destroy humanity. In their own way, they kept a balance between the world of the undead and demons and the mortals.

If Miranda Bond had the power to destroy the society that the queens had created and ruled over, Serena did not doubt the queens would want her dead.

"There is something else I must tell you." Eve poured herself a demitasse cup of the strongly scented black coffee. She lounged back and sipped it.

Serena approached her mother. Eve reached out for her hand. "Now, you must not worry about this, child—"

"What," Serena demanded. But she then saw a flash of fear in Eve's eyes. What had her mother frightened?

"Lukos has escaped his prison. He has returned to the mortal world. To England, in fact. Both he and the vampire Zayan escaped."

"Lukos has returned!" Serena cried. Jonathon and Drake were standing beside her chair and she saw their faces. They had known of this. They'd known but had not told her. But how had they discovered it? Then she guessed. Drake had been sired, as a vampire, by Lukos. He must have sensed Lukos's escape.

Eve hugged Serena. "Denby insists that you must return to England to hunt them."

Jonathon growled, "Impossible. Althea has a new baby, and Serena is going to deliver at any time. They can't hunt rogue vampires. And we have to protect them."

Serena straightened. "We must go. We must find Miranda Bond."

Yannick spoke, his voice deep, firm, and authoritative, "There is too great a risk."

Eve stood, her beautiful silk gown swirling around her. "And if you do not hunt Lukos and Zayan, Althea and Serena could be at great risk. They could be destroyed. The queens will use magic, combined with yours, to send you at once. Gentlemen, do you not understand that you have no choice?"

7

The Castle

She was beyond caring about safety.

Miranda pulled back the shade and leaned beside Lukos to take in the sight. Flames fluttered around upraised torches. Plumes of smoke rose in the black sky. The light fell upon Mr. James Ryder, casting lines of reddish gold along his beaver hat, his mocking grin, and his hands at the reins of a large black horse.

How had he ridden ahead of them? Then Miranda remembered—she had sent them in the wrong direction at first, while the vampires had been fighting. They had only turned around while she'd slept, which had given Ryder an hour or so to ride ahead. She hadn't thought he would be so determined to pursue her.

But he'd told her he had to destroy her.

The horses shied in the face of fire, and whether the vampires controlled the coachman or not, he pulled on the reins and brought the horses to a rapid stop.

She was flung forward, but Lukos caught her.

"They'll burn us all alive in here," Miranda gasped. The sweet smell of smoke grew stronger; the mob was approaching their carriage. Panic begin to claw inside her.

"We won't stay inside, sweeting," Zayan pointed out.

How could both he and Lukos look so calm? Though if he really had been a Roman general, Zayan had survived for two thousand years.

"Where can we run to? They'll capture us and kill us if we run outside." She could not understand why she felt this sense of belonging with Lukos and Zayan, along with the need to plan escape together.

"You forget that we aren't ordinary vampires," Lukos said, grinning.

As though vampires could ever be ordinary. But she understood what they meant as they conjured a deep blue glow within the carriage, a darker one than the lights that had preceded their sensual play. Cooling and fresh, like the breeze over a deep lake, the light filled the carriage, then radiated out.

At once the fires were quenched.

Zayan flashed her a reassuring smile. "There, angel. A simpleton of a vampire slayer is no match for us."

Miranda stared at Lukos. He could have used his magic to destroy Mr. Ryder at the inn. Why hadn't he? Why had he spared a vampire slayer's life?

Outside the carriage, the shouts of frightened men rose around them. Mr. Ryder had lured a group of men out here to destroy vampires, and now they'd seen magic.

"What in the bloody hell happened? Did you see a blue light?"

"Yer imagination. The wind put out our torches."

"After they were doused in oil? Bloody impossible!"

"Go for the carriage! Tear it to pieces!"

A roar was taken up. Peering through the window, Miranda saw the torches wave, along with pitchforks, clubs, and shovels. The mob swarmed toward the carriage. A flash of light blinded her, and a roar flooded her ears. She was jerked back from the window, but the pistol ball slammed into the wooden side of the carriage.

"I'm going to bloody destroy them," Lukos snarled.

Miranda jerked toward him. "No, you can't!" She grabbed for his wrists. Her fingers closed around his long, elegant fingers. She knew he could have flung her off if he wanted.

He didn't.

But she couldn't stop Zayan with her hands clinging to Lukos's wrists. She watched helplessly as Zayan gave a casual wave of his hand. One careless gesture of his long fingers and a red mist surrounded them. It seeped into the carriage.

She heard coughing and sputtering outside. She released Lukos and leaned to the window, letting her eyes look just over the sill. The men surrounding them were clutching their throats, gasping for breath.

"What are you doing to them?"

"They will collapse and sleep—they will awaken unharmed."

What about the slayer? Lukos's voice sang in her head. *I'll kill him for you, Miranda.*

"No, I can't ask you to kill someone for me."

He intends you harm. He intends to kill you.

"Even then, even then, I won't do it!" she cried. Her sin was that she gave life back—as ironic and stupid as that was. She would be a proper martyr and die for that before she would ever command that a man's life be taken.

Around the carriage, the men gathered by Mr. Ryder were falling to their knees. Some had collapsed with their faces in the dirt. Was Zayan lying? She saw the flanks of the black horse. The beast turned. Mr. Ryder was slumped on its back, fighting for breath just like the other men. Swirling around them, like clutching fingers, was the thick crimson fog.

Ryder's eyes locked on hers. At least she thought they had.

And he reached out, as though driven by his hatred of her to find strength to get to her.

The crimson fog began to retreat, and Miranda could see Ryder, hanging off the side of the horse, clinging with weak hands to the reins. His body tilted—

He fell to the ground.

Blackthorne's castle perched atop a rocky outcrop that soared above dense forest. A gray stone tower thrust out of white mist like a clenched fist. From its top, two tall stone turrets reached toward the stars that twinkled in the black sky. Dark trees massed at its base, and a road was carved out between the shadowy branches.

Miranda peered out of the window. *If you are there, Lord Blackthorne, run for your life.*

She hated herself for bringing doom to him. She might belong with vampires and demons, but Blackthorne did not deserve to die.

She'd fallen in love with him through his wonderful, lyrical, passionate letters. How could she be bringing such danger to a man she loved?

Could Lukos and Zayan read her thoughts—her most private thoughts? Fear that they were privy to her plea to Blackthorne made her head jerk up. Lukos's mirror-like eyes met hers. A wicked grin showed his fangs, and he cocked his head. The oddest look crossed his face; it was as though he was waiting on her invitation. He wanted her, she could recognize his lust, but he wasn't simply getting up and taking what he wanted.

Shivering, she shook her head. She was furious. They might say she belonged with them, but she didn't. She *didn't*. They were demons at the core, willing to kill and destroy. She could never be like that.

Miranda hugged her chest with her arms, and with a shrug, Lukos turned his attention to the window. That amazed her.

Why would he leave her alone when he wanted her? Both he and Zayan were now behaving like well-mannered gentlemen.

Fingers of cloud slid across the first turret of the castle, an imposing construction of tooled gray stone. She had read gothic novels, the horrid novels. Blackthorne's castle looked like the sort of eerie mausoleum that would be filled with ghosts and should be forever tainted by evil deeds.

She shook off the fancy. It was a fortified home, a place of refuge. People had, no doubt, died in it, both violently and not, but it was Blackthorne's home, and it should have been his sanctuary. And she was taking that from him by bringing vampires.

The carriage rattled relentlessly onward, taking her demonic escorts to Blackthorne's refuge. Rumors about Blackthorne had swirled through the London ballrooms, passed behind the fans of experienced matrons, beautiful widows, and unmarried ladies who skirted the very edges of propriety.

"They say that he no longer comes to town because he was so hideously wounded," the women would whisper. "He knows no lady will love him—he is terrifying to behold—so he hides in his castle. And since he knows he can never have a bride, he has embraced the darkest, most scandalous erotic practices. . . ."

"Orgies involving dozens of women."

"A dungeon filled with shackles in which he would imprison maidens of the nearby village. He would take their innocence and pay their families for their silence, and the girls would never return home. . . ."

Staring at the castle through the jiggling window, Miranda could almost believe the foolish rumors. But she didn't. The matrons were angered that Blackthorne eschewed London society, and the *haute volée* adored nasty, titillating gossip. Surely such a madman would reveal himself in his letters. But what she had seen in his letters was a man who longed to have someone to talk to. Someone to treat him as human . . .

She had understood what he'd felt.

"So you intend to marry the man who keeps this place?" Elegantly sprawling across the seat opposite, Lukos grinned. His hair streamed down along his face, coasting over his high cheekbones. The lock of black with the white streak brushed across his sculpted lips, making him look more of a fallen angel than a brutal demon.

She'd hoped to. She couldn't hope for that anymore. She looked to Lukos and remembered feeling bold and daring just hours ago, when she'd—she'd sat on top of him. Now, she felt empty and forlorn. Even though her heart pattered at his handsome face and his teasing tone, she now remembered exactly what he was: a demon. Her stomach was her barometer here, and it felt full of knots. "Please don't hurt Lord Blackthorne," she whispered. "He doesn't deserve to be killed just because . . . because I decided to come here."

"You ask me to willingly spare a strong, healthy meal?" The grin widened and her stomach gave a great dip, but in the next moment, Lukos's smile faded. His expression became one of weariness. "Sweetheart, he will fight us. He will not just welcome us into his home. We will have to force our way in."

"But why?" she cried. "Why do you have to come here? Can't you take the carriage and continue? Isn't that enough?"

"Not any longer." Lukos's deep growl rumbled over her.

She turned to Zayan, who sat imperiously beside her. His face was set with the stillness of a statue, lips drawn into a hard line, ruthlessness in his silvery eyes. Even in the close confines of the carriage, it was as though he were looking over the sea of his troops to the battlefield.

Miranda reached for the door. The forest sloped away on either side from the narrow, winding dirt road. She could run through the trees. The vampires would chase her, but it would buy her time to think of some way to protect—

The door handle suddenly grew burning hot. With a squeal, she pulled her hand away.

Zayan's lip curled in impatience. "I don't have time to let you flee. We need to have the castle under our control before dawn."

"But why? You must know you can't keep it." She squared her shoulders, infuriated by the amused quirk of Lukos's lips. "You will be attacked by more people than the mob that came with torches—people who will fight with every weapon they have. You will end up being destroyed."

Warmth curled over her cheek, cupping its curve. It was like the brush of a man's finger, but nothing was there. It was magic conjured by Zayan, and she sat rigidly, fighting the way her skin heated at the phantom caress. Her fingers still hurt from the heat Zayan had unleashed on the door handle, and she would not let his magic defeat her will.

The carriage creaked up the path. Stones scuttled out from the wheels. The horses strained to make ground.

"You don't belong with Blackthorne," Zayan said. "You belong with me, Miranda."

Lukos stretched his long limbs. She saw the graceful movement of the wolf in the way he almost shook out his legs. "No, sweetheart, you will belong to me." A feral gleam came to his eyes as he looked to Zayan. "I intend to claim her, Roman, and I'll rip out your throat to do it."

The soft magic stroking of her cheek ceased.

She glanced out the window again. The rough path had left the trees behind and had opened out onto the rocky hill. The turrets of the castle seemed to be hanging over them. Its bulk blotted out the stars.

"Rip out my throat, dog?" Zayan snarled in return. "I could blast you into dust where you sit."

The castle wall loomed ahead, the gates thrown open.

Blackthorne told her that he could leave his door wide open at night and no one would walk in. Every one feared him—the entire village, and most of England. *No one can see past disfigurement,* he'd written. *They see scars and think the man inside is scarred. Scarred, healed badly, and ruined forever.*

She had to do something before they crossed through the gate.

"Stop!" she screamed.

The carriage continued on, but the bickering stopped, and she had to turn her attention from the window and the gate that was only yards away, to face the vampires. Her chest rose with her frantic breaths.

"If you promise to stop, to leave Blackthorne alone," she cried, "I will let you both do what you want to me. If you want to compete for me, if you want to do carnal things to me and try to seduce me, you can. I won't fight. But we must stop. And turn back. On the way down, you can . . ."

"We can what?" Lukos prompted.

"You are in no position to bargain," Zayan said arrogantly, and she saw one of the gateposts fly past the window as the horses were urged to greater speed.

"Then I'll fight," she spat out. "With every weapon I have."

But she knew what she had to do. As soon as they reached the main door, as soon as there were servants about, she would have to sound the alarm.

Even if she died.

Lukos inhaled a long breath as the wheels crunched on gravel. "The heavy perfume of whores, it permeates the place."

Miranda gaped at him. Could he really smell that? Was it true? She could smell only the damp in the air, the loamy scent of wet earth, the tang of her sweat and other indecent things. . . .

"Heartbeats . . . but not many." Zayan stroked his blunt, strong jawline. "There should be more in a house of this size."

Her heart sank. Blackthorne had revealed in his letters that he kept only a handful of servants, and most were old. The younger ones were driven by curiosity and that infuriated him. How could a few elderly servants stop vampires? She was going to be responsible for all their deaths too.

Zayan's hand settled on her shoulder and she jumped at the sudden tingling sensation as his fingertips rested on the skin of her neck.

It was not a reaction of fear . . .

It was one of heat and awareness . . . her traitorous body responding to his magical allure.

"Keep our secret and no one will be hurt." His voice was cold and without emotion.

"If you were a general, you've killed thousands in battle. You've killed probably thousands more as a vampire. I don't believe you."

"If you race in there and tell everyone what we are, what will happen?" Lukos leaned across to her. "You will be locked up, and we'll take the castle with ease. I would not leave you in a prison, my sweet, but I will take this castle for my own. With bloodshed or without."

"Without? You mean you would spare Blackthorne and his servants?" Miranda could read nothing in Lukos's silvery eyes, but his brow lifted.

"You can take us across the threshold. Otherwise, we tempt them outside and destroy them one by one. The choice is yours, angel, not mine."

"The hand that strikes people down will be yours!" she shouted. But she knew that she was the only one who could stop violence and death, so that did make her responsible for innocent lives.

The carriage halted with creaking wheels and the jingle of the traces playing into the windswept quiet.

There were no servants about, and her coachman and outriders began to unload her trunks and unfasten the horses. Here the wind raced over the barren rock and snapped around the sides of the tower to whirl and eddy in the courtyard. Her bonnet was gone and her disordered curls were tossed over her face.

What must she look like? Mussed hair? Dirt from the inn's yard streaked her face; she felt the crusts of it on her chin and forehead, and the itch of sweat irritated beneath her corset.

Any servant looking at her would dismiss her in an instant.

But Lukos had already strode to the large oak door and he'd rapped on it loud enough to waken the dead. She had to race forward, with Zayan at her side.

The castle door was flung wide and a grizzled face leaned forward to examine them. The butler wore black, which made him appear as thin as an arrow. Moonlight caught the silver in his thinning gray hair. "The master is not at home."

Miranda both sagged in relief and gagged in fear. She'd come all this way, she'd read the yearning for her in Blackthorne's last letter, and he was gone?

Lukos's silvery eyes glinted. In the shadows, his lips drew back to reveal his fangs—

"No!" Miranda lurched forward toward the butler. She had to make a choice. What to do? She either convinced him to let her and the vampires cross the threshold, or she screamed out what Zayan and Lukos were.

The old eyes peered at her. She prayed he couldn't see well enough to realize she looked as though she'd been dragged through a hedge.

"I am Miss Miranda Bond. I have been corresponding with Lord Blackthorne for several years and I came here . . . at . . . at his invitation."

The man bowed. "I am so sorry, my lady. Sometimes the master is driven to leave. We never have visitors. He left in haste."

"Where did he go?" She spoke without thinking.

There was no answer. Either the servant did not know where Blackthorne was or he was loyal and circumspect.

"I do not understand," she said. "How could you not know where he has gone?"

"It is not unusual, my lady. His lordship travels frequently. He does not inform us as to where he travels, and we rarely know when he plans to return."

So Blackthorne was safe, at least. But to vanish without telling anyone where he was going? And he did so frequently? This was the gentleman she had wanted to love, this was the sanctuary she had wanted to believe in . . . and all she found was a mystery. "We shall have to go to the local inn—"

She saw Lukos's hand raise. Oh, heavens no, he was going to use his magic to overpower the butler's will—or perhaps kill him outright.

The butler gave an expansive wave of his hand to the large, tomblike foyer of the castle. "No, no, my lady. You are to be a guest at Blackthorne Castle, as are your companions."

Guilt struck at the thought of what this hospitality was risking, but Lukos and Zayan were already across the threshold. She hurried to walk in step as they followed the servant within.

"There," she whispered. "You are guests here. You don't need to hurt anyone now, do you? You won't have to feed on anyone."

Lukos was the one to turn, to smile down on her. Torchlight cast him in eerie shadow. "I'll hunt beyond the castle walls to feed. For you, sweetheart. But what about when the slayer brings his mob to the castle gates, love? How will you explain that to Blackthorne's gullible servants?"

Tapestries displayed the Blackthorne crest, two dragons of

royal blue against a background of red and gold. Blackthorne had described his home with love, though he admitted a woman would find it a draughty disaster.

She glanced around. Just a week ago, she had dreamed of coming here and bringing warmth and light to Blackthorne's world. And when she'd left yesterday, she was racing here to protect her family, and because she had nowhere else to go.

The butler carried a candle to light the way. The light flickered over tooled stone and was lost in the tall ceiling of the corridor. They mounted a sweeping stair, and she was caught between Lukos and Zayan, two raven-haired giants.

Along the way a maid was sent to bring other servants on the run, to light fires and bring bathing water, and to inform the kitchens.

"Your chamber, my lady." An oak door opened to reveal a massive four-poster bed, an enormous fireplace, and heavily carved furniture.

She glanced from one vampire to another. Without a word, she hurried inside the room. As the voice of the butler moved on, she peeked out. Blast, her vampires were being given rooms by hers in the long hallway. She closed the door and turned the key.

Then took several frantic breaths.

Would they leave her alone in her bedchamber?

She hugged herself and went to the window. Small and paned, it gave out on a sheer drop to the forest below. She'd never survive that if she fell, and there was nowhere to climb. There was no route to escape.

A rap at the door, followed by a female voice. Miranda took the risk and opened the lock.

A gray-haired maid brought in a ewer of fresh, steaming water and a basin. Her trunks followed, brought by an aging footman and a man in a rough shirt and breeches. He must be a groom or a gardener. They dropped the trunks, then rubbed their backs on the way out. The maid curtsied. "Would you wish me to begin hanging your dresses, my lady?"

"No, I want you to escape the house and go to the village. It's not safe to stay here. Take the other servants with you."

She expected shock, but the maid looked at her blankly. "I will go and come back if you need me."

Already, the vampires had the poor woman under control. Miranda's shoulders sagged. She wanted to command the maid to stay, but she had already hastened out the door. Alone, Miranda undid the few fastenings of her simple traveling dress—now a dirty, crumpled mess. She pulled it off, over her head, but without a maid, she could not loosen her own corset laces.

She prayed that the weak, defenseless woman did not end up being a meal for Lukos or Zayan. She went to the ewer of water the maid had brought and threw the warm water on her face. It dripped to her neck and she rubbed there.

Now, away from the vampires, she couldn't understand why she had ever thought she belonged with them.

The doorknob rattled. Miranda jerked around.

The key turned in the lock by itself and the door opened.

Zayan leaned on the doorframe, his hands bare of gloves. He had discarded his coat. A white shirt, open at the throat, clung to his shoulders.

"Leave my bedroom." She held her linen towel against her breasts, thrust up by the corset and covered only by a filmy chemise. Defiantly, she added, "I do not invite you across my threshold."

"You climaxed with me. Your invitation has already been extended."

She flushed. "That was when I was trying to save your soul."

But he strode inside, to her bed, with an arrogance that was as heightened as his strength. He stretched out on her bedcover.

His muscular legs easily reached to the end and his black boots hung over the edge.

"What do you want from me?" She strained to read his thoughts. She knew he wouldn't answer aloud, but if he thought of it, she might hear it again. But she heard nothing. "You want my power, I know, but why? I can't give it to you. I don't even know what to do with it."

Zayan levered up on his side, his eyes glittering in the flicking light of the fire and the candles. "You felt at your most comfortable having orgasms with Lukos and me. You felt finally alive, didn't you?"

I need her love.

She heard that small hint at his thoughts, and it stunned her. She did not know what to make of it—or the determined tone in which the words came to her. "I think I was controlled by the magic," she said.

"Not true." His grin slid over her from mussed hair and damp face down to her dirtied boots. "What you felt is what is truly inside you, Miranda. A passionate nature. A sensual soul. A yearning to explore and to be free in sexual pleasure."

"N-no," she said shakily.

"A lie." He sat up, and his face showed regret. "Blackthorne's dungeons are littered with lace torn from ladies clothing, corset laces, and lost hair pins, angel."

She felt as though punched in the chest. "I don't believe you."

"There are some mortal men who are much more wicked than vampires. Come with me. See for yourself."

"I'm half undressed." Again, she spoke without pause, without sense. Why remind him?

Zayan held up his cloak, and with a quick flick of his hand, it flew through the air, settled on her shoulders, and closed around her at the front. He led her to the end of the corridor, to a narrow, winding stair that plunged into darkness. She swallowed hard. He could see in the dark, but she could not.

"I don't wish to see Blackthorne's dungeons."

"Don't disappoint me, Miranda. I believe you are courageous enough to face anything."

She knew she had to be. It was just that she had one light in her life—Blackthorne's love. She could never have him, but she did not want to extinguish that, too, and be left with nothing.

8

Dungeons

In flickering candlelight, Zayan pulled a whip down from its hook upon the wall and threw it to an octagonal table of wrought iron that stood in the center of the dungeon. He looked to her, his silvery eyes speaking volumes of sympathy, but Miranda was too stunned to find words.

She had never seen such things.

The dungeons consisted of three cells cut into the hillside rock. A large oak door stood open on each cell. Iron shackles hung off the walls and ceilings. Benches of odd configurations sat in the corners. She had no idea how a human body would fit on the odd seats and strange leather pads, and she was certain that half were intended to thrust a person's buttocks into the air.

There were more than scraps of women's clothing and scattered pins, there were journals complete with carefully rendered illustrations. The pictures had been annotated. She recognized the hand from the letters she had received. These were Blackthorne's books. In them, he'd sketched his plans of what he intended to do with his female prisoners, adding his notes on what had worked and what had not, and how to make his tortures more arousing.

She dropped one of the books to the table. She was not certain what she felt. Horror. Disappointment. And after her erotic adventure with Lukos where he had been tied up, a sense of understanding that unnerved her.

She was stunned. But after what she had revealed as her fantasies, did she have any right to judge?

Zayan stepped in front of her. "You see, angel." His voice was infinitely gentle. "He would have hurt you more than I ever would."

Miranda crossed her arms over her chest. Anger boiled, and she wanted to take up the whip and lash it at the walls. "You would happily hurt me. You would drain my blood, and the only reason you haven't is that I have something you want." She was alone now—utterly alone. She could not go back to her brother and his family, or Aunt Eugenia—not without putting them at risk. All she'd had were dreams and fantasies of Blackthorne. Fantasies of love and marriage. Of hope. That's what he had been for her—hope she could have a normal woman's life. But she couldn't. Not here. Not anymore. It appeared all the dark, scandalous rumors about Blackthorne were true.

She shuddered as she looked around the dungeon. This did not arouse her. It made her sad.

Had Blackthorne sensed, even in her letters, that she was not normal? Was that what had drawn him to her? Or had it been that he'd known, once she was here, she would have had no escape?

Zayan gently cupped her cheek. "I am sorry. I know what the betrayal of a loved one feels like." Below the dark slashes of his brows, his beautiful eyes revealed anguish, and her heart gave a small leap. He caressed her face and brushed his thumb to her lower lip, making it tingle.

His mouth lowered toward hers and she arched up. Wanting his kiss. Needing it.

She fell forward and her hand touched his chest above his heart—

They were sleeping. He padded softly into the chamber in which the boy reposed. He could not assign this task to anyone else. He could not put himself in anyone else's power. Wearing a slave's robes, he had entered the house. He was believed to be far away, on his way home from battle. It would never be suspected that his was the hand that struck—

The boy stirred. He was small and frail. It would be an easy task. A hand to the mouth to muffle a scream, a quick slash with the blade. As his hand clamped down over the face, the boy's eyes opened, showing first confusion, then recognition, then—with the wisdom of the young—frantic fear and the knowledge of impending death.

Blood sprayed. He had pulled a dark cloak on top of the servant robes. This he would discard when he was finished.

There. It was done. All he had to do now was find the girl—

"Miranda?" Arms surrounded her; hard muscle pressed against her back.

Blinking, Miranda focused on the present, not the past. The horrific image had disappeared. She had fallen against Zayan's broad chest and he had embraced her. She heard one slow, languorous beat of his heart. Then she dazedly remembered what she had seen and struggled to break free.

She had seen what had happened to Lukos. Was she seeing what Zayan had done?

He let her go and she glared at him, hurt and furious. Her

heart must be thumping as loud as a drum. "You told me you were a Roman general. Is that the truth? In which case, you have blood on your hands." *Her* blood was moving like mud through her veins. "Did you kill children?"

Zayan had lit a torch in the cell with his magic lights, and his eyes were mirrors in the wavering light. Reflective eyes hid so much. "I have a great deal of blood on my hands. And though it was said that I fed from children, that I took their blood to keep me eternally young, that was not true. I would never hurt a child."

His eyes might be shielded, but his words were tired, and his voice held a heavy quality that sounded like regret. A vampire was without a soul, but Eugenia had told her that the "poor creatures" did experience emotion, and that the Royal Society was wrong in its belief that vampires could not feel anything. Eugenia believed they carried the pain of their mortal lives into their undead existence.

The images she had seen haunted her. She wanted to know what they were. "Were you forced to become a vampire? Or did you willingly become a vampire?" Wouldn't a general want to embrace immortality? To be able to fight with preternatural strength and never die? "Why did you give up your soul? To win battles?"

"Any man only embraces death when he has nothing left to live for. Even on the battlefields, when the pain is beyond belief, a man will welcome death."

"Were you dying on the field and you became a vampire to escape?"

"I saw my children dead in their beds and knew I had nothing to live for other than revenge."

His words, thrown at her without a trace of emotion, stole all the air from her lungs. The small boy she had seen—had that been Zayan's son? "H-how did they die?"

"They were murdered. Someone had entered my house and slit their throats."

Dear God, she had seen it. And she had heard the killer's thoughts in her head. This had never happened to her before. She had seen through a murderer's vicious, coldhearted eyes. The whips and instruments of torture around her dropped away. They did not matter anymore. "Who murdered your children?" She was not sure why she was determined to push to find the truth.

His silvery eyes turned oddly black, like the shiny surface of a smooth plane of coal. He turned away from her and contemplated the other whips hanging upon the cell wall. Midnight black and gleaming in the torchlight, his hair rippled around his shoulders. Suddenly, he launched forward and slammed his fist at the wall. Chips of stone flew into the air. He had drilled a three-inch-deep hole with his fist, and Miranda froze at the sight of such rage.

"That is something you do not need to know," he said, but he did not turn. He ripped several of the whips from the wall and broke the thick handles, scattering them to the ground. "By the gods, it is like I can see them again—"

She was scared. By touching him and seeing the murders, had she brought the memories back to him? She was afraid to approach him.

"I've never known the truth of who did it," he said. "I became a vampire, possessing unearthly strength and powers, but I could not prove who murdered my children. I believe one of my rival generals had them killed. My innocent children were slaughtered to destroy me. You asked if I became a vampire to escape. I did—to escape pain." He turned. "What need had I for a soul?"

"Slaughtered. I am so very . . . sorry." She had never seen a man look in so much agony—only Lukos when she had witnessed his torture in a vision.

She had not seen the face of the killer of Zayan's children because she had seen through his eyes. What would it do to Zayan to tell him what she had seen? It would not help him. And she could offer him no clue to the killer.

He pushed off the wall, and he faced her hollowly. "When immortality and strength were offered to me, I saw I could get the vengeance I craved. That's why I chose to become a soulless demon, my love. I got my vengeance and thousands of frightened, weak mortals paid the price."

Before she could respond—before she could think whether she should be angry, or sorry, or outraged by a man who selfishly hurt others to ease his grief—the long echoes of a gong filtered through the dungeon.

"Dinner," he murmured. "You were denied the chance to eat at the inn. You must be ravenous now."

It was as though the sound had broken through his anguish. Pain no longer distorted his features. He was as handsome as ever.

"Dinner? In the middle of the night?" Then she understood. Zayan had compelled the servants to serve a meal for her.

What did food matter? If only she could have been there for his children. She could have touched them and—

"You are thinking that if you had been there, you would have changed everything," he said coldly. "You would have given me my children back. You would have stopped my heart from breaking. You would have stopped me from making a pact with the devil. You might have spared so many lives."

That had been her thought, and he had seen it. "I know it's impossible, but I don't deserve your anger for thinking it." He strode to the door, then turned, waiting for her to follow. But he did not compel her to do it. As with Lukos, she went to him to ask questions. "Has it haunted you for all these years? For centuries?"

She saw a quick flash of anger. He did not want to talk about it. Which surprised her then, when he said softly, "I can still see the wounds. I can see the pools of blood behind their heads. But I can't remember what their faces looked like. I've forgotten. I've spent almost two thousand years trying to remember, but with each moment, the memory of them becomes harder to grasp. I will forever see them dead. I'll never again see them as they were alive."

His words speared her. Pain etched lines around his mouth and slashes of shadow across his forehead. She thought of the shock and the futile anger that had almost drowned her when her older brother had died. Even after she had saved him, terrible fear and grief had consumed her, as though he had died and not lived. She had wanted to do something dangerous and mad to expend all that fury and pain that had no outlet.

If Simon had died, and if someone had appeared and offered to make her a vampire, what might she have done?

You understand . . .

The words echoed in her thoughts. Miranda realized Zayan now stood in front of her. Her hair still rippled with the slight breeze of his impossibly fast movement.

He cupped her cheek again, his bare skin smooth as velvet. "No magic this time," he murmured. Then he bent to her mouth.

Aching for his broken heart, his sorrow and pain, she let his mouth cover hers, a mouth that was impossibly warm for a man who should be dead. Zayan was tortured. He had been driven to madness by an unthinkable crime. She saw that Aunt Eugenia had been correct. Zayan had the capacity to feel regret and know sorrow.

She let her lips part, shamelessly encouraging him. Her upper lip bumped his fangs and she felt the prick to her toes. Silky and hot, his tongue touched her lips, sending another jolt of sensation that streaked down through her and seemed to burst into fireworks between her thighs.

His hand tightened on her back, pulling her up to his mouth

as his lips ravaged hers and his tongue filled her mouth with heat. Each teasing plunge of his tongue made her pulse between her legs. He kept kissing her and didn't seem to ever want to leave her mouth.

A sharp clang jolted Miranda back from the kiss. Lukos had thrown the door to the cell wide open. He stared pointedly at her corset and shift—revealed because the cloak had fallen open. Then he snarled, baring his fangs.

Miranda strode down the corridor toward her bedchamber— and clothes—clutching the fur-lined cloak around her. She felt a ripple of air; then Lukos materialized in front of her and in front of her bedchamber door. His long strides and preternatural strength had easily allowed him to catch, then pass her. He braced his arm on the wall. Bolts of vivid light seemed to flash in his silvery violet eyes.

"You kissed him," Lukos growled. "You went with him to the dungeons and let him kiss you. You enjoyed it. I heard the rapid, excited beat of your heart—"

Miranda threw up her hands. Lukos's lower lip had jutted out into a boyish pout. She could not understand. He had willingly let Zayan kiss her nipples in the carriage. And now, rage crackled off him like lightning sparked by colliding clouds.

He would not step aside and let her pass. He was jealous. This was all about possessiveness. "You shared me in the carriage," she said in a fierce whisper. "Why are you behaving now like a petulant boy?"

"I was in control in the carriage—I was part of the game, allowing you to explore. In the dungeon, you were opening your heart to another man. That's a different thing."

"I sympathized with the tragedy that Zayan had experienced. Just as I felt horrified by what had happened to you—"

"You pity me?" Lukos roared in disbelief. He reached for her cloak, but she held up her hand. To her amazement, a red glow shot from her palm and hit Lukos squarely in his chest. It shoved him back and he stumbled sideways.

Heart pounding, Miranda pushed open her door and rushed into her room. She paused before closing the door. "What would you prefer? That I am afraid of you? That's not what either of you want, is it? For some reason, you both want to seduce me. Why? For my magical power? We've already proven I cannot return your souls. What is it you want from me?"

He said nothing. So she pulled off the cloak and flung it out into the hallway, then shut the door hard. At which point the shock of the dungeons, the horrifying images, the battle with a vampire in a tantrum all did their work, and shaking, she sank to the bed.

She felt close to them both—to two *vampires*. Again, that mad belief returned. That this was where she belonged. With them.

Lukos had the last word—in her thoughts. *Not my soul, angel,* he whispered in his beckoning, beautiful voice. *Someone else's.*

Why had he told her about his children?

Zayan tucked Miranda's hand in the crook of his arm and led her toward the long, laden table in the center of the dining hall. He had felt her turmoil of emotions in the dungeon's cell. She'd hated him for what he had shown her about Blackthorne. She had felt lost and alone. And then she'd pitied him, and now that emotion was strongest in her heart.

A growl from her stomach chased away some of his anger. He had not wanted to talk of his children, but sympathy had begun to open her heart to him. It wasn't seduction that would make her fall for him, he realized, but his vulnerability. She wasn't going to love him for his strength, but very possibly for his weaknesses.

He was going to have to open his own heart, slice open his

own old wounds. And he was going to use her compassion against her because he had no choice.

It was the only way to bring his children back.

Lukos already sat at the table, arrogantly sprawled in a high-backed chair. Flames flickered on candles on the table and reflected in crystal glasses. Steam wafted from the food; he remembered the aroma as being good, but food held no interest for him.

Miranda's scent teased him as he drew out her chair and watched her stiffly seat herself. She smelled of sweat, of blood, but also a trace of feminine vanilla and roses. She smelled of life. And she carried a richer natural perfume—the intoxicating aroma of magic.

He watched her lift her wineglass to her soft lips, and he remembered . . .

Once he had returned home in haste from the battlefield. He had burst into his house. He had found his children sleeping, his wife bathing. She had rejected him that night—because of the gore still on him, the stench of his body. Even after he'd bathed, she had been like wood in his bed, her body stiff and her eyes closed. He knew she took lovers while he fought. He knew she did not love him, but what he had not known was how far she would go to betray him—

He had left her sleeping and had gone to his children. He had kissed them. He could remember the curve of their cheeks, the velvet softness of their skin, darkened to honey-bronze by the Mediterranean sun. The smell of that sunshine had clung to their hair.

But he could not remember anything more.

The clink of dishes brought Zayan back to the present. His silvery gray gaze followed each motion of Miranda's graceful hands as she ate. Spoonful after spoonful of meat and sauce. Watching her try to eat daintily with ravenous hunger eased the iciness around his heart. Soft cooing sounds escaped her as she ate. She enjoyed her food with simple passion.

Lukos was drinking—demons could—and watching Miranda, flames reflected in his eyes.

Zayan took his glass, the wine not drunk, and went to the window. He had forgotten this feeling around his heart—tightness, awareness, something much richer than lust.

Then he blinked; dawn was only a few hours away. Far below, a few lights glittered in the tiny village at the base of the hill. A mass of heartbeats thrummed in the town. But above, around the moon, red clouds swirled.

Zayan...

The voice of the red power sang in his head. Christ, it had come to him.

Fingers of red mist streaking down from the sky toward the village—

From behind, Miranda cried out, "No! What are you doing?"

Zayan spun away from the window, his every muscle tensed, his body primed to attack Lukos to protect Miranda. Not to claim her—to protect her.

Then he relaxed. A maid had walked into the room—a much younger servant than the others, a fresh-faced young lady with flaxen curls and a peaches-and-cream complexion. To a vampire, she was like a delectable pastry. And with his attention fixed on the red mist, he hadn't sensed her heartbeat.

Wearing a fetching blush, the maid curtsied. "My lord? You summoned me?" Her smooth throat was a pretty column of ivory.

"Stop this." Miranda smacked her spoon on the table. She leapt to her feet as the maid padded to Lukos's side. "Let her go."

Zayan took a seat. Lukos had trained in the Scholomance,

had learned great power from Lucifer, had plotted to rule the world of vampires, but he behaved like a rebellious boy most of the time. Zayan should be pleased; it would turn Miranda's heart from Lukos, but it would also remind her what they both were, and that would damage his chances of getting those magical words from her—*I love you*—and then getting her power.

"Do not do this to try to prove something to me. Do not do this as revenge for my—my kiss."

Power rolled off Miranda in her outrage. The magical forces surrounded her like an aura of gold. And the red power would sense it.

Lukos crooked his finger, and without a word exchanged, the pretty maid flounced to him and planted her rounded bottom on his lap. She tilted her head and her curls tumbled away from her neck. Lukos grazed her lace-trimmed cap with his fangs, then leaned to that tempting curve of ivory skin and sank his fangs deep.

Zayan went instantly hard at the small pop of the penetration of flesh. The coppery sweet smell of her rushing blood flooded Zayan's head. He had not fed for hours, and now hunger pounded in him, a thousand times more demanding than lust. His fangs erupted.

Damnation, his beastlike nature was exploding out. He could not show it in front of Miranda. Not when he had to capture her heart.

The maid squealed in shock, but she relaxed quickly underneath Lukos's spell. Her face tipped back in blissful ecstasy. "Oh, aye, aye, sirrah," she moaned.

Miranda had snatched up her fork and was stalking toward Lukos.

Zayan heard the race of the Miranda's heart. He heard the healthy thump of the maid's strong one. Moaning and gasping, the maid wriggled on Lukos's lap. She rocked her derriere on him and thrust her breasts forward. Zayan could sense Lukos was playing, not slaking his thirst. And no doubt this maid had been a plaything of Lord Blackthorne's—

Miranda was pulling at Lukos's shoulders.

"Ooh, sir. I'm coming." The maid bucked on Lukos's lap. He had not touched her, just had taken her blood. Lukos lifted his mouth from her neck. Blood darkened the white fangs. Miranda had been pulling on Lukos's hair—so hard she clutched a few long black strands in her hand.

Lukos bent back to lick the smear of blood and the wounds on the maid's neck. To heal them. He gently lifted the maid off his lap and she landed on unsteady legs. A dreamy expression touched her pretty face. "Thank ye, sir." And she stumbled away to the door.

Lukos flashed a wry grin to Miranda. "With her, I can control myself. I wanted to show you that. I didn't hurt her; it was pleasurable for her. I'm not an ordinary drone of a vampire, I'm a demon. A powerful one. But with you, I can't control my hungers and desires, angel—"

A quick motion and he had lifted Miranda and planted her on her rump on the edge of the table. Lukos tossed up her skirts. She desperately, angrily, tried to pull them down. "How dare you? After biting her, don't you touch—"

The blue silk skirts were at her hips, showing the creamy skin of her thigh above her garters. Zayan loved the costume of English maidens—the filmy stockings and pretty garters, the slender flowing skirts, the low-cut bodices that lifted full, bouncy breasts up for his appreciation.

Lukos bent his mouth to Miranda's wet cunny. Golden curls covered her mound, and the lips below were rose pink and slick. Wildly, she slapped at Lukos's head, but her blows just glanced off him.

Lukos was not using magic to seduce her, only his skill and her innate, fierce desire.

He ate her cunny greedily. His heartbeat slightly quickening, Zayan watched Miranda fight the physical pleasure. She had her hands clenched into fists, and each time her body softened, she immediately jerked her spine straight and pummeled Lukos's shoulders.

Zayan could imagine her taste—the salty, primal essence of her on his lips and tongue. He tossed back the wine, unaware of its flavor. There were only two tastes he hungered for: the slickness of Miranda's quim and the coppery tang of her blood.

Damn.

Lukos was making her juices flow and their scent maddened him. It filled the air, filled his senses. Zayan wanted to drag Lukos aside and make her climax himself.

Lukos was dipping hothouse grapes into her lush cunny, scooping her juices and touching them to her lips. She looked shocked. Lukos popped the grape into his mouth, then licked his lips.

Zayan wanted to press her down on the snowy white tablecloth and tease her with fruit and wine, but he had to wait, watch, let Lukos do this. Jealousy. Lust. Need. They were weakening emotions. He had deadened emotion when he had first been a soldier. It had flared to life with his marriage—lust and love and possessive need—and had become stronger with the births of his children. With them he had known poignant sweetness, pride, the deepest, richest love. But Claudia had betrayed him and he'd lost his children—

"No!" Miranda cried; then she screamed out, climaxing on top of the table. Her hand sent a glass of wine toppling and a bowl of pudding skidding across the table. Platters of roast pig and beef rattled.

Lukos lifted from her. With her feet against his shoulders, Miranda pushed him back. "That wasn't seduction," she gasped. "And I am furious with you for feeding from that maid."

Then she lifted her hand and a stream of scarlet light flew from her palm. It hit Lukos's shoulder, and the vampire howled in pain. He staggered back, gripping the wound, a look of shock etched on his face.

Zayan stared—the stream of red light was the same color as the red power. Miranda leapt down off the table and ran from the room. Zayan shifted shape to a bat and flew after her in pursuit.

All Miranda could think of was the sight of Lukos's fangs touching the woman's neck, then plunging in. She had been horrified, then stunned by his victim's reaction. The woman's face had glowed with pure ecstasy—she looked like a woman who had seen angels.

Miranda rushed to her bedroom and locked the door, knowing the gesture was likely insignificant against the men's strength. She hugged herself as she paced the large, silent room.

Lukos had not hurt the woman. Why did it bother her so much? Was it the belief that he could lose control and kill? Or was it the fact that when he fed, the experience he shared with other women was so erotic?

Madness. It was mad to feel . . . jealous. Even a mortal man would have had many lovers. She knew men were rarely, if ever, faithful.

She thought of the horrible torture she had seen Lukos endure. Wasn't it amazing that he was not just a killer? My God, she had seen him lose his eyes. She had seen him covered in blood—

Miranda heard the soft sound—the beat of wings, faintly for it was coming from beyond her closed window.

Let me come in, love. Zayan's voice.

When she had been young, Aunt Eugenia had warned her that if a vampire ever came to her father's house, she was never to open a window or door to it. She had always agreed, while secretly giggling. A vampire coming openly to the house? That was mad.

But now she slowly walked to the window. Her fingers played

on the latch. She thought of the images she had seen of Zayan's children.

What if she could touch him again and see more? What if she could see the face of the killer?

Then she looked down at her hand and saw a red mark appear in the center of her palm. A diamond shape. It vanished but in her shock, she flicked the latch and the window swung wide.

Zayan flew in and materialized before her.

Miranda gasped in amazement. He stood before her naked. He held out his hand. She saw not a vampire before her, or a hard, ruthless general, but a man driven by desire. A man feeling vulnerability along with his need.

"I dreamed of you. I dreamed of a woman while I was held in captivity—a woman wrought of gold and sunshine. And I understand now that she was you. I know you didn't see me, I was always making love to you from behind." He bowed, his long erection wobbling in front of him. "You belong to me, love. And I remember you saucily told me that I belong to you."

Miranda stared. She had dreamed of Zayan. He had been the man in her erotic dreams, the man she had never seen. "Those were dreams only." And she frowned. "Did you put them there?"

He shook his head. "That power I don't have. I can't come to you in dreams. You have to bring me to you."

"What does that mean?"

But he grasped her hand, held it to his mouth for a kiss that made her toes sizzle in her shoes. And he drew her into his embrace, and slanted his mouth over hers.

Suddenly, she felt as fiercely hot and tense and excited as she did in her dreams. But how could she? She had just been jealous over Lukos, and she had shared dark, astonishing fantasies with him. How could she feel such a rush of excitement in Zayan's arms? But she felt as molten, as intensely aroused, as she had when Lukos had plopped her on the dining room table.

Zayan's kiss deepened, his tongue slid in and played with hers, and she moaned in approval, surrender, and pure, hungry lust.

There had been another man in her last dream. If the dreams were the truth, or some kind of prophesy, who was the man with the golden hair?

And in her last dream, she'd been bitten . . .

Moonlight shimmered in, and before Miranda's eyes it turned fiercely red and bathed Zayan in its vivid glow.

9

Daylight

The red mist swirled around both Zayan and Miranda for seconds, twirling around her throat, making her shiver. It slithered down her breasts toward her belly and hips; then it vanished.

It was the exact same deep, intense scarlet as the light that had shot from her hand. In its wake, it left images in her head. Visions from her dreams with Zayan. She was flooded by memories of the things she had done with him, with this naked man who stood before her.

"You did that, didn't you? You sent that burst of red light from my hand to hit Lukos."

He paused for a moment, and she believed he'd deny it. Then he slowly, reluctantly, nodded. "I had to, Miranda."

She should be exasperated, but gazing on him, she couldn't be. She understood the inspiration of the artists of Rome, who had turned marble into exquisite male bodies. Zayan possessed a warrior's body. Shoulders that must be as wide as the doorways in the castle and formed of straight planes of bone and solid muscle. His chest was a play of light and shadow, revealing taut ridges and two dark bronze nipples that puckered as he looked at her. She wanted to run her hands down his chest and touch the cobbled beauty of his muscled abdomen. Then grasp his amazing erection, for the thick, heavy shaft lifted proudly to his navel, and the head looked taut enough to burst.

He was beautiful. Every inch of him. Yet, she was cautious now, uncertain if she could touch him.

He grinned and emerald green stars flew above his hands. They darted to her, and pressed quickly to her lips, tickling her, then danced at the base of her throat.

Desire rushed through her, giving her bravery. She stepped forward and touched Zayan's heart. She pressed her palm to his bare flesh. His erect nipple teased the sensitive center of her hand. And suddenly, she was looking up at Zayan; but she was in the shadows, and Zayan was reclining on a chaise. She could glimpse his thoughts—he was thinking of the profile of a beautiful woman. Miranda could see what he remembered—lush black hair elaborately dressed and long-lashed eyes that flashed with anger but never with love for him.

Beware Gaius, a man's voice said. *He would sacrifice a victory of Rome to see you dead. He would pay any price to destroy you, Praetonius. The emperor fears you. You are too strong and too popular. With an army at your command, you could take Rome. . . .*

In her vision, Zayan disregarded the warning with a laugh. He was not afraid of Mucius Gaius. The man was not ruthless enough to make a true grasp at power—he was weak. And he was thinking of his children. His daughter had defied her nurse to embrace him, and how he had loved the feel of her slim body in his arms. How he had delighted in her ingenuous show of affection. He loved them both, his children.

He had everything he could wish for—success on the battlefield, the ear of the emperor along with the man's fearful respect, immense wealth, precious children, and a beautiful, sensual wife.

What he did not have was a woman's unconditional love.

But no great man, no powerful warrior, worried about such a thing—

Miranda moaned in surprise as Zayan's green lights lifted her. She floated two feet off the ground and began to move toward his naked body.

In dreams, she had shared intimacy with him. In her visions, she had seen a glimpse of his family life—the wife he loved but believed did not love him, his adored children.

She had even glimpsed a sense of emptiness. Victory on the battlefield had left him void of hope and love. She had seen that Zayan realized he had been losing the sense of invulnerability of a successful general. He had begun to realize that he was not unstoppable and untouchable. That he could die at any time.

He hadn't cared, she'd realized, as long as he left his legacy—his children.

What are you thinking, Miranda? Zayan asked. *Your thoughts are a jumble to me—I can't see inside them. But I sense you are thinking of something that hurts you very much.*

She could not speak of what she had seen. Not as he stepped toward her and began to caress her breasts through her dress. His hands cupped and gently kneaded.

In her dreams, this had made her wild with desire.

The reality was so much more intense, more pleasurable, more delicious. Zayan was more than just a vampire or a demon—he was a complex man capable of great honor, deep love, and fierce hurt and anger. She tipped her head back languorously and savored the pleasure. It seemed to last forever.

Then he slid his arm around her waist and pulled her to him. Instinctively, she locked her legs around his lean, hard waist. Her thighs rested on the hard ridges of his hipbones.

I want to make love to you. As in our dreams. There is a reason we dreamed of each other. It speaks of a deep and special connection. I've never dreamed of any woman like that. No woman but you—

He left her breasts, which were swollen and tight with pleasure, and slid her skirts up. The green lights held her up with her heels locked together against Zayan's low back. She was truly flying.

Then her drawers vanished on a wisp of magic, leaving her nether curls and her wet lips pressed to Zayan's shaft.

This would not be shocking at all in her dreams. But here—

There is nothing shocking. We desire each other and have shared this already. Do you not believe linking our thoughts in dreams is as intimate as sharing our bodies?

Yes, she whispered in her thoughts. It was, wasn't it?

Zayan used his magic to rock her on his shaft. Her heart pounded like the pulse of frantic wings. He shifted his hips beneath her, and she felt his—

My cock, angel. My cock is going to slide deep inside you. Just as you've loved to have it in your dreams.

She held her breath. She did want this, but . . .

But she had already been intimate with Lukos. She had felt her heart open to him. She couldn't make love to another man just hours later. She couldn't.

She began to struggle.

A band of pinkish light spilled into her room.

Faint light, soft and pure. A ray of dawn. But how was that possible? Had she truly been locked on Zayan's hips for hours, letting him caress her breasts?

Zayan abruptly let her down. Where the light had struck his cheek, smoke curled there. Miranda stared at him. "You must go."

He nodded, then bent and gave a lingering kiss to her hand. One that made her breath come quickly and her toes curl. But there could be no more.

Zayan stepped back. Darkness began to swirl around him, a blackness that winked with tiny lights, like firelight reflecting on polished jet. He vanished and she felt a brush of air and heard the soft flutter of wings. Before she could see him, she felt a breeze and knew he had gone.

"No!"

Miranda bolted up in her bed. At her side, the candle had burned to a stub, the fire was now only glowing embers in the grate. She was wearing her dress but was under the bedcovers. She did not remember anything after . . . after she had come to her room.

But she strained to hear. She thought she'd heard someone shout.

She wasn't certain. Had she really heard it, or had it been part of a dream?

She fought to remember. Slowly, it came back. Zayan had kissed her passionately, and she had touched her hand to him and had glimpsed inside his past—and into his heart. He had told her he did not know who had murdered his children, yet someone had told him to beware of a man named Gaius.

Then he had gone because dawn was coming.

Miranda got out of bed and hurried to the closed drapes in the room. She pulled them open. A gray light spilled in. Not the soft pink and gold glow of dawn. She glanced out and saw thick, dark clouds massed in the sky. But it was still daylight.

She heard another sound—a scraping, followed by another sharp cry. It came from beyond her door.

Cautiously, she unlocked her door—the window was also locked, though she didn't remember having locked it again after Zayan left her. Why was all that time a blank? It had disappeared from her mind. She made her way down the gloomy corridor, straining to hear.

All was suddenly eerily quiet.

She came to a junction of corridors. There was more light to the right, so she went that way, and had gone around another bend when she saw a crumpled body on the floor.

Miranda crouched down. He was a young boy, perhaps twelve. His face was ashen and his limbs limp. His eyes were shut, and fear—inhuman fear—was the last expression etched on his young face. His head had flopped to the side, and red droplets stood out against the white skin of his neck. Blood.

Miranda reached out, her fingers trembling. She brushed back the unkempt locks of hair. There, in the middle of his young throat. Two puncture wounds.

One of them had done this: either Zayan or Lukos.

She had seen Lukos feed from a woman and not hurt her. Did that mean Zayan had done this? Or had Lukos lost control here—?

She shook her head. It shouldn't matter which one had been the killer. They were both vampires. They were both capable of this.

Miranda touched her hand to the boy's heart. Had he been gone too long? Her arm began to feel hot—a scorching heat that seeped out her fingers. Her body began to hum, and she felt vibrations throughout her.

And suddenly, before her eyes, the boy's chest jerked. He sat up abruptly. He stared at her with wide, frightened eyes. She sat back, amazed at how quickly he had begun to move again. Her hand lifted from his chest and he rolled away from her. He scrambled to his feet and ran away down the corridor.

"Wait, please!" she cried. "I don't mean you harm!" She wanted to know who he was. Did he live in the castle?

But he'd vanished into the shadows farther down in the hall and she could no longer hear his light, frantic footsteps. Chasing him wouldn't protect him.

She had made love with Lukos and almost with Zayan. She had let her heart be swayed by the pain in their pasts.

The visions she had seen had made her forget they were vampires. Even Aunt Eugenia, who tried to understand vampires, had told her that they could not fight the compulsion to drink human blood. That was the real tragedy, Eugenia had said. Vampires had to be killed for a craving that was not their fault and beyond their control.

But then she had seen Lukos merrily feed from the maid. They were not even willing to try to control their cravings.

And she now knew she must stop them.

Staking Lukos and Zayan while they were trapped in sleep would be her only chance, but the thought of making a stake, then driving it into each man's chest brought bile to her throat. She had made love to them. How could she kill them?

Because she was the only one who could.

Slowly, Miranda rose to her feet. She did have another choice. She could escape and bring help to the castle. If she could get out, she could take the road down to the village at the base of the hill.

She shivered. She could be racing out in the open. But the vampires would be asleep now that it was day. This was her only chance.

Unease prickled along Miranda's spine as she hurried back to her room to dress. Hadn't Lukos and Zayan thought she would try to escape with daylight? Why hadn't they imprisoned her in her room?

Or did they think that she had been seduced by them and wouldn't leave?

As she hurried down the corridor toward her room, her half boots clattered on the floor and broke the quiet. She could feel the brisk, icy air seeping through the stone wall from outside and knew it must be bitterly cold outdoors. She rushed back to her room and pulled a pelisse from her wardrobe. Quickly, she pulled it on and crammed a bonnet on her head.

Now she had to find a way to escape.

She crept down to the main foyer of the castle, a cavernous room of stone decorated with embroidered tapestries. Her heart hammered furiously as she reached the double front doors—twin slabs of oak. She pulled on the iron handle of the door on the right. It didn't budge. And neither did the left when she tugged desperately on it.

The doors were locked, the key missing. Miranda made a rushed search of the corridors and rooms close by. There were no servants, no one who could fetch a key to open the door. She swallowed hard as she turned slowly in the huge, empty entrance hall. Were they all dead? She raced down the servants' stairs to the kitchens in the bowels of the castle. Heat wafted from the large rooms and voices within had her panic subsiding.

She rushed in to find the cook and two young girls busy at a large wooden table. The cook rolled out pastry with a wide, heavy rolling pin. One girl was laying out a plucked bird, the other placing herbs on the table.

"Good morning," she said, trying for normalcy. But the women continued on with their work as though she were not in the room.

"I wish to go out." She spoke louder, but again she was ignored. She walked past them and the cook relentlessly rolled, flattening the pastry. The other girls focused only on their tasks.

Miranda picked up a china dish and smashed it to the table. But no one flinched or jumped at the sharp sound and the flying shards except she.

Somehow, Lukos and Zayan had taken control of the servants' minds and she could not break through.

Miranda reached the narrow door that must lead to the outside. She lifted the iron bar that bolted it shut and tugged. Of course this door, like the front door, was locked and it also required a key to open it. Blast.

With no other choice, she rushed back to the main floor of the large castle and searched the rooms there. She found a gallery off a room that had been changed from an immense dining hall into a ballroom. Large windows looked out onto a small stretch of manicured gardens before the wild of the woods encroached.

Miranda grabbed the back of a chair and dragged it to the gallery windows. She hefted as best as she could and half-threw, half-rolled it.

Glass exploded, and glittering pieces rained down on the flag terrace.

Miranda felt triumph for all of one heartbeat. She was free—but would anyone believe her story of vampires? Would anyone come back with her to save the castle?

And she felt a sharp, awful pain at her heart. She was going to betray Zayan and Lukos. She was going to bring about their destruction.

To save innocents like that young boy, she had no other choice.

Miranda ran down the winding, rutted road from the castle, her boot soles skidding on the uneven ground. The road dipped and rose, following the contours of the rocky hill on which the castle perched, and she found herself quickly clear of the trees, with a panoramic view of the village below and the surrounding tilled fields.

She had to slow down, her skirts clutched in her hands to lift her hems so she could run. She'd had no choice but to try to get to the village on foot. But she'd been raised to be a lady, which meant she hadn't hiked up her skirts and sprinted for years. Already her lungs were burning and her legs ached. She rode well, but when she'd tried to approach the horses in the castle's stables, they had reared and rushed against their stalls, terrified of her—as though they feared she was a monster. She'd never had that happen before. She wanted to believe that the vampires had controlled the horses, just as they had controlled the humans. She did not want to think the horses had sensed something evil about her.

Her lungs were burning.

Miranda stopped to suck in breath, but what she saw stole that breath away.

Fog hung over the village, but it was like no fog Miranda had ever seen before. At the bottom it was a normal grayish white, but higher in the sky it appeared to be red. It was like the eerie look of the sky when Zayan and Lukos had stopped her carriage the day before.

From this vantage, high above the village, Miranda could see the mist was centered on the village, and it swirled around with the cluster of buildings in its vortex.

Had the vampires brought this eerie red mist? She remembered Zayan fighting a creature that had come out of it. And a mist the same deep blood-red color had swept around both her and Zayan in the castle.

Was it dangerous? Was it going to hurt the people below?

With her hand on her heaving chest, Miranda started off at a run again.

10

Wolf

The tall, thin, hawkish innkeeper's gaze swept haughtily over her. Miranda knew he saw disheveled hair messily drawn back in a bun, a pelisse that was only half-fastened, and splatters of mud all over her skirts. She took a deep breath, then launched into her story.

Mounting disbelief came to the man's eyes, and his brows rose as quickly as her hopes plummeted.

"You were attacked on the road by vampires?" he snapped. "Vampires who have taken control of Lord Blackthorne's castle and have sucked the blood from a young boy." He shook his head. "You're either mad or drunk, lass, and I've no use for either in my fine establishment. Be off with ye."

"It's the truth," Miranda stated hotly. "If you'd send men to the castle, you would soon find that out." Her stomach was twisting in knots. She couldn't just desert the servants of the castle. She had to find some way to get them help.

But she saw the innkeeper edging along his desk, toward an opening that would lead him to her. What would he do if he thought her mad? Throw her out? Or lock her up?

It was hard enough to betray the vampires, without having to fight the people she was trying to protect to do it.

She'd taken an unsteady step back, when a woman appeared behind the man. She'd come out of room behind the desk and hurried forward. The woman had a plump, red-cheeked face and tightly curled, iron-gray hair. "Hush, Harry," she admonished. "Now, who might you be, lass. Have you had a bad fright, then?"

A fright? The woman bustled around the counter, a kindly smile on her lips. "What's all this talk of vampires? There's no such thing, my love. Oh, there were foolish tales around here dozens of years ago, but no truth in them. Rumors and stories invented by wicked people to persecute others. Why don't you sit quietly, love, and have a cup of tea."

Miranda understood. The woman thought she was mad, too, and hoped to calm her to find out where she belonged. She nodded her head and dutifully followed the woman to a private parlor. But what she hadn't counted on was the woman locking the door as she left for the tea, imprisoning her inside.

Blast. And even as she thought the word, the lock glowed with an unearthly red glow. A fierce creaking sound came. With a crack, the lock broke and the door swung wide.

For a few heartbeats, Miranda didn't move. She stared at the twisted metal of the lock. Had she—?

Two maids passed by the opening and Miranda ducked behind a faded wing chair.

"The gentleman in room six," one maid said softly to the other, "it's his lordship. I caught a glimpse as he opened his door, and I know it was Blackthorne."

The servants stopped in front of the door, then stepped into the doorway to speak, assuming the room was empty. The second girl shook her head. "He wouldn't stay here—"

"He might if he's tupping one of the barmaids."

"The man in room six is named Casselman—"

"Aye, the man of the castle. He's not using his proper name. I think he's doing dark things in his room. Things he has to keep a secret. There's rumors he does witchcraft, you know."

"I heard a tale that he drinks the blood of young maidens."

"Oh, aye, I expect he makes them bleed. But from breaking their maidenheads, I'm certain."

With that, the two girls scurried away.

Miranda stood. Her hands trembled. Was Blackthorne, the man she had thought she loved, the mysterious inhabitant of room six?

After what she had seen in the castle dungeons, she could not just let him hurt innocent women in his room.

Something had to be done.

A naked man stood at the window, running his fingers through his collar-length coal-black hair. Beside him, a lamp threw light on the tight curve of his derriere, the hollows at his haunches, and the small of his back. He was chuckling to himself, and with his other hand, he tapped a riding crop against his solid thigh.

He was a beautiful man, almost as gorgeous as Zayan and Lukos. But was he Blackthorne? From her view of his naked rump, Miranda had no idea.

A soft sigh fluttered to her. Her heart made a sudden lump into her throat and Miranda looked to the bed. Two women slept on it. The covers had been drawn back, but one woman clutched the edge of a white sheet. She lay on her back with her large breasts half-exposed. She snored lightly. The other was curled up in a ball, and long, dirty-blond hair streamed out around her.

What made Miranda stare was the pictures drawn on their bodies in . . . in some kind of paint. Pentagrams and strange symbols and exquisitely rendered letters that looked like the sort found on old manuscripts.

"Put the tray on the sideboard, lass," said the man at the window.

Miranda froze with her hand on the doorknob. She'd stealthily opened the door when she'd found it unlocked. Not sneakily enough, it appeared.

The blonde who had been curled up stretched and uttered a groan. "Aren't ye coming back to bed, milord? Won't ye untie my hands?"

Shocked, Miranda realized the woman's hands and ankles were bound with white rope.

Then she saw it. The long scar that snaked down his right side, the puckered lines illuminated by the light. It was deep and ugly. The skin had not knit well, and it made a trough along this perfect, strong body.

This *must* be Blackthorne. He had described himself once in a letter to her. Hair that looked like he'd been dragged through a sooty chimney, he'd written—dark as coal, but it tended to stick up in odd places. Eyes that had been likened to the color of a mud puddle.

She had fallen in love with him over that teasing description. And it hadn't really been true—he was breathtakingly handsome.

But he had also shared his bed with two tavern wenches the night before. The night when he had not been at home and his servants would not divulge where he'd went.

He turned to face her, obviously surprised she had not come in. His smile widened to a leer. "Interested in joining the fun, pet?" He reached down to his privy part and her gaze streaked down with his hand. He fondled his shaft without a sign of embarrassment.

Stunned, Miranda stumbled back. She'd seen the accoutrements of his dungeon, had overheard the maids, and she didn't know why she was so startled.

She gathered her skirts and ran down the hallway. She

reached the stair, her momentum almost carried her headfirst down it, but she grasped the banister and raced down. Why was she running like she was being pursued by the devil?

At the bottom of the stair, she stopped. It didn't matter what he had been doing with those women. His castle had been taken over by vampires, and he had the right to know. She was the one who had led Lukos and Zayan to his home. She was obligated to face him and tell him.

But cowardice struck. She couldn't go up now. Not when he was naked, after he'd leered at her. Not so soon after she'd realized all the tender thoughts he'd penned in his letters to her had to be so much twaddle.

"The first coach arrived, Mr. Lorimer," a woman's voice announced. Miranda recognized the strong, hearty voice of the plump woman who had approached her kindly. But now the voice sounded strained and filled with fear. "And it seems that this odd, wretched fog is only here, around our village. The day is fine and clear everywhere else. Even in Haring-on-the-Marsh, which is only a mile to the north."

The innkeeper grunted. They were both in a parlor that led off from the stair. Miranda could see them, so she retreated in case they could also see her.

"We're in a valley, Mrs. Lorimer," he answered. "All the inclement weather pools here, as well you know."

"Then explain why three wee mites have died last night—since this foul fog settled upon us. It's witchcraft, mark my words. It's something evil and demonic."

"How is this fog responsible for three children's deaths?" Lorimer barked. "Unless they were lost in it."

"They weren't. They just . . . died."

Miranda took the risk of peeking in the room. Muttering something about gothic novels and not enough work, Mr. Lorimer left the room through a door in the back.

The vampires had brought this fog to the village—Miranda

was certain of that. What if it was some evil form of their magic that stole children's lives or their souls? She had seen a red mist around the boy she had saved. And Aunt Eugenia had told her that some members of the Royal Society believed vampires actually fed on souls not blood. Blood was the way to release the soul.

It was still morning, not even eleven. Miranda hurried into the room and the innkeeper's plump wife stared up in surprise.

"Now where did you go, dear? I was looking for you."

No convincing lie popped into Miranda's head, so she blurted the truth, "I sought Lord Blackthorne to warn him of the danger in his home, but—"

"You went to his room?" Red suffused Mrs. Lorimer's face. Her eyes narrowed and the kindly smile vanished. "Dear heaven, what did you say to him?"

"Nothing. He was not alone." Miranda drew herself up. "He had two women in his bed. Women who work here, I assume—"

"No, he has them brought to him." The woman's gaze averted downward.

"I left him—and overhead you, Mrs. Lorimer. I want to know which children died last night. I believe I can help them."

Tears glistened. "You can't. They are all dead."

"Where are they? I must get to them as quickly as I can. There might still be time."

"I am not going to tell you. Their mothers are grieving, and I'm not going to unleash a mad woman on them. In fact—" Mrs. Lorimer yanked the bellpull hard three times. "You should be taken to the magistrate. He'll find out where you belong."

Heavy footsteps approached. Some burly servant was no doubt on his way to answer his mistress's summons. Jerking up her hems, Miranda raced out the door at the back of the room, the one Mr. Lorimer had used. She was plunged into the servants' part of the house, near the kitchens. She ran through there, jostling the kitchen maids, darting around the tables. The door to the back gardens was open, the faint reddish light like a beacon.

Someone grabbed at her, but the sleeve of her pelisse tore and she pulled away. She rushed out of the house.

The fog had settled so heavily she could see only a few feet in front of her. She could barely make out the bulk of the white-painted inn beside her. But enough so she could follow it to the front street. Once there, she ran for the next building.

Without stopping to see if she was being pursued, Miranda darted inside. A bell tinkled above her head. The cheery aroma of baking bread greeted her, and she retreated to the corner near the counter.

The proprietess came out, wiping her hands on a linen cloth. "May I help you, madam?"

Such sweet, normal smells surrounded her that Miranda wanted to sink to the floor and close her eyes. But she stuttered an order for sticky buns. As the woman carried out her request, she sidled to the end of the counter. If someone burst in looking for her, she could escape around the counter and through the back of the shop.

"This fog is growing heavy," she began conversationally. She'd learned it did not work to blurt out the truth. "And I heard that it is responsible for the tragic deaths of some children. . . ."

"Oh, I don't know about that," the woman broke in. "There's some that think the fogs that roll in here portend tragedy. And there were three wee children who passed on last night. One of the boys had been poorly since his birth. The smithy's son. And there was another girl and a wee one who had just taken his first steps."

Miranda felt sick with grief. She questioned the woman until she found out the names of the families the children belonged to. The smallest of the mites had passed away at dawn. While she'd never tried to save anyone who had not died right in front of her—except the boy this morning, and she had heard his dying scream—she didn't know how her power worked. She might still be able to save the children. Time might have nothing to do with whether her magic worked.

After one night with Zayan and Lukos, she felt, oddly, more comfortable with her power. She did not feel so freakish or as frightened of it.

Armed with a basic direction of the cottage in which the smithy's son lived, Miranda hurried out, her buns ignored on the counter. The woman shouted, but she plunged into the fog and vanished.

Or rather, everything seemed to vanish around her. After walking only a few feet from the bakery, she could see nothing but the swirling red mist. Where it touched her skin, the fog was clammy and cold. She rushed on with resolute steps for another yard, then stopped.

Damnation, she really could not see a thing. She felt almost nauseous because she couldn't tell which way was up or down. Sometimes the reddish mist would swirl, leaving a small opening she could see through, and she'd take a step. But it would thicken almost at once, leaving her blind. Then she did a foolish thing. She turned in a circle. She was sure it was a complete circle— well, she thought so. It was enough to completely disorient her.

She was not going to let this wretched fog cheat three children out of their lives.

But what was she going to do? Could she will her power to lead her to the children?

Miranda shut her eyes. She focused on a vision of a cottage, one with simple walls and a thatch roof and dirt floor, from the description the baker had given. She could imagine the family, their grief for their son, and their fear. It was so real to her, but being able to envision it was not telling her which way to go.

"I must save him," she shouted aloud at the blasted fog. "Where is he? Lead me to him and I will save him."

To the right of her, the fog swirled wildly, then rolled back, as though making a path for her.

Impossible? No, nothing was impossible anymore.

Miranda ran through the path in the fog. Ahead of her, the mist kept cleaving apart, until she reached a tiny garden. Dew clung to the wilting flowers and green leaves, and rolled down the front of the door. She rapped and waited.

Just as she lifted her fist again, the door swung open. A woman with red eyes and unkempt hair peered at her.

"Please let me in. I want to try to save your child."

Aching pain showed in the tired, faded eyes. "He's dead."

But Miranda stuck her foot in the door to stop the woman from closing it. Then she pushed inside.

He was so small and fragile. Pale with death. His eyes were closed, and his body now felt cool to Miranda's touch. He was laid on a rough-hewn table in a small room that served as a parlor. Behind was a room off the kitchen, where the rest of the children had gathered to be by the fire—at least the warmth came from there, as did sniffles and arguments.

Could she save him?

Miranda bent to the boy. She touched his chest and prayed she could help him. She also prayed that God had been the one to give her this gift, and that He would listen.

The rush of heat took her by surprise. She splayed her fingers on the boy's chest, tensed, and endured the fiery agony that shot through her arm.

There was no pleasure this time in the use of her power. Just pain. Pain that started in her arm as an ache, then grew to a piercing intensity. She cried out with it. It shocked her. She wanted to snatch her arm away, and she couldn't.

She drove her teeth into her lower lip to bear the agony. She whimpered with it. And it grew so strong, she thought it would kill her.

But then it stopped. The pain ceased, and the heat in her

body faded. The little boy's chest rose beneath her and his eyes flickered open.

The mother, who had been standing behind her, gave a sob. She rushed forward and took up her small son, cradling him to her chest. But that moment of amazement and joy, the awed look of a woman who had seen a most precious miracle, vanished.

She backed away from Miranda, hugging her child tight. "Get out. What are ye? A witch?"

Another woman came forward—she must have been in the other room with the other children. "A gypsy!" she cried. "She might have cursed him at first and now she's come and lifted it. We won't give you a thing!"

This other woman held a kitchen knife like a weapon.

Miranda stared at both women in shock. She had saved the boy's life, but there was no gratitude in their eyes, only stark fear.

Now was the time to leave. And to run.

Once again, Miranda found herself charging outside, but this time the fog was fainter. And once again, it parted in front of her, creating a path to the next dead child.

The path led to a cottage at the end of the road. Miranda had almost reached it when a black shape jumped out at her. A large hand clamped over her mouth, another closed around her throat, and a man dragged her off the road to a copse of bushes.

She was slammed against a tree and her breath fled her chest as her back hit the trunk. The man who had grabbed her wore a cloak, with a hood pulled low enough to shadow his face. But she could see a hard mouth and a strong jaw—a jaw rimmed by stubble. He had his hand clamped over her mouth and his other arm kept her pinned against the tree.

The smell of smoke clung to his face and his cloak, and the stink of liquor rose from his breath.

He smelled of sweat. Lukos and Zayan had not smelled of

stale male perspiration—this had to be a mortal man. He must
be the one mortal man who wanted her dead.

Mr. Ryder.

His hand came up, and something cold and hard jabbed her
throat. "Stay still," he warned, "or I'll shoot you, Miss Bond.
And keep your mouth shut."

The hand lifted from her mouth. The hood dropped back.

She stared into Mr. Ryder's beautiful, brilliant blue eyes—
eyes that would make any unsuspecting young woman swoon
with passion, but made her gag on fear. The pistol pushed
harder against her neck.

"She ran away? How could you let her go alone?" Althea
knew she had no place to snap the questions at Miss Miranda
Bond's aunt, but she had hoped and prayed this would be the
end of her journey. But it wasn't, and she had to find Miss Bond
to have a hope of saving her baby's life.

She sank on the edge of a chaise, and she had to put her hand
to her mouth to stop the scream of fear and frustration that
wanted to come out. Baby Serry slept in Bastien's arms, and as
Althea saw him plant a kiss on the tiny forehead of the swaddled bundle, she almost burst into tears. Serry now barely
moved her limbs and rarely opened her eyes. Her daughter was
dying before her eyes, and her one hope—Miranda Bond—had
vanished.

Eugenia paced in front of the crackling fire in the home of
her nephew, Simon Bond, a baron. Despite her silver hair, she
was slender and obviously strong and spry. "I did not *let* her
go. She is a headstrong girl and she simply left." Eugenia waved
a book in front of them all. "My dear niece kept a journal and in
it, she writes of Lord Blackthorne—her grand passion. I suspect my niece had gone to him. My nephew has—well, he has
thrown most of his money away in gaming halls. Miranda saw
marriage as a way to save him."

Jonathon stepped forward. "Do you know, Miss Bond, of a vampire slayer named James Ryder?"

Out of the corner of her eye, Althea saw Yannick take Serry and hold her tight to his chest.

"Was he not thrown out of the Royal Society four years ago?" Eugenia asked, frowning.

"Yes, but it is believed that he visited your niece here, and he was seen approaching her in Hyde Park, the day before she left."

"Good heavens, why?"

Drake Swift spoke, "I would suspect the Royal Society is behind it. They like to have loose cannons under their employ, but secretly."

Eugenia swallowed hard. "The Society?"

"Lord Denby says the Society has been protecting your niece," Althea said.

Eugenia whirled to face her. "The Royal Society does not know about her. I've never told them. I have kept her power a secret—"

She broke off. Pure horror touched her face. Althea remembered what had almost happened to Serena because of rogue members of the Royal Society.

"Good heavens," Eugenia rasped. "We must find her. And we haven't much time. It has been two nights since she left London. I was going to go in pursuit, but Denby had called me to an emergency, and I believed she was safe—" Eugenia slammed her fist on the fireplace mantel. "The emergency was a lie, I see now. To keep me from going after Miranda."

"The Society usually reacts in fear to anyone they do not understand," Serena added solemnly. "And if we cannot trust the Society, we should turn to the vampire queens."

"No!" Eugenia cried.

"You know, don't you, that we are all vampires?"

Eugenia nodded. "I have never understood how you can be vampires and belong to the Royal Society."

"Perhaps because we realize that 'vampire' and 'evil' do not necessarily go hand in hand," Althea answered. "We have proved that vampires can exist without using mortals as simply their prey." Nods of agreement came swiftly from Yannick, Bastien, Serena, Drake, and Jonathon.

"The vampire queens will see her value and will be afraid of her. They will be as frightened as the Society," Bastien said. "They might want her destroyed."

"I would not trust the queens to protect my niece," Eugenia exclaimed. "I shall go after her alone before I would go to them."

"You won't be going alone," Althea declared. She did not know if more travel would hurt Serry, but she could not leave Miranda Bond unprotected. And not just for her child, for Miranda herself. "We will all be with you."

"Lord Blackthorne has a black reputation," Yannick said.

Eugenia shivered. "I had no idea my niece even knew of him. My weapons are prepared and I am ready to go." She clucked her tongue. "I thought Miranda had more sense than to expect a man to save her."

"Christ, this fog is so thick it's as dark as bloody night," Mr. Ryder grumbled, as he sliced open the front of her pelisse.

Miranda felt the push of the blade and the *pops* as the buttons gave. He'd tucked his pistol in his waistband, but the blade of his dagger was as frightening. The fog had dropped and had changed to white, curling in around them to plunge them into an impenetrable haze. She couldn't see beyond Mr. Ryder's glittering, hungry eyes and a few branches that hung around his head.

"They wanted me to kill you as soon as I caught you, thinking that I'd blindly follow the order and not realize that if they want you dead so much, you must have a bloody great value."

"D-do you mean to ransom me?" Ransom bought her time. It bought her hope.

"What I want is your power."

She stared up at him. She couldn't give him her power. "You want to force me to use it for you?"

"There is a way for a mortal to take a demon's power."

"I'm not a—" But was she a demon? She had no idea what it felt like to be a demon. What she possessed was an ability to do magic—an impossible ability. But her magic saved lives.

Mr. Ryder's breath came in heavy, alcohol-laced pants. "Are you a virgin?" he snarled. "Did you give yourself to those vampires?"

Before she could say a word, he rasped, "I want you. But I would be more gentle if I knew for certain you were untouched."

She had no intention of telling him what she had done or not done. She had to think of a way to get free.

But his gloved hands wrapped around the sides of her cut pelisse and he tore it open. His hands—the knife still held in his right one—clamped to her breasts and he squeezed them through her gown.

It was horrid. She'd never been mauled like this; it was nothing like the way Lukos or Zayan had touched her, even on their first trip in the carriage.

As he pawed her, the tip of his knife twitched around. She couldn't breathe, not with his hands crushing her flesh. He wanted to hurt her, to scare her. She could see mocking pleasure burning in his eyes.

He slayed vampires. He should have been a hero, but he was enjoying her terror. He was a bully, and her best hope was to conquer her fear and deflate his triumph.

"Let me go. There are children I could save, and you are keeping me from them. If you want my power, let me use it. Let me save innocent lives."

His lip curled in disdain. "You are raising the dead. Don't you understand what you are doing? Creating vampires."

"It's not true." Aunt Eugenia had not become a vampire. "And if you think I'm a demon, why do you want my power?"

He pinched her nipples through her gown with harsh force and she screamed in shock and pain. The back of his hand cracked across her face. She snapped back with the force of his slap.

He shoved her back against the tree again and jerked her skirts halfway up her thighs.

She clawed at his hands.

But she couldn't stop him. He pushed against her, his shoulder drove hard into her collarbone, and his hips surged forward. He rammed his legs between hers, forcing her legs apart, and the fog swirled around her bare upper thighs, dampening them with mist.

"Stop," she cried, but he gripped her thigh, driving his fingers into her flesh. She felt his other hand push between their bodies, working down to the front of his trousers.

"No!" she shouted.

A vicious growl echoed through the fog. It seemed to come from everywhere, as though wolves had crept up under the cover of the mist and surrounded them.

Mr. Ryder jerked back. "What in Hades was that?" He leaned forward to keep her trapped while he glanced fearfully around them.

She felt his quick heartbeat pounding against her. "Wolves," she gasped, feeding his fear. "It sounded like a pack." She might be trying to stoke his terror, but she was also heightening hers. What if it was a pack? Even if she could escape Ryder, she couldn't outrun wolves.

The growls grew louder. Ryder swung around to search the thick white fog. He had let her go to hold his knife and his pistol.

A dark shadow loomed behind Ryder. "There!" she shouted.

He jerked around, but the black shape had vanished. He spun back, his eyes wild, and he held the knife to her throat. "No tricks, witch."

She gulped. "It's not a trick. I saw it. A shape or a shadow."

Another growl. A low, rumbling roar, and a black animal streaked out of the white. The huge mass of it launched at Mr. Ryder.

Bang! His pistol exploded with a deafening roar, sending his arm flying back. She flung her body to the side to avoid his elbow. She tumbled to the damp ground. Dazed, she saw four legs and a huge, black furry body. It was a giant of a wolf.

Jaws snapped and flashed at Ryder, then the beast leapt on top of him. The dagger's blade sliced and slashed at the wolf. Ryder shouted, screamed. The wolf snatched him up by the shoulder and threw him. Ryder's body sailed into the trees.

The wolf bounded to her and she held her breath. Her chest thundered. She scrambled back but bumped the tree. "N-no."

Sniffing the air, the wolf moved in closer.

11

___

The Chain

Stay utterly, completely still.

Miranda whispered the warning softly to herself as the wolf cocked its regal head and looked at her. The animal's dark, liquid, beautiful eyes solemnly held hers. Reflective eyes with a hint of violet.

Lukos.

The fog sucked in around him, covering him like a white blanket; then it shimmered. In moments, he stepped out of the thick mist, his hair long and loose, his body—naked.

He had pursued her. Though she was a captive again, Miranda felt a surge of relief.

She had not seen the moment of transition, and it seemed so impossible that the fearsome wolf had transformed into this man. He held his arms wide in a sign of welcome and she stepped forward into his embrace.

He gathered her to his broad, warm chest. Her fingers curled against him, and she gave a shuddering sigh as his arms tightened. He was a vampire, but his caress was loving and gentle, even as it promised strength and power.

She should not feel safe held against him. She should feel fear. But she didn't.

His hand skimmed up to her neck, settling around the nape. He pulled her into his kiss. Possessively, his mouth took hers. It was a fierce joining, with none of the languorous tongue play he'd indulged in before. This was the kiss of a man who believed he owned the woman he was kissing.

Miranda pulled back. "Did you kill him?" Considering Ryder had wanted to rape her, take her power, and kill her, she should not feel the spurt of concern for him. But she could not help herself. She was not a ruthless woman.

Lukos's hand closed around her shaking wrist. "Come, angel, I'm weakening in the daylight and we have to go."

Though she wanted nothing more than to run, Miranda held back as he tried to pull her forward. "No."

"What do you mean 'no'?" He growled like the wolf he had been. "I just rescued you from a lunatic who wanted to rape you, then kill you. Come with me, Miranda."

"I cannot." She quickly told him of the children who had died and the one she had saved. "Ryder said the Society wants to destroy me and told me that I might be creating vampires. But I know I am not. I have the power to save these children, to save their families from the worst grief. The Royal Society just assumes my power must be evil. I believe it is good, and I intend to prove it. I have two more children to rescue."

"You will not." Arrogance showed in his up-tilted chin, in his flashing eyes. "There is too much risk."

She abruptly turned away from him and began to march through the woods, moving from tree to tree to fight her way through the mist. She was following the path of her feet, all the while asking her heart to guide her to the next child.

"Stop," Lukos bellowed. "I am not going to let you get yourself killed."

"Why should it matter to you? I found the small boy that you fed from. I saved him—"

"What young boy?" Shouting behind her, he sounded genuinely perplexed and frustrated. "I have not fed from a child."

She didn't stop. She ran so crazily her hips bumped the trees, and her feet slipped on wet roots and fallen branches. "Then perhaps Zayan did," she yelled. "Or perhaps you are lying. You turned the servants of Blackthorne's castle into mindless drones and fed from a woman in front of me. I am not going anywhere with you, Lukos."

He grabbed her arm—he'd caught up to her—and gave a strong tug. She fell back against him, sprawling, of course, against the wall of his chest. Her breasts lifted with her hard breathing, a combination of exertion and anger.

"That slayer will return. I did not kill him, Miranda. And when he does, if I am still out in the daylight, I won't be strong enough to protect you from him. Hell, if I am actually *out* in the light, I'll be burned to a crisp."

She jerked away from him. He let her move from his chest to face him but didn't release her wrist. His long fingers easily encircled her. "It's daylight now!" she exclaimed. "How can you survive in it at all?"

Lukos tilted his head, his hair spilling over his bare shoulder. She could not see how he did not feel cold in the mist. It was condensing on his skin. He rubbed droplets off his chin with his free hand. "It's the fog, I think. I woke and found you gone, and felt a compulsion to come here. Somehow I was led directly to you. And the fog kept the light from burning me. It doesn't protect me from the weakness I feel in daylight."

"I thank you for saving my life." She bit her lip. What if she made him stay in the light? Would he weaken enough that she could escape him? If he did collapse, it would be her chance to have him captured.

182 / Sharon Page

Heaven help her, she did not want to do it. "Please let me help those children." She asked it without hope. Why would a vampire, who looked on humans as prey, care if she saved a child?

He raked his fingers through his hair. "I could take you against your will. I have been indulging you as we have stood here and argued."

"And I had been indulging you by not driving a stake into your heart when I had the chance at the castle."

Low and rich, his laugh washed over her. "Why did you not, angel? Why show me mercy after I fed on a woman in front of you—for the sole purpose of making you jealous?"

"That is the very question I am asking myself," she retorted. But his smile, that slow, almost vulnerable curve of his sensual lips, was making her weaken toward him.

"Come, let us go to your children, then."

She stared. "You are willing to let me go?"

"I am willing to take you."

She explained that she did not know which way to go, and that a force of magic she did not understand had directed her to the first child. He nodded, unperturbed. "I'll follow."

Once more a path seemed to carve itself through the thick white mist.

"The fog is moving," Lukos observed.

"We must go quickly. This is exactly what happened before." She gathered up her skirts and ran for a few feet—then she stumbled over a root. The ground rushed up to her and her arms flew out. But before she smacked into the rough ground, she stopped. She hovered there, a foot above the rock-strewn, root-covered surface. Warmth sizzled around her, along with a soft yellow light.

Lukos had stopped her fall with magic. Her body floated higher; then she rotated in midair and was lowered gently to her feet. He'd used magic to clothe himself.

"Take care," he murmured. He wrapped his arm around her waist and lifted her. A great gust of wind struck them from behind, a gust that lifted them into the air.

"W-what's happening?" she gasped. She was rushing up toward the tops of the trees, with Lukos behind her.

"I can command the wind to carry me, and this time, I'll carry both of us."

The path through the fog kept opening for them as they flew. But tendrils of the mist struck her face and it stung like something caustic. Her eyes watered. She had to turn to Lukos's chest to protect her face. The burning sensation did not bother him in the least.

Then through a break in the dense whiteness, she saw the tops of budding trees below and the roof of a house. She was so high above the ground, her stomach dropped to her toes. If they fell, they'd die, at least she would. But she felt an intrinsic trust in Lukos.

"If you have the power to control the wind," she said into his big chest, "did you bring this fog here? Is it to protect you from daylight?"

Her skirts were fluttering around her, and they dipped and rose to follow the currents of the air. She clung tight to his arm, supported on the air.

"I didn't bring this fog, angel, but I believe Zayan did. There's a legend of a red-colored fog that brings evil and death with it."

That would explain the deaths of the children, and the presence of the red fog around the wounded boy in the castle. She felt a spike of rage. If Zayan had brought it, and he had been responsible for all these children's death, she would make him pay. She was not sure how, but she would.

Below, Miranda saw an old stone structure with a rough-looking cottage attached. An instinctive pull told her to go there. Lukos steered them downward and she knew he had glimpsed into her thoughts.

This time that didn't unnerve her.

When she had been twelve and had saved Aunt Eugenia's life, her aunt had warned her she must keep her power a secret. Back then, she had just wished she could get rid of it. All her life she'd felt the same way—she had just wanted to be an ordinary girl.

But now the power felt like her responsibility, and she had to protect it. No matter what.

It was the sweetest sound. The cries of a frightened child, then the *shushing* sounds made by a loving mother.

And wonderful, thought Miranda, because this child had been laid out dead and the mother had wept for so many hours, she could no longer find tears. She felt a surge of happiness, but Lukos gripped her arm and pulled her back into a shadowy corner of the small room. Ringing sounds came from the smithy's shop—in grief the father had gone back to his work. The mother gathered the child, and Miranda saw her eyes change from hopeful and happy to wary. Only now the mother was realizing that Miranda had performed a miracle. And she was now frightened.

"You should take the child to your husband." Lukos spoke from the shadows, his voice deep and hypnotic. The sound of it wrapped around Miranda and she saw he had instantly taken control of the mother's mind.

Staring at him, the woman backed away, her eyes blank. But she nodded. Once the woman and her child had gone, Lukos moved to Miranda's side at lightning speed. "He'll return wanting to kill you. The stupid man will think you bewitched the child."

Exhaustion dragged at her. "What if I did? What if this is no gift at all?" She tried to swallow through a tight, dry throat. She had saved three children today—four including the young boy at the castle—but what had she really done to them? Had she made them into something that was not human? And even if they were still normal and mortal, would the people of this cloistered little village see them as cursed or bewitched?

Lukos's long fingers clasped her chin, forcing her to look at him. "It is a gift, woman."

"It is witchcraft!" a male voice bellowed from behind the cottage.

"What is it with mortals that they will look a gift miracle in the mouth?" Lukos muttered. He took her hand and together they hurried out into the fog. It wrapped around them at once. Light crackled inside it and Miranda jumped. "What was that?"

A jolt of energy like a small bolt of lightning hit her breast. It held her, lifting her off the ground. Her limbs shook. Searing pain shot through her heart. It felt as though her heart were being pulled out of her chest. She couldn't even scream with the pain; her arms went limp, her mouth numb.

"Zayan," Lukos snarled. "He must be using this fog to drain your power, love." He swept her into his arms, freeing her from the grip of the light. "We need shelter."

Shelter proved to be a stone barn. Holding Miranda, Lukos ran to it, taking long strides through the fog that seemed to tear at them as they tried to fight through it. The mist shot sparks, she thought, like tiny fireflies sizzling toward them, pricking their flesh. Somehow he brought them to a stone barn—a tumbledown-looking structure, but it had heavy doors—and he hauled her inside.

He shut and bolted the two doors, throwing them into darkness. A whitish but gloomy light spilled in through holes in the ceiling. Miranda groaned. This could never be a sanctuary. But Lukos held up his hands, and instantly a brilliant blue light surrounded him. It expanded like a bubble and flew up to the wooden rafters above.

"It's a shield," he explained. "It will last for a while and the fog can't penetrate it." He lay back casually, resting on the large pile of hay on the floor. "But I need to rebuild my strength." He held out his hand. His clothes disappeared.

Sprawled naked on the hay, all long, lean legs and sculpted muscle, Lukos looked like something out of a maiden's erotic fantasy—the powerful groom awaiting to pleasure her in the haymow.

Miranda shied back. She couldn't let fantasy seduce her into danger. "You want my blood, don't you? How else will you re-build your strength?"

"Angel, I need you to make love to me. If I'm to get us safely out of here, I need to be powerful. And some fierce and lusty sex with you will restore mine." He crooked his finger. "Without added magic this time, only the magic that our fuck-ing will make."

> *If he does not find his mate by the first spring equinox after he has risen, he will be consumed by his own power and burned to ash.*
>
> *And the one whom he loves most will also perish. She will die in a prison of Satan, her soul condemned forever in torment, in sufferance for the sins of Lukos—*
>
> *The rest of the Prophesy of Lukos—Manuscript found in the Westwarden Barrow, Wessex, England, November 1818*

Lukos heard her sharp breath at his words. Saw her shiver with desire and uncertainty as he'd growled *fucking* at her. Strange that he would use that word with the one woman with whom joining would be so much more.

He had promised himself not to use magic. He knew, as she slowly approached him, she was doing it of her own will. His nostrils flared, taking in the rich, earthy invitation of her desire. She smelled so ready for him.

Sitting up, he embraced her hips when she was close enough. Eager, impatient, he did use his power—to lift her skirts into a bundle of fabric at her waist so he could readily put his mouth to her wet quim. Slicking his tongue over her glistening lips, Lukos savored the taste he now knew and loved.

What do you want me to do? He asked it in her thoughts. *This is the power of a vampire—he can speak in your thoughts while licking and sucking your sweet pussy.*

Her laugh was like silver tempered with sunlight. It shivered over him. *I like this,* she whispered, shy and uncertain. *What are your fantasies? What were your fantasies when mortal?*

I don't ever think of being mortal, love. Wouldn't you want to know what a demon fantasizes about?

Yes.

Not raping and pillaging and taking blood. My fantasies are either highly naughty and erotic, or richly drenched in the love I can't have. Which do you want to know?

She hesitated and he suckled gently on her clit. She leapt against him with a little cry. *Which do you wish to reveal?* she asked tentatively.

A clever woman. Right now? The naughty ones. I imagine taking you to your sexual limits. It arouses me to think of teaching you. I saw the whips and chains in the dungeon of Lord Blackthorne—you were not really engaged to him, were you? But I felt the depth of your shock and disappointment. I felt how the truth of him lanced your heart. Tying you up is intriguing, but my fantasy is to free you, not bind you.

She was looking down at him. Hanging free from her pins, her hair looked wild and sensual. With her slightly up-tilted eyes and full lips, she possessed a sensual face. A beautiful face, with cornflower-blue eyes and peach-tinted ivory skin.

How do you mean?

Lukos heard her heart speed up. He suckled her labia, drinking her juices. He did not want to lick her clit again yet. He did not want her coming yet. But to create a carnal dream for her, he was going to have to show her, with his hands, his mouth, his hard cock—perhaps even his toes, if he had to be inventive . . .

I was imprisoned for a thousand years, he murmured into her thoughts. *I had plenty of time to invent erotic dreams. And one night—on each equinox and each solstice—I was allowed to walk free. In your time, this time, I discovered brothels, where a man could arrange any sexual pleasure he wanted.*

What did you want? What would you want for me?

Even in his thoughts, her voice was breathless.

You must learn that every part of your body is sexual.

Lukos couldn't resist cheating again, using magic to bring the few objects of the barn to him. A spell undressed her, and he sent her gown and petticoats whirling across the barn to lay neatly on a pile of straw.

He touched a length of chain he had summoned, and it became new, changing from old iron in his hand to clean, gleaming gold. The links became smaller and delicate. *I've had this game played with me with strings of pearls.* He pressed the last link to her snug anus, stroking gently with the rounded, gold tip. She moaned and wriggled for him. Slowly, he felt her ass loosen for him. Gently, he pressed the first link inside her.

Her sky blue eyes were open wide.

Is it good? He slid a second link inside her, pushing the first deeper, then a third. Her bottom clenched tight around the invading chain, and when he leaned back she had a spill of gold links from her rump like a fanciful leash.

She nodded. Her cheeks were pink with desire, her breath coming in rasps. *It is so . . . unbelievably erotic to have my derriere . . . filled, yet my quim is empty and waiting for you.*

His cock reared against his belly. *You aren't filled yet.* No, it was his intention to fill her lovely ass with half the long, narrow chain . . .

And he did, link after link, while she moaned and panted and rocked in front of him. Twice she protested she couldn't take more, but he suckled her clit until she melted again, and he filled her as he desired.

I'm stuffed, she cried finally in his thoughts. *And I—I'm going to come.*

Magic, this time, though he'd said he wouldn't. A small spell to hold off her orgasm. Then he stood in front of her and threaded the second half of the chain inside his own arse. With a quarter inside him, he had to bow his head. It was so good. And each link disappearing inside him was joining them closer and closer together.

Finally, there was only a foot and a half of chain dangling between them. Miranda's nipples were hard and blushing scarlet. She was clinging to his arm, her nails driving deep. He shoved brutally at his rigid cock, pushing it down. The head brushed along her belly, leaving a trail of his juice, and when he got it to her pussy lips, she was so wet and he so hard, that he sprang immediately inside.

Let us be closer. Lukos twitched his fingers, and the last of the chain pushed inside his rear and hers at the same time, pulling them together, and drawing his cock into her to the hilt.

"I'm coming!" she shouted, aloud—up to the roof of their barn. He held her tight as she bucked and writhed on his cock, exploding for him.

Then he cradled her afterward, as she gasped his name again and again, then waved his finger and their chain disappeared. Gently, he lowered Miranda to the hay.

She looked at him breathlessly, intently, as though her ingenuously honest blue eyes could see into his mind. He had one moment of fear that she could—that she could see how deeply he wanted this.

Coaxing her to lift her leg, he clasped it, and buried his cock inside her again. Velvety, creamy, hot, and tight, her cunny embraced him.

He began thrusting into her, trying to penetrate her eyes as his cock plunged into her body. Her gaze held him. Miranda looked at him as no woman had ever done—not as a lover, but as a beloved. It made him thrust deeper—half wanting to erase the precious look, and half wanting to keep it forever, stoke it, savor it.

Her arms wrapped around his neck, and she moaned for him. They moved together, and he knew with every awkward collision and half-giggle she gave him, that he was her first.

She skimmed her hands over his shoulders and back. The scars there had healed when he'd become a demon. He was thankful his skin was smooth beneath her touch.

He usually teased his lovers, he liked blunt sexual talk, but he was almost afraid to speak as he thrust into Miranda. He felt like a callow youth. Vulnerable even as he was feeling such unbelievable pleasure.

Miranda bewitched him—there was no other explanation for it. She touched her hands to his cheeks and held him with tenderness he had never known. And she arched beneath him, suddenly a slave to another climax. She cried out, the sound ringing on the rafters. Her hips lifted, her nails raked his skin; then her hands flung away, clenched into fists. Her eyes shut, her lips parted in breathless wonder; and at the sight of her pleasure, his orgasm slammed into him, hotter and more dangerous than the fires of hell.

Even coming, he was never totally vulnerable. At least not before this. He surrendered everything to Miranda. His brain flared like Lucifer's torches, his heart expanded in his chest, and his muscles seemed to turn to liquid.

"Miranda." Her name came out in a rasp, a whisper, a softly spoken prayer. He almost collapsed on her as his body seemed to dissolve with the pleasure. And beneath him, straining to him as she came once more, she seemed to glow like the sun.

He bent and kissed her, and the magic surged between them and hit his still-climaxing body like a wave of light.

Lukos.

Then he was falling, and he had enough presence of mind to lever off her, so he tumbled to the hay at her side. At once, he flung his arm around Miranda, to hold her to him. But he was thankful that she nestled against him on her side, her face turned away.

He felt as though he had been singed by the sun, smoldering everywhere and struggling to survive. But at the same time, he could feel a renewed magic crackling inside him, something far stronger than he'd known before.

Sparks danced before his eyes when he shut his lids. His entire body hummed and sizzled.

He'd never felt more powerful. But he opened his eyes and saw Miranda's aura as she lay slumped at his side, beneath the span of his arm. It did not glow as fiercely gold as it had before.

By making love to her, he'd given her his seed and she had given him some of her power in return. It had been what he'd wanted, but it shocked him now. If he kept fucking her, he could take most, if not all of her magic, and become strong— likely strong enough to destroy Lucifer. But what would he do to her?

He'd thought he could take her power without hurting her. Was he wrong? Would draining her kill her?

But if he were not going to find his mate, in days he would be destroyed. On the spring equinox. He did not have long to carry out his vengeance and destroy Lucifer for taking his sister.

"Straw is not entirely comfortable," Miranda whispered softly, drawing his focus back away from his anger to her. But Lukos saw her teasing smile. "What were you like, when you were mortal? You never spoke of the torture I saw."

"I don't want you to know of that."

"I've given you my innocence. I've given you . . . everything I had to give."

Damnation. And for that, she believed she had the right to delve into the soul he didn't have. She stroked his cheek. "Tell me."

"I was apprenticed to Lucifer." There. No couching in gentle words, no preparation, no qualifications to dim the shock. She wished for the truth and now she had it. She had given her innocence to a beast, a demon, a thing created by the devil.

Her brows drew together, not in horror but in anger. "Apprenticed to the *devil*? By whom?"

Astonished, he saw she was not angered at him. She was not pulling away. If anything, she looked more deeply into his eyes.

He, a powerful demon, wanted to flinch away from her perceptive gaze. "My father."

"You mean you were not taken—"

"My father gave me willingly. And he had to convince me to go of my own free will."

"Why would he do such a thing to you?" Miranda cried, indignant and shocked. "How unspeakably cruel. A parent should protect a child—not give a young man away to Lucifer." Then she paused. "I did not know Lucifer actually existed."

"He does. I have lived in his hell." Lukos touched her cheek as softly as she was touching his. "What you saw must have been my initiation."

"That torture was an initiation?"

"I was being taken into hell, love."

"But how did you survive it?"

"I didn't. My throat was cut and I was raised from the dead to serve the devil."

He had never once spoken to another person—or demon—of what had happened to him. But he gently drew spirals just above Miranda's soft, pale breasts. "Have you ever heard of the Scholomance, love?"

He'd assumed she would not have, but to his surprise, she nodded. "It was a story that my aunt told me. I thought it was a legend—something that may or may not be true."

He had to smile softly at that. "It is true. It still exists today." Lying with a woman in his embrace while he revealed his past was completely foreign to him. "Who is your aunt?"

"A woman who wished to be a scholar but could not be."

Lukos wondered. It was not all of the truth, and when he probed her mind he caught a fleeting word. *Slayer.* "What did she tell you about it?" he asked cautiously.

"That the name came from the School of the Dragon. Lucifer would allow ten mortal men to enter a labyrinth of underground caves that led to his Underworld. They made a pact with the devil to acquire occult knowledge—alchemy, magic spells, and the secrets of nature and animals. She told me they would learn to control the weather—winds, rain, and storms—and that nine men would graduate after . . ." Her voice broke. "After they had undergone horrific ordeals . . . Were those worse than what I saw?"

He gave her a grim smile in place of an answer. "I was a tenth apprentice. Did she tell you what that meant?"

Miranda gasped. "She told me that the tenth would be retained by Lucifer as payment and would serve at the devil's side. You were kept by Satan?"

"Until he imprisoned me."

Stretched on her back at his side, she was all sinuous curves— a flat plane of belly, rounded hips, and two plump breasts on top, tempting his mouth to suck. Just looking at her made his cock rise again.

But as he bent his head, she stopped him by putting her palm to his chin. "Why?"

"Why lock me into the earth, into rock, keeping me alive but trapped for one thousand years?" He shifted, so he was lying on top of her, bracing his weight on his arms, and she parted her legs so he and his awakening cock could snuggle between.

"Yes, why?" She frowned. "How old are you, Lukos?"

"I was born in 854, so I am close to fifty times your age, my sweet." He did not see shock. Zayan was two thousand years old, after all—even in that, the bloody Roman general liked to crow that he was superior. Damned Zayan who had been the one to capture his sister and take her to Lucifer.

"Where are you from?" she asked. "Tell me everything about you."

That stunned him. She sounded so earnest. And she looked at him with complete fascination. As though she cared . . . "I was born in England, angel. In Wessex, during the reign of Alfred, our king. Alfred became, after he held back the Vikings, the King of the Angles and Saxons. Alfred had embraced Christianity. In those days, there were many kings—of Mercia, Kent, Sussex, and Wessex. Alfred knew the Danes wanted to destroy him. After plundering the country, they decided to become conquerors instead of raiders. Soon only Wessex still stood with an English king."

She was watching him, hanging upon his words.

"My father acted as advisor to Alfred. My father was determined to protect our world—our religion, our king, our way of life. He believed that our salvation was not with God, but with Satan. With harnessing the occult magic of the devil. He believed that a man with the intent to do good had the right to dabble in the power of evil." His father had had no bloody idea. He had never known his father's intent on sending him to be an apprentice. Control of the ultimate magic? It didn't matter now. To Miranda, he gave the reason his father had given to him. "I was sent to apprentice so I could save our people."

She put her hand to her mouth. "How could he do that to his son?"

"Better his than any other man's. He believed he could control me."

"But you did not return." She frowned. "Lucifer did not let you go back to help your people."

"My father did not realize that the devil does not necessarily do what people want."

"No." She spoke very seriously. "I suppose he does not. He is supposed to torture souls."

"He tortured mine. I went willingly, love, to save my king and my people. I was raised to be a warrior, to fight on the battlefield." He had first crossed swords with the Vikings at fourteen, when he had thrown himself into the bloody, terrifying fray. He had been almost paralyzed in terror, mortally afraid of pain and death. It had been instinct that had sent his sword swinging to cleave heads. And his survival on the battlefield convinced his father that he was more than just an ordinary warrior. "Entering Lucifer's Underworld was just another battlefield."

But it hadn't been. It was not known as hell for nothing. He had been ready to kill himself many times, and he'd even tried, but because Lucifer had brought him back to life, he couldn't die. He had been ashamed of the pain and fear and despair that had made him take a blade to his own wrists. After that failed attempt, he vowed that he *could* pay the price to be an apprentice. But he could not accept that Ara had to pay the price too.

"Ara?" Miranda asked softly. "Who was Ara?"

She had seen into his thoughts once again, even though he had not sent them to her. "My sister." Lukos kept his voice level and calm as he said her name, though his heart clenched in pain. "Lucifer had her stolen from the mortal world, and he held her prisoner to ensure I did his bidding. If I rebelled or betrayed him, she would die."

"What did you do to make him imprison you?"

He gave a sad smile. "I tried to destroy him to free Ara." He leaned back against the straw. "She was like silver, my sister. Like a source of light. She gleamed like an exquisitely crafted sword—tall, slender, with pale blond hair, and fragile white skin. She was the one thing in my world that made me believe God and heaven could actually exist, because she was too perfect to be mortal. I loved her dearly. And from the moment my father sent me to the Scholomance, I held her life in my hands."

"W-what happened to her?"

"I don't know. I was imprisoned and I never saw her again." Anger crackled in his voice. He could not block out the emotion. "She was taken from her home to the Underworld by a demon. I believe that demon was Zayan."

Miranda took a sharp breath.

"I expect, as I did, he had to serve his master, Lucifer." But Hades, he hated Zayan for what he had done to Ara so very, very long ago . . .

Hands caressed his shoulders. Suddenly he became aware that Miranda was stroking him. Then surreptitiously her left hand began to slide down toward his heart.

No, he could not let her see his past. What if she could glimpse too deeply into his heart and see that he wanted her power so he could fight Lucifer?

Grinning wickedly, Lukos drew back—and bent down to her delicate, bare feet.

Miranda couldn't help but gasp. Lukos's soft cock, which had been curled up adorably against his thigh, began to straighten again. Before her awed gaze, it thickened and became stiff, slowly rising up as though by magic.

While she stared, impressed, he closed his mouth around her toe. Warmth and wetness and a tickling sensation streaked up from her big toe. "Oh!"

Lukos, the warrior, the vampire who could shift into the

form of a wolf, who had endured torture and hell she couldn't begin to imagine, was delicately kissing her toes. He suckled each one in turn, the gesture sweet and carnal at the same time. Laughter bubbled up. She could not believe she was feeling pleasure while death was waiting for her outside.

"Do you trust me?" he asked.

That was a very terrifying question. It could only mean he wanted to take her to the limit of that trust. "How many times have you saved my life?" she whispered. "How could I not?"

"That's not an answer, angel." A swift flick of his tongue along the sole of her foot made her squeal. "I won't let you touch my heart, Miranda. I'm afraid that what you see could hurt you."

"I'm not afraid. . . ." she began.

But Lukos got to his feet, towering over her, so she couldn't touch him. "No."

Miranda stared up at him. His hair, which tumbled to the small of his back in long, untamed waves, was no longer black with its white streak. It was golden blond.

Like the second man who had come to her in her dream in the carriage. But when she blinked, his hair was the rich darkness of the midnight sky once more. Had she just imagined it? "I only wish to help you. To understand—"

"You can't save me, love. You cannot save the world. I learned that."

"Not the world—but one person—"

"Would you walk through the slums and lay your hand on the heart of every child who dies and bring it back? What would you bring it back to? Squalor, poverty, and hopelessness."

"I don't know. But life is supposed to be a precious gift." Where there was life, there was hope. But now she wasn't sure. Miranda hugged herself protectively. "You prey on innocent people," she shot back. "How dare you judge my power?" She felt a sense of helplessness—everyone condemned her for saving lives. Then she shook off the self-pity. She did a good thing—no one was going to convince her to believe that was not true.

"And if you could resurrect every soul that dies, angel? What would happen then? What would happen to a world where everyone cheats death?"

If no one died, what would happen? Would people live forever, like vampires? Would there be millions of people—poor, starving people, far too many for the world to bear?

She sensed him step behind her. She did not turn to look to him; she was too troubled to do so. What she needed was to think.

His hands settled on her shoulders. He bent to her neck, his breath dancing against the rim of her ear. "It frightens you, doesn't it? It is terrifying to not know if you are evil or good. And hell to know you are controlled by a magic power—you never control it."

She nodded. It was true. And he, Lucifer's apprentice, must understand. Everyone else was afraid of her. But she could talk honestly to Lukos.

"There is something you do need to understand about me, Miranda. I've killed, but I've never killed for pleasure. I've never enjoyed taking a life, and each time I do, I pay for it. I have to feed and I have a curse—one given to me by Lucifer when I became his apprentice. Part of the price. I suffer the pain of my prey. Lucifer never bestows a gift. He creates servants controlled by curses."

"We are alike, you and I, both cursed with power we don't want," he murmured, and his voice cast a spell around her that did not come from his magic but from her heart. "We belong together." He embraced her as he spoke and let his chin rest in the crook of her neck. She stiffened for a moment, but he made no move to bite. Lovingly, his lower lip grazed her skin.

For once, she did feel she belonged somewhere. Here—

"Christ Jesus," he roared behind her, and Miranda found

herself thrown to the pile of hay. The dry, prickly grass jabbed her hands and cheek, and she whirled to face Lukos.

Red ropes of mist were winding around his powerful, naked body. He struggled, wrenching his arms and twisting his torso, but the fog was crushing his chest.

On pure instinct, she ran forward. She grabbed at the lines of fog, hoping to pull them away from him.

She touched them and white light exploded from the contact. Sparks shot up to the air. Several landed on the hay and it began to smolder.

An unearthly shriek filled the barn and the fog dropped free of Lukos. He stumbled forward and fell to his knees on the earth floor. The red mist sucked back through the door and vanished. Miranda had to leave Lukos, but she watched him as she stomped, barefoot, on the smoking hay, gritting her teeth against the sting of the heat.

He groaned, grimaced, but straightened. As soon as the fire was out, she went to Lukos's side. Where the fog had touched him, dark red bands were left. But they were disappearing before her eyes. Healing. She blinked, realizing tears had gathered on her lashes.

Lukos lifted his head, and as his brows rose, she knew he had seen those tears. He lifted her as he stood. "You aren't hurt?" she whispered.

But he cocked his head. And to her amazement, he laughed. Wryly. Darkly. "You frightened it away, angel. But I sense vampire slayers have arrived."

12

Slayers

It was madness to go out there.

Miranda pulled on her pelisse with shaky hands. "You don't know if this will work, do you?" She stepped in front of Lukos so he had to face her—while she'd dressed and questioned him about his plan, he'd avoided meeting her eyes. "I can sense your apprehension."

Lukos had drawn in the shield of blue light he had created until it had surrounded just the two of them. It now glowed a vivid blue-violet. Miranda sensed it was stronger. But strong enough to keep them safe?

He gave her a devil-may-care grin. "Love, call it what it is. Fear. I'm bloody afraid we'll be destroyed if we walk out this door."

"By the vampire slayers?"

He shook his head. Already the fog was seeping in through holes in the roof, and between cracks in the stacked and mortared stone. And the fog was scarlet again. "By this mist."

"The mist that you believe Zayan controls."

She saw him snap his fingers and summon a white light that

whirled around him and became a linen shirt and trousers. His silence meant there was something he did not want to reveal.

"Does Zayan control it?" she repeated.

"I don't know. I thought Zayan had summoned it, I don't know if he controls it now. But it is drawn to you, Miranda. It wants you."

A shiver rippled down her spine. "Perhaps because I saved the children . . . No, that makes no sense. It led me to the children. It helped me save them."

He raked back his hair. "I think it wants your power."

"But what is it?" Then a thought struck her. "You were taught by Lucifer to control the weather. You could bring a fog to engulf a village, couldn't you?"

"I could. But I didn't, angel." Lukos scrubbed a hand over his square jaw. Around them, the blue light rippled, shimmering like a giant bubble. "I wonder if this has nothing to do with Zayan—if it is Lucifer's work."

It was like being dropped in cold water. "How would Lucifer know about me?"

"He knows about any being with power, love. He will have sensed you."

He spoke calmly, while her heart thumped against her ribs as though trying to get out. Lukos grasped her hand, threaded his fingers between hers. "We have to escape this place. Stay at my side, and you should be safe inside the shield."

Hours ago she would never have dreamed she would have gripped Lukos's hand and trusted him. Making love to him had made her believe she could. The pure delicious intimacy of sex had made her feel they had a bond—a deep bond. We belong together, he'd said. But was she letting her heart rule her head?

She had to keep that head level and thinking clearly. He told her Lucifer would know about her power. And he had admitted he'd served at the devil's side. He could be intending to capture her for Lucifer—

Thunk. The doors of the barn swung open—controlled by a snap of Lukos's fingers. Miranda could see nothing but swirling mist. It seemed to rush toward her; then it struck the blue shield. Something shrieked, and that scream vibrated through her entire body.

Lukos stopped and she stayed at his side, holding his hand. The fog rushed back and forth in front of them like a living being. Shadows took shape—into the round hollows of eye sockets, the holes where a nose should be, the wide "o" of a screaming mouth. In the fog, she saw a screaming face, a woman's face.

And as she screamed inside the shield, the face disappeared.

"Come, love," Lukos urged.

"But to where? How can we escape this?"

He halted. "Slayers nearby." Another wry grin touched his beautiful mouth. "I can even hear the stretch of the crossbow strings."

Crossbow? "It must be Mr. Ryder—"

"No, this slayer is also a vampire. And one I sired."

One he *sired*? She couldn't have heard him properly. Just as she was asking, "How can a slayer also be a vampire?" a female voice cried, "Dear heaven, it's Lukos!"

The fog suddenly retreated with a *whoosh* of air that tore at their blue shield. It exploded and flew away on the wind. Helplessly, Miranda reached out to it, as though she could catch it and bring it back. With the fog gone, she saw they stood in a field, with the stone barn at their backs, and a few yards ahead was a copse of trees.

In front of those trees stood two men and a woman. Each held a crossbow, with arrows loaded, and the silver points were trained on Lukos's chest.

Vampire slayers.

This morning, when she'd been horrified to find the servants behaving like drones and she had saved the life of the child with the wounds in his neck, she would have been relieved to see vampire hunters. It would have meant rescue and safety.

Lukos turned to her. A strange scent came to her, a sickly sweet smell, and she saw two men flanking the vampire slayers. They held lanterns and a strange smoke wafted out of those.

"It's called *solange*," Lukos muttered. "The smoke created when the oil of the plant is burned drains the strength of vampires."

He staggered and had to lean back against the stone wall. He had to turn against it as daylight began to burn his cheeks. The men fingered the triggers of their bows. Miranda threw herself forward, directly in front of Lukos, between their weapons and the vampire's heart. "Wait, no! Stop!"

She saw the raised eyebrows of the two men—one with dark brown hair, the other with pale blond locks. A startled "o" formed on the woman's mouth.

Black haired and small, with a face filled with grim determination, the woman slayer took a step forward. "What madness is this? He is a vampire. Get out of the way, you silly fool."

But Miranda didn't. She flung her arms out to the sides to make a better shield. "Put your weapons down," she begged. Earlier, she had been determined to cause Lukos's and Zayan's destruction. But Lukos had helped her save children's lives. And she'd made love with him. She could not do that, then step aside and let him be killed. She was lost already. She'd had sex with him once and had fallen in love.

"Miranda, angel, come back here," Lukos roared. With magic, he pulled her back against him, her heels dragging in the dirt. At the same instant, two bolts of red light fired past her on either side. The streaks of light hit the men and sent them sprawling back. Lukos's arm wrapped around her waist. "We'll fly on the wind."

They soared up, and as soon as they left the ground, the mist whirled in once more. Miranda looked back. The men were standing again and they were at the woman's side. The female slayer had dropped her crossbow to her side. Her other hand rested on her stomach. Miranda saw what the voluminous skirts had hidden. She was very pregnant.

The fog rushed in around the three vampire slayers, and Miranda heard their cries and saw them thrash helplessly in it. The woman's scream pierced through the mist.

Miranda turned her head to speak to Lukos. "We have to go back. The fog has done something to them."

"Go back to get shot? Those were the slayers who imprisoned me. They'd kill me in an instant. I am not going back."

She clawed at his arm, which gripped tightly around her, just below her breasts. "Then let me go."

"Stop trying to push my arm away. You'll fall, you foolish chit."

"That woman was pregnant. I can't let the fog hurt her and her unborn babe."

With the wind whistling in her ear, she heard his voice in her head—in the most intimate way they could communicate. *How do you plan to stop it? Even I can't. There's nothing that can be done for Serena.*

Serena. He knew the woman's name. Her Christian name, which implied an astonishing level of intimacy with someone who wanted him dead. *She may be your enemy, but the baby is an innocent.*

And Miranda can never turn her back on an innocent.

Derision and anger laced his voice, and it only infuriated her. *Yes, mock me. Hate me for being mortal and emotional, and for wanting to save lives.*

To her astonishment, he suddenly banked and turned in the air. They were going back.

"This is madness," he shouted into the wind. "They belong to the Royal Society. They aren't here to rescue you from vampires, love. They are here to destroy me and take you."

But still he was taking her back. Because she wanted it.

"Bloody hell," he muttered.

A dark shape swooped before them—a winged creature of shadow and mist. A red glow surrounded the giant wings. It rushed at them, and a forked tongue flicked out at them from between massive jaws. Small bolts of lightning shot from its red glowing eyes and streaked past them.

The damned red mist again. Miranda knew she should be terrified. Instead, she was just fed up.

Lukos had to dart from side to side to avoid the lightning bolts, and Miranda's stomach plunged to her toes. They would whirl and spin, so one minute she could see the ground, then the creature, then the sky. Fog surrounded them and it seemed to paw at her. It was now blisteringly cold, like hundreds of frozen, clammy hands grasping at her.

"Repel this beast with me," Lukos growled by her ear. "I think we can combine our magic and do it."

"But I don't know how to control my magic."

"Ask with me for the force of the wind to strike the creature and send it back."

"Oh, of course." She had no idea how to do what he asked, but she tried.

A sudden gust of wind hit the creature and sent it careening away through the mist. But, with a howl, it flew back at them.

Think of shielding us, Lukos urged.

She tried. She tried thinking of the blue shield, and she asked for safety and begged to be delivered from this nightmare. The blue lights reappeared. But the creature sliced through their shield with ease, and the blue bubble exploded into useless fragments. Lukos deftly plunged downward to avoid the beast, but the wing struck Lukos's arm. The edge of it sliced through his shirt and blood spurted out into the air.

The wings beat at them both. *Magic,* she shouted in her head, *I need to send a bolt of magic to destroy this creature.* Nothing happened. The creature circled around behind and she shouted "Lukos" in warning, but even though he tried to roll them away, the winged beast slammed into his back.

They were falling—

He was still holding her tight, but they were plunging through the fog, and the ground rushed at them, a sea of terrifying green.

She saw the two male slayers running toward them. Toward the place they would hit the ground. But Lukos suddenly swooped, arcing away from the death that was hurtling up to her. Miranda screamed in surprise, but the wind sucked the cry from her lips. The wind slapped and tore at them as he tried to pull up from the plunge. They shot horizontally across the field; then he hit the grassy earth, and they both tumbled together.

It seemed to take a lifetime before everything stopped moving.

"Miranda, are you all right?"

She was sprawled on top of Lukos. "Oh my god!" she cried. A branch had impaled his chest, at her side—on her right. It had not driven through his heart, but the pain must have been terrible. Yet Lukos merely lifted his brow in a wry grimace, then calmly pulled out the branch. The tip was bloody and, twisting his lips in irritation, he threw it aside.

Her gaze locked on his. "Thank heaven," she whispered. She wasn't sure what she was thankful for. The fact they were alive? That the branch hadn't pierced his heart? He had thrown himself to the ground first, to protect her.

Miranda could not believe his strength. The way he'd pulled out the branch reminded her of what he was. A vampire, and an unfathomably powerful one. But one who wanted to keep her safe.

Footsteps crunched through the grass as the slayers approached—they were still yards away.

"You could escape." Miranda had figured out the blunt truth. Without her, he could fly faster, or shift shape and run free.

"I will not let you be hurt."

Then softly, through the rolling mist, Miranda heard a woman speak. "We must save her—if she cannot use her power on Althea's baby, the child will surely die."

Lukos heard Serena's voice—the voice of the woman he had thought was supposed to be his mate. It did not make the hairs on the nape of his neck stand up in anticipation and awareness the way Miranda's did. Once he had thought that Serena Lark, the first child of a vampire and a fallen angel, would be the woman spoken of in the prophesy. The prophesy written by his father after, his father had claimed, he'd had a communion with God.

He looked to Miranda and groaned. At once sympathy, uncertainty, and pain rose in her massive blue eyes. "They want me to rescue a child."

He'd felt a tumult of emotions in Serena's words. Hatred for him had been the strongest, buffeting him in waves. As a demon, he could tap into a mortal's emotions in the same way he could control their minds. But as he tried to reach further into Serena's, Miranda shook his shoulder. "You must go."

"I am protecting you, woman, not the other way about. The child could be a trap. Or a way to find out what you can do before destroying you."

"It did not sound like that. She sounded truly afraid. I have to do it."

Miranda was struggling to break free of his grip and stand. The slayers would be upon them in an instant. He would not let the Royal Society take her.

The bushes near them parted, and skirts appeared through the leaves. Lukos followed the view upward, until it stopped on a crossbow. It was the most intricate weapon he'd ever seen—it possessed forged pulleys and hinges to enhance the user's strength. A woman held it. A gray-haired woman who wore a black pelisse, along with a black turban adorned with a long, white feather.

"Release my niece," the woman barked, and she leveled the sight line to her eye. She wasn't afraid of him. He sensed she was ready to kill him, whether he let Miranda go or not.

"Aunt Eugenia?" Miranda cried.

He didn't want to let Miranda go. But he was now surrounded. Two other male slayers stepped out from behind the woman Miranda had called "Aunt Eugenia." And within moments, Serena, Drake Swift, and Lord Sommersby would find him.

He had sired Drake Swift. That was how he had sensed the slayers earlier. And he knew Swift would use the same instinctive connection between sire and vampire to find him through the fog.

He was as good as dust.

Miranda gripped his arm. "Don't shoot, Aunt! I'm safe, and he is not what you think—"

Her aunt took a step closer. "Let him go. Move away from him, dear."

In a split second, Lukos made a decision. If he let Miranda go with the slayers, he would lose his chance to get her power. He would not be able to destroy Lucifer before his time ran out.

But now, his time had run out.

He had to let her go. He felt her trust for her aunt; he could almost taste the love the woman felt for her niece. It was deep and rich. It was the love of family, the type of devotion he had felt strongly in Miranda. It reminded him of how much he had loved Ara.

He had to let Miranda go to them and safety. Once he was blasted by a half-dozen crossbow bolts, he couldn't protect her from the fog or the rogue slayer.

What he wanted, more than anything at that moment, was to keep her safe. And that meant getting the hell out of there.

One quick kiss to Miranda's hand and he shifted shape. He used explosive power to do it, and the flash of light forced the slayers to fall back. His kiss had held enough magic to protect Miranda from the fierce glow. Then he became a wolf and streaked away into the shadows cast by the fog.

Althea cradled her daughter to her bare breasts. She did it to keep the baby warm. She knew the tiny lips—lips rimmed now with blue—wouldn't begin to suck. Serry's eyes were closed, and her chest moved with slow, shallow breaths.

Two lamps and the fire warmed the room and bathed it in gold. A counterpane of silk half-tumbled off her legs, where she stretched out on the chaise with her child.

For hours she had tried to summon the vampire queens to her, to help her keep her baby alive. She could tell she was losing Serry. But the queens had not come, and even though she had projected pleas in her thoughts, she had received no answer.

Outside the room, the few servants of Blackthorne Castle bustled about. The vampires had been gone when they had burst into the castle. Yannick and Bastien had released the poor people from the controlling spell cast by Zayan and Lukos, but they, in turn, had planted the lie that she and her men, along with Eugenia Bond, Serena, Mr. Swift, and Lord Sommersby were the guests of Lord Blackthorne. No one, it appeared, knew where Blackthorne was.

Althea had felt a pang of conscience as her demon twin husbands forced their will on the servants' minds. Were they not as bad as Zayan and Lukos?

No, they were not. They meant the people no harm.

But was it simply because they were vampires that Serry was dying?

Serena was the daughter of Eve—the first Eve fashioned by God after Lilith to be mate to Adam, and rejected by Adam.

BLOOD DEEP / 211

Eve had become a vampire, though Althea did not know how. But Serena's father had been a fallen angel, not a vampire.

There had never been a child born to two vampires. If she had known that vampires could not have children, she would never have let herself become pregnant. It was too cruel to give a child life for only a few short weeks, and force the poor thing to fight a losing battle every moment.

"Althea?" Yannick stood in the doorway. "We have Miss Miranda Bond, and she is willing to try to save Serry. But she is afraid. She says she has only ever brought children back from the dead. And she has saved only mortal children. She doesn't know what will happen."

But she heard it then—a long soft, sigh from her daughter. The body went limp in her arms. Her throat tightened and the tears rushed to her eyes, and she could barely force out the words. "She has gone, Yannick. She has died."

Yannick bent and laid his head to Serry's chest. "No, there is still a heartbeat—but it is faint and she is barely breathing. It has to be . . . now." He turned silvery blue eyes to her. "But Miranda Bond does not know we are vampires."

"I can do this. I know I have the power to do this."

But Miranda saw Aunt Eugenia frown as though in disapproval. They were standing outside Lady Brookshire's bedchamber. "You do not know that. You have never tried to help a living person. You must not be overly confident, Miranda. Magic cannot be trusted."

Miranda swallowed hard. She realized Eugenia was telling her that her power might be more harmful than good. "I believe it is a gift. I have to."

She moved to go, but Eugenia stepped firmly in front of her. "What was your intention, when you came here to Lord Blackthorne?"

That seemed irrelevant. And so far in past, even though it had only been a day ago when she had climbed into the carriage with the only plan she could concoct. But her aunt was worried about her, and so deserved the truth. "We had exchanged letters. He had saved Simon on the battlefields, as you know. I—I had fallen in love with him. Two weeks ago, it had been my plan to come to him and convince him we should be married. A way to rescue us all from bankruptcy. Simon has been avoiding the bailiffs for months now, and I knew that we were close to be clapped into Newgate Prison over the unpaid debts."

"But to rush up here, to a man you did not—"

"There's more, Aunt." And she told Eugenia about James Ryder, the day in Hyde Park, and the threats he had made. "He caught me once at an inn, after he let a child be crushed by a carriage to draw me out. And he caught me again—" She broke off. Both times, Lukos had rescued her. She owed her life to Lukos. And now she did not even know if he was safe. Had he escaped the burning light of day by transforming?

"Why did you come here, then?"

"I didn't know where else to go. I could not stay at home without putting all of you at risk. I thought to hide, and I wanted to find somewhere I could feel safe. . . ." Somewhere she could believe she belonged. She cleared her throat—it felt annoyingly tight. "I've discovered that Blackthorne was not who I thought he was. But where is he? Did he not come back?"

Eugenia shook her head. "We are not certain what happened—there was no sign of Blackthorne in the castle, and of course the servants knew nothing."

That was a reminder of what Lukos and Zayan did to mortals. Controlled them. Used them. Fed from them. A reminder she should not want to protect them. But she did. "Blackthorne had been in the village. He might come back."

"We will deal with that when it happens."

Aunt Eugenia had always felt so close to her; after her

mother's death when she'd been nine, Eugenia had stepped into that role. Closer, for her mother had never spoken of her power, had never warned her she would eventually have it. Miranda was not even certain her mother knew she was to possess it. But Eugenia had, and had always known the right words to say to ease her fears, and had always protected her.

But now, Eugenia had crossed her arms over her chest. "You must not try to share your thoughts with Lukos and Zayan, and if they come in pursuit of you, you cannot let them in."

Miranda swallowed hard. She and her aunt were now on different sides of the battle. Miranda had always thought her aunt's battles had been ones of good against evil. Now she saw it was not that simple at all.

"I must go." And she left Eugenia, to hurry into the bedchamber in which Lady Brookshire waited with her daughter.

Althea, Lady Brookshire, was a beautiful woman with long red hair that hung in curls and waves to her waist. Her eyes were green, but they were darkly shadowed, and red firelight glinted across their surfaces, as though they were reflective. Miranda realized it was because her ladyship's eyes were brimming with unshed tears—she was valiantly trying not to give in to despair. Lady Brookshire was kneeling beside the still, pale body of her baby. She stood. "If you cannot do this, I understand. I want a miracle, but I do not think I believe it is possible."

"I want to believe it is," Miranda said. She knelt by Serry, who was so tiny, her heart lurched in pain. She put her hand on the baby's chest. *Please do not let me hurt her by doing this.*

But this time the heat did not flare up in her body.

Please, she whispered in her thoughts. *I don't understand. I want to help this wee baby. Please let me help this child.*

But who was she sending the desperate words to? She had no idea whom she could pray to.

Her arm felt cold, frightfully cold, and she jerked her hand from the child's chest. If she felt cold rather than warmth, what if she was hurting the child? Killing her?

Miranda.

Spoken in a compelling, beckoning masculine voice, her name sounded in her thoughts. She heard the rattle of the paned window and looked there. A large black bat swooped by the window, and the voice that had come to her was Zayan's.

Out of the corner of her eye, she saw Lady Brookshire leap to her feet.

Then she heard the low, mournful howl of a wolf. *Are you safe, angel?* That was Lukos.

The vampires had risked coming to the slayers to find her. To ensure she was safe.

"Do not move," Miranda warned. "Do not attack them or sound any alarm, or I'll stop. I—I won't try to help your child." She hated that, using the baby as blackmail, but how else could she keep Lukos and Zayan safe?

She thought Lady Brookshire would ignore her, but her lady-ship sank back to her chair. "It is like that, then, between you and them. I—I would have thought it impossible. They are evil. The darkest of demons. They have committed the most un-speakable crimes—" She stopped. "All right, I will do nothing. Please, please help my child."

Guilt was like a lance to Miranda's heart. But warmth began to surge through her, chasing away the horrible cold. *I am safe,* she said, hoping her words went to both men. *I am trying to save a baby. Lady Brookshire's baby, who has died.*

Lady Brookshire? The baby would be . . . would be Bastien's. The voice was Zayan's. And Miranda realized Zayan had a past with Althea and her husbands, just as Lukos must have one with Serena.

Draw on our strength, Zayan urged.

We will send magic to you, Lukos added.

Miranda felt warmer, stronger. She felt energy dancing inside her. Holding her breath, she touched the baby. And felt the sizzle of power. It was stronger, yet somehow more controlled. The magic grew in her, flowed down her arm, and into the baby. She heard the heartbeats of Lukos and Zayan.

Please, please, let our combined magic do this, she prayed. But nothing was happening. The baby stayed still, the eyes shut.

Then she felt it. She sensed a tiny, faint heartbeat. Very slow, almost as slow as the pulse of the vampires, but it was there and steady, which it had not been when she had first touched the child.

Serry's lids went up, revealing enormous eyes of emerald green. Her fists lifted and waved fiercely. She let out a cry, the lusty squeal of a healthy babe.

Miranda scooped up the baby, feeling the warm of her skin, and Althea was at her side in an instant. She handed Serry to Lady Brookshire and saw the baby root at her mother's breast. Althea opened her robe, and the baby took to the breast and began to feed.

Tears shining in her eyes, her baby cradled to her bosom, Althea grasped Miranda's hand. "Thank you. It seems too inadequate, but thank you so very much."

"I don't know exactly what I have done," Miranda said slowly. "I do not know what I have done by saving a living child."

"You have given me a miracle."

"I didn't think it was going to work." She realized the slayers had to understand what had happened. "But Lukos and Zayan connected with my thoughts and they sent me their power. I do not think I could have saved her without them."

Althea stared at her. "They helped you save my child?"

"Yes, they risked destruction to find me and ensure I was safe—because there is a rogue vampire slayer hunting me, wanting to kill me because the Royal Society wants me dead. I told them that I wanted to save your baby, and they sent their power to me. It is only because of them that I could give you a miracle."

"I think Miranda Bond has fallen in love with Zayan and Lukos. She used their power, combined it with hers, to save Serry. I don't understand why, but they were willing to help save my child."

"But what happens if they become a ménage? What happens if they discover the power of a love shared between three, when she is so obviously very powerful?"

Miranda caught her breath. The first woman to speak had been Althea, and the next had been Serena. She shrank back against the stone corridor wall. The door was closed, but she had heard their voices clearly.

Blushing, she thought of the erotic things the men had done to her in the carriage. That must be what they meant by a love shared between three. Did it mean they knew—or at least had guessed—what she'd done? Did Aunt Eugenia know?

Her aunt would hate her. Eugenia had said she wanted to understand vampires, but she still obviously believed they were evil and must be destroyed.

Lukos had told her that one of the slayers was also a vampire. She had asked, *How can a slayer be a vampire?* She had no answer and she didn't understand. Why would the Royal Society use vampires as slayers? Or where they rogue killers, like James Ryder?

But Aunt Eugenia was here, and if Eugenia was with them, she must believe they were safe. Miranda was certain of that.

Did it mean, then, that vampires could change? They could control their predatory urges?

"Can we convince Miss Bond to stay with us until our twins are born?"

The male voice behind Miranda startled her. She whirled around, but there was no one in the corridor. She heard footsteps and low voices from an intersecting one. She had best make sure she wasn't caught eavesdropping. Quickly, she eased back in a shadowy doorway just as Drake Swift and Lord Sommersby walked into her corridor from another.

The light of a torch flickered across Lord Sommersby and Drake Swift's eyes.

Both men's eyes reflected the light like mirrors.

She remembered now, when she had been in Lady Brookshire's bedchamber, she had seen a glint of light on her ladyship's eyes. She had thought it was tears. *It wasn't.*

"She saved a vampire child," Lord Sommersby said quietly. "I have not been able to rationalize how."

"With science?" Swift cocked his brow in a wry look that reminded her of Lukos's. She felt a sudden tightness around her heart. It was dawn now. Were Zayan and Lukos safe? The vampire slayers had taken over Blackthorne castle. So where had they gone to protect themselves from daylight?

"It's a miracle," Swift said. "One we might desperately need."

The men passed by and went into the room where the others were.

A vampire child. That was what Lord Sommersby had said. It had to mean Althea's child was a vampire, and she had saved it.

But had she returned its soul?

There was so much she wanted to understand. How could vampires also be slayers? Who had brought the red fog? Why had Althea called Lukos and Zayan the darkest of demons?

And most importantly, why did she feel, deep in her heart, that though she wanted to stay here and answer these questions, and help Lady Sommersby's unborn child, her place was with Lukos and Zayan?

Even now, she felt the tug to run away from here and go in search of them.

But she couldn't. Not until she knew the truth of who—or what—they really were.

13

Danger

They were in the carriage again. . . .

Miranda was on the seat, staring in astonishment as Zayan and Lukos grappled on the floor. Lukos grabbed Zayan's broad shoulders and flipped him, smacking against the seat in the narrow confines. "We could fight to destruction to win her."

"That's my plan, wolf." Snarling, Zayan landed a punch to Lukos's jaw that sent his head reeling back.

"Or we could let her choose."

At those words, Miranda felt a flare of panic. She had given her virginity to Lukos and had battled the fog with him. When she imagined his eyes, or his sensual smile, she grew hot between her legs and achy in her heart. But Zayan had been with her in her dreams, and when she looked at his darkly reflective eyes, her heart glowed as she thought of the intimacy she'd shared with him there. When she thought of his children's murders and of how deeply he'd loved them, how capable of love he actually was, her heart ached in anguish for him. And equally, the thought of Lukos's torture broke her heart.

How could she choose?

A love shared between three. What did it mean? Was it even possible? Not just erotic games, but love?

"Erotic games?" Zayan's voice rumbled to her. He had read her thoughts.

"The lady wants carnal games." Lukos grinned. "As we promised her but haven't really delivered."

"You made love to her, but did you show her all the delicious parts of her body, all the pleasure she must learn, before she can be shared?"

"Before I can be shared?" She heard the tremble in her voice as she retreated on the seat.

But Zayan shifted shape to become a bat, and his clothes dropped off him. Lukos stripped naked with a wave of his hand.

Both men leapt to their feet, then settled on either side of her on the carriage seat. Lukos tugged at her bodice. The tight circlet of her neckline resisted, tore, then dipped below her breasts so they popped above it, served up to his mouth.

Zayan was behind her. He coaxed her to her knees, pulled up her skirt, and caressed the cheeks of her rump. He bathed the nape of her neck in kisses. The scrape of his fangs sent shivers to her wet quim. "Do you want us both inside you at once?"

Yes. No. Yes. She was afraid. She was—

It was too late. Lukos lifted her right leg over his hip at the moment he thrust deeply inside her. Filling her to the brim, to the hilt, to exquisite agony. And Zayan gripped his shaft and began to rub the weeping head to the tight, pucked entrance of her derriere—

She came. Before he was even inside her, the orgasm hit her. She cried out. Her body writhed in their arms. Stars shot across the darkness of her shut lids.

Stars. Explosions. Pleasure that made her shout, laugh, and weep . . .

Blinking, she opened her eyes. She was alone, alone on a bed that was now plunged into darkness even with the drapes open, and her quim still pulsed in the dying pleasure of her orgasm.

It had been a dream.

She was still dressed, in a gown brought by Aunt Eugenia from her home, and she'd fallen asleep on top of the counterpane.

"How did I get here?" She rubbed her head. Vaguely, she remembered that she had been too cowardly to confront the vampire slayers with her questions. And using her power to save the baby had left her exhausted. She had come to a bedroom to think. She must have fallen asleep here.

A rap sounded at the door. "Miss Bond?" called a maid.

Miranda bade the woman entry. The maid curtsied. "Miss Bond, Lady Brookshire has asked if you would come to the library."

"I want to know—" Miranda paused as she glanced from Lady Brookshire to Lady Sommersby. "Everything. I want to know how vampires can be vampire slayers. I want to know why you, who are members of the Royal Society, seem to want to protect me, not kill me. And I want to know everything you know of Zayan and Lukos."

She saw Lady Sommersby bite her lip. And heard Lady Brookshire's thoughts. *You were right. She is in love.*

The two women were seated by the fireplace, and all around them, books reached to the high, arched ceiling of the room. Two axes were mounted, crossed, above the thick, stone mantel, and a fire crackled merrily in the grate.

"I can hear the thoughts you send to each other," Miranda said, "so you might as well speak aloud."

Both women flushed guiltily. "Cards on the table then." Lady Brookshire placed her hands on the occasional table in front of her, faceup. "We fear that you have fallen in love with both Lukos and Zayan, but we believe that you do not know what they really are."

Miranda was on her feet, too restless and nervous to sit. "Then tell me," she implored. "But you must remember that they did come to protect me, and they did choose to protect your child. I want to hear everything that you believe they've done. In the past, my aunt has told me that tales about vampires are often exaggerated, because people *want* to be frightened."

She feared Lady Brookshire and Lady Sommersby had accepted whatever the Royal Society had told them.

"These stories did come from the Royal Society, and I do recognize that obviously does not mean they are the gospel truth," Lady Sommersby said. Then she added, "And you must call me Serena."

Miranda swallowed hard. Lady Sommersby could see her thoughts. Miranda had not even thought of masking them. It was proof, along with the silvery glimmer of her ladyship's eyes, that she was a vampire too.

"I want to hear them, and then I want you to tell me which stories you think are the truth," Miranda demanded. If she *was* in love with both Zayan and Lukos, she wanted to face the truth about the men whom her heart was torn over. She couldn't be certain if what she felt was love or just the need to save them. This was her power—to rescue, to resurrect, to save.

And she wanted to do it with Lukos and Zayan.

"That's very dangerous," Lady Brookshire advised. "And of course you must call me Althea."

Serena looked to Althea. "It is, of course, what we both wanted to do ourselves, isn't it? Rescue our men." She leaned back on her chair with one hand at her low back and the other on her rounded belly. Her black, waist-length hair was caught up in one long braid that lay over her shoulder. "I assume you have made love with them. That's why they have both captured your heart, I suspect. I would like to know what Zayan and Lukos have told you about themselves?"

Miranda paced along the long table that held stacks of books. She had never had such direct conversation with women about such scandalous matters. But she preferred this. This was much better than the gossip and whispers, allusions and lies that had been part of her life as a normal young lady of society.

Honesty. She wanted that. "Zayan told me that he was a Roman general named Marius Praetonius in his mortal life. Lukos told me that Zayan had taken the blood of thousands of innocent women and children." Did vampires feed each night? Zayan had lived for two thousand years . . . Dear heaven, that must mean he had claimed seventy thousand lives. "But I never saw him feed. And he controlled himself around me." She forced herself to stop defending him and just speak. "He told me that his children were murdered, and that was why he embraced the chance to be a vampire—to get his revenge." She paused. "I also saw it. I—I saw the murders. They had their— their throats cut. It was cruel and gruesome."

Althea blinked and Miranda saw her hug herself. As a mother, Althea must be able to sympathize. "Those murders took place two thousand years ago," she said slowly. "How did you see them?"

"I don't know. I had a vision of them. It was as though I were looking through the eyes of the murderer. I also saw Lukos's torture, when he was given to Lucifer as an apprentice."

Serena stood, her hand at her back. "But with Zayan, you saw visions that he could not have seen."

Miranda nodded. "That's true. He said he did not know who killed his children." She looked from auburn-haired Althea to dark-haired Serena. "Who did it?"

Althea's brows drew together. "The truth of that is lost to the past, Miss Bond. My father is a vampire slayer, and I helped him with his research, combing ancient books. It was my father's original intent to destroy Zayan. You see, Zayan sired my husband Bastien. He was the one who turned him into a vampire, when he lay dying on the street."

Althea told her of how her husbands Yannick and Bastien de Wynter had been known as the Demon Twins. "I would like to tell you the truth," Althea said. As she spoke, Miranda was amazed that Althea would reveal such personal things. Althea revealed they had hunted Zayan; then Bastien had asked for him to be imprisoned and not destroyed.

"After Zayan's imprisonment, I had to learn as much about him as I could. Yannick—my husband—told me about his past. It was said that Praetonius drank the blood of his victims, even as a mortal. Then he craved the blood of pure strong men, to keep him vital and strong. And as he aged, he sought the blood of the young to give him life." Althea paused. "Like Countess Elizabeth Bathory, drinking the blood of young women in the belief it would keep her young."

"It was said," Miranda repeated. She had felt Zayan's agony over his children's deaths. How could he be the instrument of death to others? Lukos had said so—but she didn't want to believe it. "But is there any proof?"

Althea pointed to one of the stacks of books on the long desk. "The one on top is a diary—the journal of a vampire slayer from the seventeenth century, who had battled Zayan. I brought it with me. It was in there that I learned about the murders of Zayan's children. That slayer believed that Zayan's wife was the lover of another general, a compatriot of Zayan's. Mucius Gaius. The slayer believed that Gaius was the man who killed the children."

Miranda remembered that glimpse into Zayan's thoughts.

"In the journal, the slayer wrote that he believed that Zayan's wife betrayed her own children. That was different than the story Yannick told me of Zayan—it had been believed she had been betrayed too. But it appears she knew of the general's plan to murder them but did nothing to either stop him or protect them."

Miranda was appalled. "Dear heaven, why? Why hurt her own children?"

"For power, it was believed. She wanted Zayan, who was then Marius Praetonius, to be crippled by grief and pain, and to lose in battle, to perhaps even be killed there."

"But why not just . . . just have killed Zayan? As his wife, she could have done so and spared the lives of her children."

Althea shook her head. "I cannot understand it, but that vampire slayer believed she did it because she wanted to destroy the children she had given to a man she hated."

"I can understand," Miranda said softly, staring down at the journal but not touching it, "why he might have become a vampire in anger, after he was so viciously betrayed, and so mad with grief."

Althea rose from her chair. "Zayan became a vampire before his children were killed."

But that was not what Zayan had told her. She held her breath as Althea glided to the table, then held the journal to her. A strip of leather marked a page. Miranda opened it, forcing her eyes to become accustomed to the cramped handwriting.

The first paragraphs explained the tenuous hold on political power of Rome's emperor. He feared the popularity and power of Marius Praetonious. Mucius Gaius had fed into the emperor's increasing paranoia, until the emperor had begun to plot Praetonius's downfall. Finding himself subject to sabotage, Zayan had faced losing a battle. And he had made a pact with Lucifer to survive. And to win.

Miranda looked up at Althea. "Did he become an apprentice to the devil, like Lukos?"

Althea shook her head. "Zayan bargained to walk as a devil among the human world, to enter into the service of Satan for eternity, and in return, he would turn living, breathing people into the undead, delivering their souls to the dark lord who craved them. But he began to believe himself stronger than the devil he served. And so Lucifer tried to have him destroyed." Her ladyship walked over and laid her hand gently on Miranda's arm. "He was not driven into brutality by grief. He was always brutal. According to that journal and others I have found since his imprisonment, he was one of the most brutal of vampires. He never tried to control his urge to feed. We are vampires—all of us—but we do not kill for blood."

"You should have some brandy brought for Miss Bond," Serena suggested.

Miranda thought to refuse, to prove she was strong enough for truth, but then she relented and nodded.

"You did know we are vampires, didn't you?" Serena asked softly as Miranda tugged the bellpull.

"I saw your eyes. But I assume my aunt also knows, and if she trusts you, I believe I can too."

Serena gave a little gasp and put her hand to her tummy. "A kick," she explained. Her soft smile faded. "I must now tell you about Lukos. There is a prophesy, you see, and the end of it was only discovered last year."

Before Serena began, Miranda stroked the book she held. The story told in this journal might not be true, she realized. The vampire slayer had not lived in Roman times. He was working from stories that would have been distorted over hundreds of years. And if the emperor had been afraid of Zayan, he must have tried to destroy Zayan's reputation. If he wanted to kill Zayan, he would hardly object to spreading lies. What she was being told were stories. It was not necessarily the truth.

She laid the book firmly on the table. "And after you tell me about Lukos, I want to know what you meant by a love shared between three."

"Oh, you overheard that?" Serena asked.

"Definitely brandy, then." Althea managed a smile. "Both

Serena and I are married to two men. Two men each. My husbands are Lord Brookshire and Bastien de Wynter. And Serena is pledged to both Drake Swift and Lord Sommersby. English law believes we each have only one husband, but that is not the truth. To defeat our foes, we had to learn to harness the magical powers created by a ménage à trois. And our foes, Miss Bond, were Zayan and Lukos."

He approached a placid pool of water. It was an elaborate bathing room, the pool itself in tile the rich blue of the Mediterranean. The deck was startlingly white, and elaborate patterns had been created in the mosaic on the walls. Naked women cavorted and giggled in the water. Some pairs sucked at each other's nipples. Two women lay face to cunny, like the numbers six and nine, and they were . . . were kissing each other's vulvas.

Their play amused him. He had Praetonius's wife, and she was wild in his bed, obsessed with him, but he liked this play.

This small pool was empty, and the mirror-like surface of the water threw his own image back at him.

He saw it. Blood—spatters of it on his cheek. The women would see it. They would be revolted by it. The blood of Praetonius's children. He kept seeing it on him, though he bathed over and over—

He knelt by the pool, dipped his hand into the center of his condemning image, scooped a handful of water, and desperately scrubbed his face—

But he knew when he looked again, he would see the blood. He would never be rid of it. He shuddered. As long as he did not hear their screams again. They haunted him.

Miranda grasped the post of her bed to keep herself from falling forward. She had been standing by her bed one moment,

thinking of what she had learned about Zayan, then the next—
the next moment she had been seeing a bathing room through the
eyes of the blackguard who had killed two innocent babes.

She sank to the edge of the bed and drew up her knees. She
shivered, hugging them.

She had seen the face of the man who had murdered Zayan's
children.

If she described him to Zayan, would he know who that
man was? Would it help him to know the truth? Or wound him
even more?

Her window rattled and she saw the subtle play of moonlight on large black wings. Zayan. He had come to her room.

He was always brutal, Althea had said. He was not driven
by grief. . . . Althea and Serena had showed her many books
that substantiated their stories of Zayan and Lukos. . . .

She should keep away from him, as Aunt Eugenia had demanded. But she wanted to know the truth. Had he lied to her,
or were the words of history and journals the lie?

Perhaps she was mad, but she wanted to believe Zayan could
open his heart to love, and that it could, somehow, redeem him.

And why was he insane enough to come to a castle that
housed seven vampire slayers determined to destroy him? Could
it really be for her?

Would she let him in?

Zayan circled in front of Miranda's window. For long minutes, she stared at him through the streaked glass as he slowly
beat his wings to hover where he could watch her. Moonlight
poured on her, illuminating her oval face, her remarkable china-
blue eyes. He witnessed the war of emotion on her face, and felt
her turmoil as strongly as if it were his own. He sensed her
heart demanded that she let him in, but her logic warned her
not to be so mad—that letting him inside could mean her death
or the deaths of others.

No, Miranda, he murmured into her mind. *I would never hurt you.*

Damn, he felt a spurt of guilt. He was lying to her. Tonight, he had to take her power. He had to absorb all of her energy to take it inside him and bargain with the red power.

Because once he had risen tonight, the voice of the red power had come to him. It had warned him that it was going to take Miranda's power itself, if he didn't do it for him. . . .

If you rebel, if you refuse to do my bidding, you will lose any chance to ever have your children again. The red power's voice had purred to him, sounding eerily like Claudia, his former wife—the wife who hated him to the point of madness.

Zayan, I can subject your children to great torture in their afterlife. I could condemn them to hell, if I wished.

What are you? he had shouted to the dark sky in rage. Though he had searched for two thousand years for some clue to what this red fog—this mystical entity—really was, he was still as ignorant as he had been when he had finally succumbed to its lure.

And fear welled up. He'd never known such horror. *Do not punish them to hurt me. Punish me. Destroy me. Torture me. I don't care.*

Serve me, and they will not be hurt at all. Serve me and I will give you the man who killed them. He is immortal, just as you are. He has lived also for two thousand years. You've hungered for vengeance for such a long time. I can give it to you. If you give her to me . . .

What he should do was warn Miranda away from him. Tell her to run.

He couldn't bear to hurt her. He had taken the magic force away from others—from angels and demons—without regret, without emotion at all. It should be as easy with Miranda. He had known her only a couple of days. She should not matter to him.

But she did.

Miranda began to walk resolutely to the window to let him in. She was doing it on her own volition. He had tried to compel her but felt that power bounce off her, like dull arrows on armor.

No woman who knew what he was had ever willingly let him in before.

But if he spared her, if he didn't drain her power, which would likely kill her, he would lose everything. His children . . .

It would be like losing them all over again. And the grief was just as unbearable, as agonizing, as it had been two thousand years ago.

Miranda ran the last few feet to the window. She darted to the lock as though determined to do it before she lost her nerve. Her hands closed on the sash and threw it open. Open for him.

He swooped through the beckoning window and shifted shape in front of Miranda.

"What is wrong, Zayan? You look . . . haunted." She reached out and traced the tight lines that ringed his mouth. "Are you in pain?" She frowned and looked to the door. "Why did you come? Are you mad? They'll destroy you if they catch—"

He silenced her words by drawing her into his embrace. He didn't want to speak. Slanting his lips over her warm, plump ones, he let himself sink into the heat of the kiss. Her fingers stroked his cheek lovingly. A woman's caress—he'd never known one so gentle, that spoke so much of emotion and caring. The stroke of just her fingertips along the line of his cheekbone sent shivers of pleasure down his spine.

Why did you come? What do you want? she asked.

You. This. Her mouth was more intoxicating that any wine he'd drunk, sweeter than any plump grapes held to his lips by a beautiful slave, richer than any pleasure—

You've captured me.

He knew how she had tried to protect Lukos. How she had

risked her own life to save three children. It was true. She had captured him.

His hands slid down over silk. She wore a nightdress, a thin creation of silk that clung to her round, high breasts, and fell sinuously from her hips to hint at the long curves of her legs. Shimmering white, the gown threw off light like the moon, and she called to him the way the moon did.

Miranda. Zayan moaned her name in need and hunger— something he had not done since he had been a general, but still a young man, and had first kissed Claudia, his wife.

Zayan's tongue was playing with hers, doing delicious things to the inside of her mouth, making her melt, and Miranda drove her fingers into his broad, naked shoulders to keep from puddling at his feet.

She wanted him. As much as she had wanted Lukos. It seemed sinful and wanton, but as she surged into Zayan's kisses, hungrily savoring his mouth, she knew she couldn't deny her desire for him.

Teasing gently, his long hair fell against her cheek as he devoured her mouth. What had he looked like as a mortal man? Strangely, she wanted to know.

Stop. She shouted it into his thoughts. *You lied to me, and I want the truth. When I asked you why you gave up your soul, you made me believe it was because you had lost your children.*

His hands skimmed down her back, ruthlessly igniting her need. *That is the truth,* he murmured, his voice husky even in her thoughts.

Lady Brookshire told me that you became a vampire before your children were killed.

Lady Brookshire was not there. With a push on her shoulders, he drew back from the kiss and faced her. "What I told you is the truth. When I was a general, once when I was facing a huge defeat, a voice came to me—a voice that came out of the sky around me. It promised me great victories in return for my soul—and ultimately, my servitude. I refused. I won the battle using my own wits, the courage of my men, and perhaps some mad and ruthless moves. I was taken prisoner once, and the rumor was that I survived by becoming a demon. But those were stories spread by my enemy. By another general, Gaius, my wife's lover—"

"And the man who murdered your children. I saw him." She impetuously gripped his biceps. "I've had visions of the man who did it. And in the last one, I saw his face reflected in the water of a bath."

His hands tightened on her arms and she almost squeaked with fear. It was as though he would snap her arms in his anguish and anger. "Tell me. Please tell me what he looked like, Miranda."

Straining to remember every detail of the face she had seen in the pool of water, she told him. All the while, he stroked her shoulders, and his touch made it easier to see that face again.

"It was Mucius Gaius. He did it himself. I assumed he sent someone else to carry out the crime—"

"No." She could barely speak; her throat seemed to be closing tight and she could not breathe. "He killed them with his own hands. I saw it—I saw what he did—"

"By the gods, Miranda, at least I was spared that."

"I—It—" No words. There was none she could give him. It had been horrific, but it would not help Zayan to be told that. Her eyes itched and burned and she blinked at him. "I am so very sorry."

"Those stories about me—about drinking the blood of children, about becoming a demon and serving Lucifer. They were not true. I was brutal. Yes, I cannot deny that. I took human lives to satisfy my hunger. But I want you to see—" He broke off. And time stood still as he bent to her neck and she forgot to breathe.

Perhaps she was foolish, but she tipped her head to the side to expose her skin. For her, it was like shouting to him that she trusted him. That she believed him. Tensing, she waited . . .

He kissed her there. That was all. His lips touched hers with the softness she remembered from her mother, long ago. The touch of someone who loved her.

"Did you summon this fog?" she asked. "Are you controlling it?"

"It came to me, but I didn't summon it. It controls me. Don't ask me what it is, love, because I don't know. I cannot tell you. But it made me into a demon, two thousand years ago, and has haunted me ever since."

His mouth traced the scooped neckline of her silky nightgown. Her most beautiful one. He reached the swell of her right breast and she giggled, then sighed in desire. His mouth made her feel like she was floating, without any magic lights or stars or spells.

"I've never shared as much with any woman as you, Miranda," he murmured before tracing a circle around her puckered right nipple. Through her nightdress. With his fangs.

Sensation streaked from her breast to her quim. "Oh!" Her nipple stood harder, her breast seemed to swell and lift toward him in her pleasure.

"If you want me, lie back on the bed, Miranda. Let me make love to you."

"In my bed? You're surrounded by vampire slayers—"

"Then you must be quiet, angel."

To save him, she should not fall back. But he began suckling her nipples—one to the other, a quick, hard suck, a flick or two of his tongue, a brush with his fangs, and she was on fire. Throbbing with need between her thighs. She felt so empty, wanting to be filled.

She was falling back—

He moved on top, and her world became the sight of his straight, wide shoulders—perfect and bronzed, without a scar or a flaw. And the taut muscles of his pectorals. And the squared line of his strong jaw. His muscled throat.

Her legs had opened wide in welcome, and she moaned as he entered her. Thick, thick, so wonderfully thick, his shaft spread her open and she clutched his arms. *A quick orgasm first*, he promised. Each thrust teased her tight, erect clitoris. Each thrust made her see stars.

His hand slid beneath her bottom, as he slid in and out of her on a cushion of her creamy juices. His mouth played with her breasts and she was bouncing up to him, clinging to him. Driving him . . .

Fingers parted the cheeks of her derriere as his erection filled her to the brim. Then his thumb pushed lightly against her entrance. He arched his hips to push his cock impossibly farther, and his thumb went inside her.

As though he'd snapped his fingers and commanded it, she exploded in orgasm. Pleasure swamped her. She felt as though floating in ecstasy. She dragged in desperate breaths. Inside her, he was still rigid.

And now . . . He grinned. *Some other delicious positions, love.*

But she realized what she had done. She had cried out. Her shout of ecstasy must have been heard by every vampire—vampire slayer—in the castle.

14

Soaring

Footsteps thundered on the stone steps of the corridor beyond her locked door.

You have to flee, Miranda cried in panic.

But calmly, as though they had all the time in the world, Zayan eased her up onto her knees, with her rear end facing him. She was on all fours, and he cradled her derriere, which jutted toward his face. *Mmm. A delectable view.*

For heaven's sake, he was so caught up in lust, he would end up staked. *I fear the lock won't hold them long.*

I am not going, because I don't believe you are ready to leave with me, Miranda. He patted her rear. She shivered. What was he seeing of her in this position? Her hair tumbled over her shoulder, but more scandalously, her rump was almost open to him because her legs were parted on the bed. Her breasts hung down, and if she tried to look through her spread legs, her chin bumped her bosom. She suspected Zayan could see the lips of her quim from his vantage. And her nipples too.

"Then what are you going to do?" She asked it softly, but with more bold courage than she really felt. And she didn't doubt he could hear her hammering heart, and knew she was rigid and icy cold with fear over his safety.

"Make love to you this way." His fingers slid between her legs from behind and toyed with her nether lips. She could see her pubic curls glistening with the juices from her climax. He stroked her, making his fingers wet and sticky; then he caressed her clit with his slick fingertip. "Relax, love." He made teasing circle that set up fireworks in her brain. "Let your body heat up for me."

There isn't—

He arched his hips forward, his cock filled her from behind and she couldn't speak. Her passage was so juicy, he'd glided in with ease.

The door suddenly rattled against the lock. Fists slammed against it. Several voices shouted her name from the other side. "Miranda?" "Miss Bond!" "Open the door!" A furious male voice demanded that.

"Think of what you are doing!" That was Serena's voice.

Oh, Miranda wished she could think. But Zayan's cock surged in and out of her. In to kiss her womb, out to reach the sensitive rim of her quim, and leave her trembling in need before he pushed in once more.

The slayers would break through the door. She would be caught. They would attack Zayan who was more than vulnerable right now. She would have to stop them from destroying him—

His hips slammed against her buttocks as he thrust, making her cheeks quiver. Even that was unbearably erotic. She pounded back against him, wildly slapping her arse to his groin.

Yes, he groaned. *Be wild. Be the powerful woman you were meant to be.*

I—I'm coming. She managed to shout it in her thoughts, hoping to share it only with Zayan.

He laughed behind her, rocking his hips to make her burst,

and to keep the pleasure roaring through her, until she was sobbing with it, and had to rest her head on the bed as she swayed with each amazing wave.

You must go, she begged.

A wise man should. But a man falling in love? He is never wise.

Was he truly falling in love with her? He was risking his very existence to be with her. Instead of fleeing, he lifted up her derriere. "Do you trust me?" he whispered out loud.

She did. She believed him. And trusted him, just as she did with Lukos.

His cock nudged between the full cheeks of her rump, and trust or not, she froze. With a shiver of anticipation, she remembered Lukos's game with the chain.

She knew what he was going to do. But the swollen head of his cock and the thick shaft that followed were so large. Could she do this?

The chain hadn't hurt, it had been wonderfully stimulating. She *could* do this. Her rump tingled in anticipation, her chest was tight with excitement, her mind swimming with arousal.

He stroked gently, making teasing circles with the wet head to her tight, furled opening. She tried to relax, wriggling against his cock as he stimulated her.

The banging on the door grew louder. "He's used magic to prevent us from breaking through the lock." Miranda recognized Drake Swift's voice.

"There's the window."

"He'll guard it with magic."

"What does he want with her? I can hear them in there—he hasn't taken her from here."

Serena's voice came through the door. "He must want her power—"

"Or he is intending to make her fall in love with him."

Miranda could do nothing but moan. She could not shout

any reassurances. Not with Zayan's cock pressed to her rump, slowly, slowly, exquisitely making her anus open for him. Her fingers curled into the covers on the bed. Her toes had tightened. And she was fiercely gasping for breath and moaning.

With a pop, the head pushed inside, and her ring of muscle snapped tight around him. Dear heaven.

Good?

Amazing. It is more . . . more intense than magic. I feel on the very brink of my . . . Every part of me tingles with awareness.

Wait then, love, until I thrust.

And he did. She arched her head back with the shooting sensations of pleasure. It was so intense. Her feet felt like they were on fire. She moaned in sheer ecstasy. With long, easy thrusts, Zayan filled her bottom with his cock. She felt the brush of his nether curls against her rear. She was on all fours, splayed in front of him, with his hard cock inside her rear.

You are beautiful, Miranda. I can explore everything with you.

Her quim pulsed with the pleasure as he began to withdraw, as he drew his cock back until the head was ready to pop out; then he surged in again. After a few thrusts, she was pushing her rump back to him to make his thrusts even deeper.

It was so intense. As intense as the play with the gold chains had been with Lukos.

Zayan leaned over her, now giving her fast, hard thrusts. She was thrown forward with them, but he had one hand on her left breast, and that kept her from being pushed away from him. He fondled her nipple.

And kept banging relentlessly against her arse.

Pleasure built and built.

Oh, even like this, I'm going—going to come—

Ah, but your arse is so sensitive, angel, of course you are going to come.

She tried to hang on, to draw out the pleasure, but he gave one thrust that lifted her legs off the bed, and she screamed in delight. It was the trigger, the one thrust that threw her over the edge. Her climax pulsed in her rump, in her pussy, made her nipples stand up hard, and made her brain burst into flames.

She saw shooting colors, like fireworks and rockets, on the inside of her lids. She wailed his name. *Zayan. Zayan.*

Oh, she loved him. Loved him for giving her this pleasure, for seeing the wanton woman she was made to be.

But he was not done. He did not even let her rest before thrusting again. Her third orgasm took her almost at once. He took her to a fourth, a fifth, until the climaxes came in one long wave and her feet were so sensitive that just the brush of air made her scream.

Then he plowed into her one last time and embraced her tightly as his body pressed against her back. *I'm coming, angel. Like never before.*

He moaned harshly after that, his body bucking against her.

He withdrew, slowly, to make it easier for her, and she was touched by his tenderness. And then she gave a weak giggle. She felt formless now, so ravaged by orgasms.

And she knew what she had just experienced.

A lesson to prepare her for a love shared between three. She had been stunned by what Althea and Serena had told her. She'd known she'd felt the pull in the carriage, when Zayan and Lukos had played erotic games in front of her and she had been hot enough to burst into flames.

But to think it could always be that way . . .

She could be like Althea and Serena, with two devoted men to make love to her. Imagine what it would be like to be filled by them both—one pumping into her wet, steamy cunny, the other pounding fiercely into her sensitive bottom.

No. Lukos believed Zayan had taken his sister to be the devil's prisoner. Zayan had sneeringly referred to Lukos as "wolf."

Lukos hated Zayan, and Zayan, in turn, appeared to despise Lukos. It could never be.

Miranda lay down on her bed, exaggerating her ragged breathing because it gave her time to think. Zayan wanted her to leave with him. But she was not certain if she could choose Zayan and forget Lukos. Not yet. Perhaps not ever.

She loved them both—desired them both, cared for them both, wanted to heal both their wounded souls, their broken hearts.

They might be vampires, but to her, they both possessed souls.

"If we all work in unison, we might be able to defeat his magic," Althea said, from the other side of the locked door.

Weakly, Miranda realized that while Zayan had been making love to her, the vampire slayers had been trying to rescue her. She didn't want to be rescued. But he needed to be protected from them.

"Come with me," Zayan urged. He rose from the bed.

"You could leave without me—" But his expression became instantly stubborn and she knew he would not. "I will go with you because you must escape the slayers. But how are we going to escape? Can you fly without shifting shape, as Lukos can?"

Zayan scowled at the mention of Lukos's name. "No, I intend to teach you to shift."

"Shift *shape*?"

He nodded as though it were the obvious solution. "You have all this magic inside you. I believe you can."

Miranda spread her wings and caught the current of air. Her entire body hummed and sizzled. She had not been able to control her power and shape-shift, but Zayan had transformed her with his magic. She had changed into a shape like a large bat. How it had happened, she was not entirely certain. He had thrown a strange spell at her—a brownish black swirling light that had surrounded her.

Outside of her bedroom door, Aunt Eugenia had joined the slayers and they had all been trying to break into her room. It had been heartbreaking to ignore the plea in her aunt's voice. Then the light had engulfed her and she'd felt intense heat, just as she did when she used her magic. Her body had changed—it had become molten and pliable, and she'd known one second of extreme pain. But then the pain vanished, and she had spread wide wings and had thrown herself out into the night, trusting Zayan.

Follow me, he urged.

It was tempting to play in the sky. She had watched birds swoop, had even thought of what it must be like, had dreamed of it sometimes in her childhood but had always known it was impossible. And here she was, flying.

Perhaps nothing was impossible.

She tried to tip her wings to follow Zayan. She went wide of him, then too far to the other side. It was hard to master her wings.

He circled back for her, patiently, as she tried to get accustomed to flying. He was the larger winged creature and he would glide close to her, beat his wings around her as though controlling the currents of air to make her journey easier.

Then, out of the corner of her eye, she saw tendrils of the red fog starting to weave up the hillside toward the castle.

We have to hurry, Zayan commanded. *Follow me and do exactly what I do.* He dove down into a tight grove of tall trees.

Miranda swallowed hard. She couldn't do that. She would hit the trees and be killed. There was nothing so certain—

A stream of blue light came to her. It wrapped around her like a cocoon and dragged her behind Zayan. The light moved her to and fro, taking her safely between the tall trunks and through the gaps between branches. She was brought to a small circle of stones in a clearing.

Moonlight darted between the trees to touch this spot, but the light was tinged with red. The instant her feet settled on the ground, Miranda groaned in relief. It had been exhilarating to fly, but terrifying to think she might die that way.

Zayan transformed before her eyes and she tensed, but the return to her normal form was quick, and the pain did not seem as intense. The ground chilled her feet and her skin pebbled in the breeze. Of course, she was *naked*.

Easy, love. Zayan pulled her into his embrace. A wave of his hand created cloaks of velvet, and Miranda snuggled into hers. She had no idea what was going to happen now. Zayan released her and walked over to one of the stones, a flat one that was like the seat of a chair. Miranda looked around. The grass in the circle was lush and a darker ring followed the line of the stones. She remembered pointing out a ring of darker grass on the lawn of their country house to her mother, when she had been eight. Her mother had called it a "faery ring," and Miranda had slipped out at night to spy on the faeries as they'd danced.

But she'd waited and waited, and had fallen asleep. Simon had followed her; he had been the one to lift her up and carry her back to bed. She'd lost her mother the next year. But she'd had Simon, her father, and Aunt Eugenia. And strangely, she already felt as close to Zayan.

This ring felt as though faeries did dance here. A gentle humming came from within it. It felt like a place of magic.

Zayan was now pacing with long, angry strides across the circle, watching the sky. He'd created boats for them.

Zayan could hear the red power's gentle, triumphant laughter on the murmur of the wind. He also sensed fear and anger rolling off Miranda as she stalked up behind him. "What is it?" she demanded. "What are you looking for? The red mist? Are you bringing it to us?"

Strong and determined, her blue eyes held his. The woman was fearless. He had always admired Claudia's strength, but he saw now that hers had been more ruthlessness and selfishness than strength. Miranda had a bravery that felled him. He knew she had risked her life to save children whose very lives had been sucked out of them by the red power.

Facing Miranda, Zayan realized that, for once, he could not hide behind superior power or strategic lies. Needing time to create an explanation that spared him from giving her the truth, he averted his eyes from her and turned away.

Miranda marched in front of him, her cloak flapping around her bare legs. She slid her hands beneath his and embraced his waist. "The truth. Why did you bring me here? What do you want of me? I do not believe it is love. There's something in your face—an emotion that I do not entirely understand."

It was a blend of pure fury and self-loathing, he suspected. "You deserve to know. Everything. I told you a voice came out of the sky to tempt me with immortality. When it came to me again and I accepted, it appeared as a heavy red-colored fog that surrounded me. In return for making me into a demon with increased strength, magic, and eternal life, it demanded that I gather power for it. I have sucked the power from other demons, even from fallen angels."

"How?"

"Blood and sex, my love."

Understanding dawned. "It wants my magic power. And you are going to give it away. Is that why you made love to me?"

He shook his head, his long hair rippling over his shoulders. "No, I refuse to take your magic, to hurt you in any way."

He told her more then. He told her that the "red power"—as he called it because he had never known if it had a true name—had promised to return his lost children to life, if he drained her magic. Her eyes went wide with astonishment, and her shock lanced him through his heart. For all Miranda had known he was a demon, she'd expected him to be noble and good. Once, he would have coldheartedly thought it nothing more than her foolish error. But with Miranda, it made him feel like garbage.

"I didn't trust it," he admitted, his voice raw and hoarse. "But the truth is that I had originally planned to take your power and use your magic as bait. I believed the red power would betray me and not give me my children, and I intended to use your magic as blackmail."

Her color drained away. He stepped forward, intending to grasp her and pull her into a kiss, but he suddenly found he didn't dare touch her. "I would never do that now, Miranda. And that is the truth."

The wind gathered strength and it threw her long, loose blond hair around her pale face. "But what of your children?"

He stepped back, toward the direction the red power was coming from. "I can't hurt you, even to save them."

She came to him. He, a vampire, was transfixed as she lifted her hand. She smoothed the tense lines around his mouth. "You loved them very much. I see it in your eyes, I see the love there, even as your face reveals the pain you also felt."

He grimaced again. "I wish to the gods that they had not had to suffer for me—"

"It was not your fault," she cried. "Althea—Lady Brookshire told me about your past. I can understand, after you were betrayed by Gaius, by your emperor, by your *wife*, why you would want to become a vampire." She gave him a level gaze. "But Althea told me history claims you drank the blood of your victims before you became a vampire. And that you accepted the red power's offer before your children were killed."

"The red fog came to me before my children were killed, but I was not ready to serve evil." He felt his lips kick up in a cold smile. "Strangely, I believed I was on the side of right."

"I know Lady Brookshire hunted you, because you were supposed to be one of the most evil vampires in existence."

"So says a vampire slayer. But the truth was, I was as evil as any vampire. I created more vampires, but only out of the dying. And Althea Yates—Lady Brookshire—has a personal reason to despise me. I used her as bait in a plan to destroy her husbands, the Demon Twins, who planned to destroy me. I hoped to pit the two men—Bastien and his brother—against each other, using her as the reason for them to tear each other apart."

"That plan failed. Instead, they found a love shared between three."

He stared. "What do you mean?"

"A threesome—a sexual and loving one—apparently makes magic stronger. It was what defeated you."

"And sent me to imprisonment. Bastien asked for my life to be spared, and one of the vampire queens had me banished to paradise." A gust of wind threw his hair about his face. He should stop talking and start inventing a plan of protection. But it felt strangely good to pour out his tale.

"Was it really paradise?" she asked, concerned, her eyes revealing her doubts.

He shrugged. "In one sense. But then, roses have thorns." She did not need to know the details. It had been a place as beautiful as paradise, yet he'd had no food for months on end. Lukos had tried to destroy him numerous times, over his supposed capture of Lukos's sister. And the damned wolf had been too stubborn to listen to the truth.

He looked down at her. "Do you believe my story? Do you believe it is true?"

"Should I doubt it?" she threw back, and as he inclined his head at her question, she frowned. "Althea told me that your wife knew your children were to be killed, but that she did nothing to stop it. Is that true? How could it be? What sort of woman would do such a thing to her children?"

One obsessed with herself, and seeing her youth and beauty fading. A woman willing to sacrifice anything to be an empress, who saw one fleeting chance to grasp that goal. "It was true of Claudia," he said softly, for keeping his voice low could hide the pain. "I could say she did it because she was selfish. Or she did it to brutally hurt me." He twined his fingers through hers and led her to one of the stones that ringed the circle of grass, a stone touched by the red glow of the mist and the silvery blue moonlight.

"Did you love her very much?"

He sat, spread his legs, and drew her between. But she crawled over his thighs, holding up her cloak with one hand, balancing with the other. She perched on the rock at his side.

"I was infatuated with Claudia." He looked to her, then off toward the trees, where the shadows were black as pitch. "She was exquisite, with an oval face and large dark brown eyes, full lips of the most unusual pink—a color that was earthy and tempting. Her lips almost shone as though moistened by a man's kisses. She was more beautiful than the goddesses who graced the statues of her palatial home. I became obsessed with her. She was the reason I waged battle, the reason I took the risks that made me a hero, and brought me great wealth. I was determined to prove myself to her, to win her, to become the powerful man that I believed she yearned for."

"Are you really certain it was because of her that you did those things? Or perhaps she represented just another prize for your ambitions."

He sat in silence for minutes, then bent to her neck. Gently nuzzled there. "You are a very wise woman, Miranda. When I look into my heart, I could believe what you say to be true. But I was obsessed with Claudia, and she was shallow, vain, and selfish. She had no true capacity to love—" He stopped. "Or perhaps she hated me so much that, while being my wife, she lost any ability to open her heart. She closed it to me, and closed it to our innocent children."

"I still cannot understand why she would let innocent children be . . . be hurt. Are you certain it was true? Perhaps your enemy made up that as well."

"I wanted to believe that, Miranda. After my children died, after I saw the coldness in Claudia's eyes and knew that she did not care about them, I vowed never to love again. My heart became a lump of ice in my chest. I never thought I would open my heart again. And all I wanted was revenge . . ."

"What happened to Claudia?"

"I did get my vengeance on my wife, but it was by accident," Zayan said. "I thought I wanted her dead—I was driven by rage. And my rage summoned the red mist. I had confronted her, the mist wrapped around her and choked her to death."

Miranda tried to sense Zayan's emotions over his wife's death, but she could feel nothing. It was as though she had stuck her hand into a pool of dark, icy water. It was unfathomable and cold. Had Zayan commanded the red fog to kill her so he did not have to do it with his own hands? It was still murder—and how did that make anything right?

"I know you are wondering if I did it deliberately. But I didn't. Once the fog came, it was beyond my control. I was sorry it happened. Even after all she had done, I was a damned fool—I wanted to love her still. And as I realized that, the fog let out a shriek and attacked her."

Miranda heard the agony behind his words. *I wanted to love her still.* Was that also behind Zayan's pain? Not just that he felt responsible for his children's murders, but also that he had still wanted to love their ruthless mother?

She could imagine how agonizing that must be. Did he love Claudia even now?

Zayan tipped up her chin. She saw the glint of his fangs, but they no longer mattered to her. What she cared about was the man inside the vampire.

"We have time, a while before I will have to confront the fog to protect you."

Just as with Claudia, she realized. The fog was coming to him, because of him, and he knew he couldn't control it. She saw it in his eyes, even as they threw the moonlight back at her. "You're planning to sacrifice yourself to protect me, aren't you?"

"I made a choice. I couldn't hurt you, not even to bring my children back. Nor could I live with the guilt of that choice for eternity—knowing that I had cheated them of their chance to live again."

Dear heaven, that was the choice he had made—for her. "There has to be another way," Miranda insisted.

He clasped her hand and lifted it to his lips. Never had the gesture touched her heart more. "What worries me is that I don't believe I have the strength to defeat it."

"Lukos and I were able to force it to retreat." She quickly told him of what they had done to combat the red fog when it had tried to invade the stable. She saw admiration in his eyes, but then any sign of hope drained out of them. "You got it to retreat, but you weren't able to destroy it."

She thought of what Althea and Serena had told her. "The vampire slayers told me that . . ." He was watching her intently and her courage almost failed her. "They told me threesomes enhance magic power."

"Threesomes?"

"You and Lukos threatened to share me when you captured my carriage."

"Indeed, we did."

His eyes were mirrored planes of silver, telling her nothing. Would he agree to it? Could she . . . do it? Even to save her life? In the carriage, she had been shocked by her wanton side. She had realized she could not be the normal, proper woman she wanted to be, if she had such scandalous sexual desires.

Now, if she gave herself to a threesome, there was no turning back. She could never be Miss Miranda Bond, decent English lady again. But what *would* she be?

Miranda was suggesting a threesome.

If it were not for his powerful, preternatural hearing, Zayan would have believed he was mistaken. No, she had never looked more serious. Or more frightened. She looked more frightened of having an erotic, unusual sexual experience than she had of the red fog.

Did threesomes really enhance magic power? Lukos had told him how Serena Lark, the woman Lukos had believed was his destined mate, had used the power of a threesome to grow stronger. Zayan knew Althea Yates had used it.

But in both those cases, the joining of the three had been more than just sex. He believed the magic came from the power of two strong men who were devoted to one woman. And there had been deep, intense emotion between the two men. Yannick and Bastien had shared the bond of brotherhood. Sommersby and Swift had, it appeared, been vampire hunters together—they had saved each other's lives. They trusted each other.

What was between he and Lukos but hatred? Lukos believed, stubbornly, that Zayan had delivered up Lukos's mortal sister to Lucifer. He had not—he had never served the devil, only the red power.

The red power had controlled him just as Claudia had done. He had done unspeakable things to please the feminine voice that spoke to him from the red mist. He had been a damned fool, just as he had been over his wife. It had enraged him that his wife had cuckolded him. He'd vowed never to let a woman break his heart that way, never to give a woman power over him by giving her his love.

But he would not be a damned fool and let Miranda be hurt. To protect her, he would share her with Lukos. He would grit his teeth and do it willingly, damn it.

Wind whipped the trees. He turned to Miranda, shouting, "Get down. Go behind the rocks, behind me."

Miranda did, and he planted himself between her and the

wild, fierce gusts. One slammed into his chest, and shoved him back so he almost sprawled over the rocks. He drew on all his strength to straighten up, to forge forward again.

"No," he shouted. "No, you cannot have her. I'm not going to let you take her."

15

Power

She was not going to cower behind a rock. Miranda laid her hand on top of Zayan's, which was outstretched and clamped to the rough, hard boulder at the top of the circle, farthest from the direction of the wind and the fog. She stood at his side to face the red fog that was racing toward them through the trees.

Strangely, when she was facing death and should be petrified, numb with terror, or steeling herself for battle, Miranda remembered Althea's words. *I had dreams about Yannick and Bastien. Erotic dreams of loving and making love to two men. They proved to be premonitions. Both Yannick and Bastien possess special powers. We were destined to be together, the three of us, because our combined love makes us stronger.*

Both women had become vampires and had willingly done so—they had been made by the men they loved. Could she still tap into the magic of a shared love if she remained mortal? But then she wasn't mortal. She didn't know what she was . . .

Zayan threw a bolt of his blue magic at the red fog that was now advancing through the trees, rolling over upon itself like a crimson wave. His spell merely bounced off it, scattering through the trees. Branches exploded as the power hit them. Sparks flew and acrid smoke plumed up. But the fog kept moving.

Miranda. Come to me, Miranda, and I will not destroy the vampire you love.

The voice rang evocatively in her mind. It beckoned her, so rich and pure and sultry and powerful, it made her want to obey. She remembered how she had tried to fight against the rich, beautiful sound of Zayan's and Lukos's voices in her head, only days ago.

She hesitated. If Zayan could not defeat the red power, she would be dead anyway. She couldn't let him die senselessly for her—

"Do not even think of it," Zayan warned, revealing he was connected with her thoughts.

Behind them, leaves snapped in a sudden breeze and branches clattered. Miranda jumped around, still clasping Zayan's hand. Lukos stood there, naked, his hair flowing out behind him like a black cape.

"I saw into your thoughts, Miranda. I saw what you want. I did not come before because I did not think I could share you with . . . with the damned Roman general who gave my sister to Lucifer."

"I didn't," Zayan snapped. An unearthly blue light swirled in his reflective eyes. Miranda had never seen that before. "I never served Lucifer, and you are a bloody hardheaded Saxon—"

"Stop!" Miranda cried. "But you came. Why?"

"Because I am willing to lay down my sword—in a sense—to protect you. If this is the only way we can stop this bloody fog, I'm willing to try." One long stride brought him to her side, and he clasped her hand.

"Together," he growled. "We will have to concentrate together. Remember, Miranda, as we did in the barn?"

"I will never forget what we did in the barn. Not one moment of it." It was her way of telling Lukos what he meant to her, her way of doing it while still preserving decorum, which oddly, madly, she felt she should do. "I have realized," she said as the fingers of fog slithered between the trees into their opening, "that I love you both."

And she shut her eyes and thought of a quenching, powerful light—something that would burrow into the heart of the fog and blow it apart forever, so it could never wrap around a person or a village again. It could never take life or power or a soul or whatever it craved—

The force of the energy that seemed to explode out through her bare skin drove her back. Zayan and Lukos held her hands tight. She opened her eyes. There was nothing to see, but she felt *it*. Then she saw a ripple in the air. A ripple of movement that tumbled over on itself like a black ball rolling through the night sky.

Instead of exploding, the black ripples spread through the air; Miranda could see them where they blocked out the trees. They looked like dark arms reaching out to embrace the fog. At once, the fog began to race back on itself. But the black tendrils reached it—touched it—

A unearthly shriek almost burst Miranda's ears. The vampires at her sides flinched too. The fog raced back with such force, it brought trees falling. Tall trunks that fell like dominoes and slammed against each other. Some hit the ground, shaking it.

The fog was gone. For the first time since they had reached Blackthorne Castle, days before, the sky was clear. Black as jet, like velvet, and festooned with winking stars.

Miranda looked to Zayan. He was straining to listen.

"It's not destroyed," he said grimly. "It just retreated. I can still sense it. What went wrong?"

Lukos shook his head. Miranda found her gaze straying down his naked body—it was a beautiful, lithe, powerful form. And now, spared from death, she felt giddy with relief, heady with the need to celebrate life. She wanted to kiss each man. She wanted—wanton woman that she was—to touch their bodies. At the same time. One hand to caress and fondle Zayan, and one to do the same to Lukos.

Althea and Serena had done it. They did it every night, and had frankly admitted they enjoyed it. She'd pushed the thoughts aside when talking to the women, because they made her blush. She'd had to admit she was curious . . . And now, standing in the quiet grove with Lukos and Zayan, she saw the allure of shared love. At once she was aroused—hot, wet, creamy, and completely ready. She wanted to savor the beauty of both men. She wanted—

Oh heavens. Four hands on her. Four legs to stretch out along hers. And fingers—all those fingers to make magic on her skin. Two mouths to take her nipples, to kiss in her most private, most deliciously sensitive places. Two tight, beautiful masculine derrieres for her to touch, perhaps even to . . . to kiss.

And two long, hard, swordlike cocks—

Oh. She'd confronted an intense power with courage, but thinking of all the sexual games she could imagine, her strength was draining away, making her weak with need and desire, making her breasts ache and her cunny throb.

She wanted to recapture the pleasure she'd known with each man. They had not been able to destroy the red power. And she knew, before Althea and Serena had gone after their foes—she tried to forget that was Zayan and Lukos—they had shared their beds with two men.

"Perhaps we are supposed to . . ." *Courage, courage, Miranda,* she advised herself. "To go to bed all together first."

"What normally happens," Miranda whispered. "What should I do? Do I lie down? How do we begin?"

"Not so clinical, angel," Lukos laughed. "We begin like this." He dropped to his knees, lifted her velvet cloak, and rained kisses over the curves of her rump. She giggled—a sound out of place in the now-hushed grove, beneath the dark sky, in the aftermath of a battle.

Zayan captured her lips. Having two men's mouths on her was dizzying. Hot lips skated over her everywhere—Zayan's along her throat to her collarbone, then to the tops of her breasts, lingering there and teasing until she grasped his shoulders to stay standing. Lukos kissed her bottom, licked her inner thighs and set her trembling. He teased her calves with her fingertips—she'd had no idea that would feel erotically pleasurable.

Lukos turned her abruptly, rotated her away from Zayan, and put his mouth to her nether curls. He drew patterns through with his tongue. It tickled. It was wet and compelling.

He was good at this, and he knew it; he smiled confidently as he slicked his tongue over her nether lips and made her quiver.

He gripped her thighs, holding her to his mouth, and she soon knew why. Gentle caresses turned to fierce, exquisite torment. He flicked his tongue fast and hard on her clit. If he hadn't kept her prisoner, she would have backed away. Zayan parted her cheeks, his hands cradling them, and he licked the puckered entrance of her rear.

Zayan's tongue plunged, Lukos's flicked. She clutched Lukos's shoulder as sensation built. She rocked her hips—forward to Lukos, back to Zayan, sandwiched between their mouths. Their hands stroked, over hips, down her thighs, on the small of her back, the planes of her belly. She was engulfed in delight. Smells came to her—of the new leaves, the sweet night air, of her lovers—

Lukos sucked at her clit and she exploded. Before her climax ended, she was laid gently down on her outspread cloak. She couldn't remember either of them removing it. Zayan laid on it, and lifted her, so she sprawled over him. His hard cock pressed to her sopping cunny.

She joined him in a heated kiss. They devoured each other's mouths; he shifted his hips, and his cock filled her.

Lukos's thumb pressed to her already pleasured anus. Yes. Yes, she did want this. A caress of his finger, and she felt wet and slick back there. As he held his cock to her, he stroked and teased, until she was panting.

Pressure. A twinge of pain. The amazing sensation of opening for him. Pleasure claiming her from both front and back. Then he was in her, in a few precious inches, and she was amazingly full.

Braced on his powerful arms, Lukos stayed in her, without moving. Zayan shifted his hips, pressing his cock deeper, so deep, and she gasped. She gripped his biceps. *Lose your control,* she begged. *I am ready.*

She had never expected to release such passion. Lukos drove deeply into her, too, drawing out to the sensitive rim of her anus, then filling her again. She rocked between them both—

Oh!

The climax took her quickly. And the men kept thrusting, taking her to another. And another.

"God, my angel, you are precious." Lukos managed to rasp those words aloud; then he bucked into her, filling her snug rear passage with his hot come.

"Beyond precious," Zayan shouted, and he surrendered to his climax too. He reached down between their bodies, tweaked her clit, and made her explode once again.

Oh, she cried. *I adore you both.*

They collapsed together on the velvet cloak. She should be chilled, to be covered in perspiration in the cool night air, but the men cuddled close to her.

We adore you, Lukos said, gruffly.

"But you seem to hate each other."

"If you want me to forgive Zayan for what he did to Ara. If you expect me to kiss and make up, I will not do it."

"It's not the truth, damn it, Lukos. And the price for your blasted stubborn stupidity could be Miranda's life."

Miranda levered on her arm and faced Lukos. The truth had to be gotten at. "Why do you think Zayan did it? How do you know?"

"Lucifer revealed it to me. Why would he incriminate Zayan if the blackguard was innocent?"

Zayan leapt to his feet. "Because of this. Lucifer has demons with the power of prognostication. He could have looked into the future and seen that we would join together with a woman of incredible power."

A woman of incredible power. Miranda sat up, and Lukos draped his conjured cloak around her shoulders. She twisted to face him. "It does make sense."

Lukos frowned. "There was already a prophesy written about me. It claimed my mate was Serena Lark, a half-vampire woman."

Miranda stilled. "Lucifer might have seen something different."

"The truth is I never served Satan," Zayan said. "I was the red power's slave. I was never an apprentice to the devil, as you were. And your sister was imprisoned only because you went willingly to the Underworld to gain the devil's magic—"

"I damn well did it to save my people."

Zayan bowed his head. "Your sister was hurt to punish and torment you. I understand how that feels—"

"He does," Miranda cried. "Don't you both see that you should sympathize with each other? You could help each other with the pain and the grief of your pasts. If only you would stop believing lies and would put your pride behind you."

The men stood, silhouetted by fingers of moonlight against the night sky. "She is right," Zayan groaned.

Lukos simply growled. Rising onto her knees, she knew she had to try to break through to him . . .

She realized she was between them, her mouth at the level of their crotches. She could smell the blend of her aromas and theirs.

Sensual desire heated in her again. Althea and Serena had told her that passion could break through reluctance, that pleasure could allow the men to push aside anger and mistrust.

She had to try.

Miranda grasped both shafts and drew her men to her mouth.

Zayan looked up to Lukos. "A truce to pleasure her?"

"All right." They both waved their hands and created two long, slim wands of green light—the wands were about the size of the men's cocks. She trembled with nerves and anticipation. But she was so wet from so many climaxes, the lights easily went inside her. The columns of magic thrust slowly in and out of her quim and derriere, as the men's erections had done. Both magical cocks surged in at once, and the sensation was so intense, she found herself squeezing the two cocks hard. Too hard. The heads both turned a dark purple.

"Heavens, I'm sorry." She relaxed her grip, slid her hands up and down.

Both men protested she had nothing to be sorry for, but she knew how to acquire their forgiveness. She opened her mouth and took Lukos's rigid cock inside. His velvety skin slid along her tongue, her lips lightly bunching it. She really had no idea how to please him, but she liked the earthy taste of him. It was naughty, exciting, to hold him in her mouth. Each pleasurable thrust below made her moan around him, and he moaned in response.

"I love that, angel."

Even Zayan groaned his approval, though she'd forgotten to stroke him while plying her tongue around the intriguing ridges and vein lines of Lukos's cock. She glanced up. Both men looked in agony, their mouths tense, their lashes shielding their eyes.

Zayan rocked his hips so his cock slid slickly against her palm. Lukos was thrusting harder into her mouth, but she felt his restraint. He was fighting for control.

Take him beyond control. Instinctively, she sensed she had

to do that, if she wanted to release magic. But how did an untutored woman do that?

Playfully, Lukos urged into her head.

It had been years since she'd played. Not since Simon's drowning—after that, after she'd discovered she had power and no longer understood herself, she'd never felt playful again.

Naughtily, she stroked down Zayan's shaft and reached for his dangling balls. She wobbled them, stroked them, let them roll around her hand and pour off, tugged them. *God, yes, love, you are a wonder when you're playful.*

She pulled on Lukos's member and gave Zayan's a kiss. She gripped Lukos's rump and squeezed, while fondling Zayan's balls and suckling him. Both men were breathing harshly.

Could she make them come this way?

Angel, you are no longer pleasuring yourself, Lukos chided. *We want you to come again first, sweeting.*

Two fevered bounces took her there.

Then both the men exploded in ecstasy with shouts that rang up to the sky.

She was still mortal, and dawn did not drag at her and force her to seek sleep. Miranda trudged up the last few yards of the rough, rutted road that led to Blackthorne's castle. Exhaustion weighed on her, pulling her down, making her take steps with annoying slowness. Last night, with Zayan and Lukos, she had not slept at all . . .

They had taken her to the closed-up manor house they had been hiding within. Empty of a family, it held only a handful of servants. They had crept through the quiet house to one of the farthest bedrooms. Magic had provided blankets. And they'd savored more pleasures all through the night . . .

She took a deep breath, kept walking, and tried to force herself to move faster. This was more than just being tired, and more than the draining effect of several hours of intense and acrobatic lovemaking. The air felt as thick as water and she was trying to wade upstream against the current.

What if making love together did not give them the strength to stop the red power?

That fear had haunted her as she had watched Zayan and Lukos succumb to sleep. They had both tried to fight their day-sleep, determined to watch over her, but the compulsion was too strong. It must be the price for being able to survive beyond death—their bodies *had* to fall into that dormant state.

Once both vampires were slumbering, Miranda had left their bed. She'd slipped from room to room until she found a wardrobe of woman's clothing. She borrowed a dress and shoes, and put on the cloak Zayan had created for her. To fight the red power, she believed she had to understand. Just as Aunt Eugenia had told her a slayer had to understand a vampire to destroy him—or her.

Perhaps she was mad, but she believed she'd find answers from the vampire slayers. Assuming they did not lock her up for her own good.

"I need to know everything you know about the red power."

Althea and Serena stared at her, perplexed. "I've never heard of such a thing," Althea said.

Miranda pointed to the window. "You've seen the fog that is settled on the village. It seems to be a living being. It can speak if it chooses. And it drains life and magical power. It thinks—like an entity. Zayan says that it was that red mist that made him into a demon."

"I know nothing of a red mist." Althea crossed to a trunk that sat in the corner of her bedchamber. In a bassinet beside her bed, her baby slept. Miranda was pleased to see the bond between mother and child was so strong that Althea wanted her daughter with her. The drapes of the room were drawn, blankets had been tacked up over the windows behind them, plunging them into the darkness of night.

The male vampire slayers were sleeping. Women vampires, it seemed, did not need as much sleep, and as long as the room was dark, they could move around in the day. Serena had ruefully rubbed her back and confided that apparently sleep was as hard to achieve for a pregnant vampire as for a mortal.

Althea gathered two leather-bound books—one in burgundy, the other royal blue—from the top of the clothes in the trunk and brought them to Miranda.

"I wrote these," Althea said, "to gather all the information I could find on the fiercest, most evil vampires we had encountered. I brought the ones I wrote on Zayan and Lukos."

"The things you told me about Zayan." She told Althea about Zayan's enemy, about what Zayan had told her. "It is logical, isn't it? Gaius and the emperor invented those horrific stories to destroy the man they hated. They wanted to make Zayan appear to be a demon before he ever became one."

"It makes sense, but—"

"Did you see him kill a child?

"In truth, no." But sorrow radiated in Althea's gaze. The words hung, unsaid but understood. Zayan had been a vampire for two millennia. Miranda could not wave her hand and turn him from predator to hero, no matter how much she wished to.

Miranda lifted the journal on top and put it to the side. She drew the one marked "Lukos" to her. It was like Pandora's box—once opened she could not put things back. She would never forget what she would see. As with Zayan, whether she believed it or not, it would change forever how she felt about him. Once she knew the evil he was supposed to have committed, she would be always trying to disbelieve it—but it would never leave her.

Holding her breath, she opened the cover. But before she

could read beyond the first few words, the room trembled. She jerked her head up—

Red light swirled in the center of the room.

Ready to attack, Miranda got to her feet.

"You have been asking about *Pravus Semper*," called out a female voice. "You called it the red power."

Miranda stared at the woman who had materialized in the room. She wore a gown of green silk, it clung to her perfect form; it was unfashionably tight at her waist and followed the generous curve of her hips. Her bosom was full and plump, barely restrained by the neckline. The woman settled herself in a seat. "Well, child, do not gape at me so foolishly. Sit."

Serena frowned. "Mother? What do you know of this?"

They had wanted her to wait, but she knew she couldn't. And Miranda did not think vampire slayers would want to help Lukos and Zayan.

She knew so much more, she realized, as she rushed down the road away from the castle. She knew of the prophesy of Lukos, and she knew that he had believed Serena, Lady Sommersby, who had been Serena Lark before her marriage, had been his intended mate. She knew it had been Lukos's plan to sire an army of demons and control the world. And she had read the last part of the prophesy, sent to Serena by Lord Denby of the Royal Society. She could remember the words: *If he does not find his mate by the first spring equinox after he has risen, he will be consumed by his own power and burned to ash. And the one whom he loves most will also perish. She will die in a prison of Satan . . .*

She knew that Zayan had imprisoned Sebastien de Wynter, who could have destroyed him. She knew that Althea and Serena did not believe.

"They are tricking you," Althea had said firmly. "There must be something they want from you."

In her heart, as much as she wanted to deny it, she knew what it was. Both vampires had both lost people they had cared about to death. Zayan had lost his children; Lukos had lost his sister. Zayan had told her that the power—the *Pravus Semper*—had promised to give him his children in return for her magic.

Could Lukos also have wanted to gain control of her magic? Was that why he had proposed sexual games in the carriage? To capture her—or her heart?

"Miss Bond."

The masculine voice brought her to a stop. Foolishly, she had been thinking and watching the red-colored clouds amassing again over the village.

Two men had stepped out into the road, at the sharp turn ahead of her. They must have been behind the trees that crowded the road. One, with gray hair and a cane, bowed before her. "Miss Bond. I am afraid you cannot be allowed to return to the vampires. It is obviously too dangerous for you."

She seethed in exasperation. "And who are you?" She glanced to the second man to include him in her demand—he was a tall pale man with dark hair and cheekbones so prominent the shadows beneath them were black. He looked like a cadaver.

"I am Lord Denby," the first man said. "Of the Royal Society."

Miranda took a step backward, but she knew she could not escape. The cadaver put his hand in his coat and withdrew a pistol.

But Denby looked astonished as the man leveled the weapon at her, and she froze, waiting for the explosion of powder, and the pain that would be searing and brutal.

"Rothswell, what is the meaning of this?" Denby was waving his cane in anger.

"You are blind to what she is, my lord. How dangerous this demon is. We cannot continue to allow her to exist."

"She is not a demon, Rothswell."

"She is not human!" Sweat broke out on the cadaver's high, lined forehead. "Gone are the days where we can indulge ourselves with study and speculation. It is our task to rid the world of evil—"

"If that's our role, then we should likely start in the Houses of Parliament or of the Lords. Probably much evil there." Denby reached out with the cane to lower the pistol. "Our duty is to try to understand what we as yet cannot. Violence is no solution. Miss Bond gives life."

Rothswell swung the pistol around to Lord Denby and the elderly man lowered his cane. "A travesty of God," Rothswell spat. Then he looked down the road and became infinitely more at ease. Miranda twisted to see what he had spotted.

James Ryder had stepped out from the forest to the road.

Rothswell hailed him at once. "Mr. Ryder, we must work quickly—" The man's voice died away in shock as Ryder lifted his arm. Miranda saw a black shape in his hand and she took a step forward. She wished she could throw magic as Zayan could. But Ryder's arm arced and the black bar slammed down against Rothswell's head.

He cried out, then fell hard to the ground.

Ryder laughed at Denby, who lifted his cane in a threatening arc. "I could snap your neck with my fingers," the slayer laughed.

"Do not do this," Denby begged. "You were one of us."

"Shut it. You considered me to be nothing more than a lowly thug." He pointed at Rothswell's limp body. "He was a member of your precious Society also, and he wanted her dead more than I do. I'm doing this for the blunt—he and the others are doing it because you are a weak man, Denby. A weak man with a pitifully soft heart."

Miranda vowed not to be taken easily. As Ryder approached, she spun and tried to run. He grabbed her around the waist.

"I'm not waiting around to take the chance of your werewolf coming to your rescue now, love."

"Where are you taking me?" To the Royal Society's men, she guessed. Where they would swiftly kill her because they were afraid of what she was.

He grinned. "No, not to them. To my new master, angel."

16

Battle

He parted her thighs and she moaned her welcome. Golden, twinkling in sunlight, her hair fanned around her. Laying on the grass, Miranda giggled, then gasped in need as he bent to her cunny—wet, glistening, ready for him.

He tasted her, and at that—just one lick of her while being bathed in warm sunshine—he lost control and climaxed. Scalding hot, his come shot out to his thigh. His body jerked with it—almost as intensely as when he shifted shape.

She had done this to him. Miranda had brought him to his knees.

But she had done more than that—she'd opened his heart to light . . .

Zayan jerked out of his deep vampiric sleep. It had claimed him at dawn against his will, and he blinked slowly. It took a few moments for all his senses to become alert, but he knew, instinctively, that Miranda was gone, even before his eyes could see the empty room in the house they had found.

He remembered her whispering that the rooms, with the furniture draped in covers, looked to be filled with ghosts.

His heart was filled with ghosts, she had told him that too. He'd felt the pain in her heart when she'd told him she wished she could bring his children back for him. But he did not think even her power could do that.

But where had she gone?

At his side, Lukos groaned and rolled out of the bed. Zayan saw the flash of surprise, then irritation on Lukos's face as he realized he had slept beside Zayan. Miranda had been between them at first, when they had first fallen asleep.

Panic flared in Lukos's eyes. He cocked his head, listening in stillness as a wolf would do. "I can hear her, Zayan." His voice was hoarse. "I can hear Miranda's thoughts, and she is terrified. She speaks of the red power—"

Ice-cold fear swamped Zayan. Sending out his thoughts, he tried to find Miranda, but he could not. His panic ramped higher. *Miranda, where are you? Where in the blue blazes are you?* Aloud, he rasped to Lukos, in desperation, "Where is she? Can you find her?"

Another fear took root in his heart. What did it mean that Lukos could communicate with her and he could not? Was it just the red power blocking his mind, or was it more? Could it be proof that Miranda was closer to Lukos than he? That Lukos was the man she loved?

Was it really possible for a woman to share? To love two men equally?

By the gods, did it matter? All that mattered was to have Miranda safe, even if he lost her to Lukos . . .

"Christ Jesus!" Lukos shouted as the air in front of them began to ripple. It moved faster, then spun in a maelstrom. A red vortex appeared before them, turning at fierce speed. The coverlets lifted off the bed, and flew into the eye of it. In a flash of light, the fluttering blankets vanished.

"Bloody hell," Lukos shouted. He clutched the bedpost. Zayan gripped the one on his side, willing his preternatural strength to hold him. The force was sucking at him, pulling him backward. His fingernails drove into the wood, scratching it.

On a howl, Lukos was pulled from the post and drawn into the vortex. The bedpost he had been holding snapped free of the canopy and fell. Distracted for the moment, Zayan loosened his grip.

The force yanked him free, pulled him through the air, and he hit the swirling red lights feetfirst. It was like having his body torn apart—

"Marius Praetonius."

At the shout of his mortal name, Zayan turned slowly. The wind threw his hair around his face, and suddenly, in his mind, he was again standing on a rocky ridge in Gaul, two thousand years ago. His legions were massed behind him, a valley stretched out before him—a valley filled with the soldiers and armaments of the Gauls.

He had that moment of pause before he commanded his army to attack with a sweep of his sword. That moment when he could choose life or death, simply by either surging forward or turning back. He could savor the power of the choice, even though he knew his choice had already been made.

An unnatural stillness would settle on the thousands of men in that moment.

That stillness settled around him now.

The red vortex had brought him here. The force of it had sent him hurtling through the fog-drenched night and had thrown him into the standing stone circle. He had risen, disorientated and battered . . .

Now he slowly met eyes of the man who had shouted his name.

He had hungered for this for two thousand years. The chance

to cut out his enemy's heart and eat it before the man's dying eyes. The heat of rage set Zayan's blood on fire as he met the triumphant dark eyes of Mucius Gaius, the man who had stolen his wife's heart and had killed his children. Thanks to Miranda, he knew the truth.

What he was about to do was not murder—it was justice.

Gaius stepped forward. A broadsword sat comfortably in his meaty hand. Blond hair fluttered around his face, and he wore armor that gleamed in the moonlight. "I'll slice you in half where you stand, Praetonius."

A snarl twisted Zayan's lips. He sent a bolt of magic to his hand. At once a sword appeared there, and he held his weapon up to the sky. It almost hummed in his hand.

Blue-white moonlight slanted along the beautiful swirling pattern of the forger's work. This weapon had been imbued by the magic of the hand of a mortal craftsman, a man who lived for his metal, his flame, and his art.

Zayan had used it in every battle two thousand years ago. In all those conflicts, after all the bones it had cleaved, the blood it had spilled, it did not bear even so much as a nick or a crack. He had conjured it perfectly from memory, but now, it did not feel as it once had done. It no longer seemed an extension of his arm.

It felt as though it was another man's weapon that he had picked up, foreign, awkward, cold.

Gaius leapt forward and slashed wildly. Zayan jumped backward. On a stream of blue light, he turned a somersault in the air and Gaius's blade heaved a clean arc where he had stood.

Gaius was intending to cleave his head from his neck.

Zayan had landed on a standing stone that had toppled over. Lifting his hand, he tried to send magic, but he felt nothing but cold in his palm. His powers of sorcery had been drained after he had summoned the sword.

Damnation, he had not fought with a sword for centuries,

and he felt awkward and unpracticed. But he didn't have time to think of that.

"Come here and fight, you damned coward," Gaius shouted, and charged at him again.

Roaring, Gaius reached him and slashed. Leaping from his stone, Zayan clashed his sword with Gaius's blade. His foe's eyes had narrowed into vicious slits. Harsh breaths sent Gaius's chest heaving beneath the metal of his armor.

"You are the coward," Zayan spat back. He swung his sword to throw Gaius's weapon back. "You sliced the throats of my children . . . my innocent, defenseless children."

"Children you begot on Claudia against her will." Gaius threw the words at him as he powered forward. Gaius had a demon's strength and he was swift on his feet. Zayan found himself forced back by a volley of hard blows of Gaius's sword against his.

Gaius was more driven than he. He realized it then, as he blocked the swipes of the sword, but did not move in for the kill.

Miranda. Her name was flowing through his thoughts. He was worried for her, and that was taking his focus from this man he should yearn to destroy.

A swift jab almost sent Gaius's sword through his stomach, but he somersaulted again to avoid it.

"You condemned me to this," his enemy shouted. "An endless life where I am always haunted by the screams of your children. Their wails ring in my head in my every conscious moment. I became immortal as some sort of jest on you. After two thousand years of anguish, I learn that now."

For a moment, Zayan was rocked. He saw why he had been given his old foe on all but a silver platter. The red power thought it could distract him this way. It had given him what he'd yearned for, believing he would abandon Miranda so her power could be drained.

He had a choice, Zayan saw suddenly. He could walk away from this battle, go in search of Miranda, and sacrifice his need for vengeance. He could walk away from his past. Or he could fight, he could carve Gaius into tiny pieces, but lose Miranda—and lose his future.

But without magic, he could not find Miranda, or shift shape and hunt for her.

Zayan drove forward, surprising Gaius. What did he remember of the general from so long ago? Gaius was cocky, bold, sometimes stupid. And arrogant. He overestimated himself.

Spinning, Zayan blocked a series of fierce blows. His blade clanged against the armor around Gaius's hips. Gaius's blade whistled toward him, but the man was half-twisted to give the blow, and off balance.

Zayan jumped to the side; Gaius tried to redirect his force and staggered—

There, he had it. Zayan drove his sword up into Gaius's side, in a small space between the breast plate and the jointed armor at his hips. His enemy fell to his knees, clutching his side. Gaius sputtered out curses, but Zayan was not listening to him. There was a sound, like a roar, in his ears.

It was the sound of anguish he had made when he had gone from his son's chamber to his daughter's—

With his boot, he shoved Gaius to the ground. Too weak to move, Gaius whimpered at him. "Two thousand years. I have spent an eternity of hell waiting to fight you, Zayan. I hunted for you, but that damned red mist protected you. As though waiting—"

For a moment, Zayan paused. Waiting . . . had the red power been waiting for Miranda all along?

Then he lifted his sword.

A brilliant light blinded him and froze his arms in position, raised above his head. One of the vampire queens appeared before him, dressed sumptuously, as usual, in a gown of rich purple silk, with furs swathed about her graceful shoulders. She was Elizabeth, the queen who had imprisoned him in what she called a paradise, and what he called hell. "Let him live, Zayan."

Sweat poured off him, as it had done when he was a mortal man. Salty rivulets dripped into his eyes. His body burned with exhaustion. It sang with blood lust.

He felt like a mortal again.

Miranda. This battle had likely cost him Miranda.

"I've waited an eternity for this. I've lost everything to him . . ." Everything in his past—his children, his wife, his fame as a general. And the most important thing of his future—Miranda.

Elizabeth moved toward him from the outskirts of the standing stones. Her feet did not touch the ground. The light surrounding her was a deep purple. "Miranda is not dead. The *Pravus Semper*, the red power as you call it, cannot kill her. Miranda is too powerful a being. She is not like Claudia. Her power is to give life and to cherish it. And no evil can vanquish that. But evil can play dirty tricks."

Zayan stared at her.

"The *Pravus* has bonded Miranda's life to that of your foe. He is not a vampire, but the *Pravus* has allowed him to live this long, waiting to make use of him." Elizabeth waved her elegant hand to encompass Gaius, who lay gasping and weeping in the field.

"You are saying if I kill him, I kill Miranda."

"The *Pravus* needs Miranda's soul to steal her power, but it cannot kill her."

"So it tried to make me the instrument of her death." Or was Elizabeth lying? Did he believe Elizabeth, who had wanted to destroy him before, but who had agreed to imprison him?

Zayan, kill him. He heard the seductive voice of the red power, the *Pravus*, in his head. *I will show you what he did to your children. You must make him pay. He did not make it swift for them. He wanted to see the terror in their eyes—*

An image speared him. Of his son, lifting his small hand to protect himself, horror and fear stark in his large brown eyes.

Zayan lifted his sword higher, both hands clasped around the handle, and swung.

"Yes!" He heard the word as he cleaved his sword through the night air. A quick cry of triumph given in the seductive, magical tone that had possessed him. The red power's excitement surged through him.

It was the thrill of a Judas. The anticipation of a siren who had lured a dupe of a man to kill.

Zayan twisted his arms, and his momentum sent him stumbling. The tip of his sword drove into the rock by Gaius's head. All his strength was in the blow. A clang rent the night air as metal struck rock and sparks flew up. His arms almost jerked out of their sockets as the force of the strike slammed back through him. The blade broke and the tip bounced up, then landed in the grass with a thud.

In his hand, he held the stump of his beloved sword.

He had no weapon any longer and no magical powers. But he felt the red power—the *Pravus Semper*—retreat on a blast of icy wind. With his broken sword clutched in his hand, Zayan turned to Elizabeth. "Can you take me to Miranda?"

"No." She hovered a foot off the ground, purple silk fluttering around her long legs. She pointed to his fallen, but breathing, enemy. "You are going to leave him alive? You will walk away from vengeance?"

"Yes," he roared, knowing that his goal for two thousand years—vengeance—meant nothing anymore. Not now. Not compared with Miranda's life. He threw his sword into the air, where it exploded into a shower of stars. He was tired of hatred and anger, of anguish and pain. Miranda had shown him something more. "All I want," he shouted into the night, "is Miranda."

He groaned then. "And I have no magic. Nothing—"

"There are other types of magic, Zayan. There is, after all, the magic of love." Elizabeth folded her arms across her chest. "I did not believe it could ever be so. That you—or Lukos—could be redeemed. That you could set aside vengeance and darkness."

"I am a vampire. How in blazes do I set aside darkness?"

"Look to the Demon Twins, Yannick and Sebastien. Even though they are vampires, they have found light in their lives. Miranda came to you in your dreams, and you also traveled to her in hers. There is no reason you could not do that again."

A dream. An erotic dream.

"A love shared between three. I suggest that to save her, you take Lukos with you."

To do it meant risking losing Miranda to Lukos completely. But to save her, he would do it.

Lukos picked himself up from the cold, wet earth. The vortex of whirling red mist had thrown him here, on top of a pile of rocks. He'd hammered against them when he had landed. His body ached only slightly now as his demonic powers healed wounds and bruises that might have killed a mortal man.

He closed his eyes, drew on his strength, then shifted shape. His body went fiery hot as it transformed, his skin tingling as fur quickly covered it, his muscles changing from strong human ones to the powerful ones of a wolf.

He could scent Miranda now, and he charged toward her, drawn by his instincts . . .

Bother that insufferable Ryder; he had chained her up in a mausoleum on the grounds of a large manor house. One on the other side of the village to the one Zayan and Lukos had claimed.

Ryder's eyes had glowed at her in the dark as he had dragged her along the aisle between rows of stone coffins. They had gleamed with a vivid red light. And he had been so strong, as strong as Zayan or Lukos.

The red power. What had Althea called it? The *Pravus Semper*. Miranda had seen two puncture wounds on Ryder's neck, and she could not understand how a fog could have done that. But what mattered was the result—Ryder was not human anymore.

He had slammed her back against the wall, had pawed at her skirts. His breath, which stank of sulfur, had made her gag. Cruelly, he had squeezed her breasts.

"Damnation," he had groaned. "I want you. I'm rock hard. And I cannot do it. Not anymore."

He'd growled in fury, in agony, and in frustration. Then a sultry, hypnotizing voice had whispered over them both. "Come to me, James. You know where I wish you to be."

Then Ryder was gone. He had vanished from the dank mausoleum in a sparkle of red light, leaving her alone.

Strangely, that was when fear crept in. It was worse to be trapped alone in the dark. She kept imagining a stone sarcophagus lid sliding open, a bony hand appearing at the rim of the coffin.

What a foolish fancy. She had made love with men who were undead.

A wolf's howl floated on the air. Far above her, a faint red mist hovered, almost like a gaoler.

If she could control her magic—as Lukos and Zayan could—she was certain she could break the shackles at her wrists. She squinted and glared at the silver circlets, but nothing happened.

But then something did happen. Lights glittered around her. From the center of the beautiful twinkling lights stepped Lukos and Zayan, but she sensed it was not real.

She felt at once aroused—wet, shivering with anticipation. This was like one of her dreams.

They shimmered like they were flights of fancy, all silver and gold, naked against the blue-white moonlight.

"I don't understand. Is this real or not?" Miranda whispered it aloud.

"I don't know," Lukos admitted. "I can smell the sweet, delicious perfume of your skin. And my erection feels real—and agonizing."

She was bound, and though Zayan stepped forward, his hair flowing behind him, and threw his magic at it, the cuffs did not open. "Damn," he growled. But to Miranda's astonishment, he caught hold of her chin and kissed her deeply. Her lips sizzled at the slow, luxurious kiss. *One of the vampire queens said we could come to you this way. In an erotic dream . . .*

Lukos kissed her shoulder on the other side. It was a soft caress, a tender one. He lifted her hair to coast his mouth over her neck, and she heard his ragged groan. *Not of a need to feed,* he murmured in her head. *Out of the need to love you.*

She was magically shackled to a stone wall, her dress torn by Ryder. But she felt the love in Zayan's and Lukos's touches, and felt safe.

She trusted them. And understood. This was not a fantasy where she was ravaged by two vampires . . .

It was one in which she was loved by them both.

We want to share you in the most intimate way . . .

The red mist poured into the room; it slithered around the closed door, and in through any crack in the wall, any gap in the roof. She knew panic. This was an erotic dream. Zayan and Lukos were not really here to stand with her against the red fog—

"We are," Lukos insisted, his mouth brushing her earlobe. She whimpered at the teasing sensation of his hot lips caressing there. "Our spirits are. Our strength is. Our *love* is. You must believe it."

Lukos lifted her skirts. His hand cupped her derriere, but it felt light, thin . . . ghostly, as though it wasn't there.

"I believe it," she said. "I believe in the power of our love." She would, because saying it meant she had to . . .

Lukos's hands were caressing her rump and they became more firm, warmer. The roughness of his palm teased her sensitive skin. His hands felt real. They were real—the power of believing had brought the men to her through her dream.

Fear mixed with passion inside, sending her heart pounding faster than it ever had before. "Take me now," she moaned, before her courage and her faith fled completely.

"These are erotic, but are making this too damned awkward." Lukos reached up and grasped the chains that held her back to the wall. She wanted to be free, so she could be held between her men's bodies and loved that way.

Snap! The chains broke as Lukos wrenched on them. Links of chain flew around them and rattled against the stone floor.

"It works, love," Zayan whispered.

"Yes." Her heart soared with hope. "Love is a magical power, isn't it?"

Lukos turned her to face him, and she gazed up at him, her eyes alight with desire, her body molten with need. He cupped her cheek, tweaked her nipples, and slid his magnificent length deep inside her on the first stroke.

All of them were behaving as though the red mist was not even in the room. But around them, Miranda heard a soft, smothered cry of anger.

She arched back in welcome against Zayan. How she wanted him in her too. She *had* to have him. She wanted the utter completeness of having her two men filling her at once.

The red fog screamed and roiled back, pressing to the mausoleum's walls. Stunned by its reaction, Miranda surged up and kissed Lukos. She poured everything into the kiss, making it deep and intense. She moaned fervently into his mouth. Evoking hoarse groans from him. Again, the red power's screech reverberated through the air.

This was the secret. "Make love to me," she urged. "If you both can love, if you truly do, show me."

"By the gods, my angel, I love you," Zayan whispered harshly. He cupped her breast from behind her. His other hand slid down between her body and Lukos's. His finger caressed her clitoris until she whimpered.

Lukos thrust his hard cock deeply inside her quim. "I love you, Miranda. I've loved you from the first moment you tried to look into my heart."

Zayan pressed his cock to her anus, but his cock skidded ahead, and by . . . perhaps by magic, he began to slide into her sopping wet quim just as Lukos's thick erection invaded on another long thrust.

She cried out in arousal and surprise. It was . . . so much. It could not be possible—how could she take both inside her cunny at once—?

But the very intensity made it so exquisite. She could tell them no, but in truth, she didn't want to. And the screaming had died away, but she could feel the very agony of the red fog, as Zayan and Lukos slowly, carefully, pumped into her.

At her gasp, they slightly withdrew. "More," she breathed. "I want more."

"Do you?" Lukos asked it, almost as though he expected her to refuse.

"Yes." Though she had to drive her fingers into Lukos's shoulders as they tried one more unbelievable inch. "I—I cannot imagine anything more intimate than to share you both this way."

"You are so exquisitely tight with both of us inside," Zayan murmured.

She had to shut her eyes. The thought of what they were doing—the thought of their two long cocks pressed together, sliding beside each other—

It was an erotic image that left her as hot as flame.

They slid in and out, and she became so creamy there was no pain, only the most intense sensation of being filled. Lukos's cock slid on top, each thrust of his long shaft teased her clit. And Zayan, being as wicked as she expected Lukos to be, stroked her anus with his finger, while his cock plunged in and out of her quim.

Oh, she could not—

Not his finger inside her—

But he did it, and she was filled everywhere, and both men played with her breasts. They thrust faster and faster, squeezed her hard nipples more ruthlessly, and she screamed her pleasure to the sky.

She couldn't even speak. All she could do was cry out, over and over, and they thrust relentlessly until her second orgasm hit her before the first was even done.

Zayan. A plantive, desperate voice rose from the fog. *Your children. I will give them to you. Stop. Stop doing this to her—*

Then the voice implored to Lukos. *Your sister. She lives still. This is the truth—Lucifer has kept her for a thousand years, and I can reunite you if you stop this. If you promise to help me—*

"We love you, Miranda," Lukos vowed. Then he thrust hard, pressed his body tight to hers, and released deep inside her.

"I knew you would lose control and come first," Zayan laughed. Then he groaned. And came, and his seed rushed into her, filling her too.

This time sex made her feel stronger. More alive. Vital and powerful.

Dazed, Miranda realized the red fog had surrounded them once again in the confines of the mausoleum. Sparks of lightning shot within it, and it began to mass and take form right before her eyes. The fog gathered and darkened until it began to take a woman's shape. The mouth was a black cavern of a scream, the eyes large and dark. One wretched wail came from inside the fog.

Then it burst—and the force pummeled them just as her vampires' cocks were sliding free. Lukos and Zayan moved tightly to her, holding her, and together they withstood the great gust of wind and the wave of energy that hit them.

Red dust scattered around them and the wind subsided.

Miranda drew in ragged breaths. "Is that it?" she asked. "Is it gone?"

Zayan hesitated, then nodded. "It has."

She slumped against Lukos in relief, then tipped her head back to touch Zayan, to include both men in her relieved embrace.

That had been the way to destroy it. Not violence. Not a fierce attack, but a true, enraptured, honest expression of pleasure and love.

She never would have thought of such a thing.

But then, she still did not know what the red being was. Even Serena's mother had not been able to explain exactly what it was. She had been able to say that it was female. It seduced men, but not sexually as a succubus would. Eve had described it as a counterpart to Lucifer, who was seen to be a male embodiment of evil, a fallen angel in the Underworld. The *Pravus Semper* was a female who had no form, and suffered torment because of that. An entity that flowed eternally amidst the mortal world.

She did not know if they had destroyed it completely. She doubted it. But they had driven it away.

Miranda reached out and caressed Lukos's cheek. He stared at the red dust that lay scattered on the ground. "Do you think it is true?" she ventured. "About your sister?"

He did not look to her. She was certain she saw a glint of a tear in the corner of his mirror-like eye. "I don't know."

And he spoke those words so softly, with such restraint, but with his tone hinting at hope, that it broke her heart.

"Well, my dark and dangerous vampires, you have both performed well."

Before them, a beautiful woman stepped out of the shadows. Miranda self-consciously put her hands to her breasts, for all the good that would do. She was naked, sandwiched between two naked men.

A pleased smile curved the newly arrived woman's full, richly red lips, and revealed her sharp, elongated canines. The woman waved her hand, and Miranda shivered as silk appeared out of the air and spiraled around her skin, cool and soft. In an instant, she was clothed in a flowing white robe. And black ones appeared around Zayan and Lukos.

Miranda realized that nothing surprised her anymore. In just a few days, she had changed from the frightened woman who did not know what she was. She now felt she could face anything—and it was Zayan and Lukos who had made her believe that.

"Elizabeth."

Miranda heard the apprehension in Zayan's deep, rumbling voice.

The vampiress turned her large, beautiful eyes to him. "Zayan. We, the vampire queens, know you served the *Pravus* in the hopes of bringing your children back. What you did not know was that she was not the only one with the power to give them to you. The *Pravus* wanted to absorb power to destroy all of us—the vampire queens. Because you have done us a great service, I will attempt to give your children to you."

"A—attempt?" Zayan managed to say.

"Miranda is the only being who can bring them back to you. I can bring their bodies back, and their souls, but I cannot resurrect life. There is no one who can do that, except Miranda."

Elizabeth turned, her robes fluttering around her, and crooked her finger. From a space between two tall stones, two children took tentative steps forward.

Zayan's preternatural heart skipped one of its slow beats. At a soft command from Elizabeth, the young, thin boy jerked up his head.

Brown eyes, rimmed with the thickest black eyelashes, stared steadily at Zayan, and he reeled in shock. The eyes were his own—gazing blankly at him.

No, they were *like* his eyes. A memory nudged its way through his shocked mind. A vision of a boy watching quietly as he practiced his sword work.

His son. This boy was his *son.* This was the face he had forgotten. Love surged into his heart as he studied his child's features with an intensity he had probably not given the boy when the child had been alive. The boy had a straight, aquiline nose. High cheekbones and a point of a chin. Large dark brown eyes and long, long lashes. His boy had been gifted with a handsome face.

His precious son.

Memories flooded back as he slowly walked toward the thin boy and the small, trembling girl. He saw two beautiful faces—his daughter also had huge, dark eyes, and her lashes reached her black, arched brows. Both had cupid's bow mouths that were full and soft.

Their faces were not lost to him anymore. They were here.

In his chest, his heart thundered. He remembered how his son's mouth had learned to be grave and serious—to show the stoicism and bravery of a warrior. But he also remembered the velvety feel of a baby's cheek against his rough skin, and he remembered the slightly sour smell of an infant cradled to his chest.

Blinking at a burning sensation in his eyes, Zayan bent down to the children. His daughter stared vacantly beneath a fall of tangled curls. When she had been alive, her mouth had always flowed readily into smiles. Smiles that had pushed away his brutal memories of battle and that had warmed his heart.

His daughter had been nine. His son eleven.

Zayan sank to his knees. His children had no smell, and they made no move to touch him. He heard a soft sob behind him and knew the sound had fallen from Miranda's lips. He held out his arms, but his children did not move.

"They cannot respond to you," Elizabeth said. "As I told you, I have brought their bodies back into this world, but they are not yet alive."

He stood and backed away from his children. They did not move, did not acknowledge he had left them.

The softest touch whispered over his wrist and Zayan turned to see Miranda reaching to grasp his hand. Lines crossed her forehead, and pain showed in her eyes. That she felt such agony for him lanced his heart. "Can you?" he asked her. "Would you do this for me?"

Moonlight glinted on tears at the corners of her large, cornflower blue eyes. Gravely, Miranda nodded. She knew, he was certain, that she held his heart in her hands.

"It is a great risk, of course," Elizabeth interjected. "They have been gone from this world for a very long time. It will take great power to return their force of life."

Lukos strode forward. "What kind of risk? What evil conditions have you vampire queens concocted?"

Zayan saw Miranda hold a quelling, graceful hand to Lukos. "I want to do it."

Lukos shoved back his long hair with an angry pass of his hand. "The risk is her death, isn't it? I know the way you witches work."

"No, you do not, Lukos. You have no idea about us," Elizabeth snapped. "Yes, her life would be at risk, but not because of some game of vengeance, or mischief. Miranda would be at risk because this resurrection would drain her greatly. She is bestowing some of her life force onto them."

Zayan leapt to Miranda and scooped her into his arms before she could lay her hand on his son's frail chest. "I can't let you take this risk."

"I have to do it. I can't turn my back on two children who deserve to live."

He had never admired a woman more. She was not doing this for him, but for them. Lukos stepped to his side and reached out to stroke Miranda's cheek. "The power of a love shared between three. If Miranda needs greater power, I suspect we can both provide it for her."

Miranda's blue eyes lit up. "Yes," she cried. "That must be it. We destroyed the *Pravus* with our combined power. Surely, we can give life with it."

Zayan nodded curtly. His throat was too tight to allow words to escape. Then he swallowed hard and managed to force out a warning. "If I sense you are in danger, Miranda, I'm stopping you." He gazed to his children, his heart ready to crack and splinter in his chest. He wanted them to live. But he could not let Miranda die.

She had no idea how to harness their combined power. And when Miranda turned to ask Elizabeth what to do, she could not see the vampire queen anywhere.

"She's gone," Lukos growled. "The queens do that. They always vanish when they could actually be of use."

The children were holding hands and stood eerily still. "I don't know where to begin—how to make our power combine. Not without—" But perhaps making love had given them some kind of a connection. She had felt a small sizzle though her blood when she'd touched Zayan's arm.

She faced both men. "I have no idea what to do, but I would like to try touching one of the children. The way I always do, with my hand over the child's heart. Then I want you both to put your hands over mine. I think that gesture—of union and of trust—might work."

But it was a wild guess. And if she was wrong, she did not believe Zayan *could* stop her. Once her energy began to flow out, she did not think he—or anyone—would be able to stop it.

17

Beloved

Miranda's heart lurched in her chest as Zayan gathered his son into his arms. The boy was long-limbed but thin, and distressingly fragile when embraced against Zayan's solid, powerful body.

Two strides took father and son to a slab of stone that lay like an altar, at the edge of the circle. Miranda followed behind them, taking calming breaths. The boy did not protest as Zayan laid him gently on the stone. He just lay limply. She sensed Lukos had come to stand at her other side. Her senses were heightened; she knew his scent, but also, she just instinctively felt he was there.

As she bent to her knees on the left side of the boy, she smiled down into the child's blank eyes. Lukos followed, behind her. His warmth whispered against her through their loose clothing. Slowly, Zayan dropped to his knees on the opposite side of the stone. She saw his hands shake slightly. It deeply touched her heart to see Zayan, who had been a battle-hardened general and a man who had known the worst betrayal, openly reveal so much loving concern for his child.

Zayan looked up and met her gaze. "Remember, Miranda. If there is danger to you, you are to stop."

The tremble of his hand—she realized, with a glimpse into Zayan's thoughts—it had been for her. She held out her hand so it hovered a few inches above the boy. "Put both your hands on mine now."

"Is there anything we should say? Any incantations?" Beneath the soft glow of the moonlight, Lukos wore the most serious expression she had seen him reveal. He had not looked so grim even when they had fought the red power.

She shook her head. "I simply touch and it happens. In all cases, I have truly wanted the child—or the person—to live. Think of that. Think of a deep desire to bring the boy to life."

"His name was Marc," Zayan murmured, and he gently rested his hand atop hers. Lukos put his on last, so his hand covered Zayan's but the tips of his fingers touched her skin.

"Marc, then." She swallowed hard. What would it be like for Marc to open his eyes two thousand years after he last shut them? *Do not think of that,* she warned herself. *Think of joy. Think of how he will have the chance to run again, and play, and know his father's embrace.*

She touched her hand to Marc's chest, over his heart.

There was no warmth this time. Her skin began to glow instead, all along her arm, in a soft, pulsating shimmer of gold. She could see it through the white robe. The golden glow increased at their joined hands. Zayan's grip tightened. "Is something wrong?"

"I don't know. It is different—" She quickly added, "But it does not feel bad." Instead, she felt a lightening at her heart. It was as though she was experiencing every joyous moment of her life at once.

Beneath her hand, Marc's heart took on a strong and steady beat. She saw the twitch of this arms and legs. His eyes shut abruptly, and when the lids flickered open again, life gleamed in the deep brown eyes. The vibrant glow of life—of a soul.

It was done, and it had not been hard at all—

Suddenly, the gold shimmer drained away down her arm. It sucked between their hands, drawing a shock of cold air behind it. The light vanished into Marc's chest. Miranda gasped as an icy sensation gripped her everywhere.

Her fingers went numb, as did her toes. She felt as though they had become instantly brittle with the cold. She could not even shiver, she felt too frozen to even move.

"Stop it," Lukos cried. "Take you hand away."

But Marc had not tried to move. She could see the light in his eyes slowly extinguishing. They were losing him . . .

Zayan clutched her hand and tried to pull it up. But her power gave her the strength to fight him. "No," she gasped. "Let me try. I think this is a test. This is what Elizabeth meant. It takes the conviction of love to do this."

Lukos growled in fury, but he pushed his hand down, which forced Zayan's on top of hers and splayed her palm tightly on Marc's chest.

Marc's eyes opened again. Shock and surprise and fear touched his face. Then his gaze settled on Zayan, and Miranda felt a feeling of safety rush over him. He knew his father, and he knew, with Zayan, he was safe.

Miranda eased her hand up. This time, Lukos released his hand, then Zayan let hers go. Now freed, Marc struggled to sit, but before he could, Zayan lifted him into a great hug.

The cold was slowly abating. Miranda stood, shakily, and held out her hand to the small girl. Lukos held her shoulders, but Miranda whispered, "No, I am all right. Bring Zayan's daughter to me." Obediently, he went and carried the small girl to the stone altar. Tears were leaking down Marc's cheeks, as Zayan stroked his hair, and he looked ashamed of them.

Until he saw the tears in his father's eyes. And these he stared at in honest surprise.

Zayan shook his head. "It is not the measure of a man to battle his emotions. It is a man's strength to give his devotion to those he loves, to *reveal* his feelings and not to hide them, and to earn the reward of love."

At the boy's confusion, Zayan lovingly ruffled his hair, then set him down. The child cuddled against Zayan's legs. He spoke, but Miranda could not understand the words. He was speaking a language from two thousand years ago. Zayan answered him in gentle tones. The boy stepped back.

Lukos planted a kiss on top of Zayan's daughter's glossy brown curls and arranged her on the stone. "She reminds me of Ara," he said, as though an explanation was needed for that emotional touch. "She does not look like my sister, but she is . . . I sense she is very much the same."

"Lina," Zayan whispered. "That is her name."

Miranda lifted her hand, and at once the men joined her, again placing their hands over hers. Knowing what to expect took Miranda's fear away as she felt the rush of joy, then the sudden onslaught of cold.

As Lina awoke, her face crumpled up and she began to cry. Shock and fear, Miranda supposed, but as she moved to comfort the girl, dizziness struck her. Her strength drained away. She slumped back, and Lukos held her. Her legs felt as though filled with feathers—with no substance or strength. She had to gasp for breath.

"Are you—" Lukos began.

"I'm fine," she managed to speak, and her heart was slowing to a steady beat.

Zayan lifted both his children, settling his son on his right hip and his daughter on his left. Then he bent to her. Seeing such joy in his dark, silvery eyes, Miranda smiled. "Perhaps this is why we shared dreams," she whispered. "I was meant to find you, so I could give you this."

"You were meant to find me, because I was meant to love

you, Miranda. I've existed for two thousand years. Now, with you, I finally understand what it is to live."

Before she could protest, Lukos stood and scooped her up. He carried her in his arms.

"We have to get to shelter," Lukos said abruptly to Zayan. "Miranda's cold and weak. And I don't trust the vampire queens. There may be a catch to this. A trick."

She shook her head. "No, I think the trick was to have faith. I think we've—we've done it."

But she saw the disbelief in Lukos's eyes. He did not believe she was safe yet.

Out of the corner of her eye, Miranda saw Zayan's children falling into sleep, perhaps the ordeal had exhausted them too. His son had clasped his hands to his father's shoulder and rested his head there as his eyes shut.

His daughter had laid her head to Zayan's chest. For a sizzling moment, her gaze held his mirror-like eyes. *I love you, Miranda,* he murmured in her thoughts. *The children are sleeping. Once they are safely tucked into beds, I intend to show you how explosive a love that will last forever can be.*

Not alone, Lukos added. *I intend to show you, too, my love.*

"Not the nursery. I want them to share my bed tonight. I need to have them close to me." Zayan laid his sleeping son on the enormous bed in the chamber of their borrowed manor house. Miranda stroked a stray curl from his daughter's cheek, then drew up the crisp, white sheets and the heavily embroidered counterpane. Marc and Lina were dwarfed in the bed, but they looked adorably cozy.

Maids, easily controlled by the vampires, had fed the children treats, had found them nightclothes that had been long tucked away, had bathed the children with soap and warm water, and then had vanished upstairs to the attics.

Miranda took a deep breath. As far as she could tell, none of the servants had been harmed in any way. There were no bite marks to be seen on anyone's neck. So what were Lukos and Zayan doing to feed?

Lukos spoke suddenly in her mind. *We can control our feeding because we have existed for so long. And I learned to subdue the urge during my imprisonment. We can survive on little blood and quickly heal the human's wound.*

She realized that like Bastien and Yannick, Jonathon and Drake, these men could be merciful to mortals. They only had to want to be.

Zayan kissed his children on their smooth, soft-as-silk foreheads, and Miranda slipped into Lukos's bedchamber. He was sprawled on the bed, naked. And erect—his cock stood straight, arcing along his belly. His black hair fanned out around him. *I want you, Miranda. One last time.*

His words stopped her on the threshold, her hand on the door frame. *What do you mean?* The cold sensation of using her power to the extreme had faded away, but a new frostiness swept over her at his ominous words. *Do you mean the prophesy?*

Come, strip off your robe, and I'll tell you.

Lukos watched as Miranda let the white silken robe puddle at her feet. She possessed a beauty that would make any mortal man believe in goddesses. The way she stood, her knees together to enhance the rounded curves of her hips, and the graceful lines of her legs—legs, he thought, that delectably went from a plump, taut rump all the way to the floor. Her naked breasts bobbed as she walked toward him. Peaked by her pink, hard nipples, they almost mesmerized him with their seductive, enticing wobble. They were so sweetly sensual, he wanted to gobble them whole.

This was all he could have with her. One more night.

He managed a smile for her. *Tonight, I'd love another peak at your fantasies, angel. What would you want me to do?*

Even after all they'd been through, she still blushed for him. She rested her knee on the mattress, clutched the bedpost, and turned a fetching shade of pink.

Do you want to be tied up? He was teasing her. Savoring her for this one night. *Or would you like to have me bound again, for your pleasure?*

"No, freedom tonight," she whispered. "No ropes or magical chains. Though I do have a rather illicit fantasy about highwaymen—"

"Highwaymen? Capturing you and ravaging you?" Zayan stood in the doorway, behind Miranda.

She gave a smile that glittered like sunlight on water. "Hmm, I suppose I have already lived that fantasy." Melodic and filled with naughty amusement, her voice made Lukos's cock bob and his ballocks tighten. "I've done rather a lot of scandalous things with both of you. I've even watched the two of you pleasure each other—"

Zayan flashed a grin. "I think the thought of it—the memory—is arousing her."

"I have to agree." The luscious smell of her juices came readily to Lukos's heightened senses. "Perhaps you would like to watch again, angel."

It would signify a truce between he and Zayan—a sign he believed Zayan's claim that he had not taken Ara for Lucifer.

The vampire queens had told him that originally. After the power that he had unleashed with Zayan and Miranda, Lukos believed he knew why. The queens had fed him lies to make him and Zayan enemies, to ensure he and Zayan did not combine their power. He suspected that together they could destroy the queens. The vampire queens were accustomed to being at the top of the hierarchy of the vampire world. Only gods, goddesses, and Lucifer held greater power than the queens.

Which made him worry about what could happen to Miranda. She had incredible power, and she was joining in a threesome with two strong demons. The queens would not be happy with that. Had Elizabeth suggested they work together to defeat the *Pravus* and resurrect Zayan's childrens as tests of their combined power?

Right now, he imagined Elizabeth, Eve, and the other queens were afraid. He suspected those witches would want to see Miranda destroyed—

"Do you not want to pleasure her, wolf?"

Zayan was prowling toward the bed, his hand wrapped around his thick shaft. Lukos had to admit he possessed a handsome cock. Not as appealing as Lukos's long, straight rod, which was a magnificent twelve inches in length, but he could understand why Miranda's heart raced when she looked upon it. "Yes," he growled in return.

"I want to be sucked," Zayan rasped. He got onto the bed from the opposite side to their delightful angel, who licked her lips as she watched, her hand wrapped around the post and her knee resting on the bed.

"As do I. I expect it would please her to watch us suck each other at once."

Miranda's eyes grew wide. "Ooh, yes."

Lukos had to laugh. Her response was so ingenuous. And his cock bobbed again as another surge of blood went into it. God, he'd never been so hard. His fluid leaked out, and he swept it away with a rough brush of his hand. Even the smack of his palm against the straining head felt damnably good.

Zayan straddled him, so he was looking up at a pair of heavy bollocks and a long, swaying member. Their audience—Miranda—gave a gasp of delight. Lukos drank in Zayan's scent— vampires had a rich, clean smell, an enticingly sexual aroma. A smell that made him want to suck fiercely at Zayan's cock.

The sudden grip of Zayan's hot mouth around his own rigid prick made him groan in agony. Hades, it was good. The brush of fangs, the tease of firm lips, the incredible suction . . .

He arched up, his fingers gripping Zayan's thighs, and he took the taut, bulbous head of Zayan's rod between his lips. *I'll make you come first, General,* he threatened. He meant to tease, and he saw Miranda wag her finger in playful discipline. *If I'm naughty,* he said to her in her thoughts, *come and spank me.*

Zayan's mouth moved expertly over Lukos's shaft, ramping up his arousal. But Lukos had no intention of giving his climax to Zayan. No, his orgasm was for Miranda, and he would hold on to his control. In challenge, Zayan began to play with his balls—exactly as he liked it, not gently, but with a roughness that took the caress to the brink of pain.

Lukos raked his fangs along Zayan's shaft. Strange to think he was sucking at the man he'd hated, and doing it to please Miranda. He knew Zayan loved Miranda, and he understood how that felt. He might not have a soul, but he had a heart. It gave him a kinship with Zayan—a closeness.

For Miranda, he could share.

He released Zayan's rigid cock and held out his hand to her. "Join us, angel. I want to be inside you. I want to explode in your tight cunny. I want your fingernails digging into my shoulders as you climax. You belong between us, love."

She climbed onto the bed, and Zayan shifted, so she was sitting in the middle, her thighs pressing against theirs. She frowned playfully. "If I were to suck one of you now, it would be like kissing the other."

Convoluted woman's logic, but the thought was erotic and Lukos was more than game. Demurely holding back her hair, she bestowed a kiss to his weeping cock head. After Zayan's fierce sucking, it amazed him that her gentle caress was so potent.

She bent and gave a gentle suckle to Zayan's prick, and let her fingernails tease the sac between his thighs. She looked at ease, her cheeks flushed with arousal, her mouth plump, wet, and tempting.

In his mortal youth, he'd enjoyed foreplay. With little freedom for one thousand years, he'd always rutted quickly. He'd
wanted to slowly enjoy this night with Miranda.

But he couldn't wait any longer.

Miranda climbed on top of him, taking his cock deep inside
her tight, fiery hot pussy. Zayan swiftly worked three fingers
into her tight derriere, making her moan and whimper in ecstasy.

In no time, she came for them. And fell to his chest, gasping
for breath.

"Another position, angel," he whispered against her ear.
"We have all night . . ."

"Oh, dear heaven, yes. I never want to stop making love to
you both."

Lovemaking had never been like this.

Lukos fell back on the bed. He had been the last to surrender
to climax, and he felt as though his brain, his spine, his every
muscle has dissolved into semen and had shot out of his prick.

Miranda's arm slid over his chest. "That seemed to be . . .
very intense."

It was. He patted her arm, and she nestled against him. After
such strenuous sex, and such powerful orgasms, she would
likely succumb to sleep. Once she did, he needed to be able to
slip away.

So he coaxed her to roll over to face Zayan. He stroked her
hair, and the look Zayan gave Miranda spoke plainly of love.
Hell, Lukos knew that expression of wonderment. He suspected
he'd been wearing it several times in the last few days. Zayan
was marveling over this just as he was. How in blazes had they
both been fortunate enough to find love?

Lukos snuggled up to Miranda from behind. Her derriere
was a lush cushion for his softening cock. She was warm, and
deliciously damp with sweat. Her hair tumbled over her shoulders in wild curls. *Go to sleep, angel,* he urged.

He saw Zayan relax against Miranda. Dawn was near, and

Zayan no doubt intended to stay close to her until she dropped off into sleep.

Zayan would keep her safe. He was certain of that. And that meant he could leave her now.

He wanted to stay forever at Miranda's side. Hades, he was willing to share with Zayan to do that. But he had another responsibility. And fulfilling it would likely destroy him.

"You did not tell me why you believe we were making love for the last time."

Lukos jerked away from the balustrade, looking guilty. He also looked exotic standing there. Even when he was in the form of a man, he exuded the primal power of a wolf. A sharp gust of wind whipped his waist-length black hair around him.

Miranda waited, but suspected he intended to avoid an answer again.

"I never knew making love could be so exotic," he murmured instead.

"You won't distract me," she vowed. "I want to know." She held her robe—a heavy brocade one she had found—more tightly around her. The night was clear, and she had never known anything more reassuring that the velvety-black sky. There was no fog. But dawn was close. The mantel clock had put the time at a quarter after four.

She approached slowly. "Tell me."

He laughed. How differently he did so than Zayan. Zayan's laugh was gusty and bold, the sound of a man with the world spread out at his feet. And with his children, his chuckles were rich and poignant and filled with love. Lukos's spoke of irony, of a joke he was making at his own expense. It was the sound of a bitter man.

"I never expected I would make love to a woman who makes my heart soar, angel. I never thought I'd make love to a woman I loved."

"And we can do it again. Tomorrow night. And every night after that—"

He clasped her fingers and drew them to his lips. He bestowed a courtly kiss to their tips, but with such a heated gaze that it set her toes on fire, even as it made her heart ache.

"I love you, Miranda."

The wind had died, letting his softly spoken words hang in the crisp air.

"But?" she asked on a wry smile. She'd guessed exactly which word would follow his declaration.

He drew her index finger into his mouth and suckled. Then he stopped. "I can't have you, love."

There would be more to follow. Miranda wanted to prompt but saw darkness shroud his eyes, a blackness that seemed to come from inside him, and suck away the reflected moonlight.

He straightened and turned to look out over the terrace railing once more. "I don't know if the red power, the *Pravus*, was speaking the truth when it told me my sister Ara is still alive and has been Lucifer's prisoner. It could have been a bluff. But it could also be true. I have to go to her, Miranda, and rescue her."

She stroked his shoulder, savoring the smoothness of his skin. "And then you could come back."

"I wish I could, angel. And I believe you are the one who can save me from the prophesy. But if I go into the Underworld, I won't get out alive. Lucifer made me an apprentice to serve him, and I betrayed him. I even tried to destroy him out of revenge for taking Ara. I'm not strong enough to take on the devil and win. But I suspect he would be willing to trade Ara for me. He'd let her go so he can have the pleasure of torturing me."

"But our power combined—"

He put his finger to her lips. "Too great a risk for you. And resurrecting Zayan's children has weakened you. You've tried to hide it, but I can sense it about you."

He moved away from her abruptly, striding along the terrace. She rushed toward him but was too late. White clouds surged around them, then scattered in the burst of wind. She glimpsed a wolf racing across the dark lawns. Lukos was gone, running away to enter the Underworld.

She did not even know where the entrance to Lucifer's labyrinth was. She could not stop Lukos, and now she could not even follow him.

In his dream, he saw Lukos. He stood naked on the terrace, and Zayan groaned as cool night breezes whispered over his skin. He felt them as though he were in Lukos's body. As though his mind was deeply connected to Lukos's experiences.

Demure lavender scents teased him, and he saw Miranda pad across the flagstones toward Lukos. Her hair rippled behind her, a cape of gold. Her arms slid around Lukos's waist, and at the shared sensation of touch, Zayan went instantly hard.

Heat flooded him—not the quick sizzle of lust, but the sharp, fiery pain of a shape-shift. Lukos, in wolf form, bounded over the terrace railing, the rough stone brushing the underside of his belly. His claws tore into the earth, his paws threw up a spray of dirt as he loped in the night.

Zayan saw Miranda turn back to see him, where he waited in the bedchamber. He felt the quickening of her heart. Then he felt it suddenly stutter—her pulse skipped a beat or two, and she pressed her hand to her breast in shock. Her heart began to beat again, slower. He could almost feel the strain on it.

He struggled to wake, but he could not escape the daysleep. His senses were still alert, even if he could not move physically. It was one of the traits that distinguished him from lesser vampires. He could sense Miranda's energy, her life force, was less than it had been before Lukos had left.

Was it the truth, or just a trick of his dreaming mind? And if it was the truth, what in blazes did it mean?

His gut instincts knew, even as he tried not to think of it.

Lukos had left. After Miranda had joined with them both, and their magical powers had combined. Somehow, Lukos's disappearance meant that Miranda was dying.

"You intend to calmly walk into Blackthorne's castle and ask the slayers to help you save Lukos?" Miranda could not believe Zayan would do such a mad, irrational thing.

Zayan drew on a greatcoat he had commanded a footman to fetch for him. He quirked a brow. "Yes, love, that's exactly what I intend to do."

"You would take such a risk, after your children were returned to you?"

"Does your aunt, the vampire-slaying one, love you very much?"

"You think she would help us? I did save her life. Years ago, when I was a young girl. I used my power then to save her life."

Zayan drew on a pair of fine black leather gloves. "Then she owes you."

"But what of your children? They are confused and will be frightened if you leave them—"

"I will take them with me to the slayers. Your aunt should be gentle with them."

Miranda caught her breath. To have the chance to spend time with children who had been resurrected after two thousand years? She imagined Aunt Eugenia, Althea, and Serena would be delighted.

But it astonished her that he would have such trust in people who wanted to destroy him. She had told him of her encounter with Lord Denby on the road to the castle, and he had realized the implication at once. There were members of the Royal Society determined to wear blinders, to see the unknown as evil, but there were others who wanted to understand more of the magical world surrounding them.

"You are willing to trust the slayers, those who were your enemies, for Lukos?"

"I am not doing this for Lukos." He tipped up her chin, the leather of his glove a soft caress against her skin. "I am doing it for you, Miranda. I am afraid that breaking up the threesome is draining your life force in some way. And the only ones who can help me understand why are the vampire queens."

Miranda bit her lip. Lukos had not trusted the vampire queens, but they had helped her. "I think Lukos believes he must sacrifice his life for his sister's. He isn't planning to return."

Zayan grimaced. "He thinks he can strike a bargain with Lucifer, doesn't he? His life for his sister's."

"You don't believe he can?"

"Any bargain he could make would involve so much trickery, he'll end up sacrificing both himself and his sister."

Miranda accepted a cloak from a maid and threw it around her shoulders. "I do not know how to get into the Underworld."

Zayan looked grim. "Well, love, I do."

"Aunt Eugenia, I want you to put down the crossbow. Please, he can be trusted. He's brought his children here!"

Miranda held Lina on her lap. The girl had been afraid of her at first, but now, only hours after she had saved the child, Lina was already beginning to trust her.

Zayan stood by the fireplace, holding Marc's hand. The fire roared behind them, and Aunt Eugenia, along with Althea, Serena, and their husbands, stood between Zayan and the drawing-room door.

"I would never trust him," Aunt Eugenia declared. But she did lower the weapon. "He was the vampire I was hunting on the night you saved my life, my dear."

Miranda's heart plummeted. Suddenly, Zayan's past was personal. She remembered how wounded her aunt had been. Heart in her throat, she faced him.

"Do you hate me now, love?" he asked gently. "Your aunt was going to stake and destroy me. I didn't hurt her. I retreated because I could not bring myself to destroy a lady. Instead, another vampire attacked her. A younger one than I."

Miranda looked from her resolute aunt to the man she loved. "I can't choose," she finally said. "I want to love you both and have you both love me. If you cannot, Aunt Eugenia, I understand."

She saw her aunt bite her lip, a gesture of uncertainty she'd never seen Eugenia make. "I suppose I could not expect him to simply stand there while I stuck a stake in his heart. But are you certain of this, my dear? You say you love these vampires. But perhaps—"

"No, Aunt. I am not under their spell. I've found where I belong. With them."

Her aunt placed the crossbow on a table. And walked to her side. "I will look out for you always, Miranda. I promised you that when you saved me and I saw your power. No matter what choice you make, I will support you. I want you to feel you belong. I want you to be happy."

Miranda's throat tightened. "You will accept that I must follow my heart?"

The Earl of Brookshire stepped forward. "Are you sure of your heart, though, Miss Bond?"

"I am," she declared loudly. "Do you not understand? Zayan became a vampire because he had been betrayed by everyone who was close to him, and he had his children viciously taken from him." She pointed to the earl. "Would you not go mad if your daughter was taken away?"

His silvery blue eyes held hers. "Yes, I believe I would. The grief would tear me apart." He turned to Zayan. "I can imagine the rage. The need to destroy."

"When I transformed your brother," Zayan said softly, "it

was my intention to save him. I cared deeply for him. I could not just watch him die."

Miranda faced Serena, Drake, and Jonathon. "I wish to help Lukos. He was sent to be the devil's apprentice, forced to sacrifice himself to protect his people." She had recounted to them all the story Lukos had told her of his past. "Can you imagine the guilt, pain, and anger he felt to learn his sister had been taken a prisoner to ensure his obedience?"

Both men solemnly nodded.

"If you, dear niece, have fallen in love with him without bewitchment, there must be something of value to him." Eugenia stepped toward Zayan. She held out her hand to Marc. "We will take care of your children, Zayan. I, for one, am willing to begin again."

18

UnderWorld

Moonlight washed the stretch of quiet, empty field. Snow swirled around the large, dark mound of earth that was West-warden Barrow. And within it was one of the few magical entrances to the labyrinth that led to the Underworld.

With her goal in her sights, Miranda lengthened her strides, until she was almost running across the uneven field, holding her sable-lined velvet cloak tightly at her throat, trying not to stumble.

Zayan grasped her wrist and pulled her back with such force, she fell against him. He stopped dead. "Wait, Miranda," he cautioned. Maelstroms of snow spun at his face, but his silver eyes fixed harshly on her. "I sense he was here, but I am not letting you rush into the Underworld to save Lukos from himself. You will wait out here while I go within."

"I would have thought you knew me better by now, Zayan." Miranda pulled her hand free of his grasp and sped up her pace. "I faced the *Pravus Semper*. I might be afraid to face Lucifer, but I'm not going to cower in fear. And if it is true, that we have all bonded through a love shared between three, then I believe our best chance to defeat the devil is to be together."

Zayan growled, and she knew he had no argument against her logic. She appreciated his need to keep her safe, but there were some things worse than death. And she knew of one—living a lifetime of regret and sorrow for not being there to protect a loved one.

Both Zayan and Lukos had lived through an eternity of grief and regret—Zayan over his children, and Lukos for his sister, Ara.

During their voyage here, when Zayan had magically shifted her shape again and allowed her to fly, he had insisted, in her thoughts, that she should turn back. She knew he had only allowed her to come with him because she had glimpsed this place in his mind. He had tried to shutter it from her, but she believed his worry over her had weakened his mind and allowed her to see his thoughts when she had touched his chest.

She was certain he knew she would have come alone if necessary.

Ahead, the barrow looked fancifully like a slumbering dragon that had curled up on the field. Zayan had sprinted ahead of her, making it easy to find the entrance—in seconds, he stood in front of it with his arms crossed over his chest.

Shouldn't love mean she and her men would not be adversaries again? It didn't, though. Lukos has flown away before she could argue with him. Zayan was determined to do nothing but argue with her tonight.

Behind Zayan's broad body, Miranda spied the narrow opening topped by a thick stone lintel in the earth-covered banks. Fallen rocks filled part of the doorway.

"Let me pass," she said simply.

But like the rocks piled there for a millennium, he did not move. Sighing, Miranda stepped to him, rested her hand on his crossed arms, and leaned up to kiss him. She brushed a tender peck to his firm, unyielding mouth.

"Flirtation will not weaken my resolve." But his voice sounded hoarse, as it had done in their shared bed when he was aroused for her. "I intend to wait until you turn around and walk back to the carriage." He had summoned a coach from the nearest village by the will of his mind, when they had flown there.

She'd wondered why he had wanted a carriage—now she knew. It was a place to deposit her, to keep her out of the way.

"I could follow you in," she argued.

"I'd sense you, love. Give me your word that you will not."

She tried darting around him, but when she moved quickly, dizziness struck her and she lost her balance. She almost fell headlong on the pile of rocks in the doorway.

Zayan grabbed her arm. "Whatever your power is, you are not a witch or a demon. You give life—which, in my mind, makes you closer to a goddess. Entering the Underworld could suck the power from you. It could destroy you."

She wished the fiercely protective gleam in his eyes did not leave her breathless. "I am dying anyway, Zayan. This is my last hope."

But his grip tightened. "I am afraid this is a trap, Miranda. The *Pravus* is considered the feminine form of evil. I believe she lied to Lukos to lure him here; she tempted him with the one thing that would send him stupidly back into Lucifer's lair. Lucifer gambled you would follow. Lucifer and the *Pravus* could be two halves of one whole. Man and woman. Combined, they represent the whole of evil in the world. I think Lucifer wants your power."

"You think he wants to capture me?" she asked slowly. At Zayan's curt nod, she tipped up her chin. "Then I had best go in. How else will he capture me if I don't?"

Zayan's jaw dropped. Her cavalier words had left him so stunned she readily slipped past him and scrambled up the rocks. At the very top of the pile, she spotted a small hole. For-tunately, she was slim and tiny. In a blink of an eye, she was in-side.

* * *

Blasted snow. It whirled around Zayan suddenly, blinding him. It had changed to hail, into stinging lumps of ice that pelted him. Snow could halt an army in its tracks. It could crush a man and smother him. It had the power to destroy a mountainside and raze trees.

And, damnation, he had tried to stop the snow with his magic, but it had not worked. Which meant that here, so close to the Underworld, his power was drained.

Zayan ripped out a large rock from the walled-up entrance and tossed it over his shoulder. Three more quickly followed, shaking the ground as they hit. Hades, this threesome magic was not going to work. He wanted to possess Miranda for his own. He had captured entire civilizations for Rome. He had taken thousands of slaves, treasures worth a king's ransom. He was not a man who willingly *shared.*

But he had to. That was the madness of it. If he did not learn to play nice with Lukos and share, Miranda would die.

Cursing below his breath, Zayan plunged into the tunnel that led into the burial chamber of the burrow. He scented Miranda—the sweet, fresh smell of her. Here in the dark, with the snow hurtling behind him, Miranda smelled of sunshine.

Her gown swished, revealing to him she was striding somewhere in the dark ahead. In a heartbeat, he could see her—the gold of her hair, the fluttering movement of her cloak. He rushed forward with inhuman speed, caught her as she ducked low, and stepped into a stone chamber.

At least she did not try to outrun him, or even to shake him off. She looked relieved on seeing him. With a shudder, she whispered, "I glimpsed Lukos's thoughts before. I saw what he went through to enter the Underworld. I saw what we have to face to get from here—"she swept her hand to encompass the room—"to Lucifer."

Zayan surveyed the chamber they were in. Primitive. Large

stone blocks fashioned the walls, and long, broad flat stones had been laid across them to make a roof. Dirt had been mounded over top. Inside, there was nothing except a stone table that held a chalice and spear. There were hundreds of these burial chambers across the country. But this one was not a grave. It was an entrance.

"There is a portal," Zayan said gently, "but mortals do not survive passing through it." Miranda was not entirely mortal. Did that make her safe? If Lucifer did want her, he would acquire her. For now, Zayan would play the devil's game. He would make it appear he was allowing Miranda to go in search of her beloved Lukos. "Most mortals, though, do not possess magic." He heard the heart-wrenching sound of Miranda swallowing. To moisten a dry, frightened throat, he suspected.

"Have you been here?" she asked.

"No." But he had heard the tales from demons who had. "There are tests. The very instant you cross the threshold of the labyrinth, you will believe a thousand insects are crawling on your skin. Most people rake themselves bloody tearing at them. But they exist only in your mind. You have to remember that, Miranda."

She gaped at him, and he could hear the rapid beat of her heart—an undercurrent to the motionless air in the tomb and the suffocating sensation of silence.

"It's a test, love. Entering the Underworld is not as simple as rapping on the doorknocker of a London home."

Miranda looked grim. But her lips lifted in an ironic smile, and he knew she had found courage. "I know that. I am not afraid. But I truly hate bugs."

Zayan clasped her hand in his and led her to the most easterly side of the chamber. He quickly found the rough circle, made of stone laid in the earthen floor of the chamber. Miranda stared at it, slowly turning to examine it. Zayan crouched and touched four of the stones, one after the other—the stones that would make the points on a compass. Suddenly the earth dissolved beneath their feet but instead of falling, both he and Miranda lowered slowly to a chamber below. As their feet touched the rough, rocky surface beneath them, the hole above them sealed over. His vision easily detected the series of pitch-black tunnels leading off in different direction. And his demonic senses allowed him to immediately select the one they wanted.

"Welcome, Miranda, to the labyrinth," Zayan murmured.

Something was crawling up her neck. It moved slowly, a tickle along her skin. It was driving her mad. There had to be something there. It felt so real. It even . . . slithered . . .

Miranda choked down a scream. In the darkness of the tunnel, she couldn't see anything, not even her own hands, but her mind could not possibly play tricks like this. She had to get it off her neck—

Zayan's hand closed around her forearm, restraining her. "Don't touch. Don't scratch. Once you begin, you won't stop. You'll claw at your skin until you tear through it. Until you are so desperate and mad, you gouge your eyes out."

"It's real," she gasped. She knew what he had done . . . "You *lied* to me when you said it was all in my mind. You did it so I wouldn't panic—" Something tickled her *cheek*. "This is real. All these horrid little legs are really walking on my skin."

Zayan's left hand, surrounded by a faint emerald green glow, settled on her shoulder. The glow slowly washed over her body, and the revolting sensation of a million little insect feet on her flesh vanished.

She turned gratefully to Zayan, then shrieked.

He was covered in insects. These were real—awful, crawling, smelly ones. And everywhere on his body.

Casually, he blew one away from his lips, before grinning at her. In the dark, his eyes had turned an eerie blood red—the same vivid red as the *Pravus*. She reached out, intending to brush a—a large, ugly, furry spider off his back—

He caught her hand. "Don't," he repeated calmly. "Once we pass far enough, they'll vanish."

"Aren't they biting you?"

"Of course. I'm undead, so they can fill me with as much venom as they want."

He was mad, utterly mad. Bugs were literally dripping off him, clinging to his cloak, vanishing into his long, thick hair, yet Zayan stormed relentlessly onward. Every inch the Roman general. Yet now, when she looked at him, Miranda saw more of the devoted father.

She cringed with her every step. Zayan waited, then grasped her hand.

Once they had soldiered onward for another yard along the rocky passage, the insects began to buzz, and the sound heightened until it was a high-pitched scream that rattled Miranda's teeth in her head and made her ears pound. She clamped her hands to her head to block out the sound.

It grew so bad, she feared her head would burst.

Then it stopped and the bugs had vanished. The green glow faded from her body, and she felt . . . normal. Her skin no longer felt as though it were alive with insects, and the horrid, rancid smell of them was gone.

Zayan had protected her from the worst of it, and as she looked up, he gave her a slow smile.

"What's next?" she asked.

"The succubi."

Shuddering, Miranda remembered the vision she'd had of Lukos and the woman in this place. Zayan inclined his handsome head. "What would the devil be without an army of female slaves designed to fuck you to death?"

She caught her breath at his coarse word, and his smile—a smile that would encourage any succubus to leap upon him. "You are enjoying this." It was a battle—and he had lived for battle. He all but burned with excitement now. Was that who

Zayan was at his core—a general in constant need of a war? Did it mean he could ever accept peace and happiness? Could he ever be content with love?

Miranda swallowed hard. She had to find Lukos, or she would die. Her world, for the last few days, had shrunk down to the immediate—live or die, fight or be destroyed, seek the truth or perish if she didn't find it. She had not thought of the future. She had an impoverished baron for a brother, and a lovely, thoroughly normal sister-in-law. But she was in love with two vampires. How could she ever think to blend those two worlds? Did loving Zayan and Lukos mean leaving her family forever? And she did not have forever. As far as she knew, she was mortal.

She would die and they would live on without her.

She shook off the thoughts. Right now, she was very, very mortal—she felt her strength fade with each passing minute.

Come forward. Come to us. Oh, come to us, please.

Soft, melodic feminine voices seemed to fill her mind. The sound was lovely, like the whisper of a breeze through leaves on a decadently warm summer's day or like the gentle music of a brook. Their voices, while faint, were low-pitched and filled with aching need.

Miranda tensed, certain the women would appear around Zayan.

She was not prepared for a female hand to come out of nowhere, reach out, and squeeze her breast. *This one is delectable. Her breasts are full and ripe. The nipple puckered as soon as my fingers brushed. And it is so perfectly round.*

A flush swept down from Miranda's cheeks to bathe her throat and chest. "Show yourselves," she demanded, hoping the waver in her voice was not so obvious.

Of course, came the melodic answer in a chorus of high-pitched voices. Mist streamed through the dark, then swiftly took solid form. Six women. They stood in order of height. All were naked—why was she surprised? Each was an astonishing beauty. All possessed glossy hair that flowed to their hips. Two had red hair, two were dark haired, and the last pair had golden blond tresses, paler than hers.

One of the blondes clapped her hands. *Look at him. He is so very beautiful—*

Wait! Look at his eyes.

The naked women all stared at Zayan. His dark, reflective eyes had become narrowed slits and the irises glowed red between his lids.

This one was made by the power of blood. By the Pravus Semper.

One of the redheads moved forward, her hips swinging alluringly. *I am strong enough for him. Come, sisters. Three of us together can have him. The power of three will be enough.*

Miranda jerked in surprise. The power of three?

Three women rushed to her. She was pulled to a divan that appeared out of nowhere, that looked like a soft, white cloud. Six surprisingly powerful arms pushed her down on it. The softness broke her fall. Hands hurriedly tore at her clothes, opening her cloak, then wresting the buttons of her gown free.

"Stop!" she cried. Out of the corner of her eye, she spied one succubus drop to her knees in front of Zayan's crotch, and another bend to fondle, then kiss, his derriere. All the while he laughed, while the third woman lifted her large breasts to point her nipples suggestively at his mouth.

"Leave me," he rumbled. "Pleasure my partner. I would like to see her with six naked women intent on making her come."

Miranda sputtered in shock. The women chorused, "No, sir. We have waited so long for another man to venture here. We have been so lonely, so empty inside. We wish you to fill us, fill us all."

"Our cunnies," the blonde cried.

"And I would like your rigid rod inside my rump," added the brunette.

"It would give me the greatest pleasure to suck you," whispered the redhead.

Miranda gasped as a warm waft of air teased her breasts. She had been so intent on watching Zayan, she hadn't noticed the women ease down her bodice. Two women bent to her breasts as one, tongues out, licking her curves. Eagerly, they both took her nipples into their mouths and suckled vigorously.

She melted. There was no other word for it. As the women teased her erect nipples with their hot mouths, her lower body felt like liquid honey. An orgasm rippled through her—in slow, deliciously gentle waves of pleasure. But they did not have time to waste. "We want to go to the Underworld," she said crisply, pushing the women away. She felt like a puddle of desire, but pulled up her bodice. "We must go to Lucifer. I believe," she added, "that he wants me."

Five of the women retreated, but one of the brunettes stepped forward. An evil smile played on her lips. "Indeed, he does. And we should not delay you from your appointment with our master. But there is only one way to enter his lair. You must be either dead—or undead."

"I am not either." As she spoke, she backed up on the divan. She saw a red mist suddenly wrap around Zayan. He roared, struggled against it, and threw magic at it, but it held him. She'd expected a blow from the brunette—but another hand launched out and a blade glinted. The blade hit her throat and dug into her flesh.

Then the lethally sharp edge swiped across her neck. It tickled at first, then stung. Coldness seeped into her throat. Then the pain was excruciating and her throat filled with fluid.

It must be her blood.

She couldn't breathe.

"Damnation!" Zayan stumbled toward her, as she helplessly clutched at her throat. Sickeningly, the blood poured over her hands. A pass of his hand, and searing purple light hit her throat.

The blood stopped, but her hands fell away. She couldn't control them. They were numb. She could not focus on the women anymore. Her body was limp.

Zayan pressed his arm to her mouth. She could not understand why. Magic? What did he want her to do?

"Drink, angel. Drink now."

Something smeared her lip. She tasted copper and sweetness, and it flowed suddenly. But she was growing weaker—

"It's not working," he roared.

Miranda felt her arm lift. She had not commanded it to do so—Zayan had clasped her hand and he was moving it. He pressed her hand to her heart and laid his overtop. "Don't—" His raspy voice broke. "You can't die. I won't allow it." Dimly, she saw him tip his head back and shout to the darkness, "I will trade my life for hers. My power—damn you, you can have it all."

Warmth. She knew the familiar warmth of her own power, but it flowed down her arm, through her heart, and back to her arm again. A circle. An impossible loop giving her life.

She struggled to sit up. Suddenly, her hand flew up. She'd been trying to lift it, and it unexpectedly moved at her command. She touched her throat. Afraid. But her fingertips skimmed over smooth skin. There was no wound.

"You're alive," Zayan said in amazement. Then she heard the choked laughter. A broken sob of relief. In his eyes, she saw joy—the same deep happiness he had shown toward his children.

She managed to nod.

"I couldn't change you." He sounded more frightened than she had ever heard him. "I could not make you into a vampire. It was your own power that saved you."

"I'm not undead." And, thankfully, not *dead*. But she couldn't enter hell unless she was.

Wrong, my dear angel. A deep baritone flooded the room, echoing in her head.

Miranda felt the air whip around her, like frothed cream. The succubi disappeared. The divan remained beneath her, thank heaven, for she was laid out on it, her arms spread wide, her chest heaving to catch breath.

She flew up into the air off the sofa. She reached down and clasped Zayan's wrist, as though he could keep her moored to the ground. He held her tight, and she saw his stark fear.

Then everything around her, the chaise, the rock walls and floor and ceiling of the passage, vanished.

The darkness melted away.

Miranda was aware of white. White surrounded her, so pure and gleaming it was almost painfully blinding. It wasn't a bright light—it was a solid space with a floor and walls. A gentle rushing sound flooded her ears. For several moments, she could not believe what she was looking at.

This was the Underworld?

Miranda felt as though she was in a seraglio; she had seen paintings of the eastern harems. She stood in a room entirely covered in white tiles, though fanciful patterns of small colored tiles decorated the arched openings and the floor. The scene reminded her of the ones she had seen through the eyes of Mucius Gaius. Water cascaded down a series of steps, to splash in a luxurious pool in the center of the massive room. Women reclined around the pool or sat on the edge and lazily kicked their legs in the blue depths. The soft sound of their conversations, the hushed murmurs, the giggles, danced like seductive music in the humid air.

Where were the fires? The eternal darkness? The brimstone?

Desperately, Miranda turned in a slow circle. She could not see Zayan. There were no men at all in the room—except one. He was naked, and horns rose from his sharp-featured and merciless-looking face. He reclined amongst silks and pillows, but steam in the air from the water hung like a veil in front of him. Through it, she could make out the long, curved horns, then broad shoulders, a chest heavy with muscle. She'd expected a creature like a satyr, with the hindquarters of a beast, but he possessed human legs. And a massive erection that had to be two feet in length.

"Approach, my lovely Miranda," he urged. His voice filled the bathing room. It wasn't loud, it simply consumed her every sense. It was as though she could also taste his voice and smell it. It sent a quiver of awareness down her spine. Though she tried to fight her instinctive reaction, her nipples tightened, her quim grew warm and wet.

"Where is Zayan?" she called out, and her voice echoed off the tile. The other women ignored her as though she did not exist. "And Lukos? What have you done to him?"

"No curiosity about me, my dear? Or perhaps you would like to see me in a more palatable form."

He changed—she watched him the entire time, stared at him, and she could not explain how his face distorted, how his body took on a new shape, how his hair changed from an unearthly red-black to a pale silvery blond.

In mere moments, the transformation was done.

She was staring in to the handsome sky-blue eyes of Mr. Ryder.

"After all, my angel," Lucifer said through Mr. Ryder's beautiful mouth, as he rose from his silver throne, "all people who surrender to the temptation of evil have a little bit of the devil in them. You are perhaps one of the few mortals I have encountered who does not. Which is why you can walk here without harm, and why you have the power to give life. The *Pravus* was the embodiment of evil. I do not know what you are—there are more things in heaven and hell than even Satan can contemplate." He stopped and bestowed a wicked smile on her. "But I believe you are the embodiment of love. When you love, you give life."

The embodiment of love. The words stunned her, stealing her capacity to speak.

Lucifer clapped his hands again and the wall behind him disappeared. Miranda saw a sheer wall of gray rock. And Lukos chained to it, hand and foot.

An evil chuckle rippled up her spine.

"You are too late, Miranda. Lukos made his deal with me. His sister has been freed, and he is now mine. Your love cannot rescue him. I won't take anything in trade. You are mine, whether I free him or not."

No, she wasn't. She would not be. "Where is Zayan?" she croaked.

"Imprisoned within rock in the labyrinth."

Damn the devil and his bloody silver shackles and his damned cell carved into a wall of rock. Zayan roared his anger, but the rock in front of him was brushing his nose. His shout bounced around in the narrow opening in which he was confined, almost deafening him.

Two stoop-backed stinking demon serfs had chained him here; then Lucifer had clapped his hands and a wall of rock had slammed down in front of him.

Where was Miranda?

He'd been a damned fool to let her come here. The devil was the most powerful evil being in existence. How could he have dreamed he could protect Miranda from Lucifer?

Miranda, who had, against all odds and all that was possible, given him his children back. He would do anything for her.

There had to be a way out. He'd defeated the Gauls with his wits more than his might. Even the most powerful army would fall if led by an idiot.

He had to think . . .

Whatever Lucifer wanted from Miranda, he would not take it quickly. The devil would believe he had all eternity to do it.

Zayan?

He heard it. The whisper of Miranda's voice—that soft, husky, bewitching sound. She spoke his name. She was searching for him.

He threw his thoughts to her—a reassurance he was safe and alive, but imprisoned. A promise he would escape to rescue her. Where are you?

Essentially I am in the devil's bathtub.

What?

I thought hell was a place of putrid brimstone and fire. But the devil actually resides in a pristine-white bathing chamber like an indulgent sultan.

He marveled at the trace of humor in her voice. Miranda was remarkably strong. *The devil shows you what he believes you want to see, to entrance you and entice you before he takes your soul. Stay strong, love, and resist him. I will come to you . . . Miranda?*

But no answer came to him. Panicked, Zayan dragged hopelessly on the shackles and chains once more, but the magical silver held him tight. In anguish, he slammed his forehead against the rock.

Freeing Ara was worth his life, but he'd never dreamed Miranda would come for him. Lukos let his head lean back against the rock behind him so he could see Miranda's face. Blood oozed from slowly healing cuts. In the Underworld, his vampiric powers were reduced. Pain lanced him everywhere. He had been beaten by Lucifer's demons and tortured by Lucifer himself with burning rods.

Where was Ara? Lucifer had released her, but to where? As soon as the devil had agreed to the bargain—his life for her release and her safety—Lukos knew the mistake he'd made. He had not been specific enough. Lucifer could have sent Ara anywhere. She would be lost, alone, in a world that had changed drastically in the thousand years of her imprisonment.

She could be in danger.

And Miranda was in deadly peril. The feisty woman had faced Lucifer with her chin tipped up and courage gleaming in her blue eyes. He could sense her fear, but also her mastery of it. She amazed him.

Lukos, can you hear me?

Miranda's words came to him. *Yes. Are you hurt?* he answered. *How did you pass through the labyrinth? Christ Jesus, angel, the only way to enter Satan's world is to—*

No, not for me. Some horrid woman sliced my throat, but the wound healed and I survived. I was able to heal myself—

With your strength.

With all our strength, I think. Now that I have heard your voice and Zayan's, I feel stronger again.

Not strong enough to defeat the devil, love.

No, she answered. *Strong enough to save him.*

Save him. What in blazes did she mean? Then he remembered her touching the small village children, and he remembered her resurrecting Zayan's son and daughter. He knew what she was going to do. *Don't. Christ, Miranda, don't go near him.*

I love you, Lukos.

God, no. Miranda—don't. Don't touch him. He'll kill you— he'll take your power. Stop, Miranda. Then desperately he shouted to her, *I love you.*

*Miranda—*Zayan's hoarse voice broke into his shared communication with Miranda. *I love you. I love you too. I believed I had to have you for my own. But my love for you is so great, so all-consuming, I'm willing to share.*

"I am too," Lukos hollered aloud. "Anything for you, angel."

He fought in vain to free himself, and as he watched, magically, the scene in Lucifer's lair, he saw Miranda calmly approach Lucifer—the being who had taken his life, then his soul, then his precious sister's future and hopes and sanity. He would be damned if he let Lucifer take Miranda, the woman Lukos loved.

And then he saw something else.

Sparks of light crackled in the air around her.

Miranda had never felt so powerful before.

The declaration of love had heightened her magic. Her feet were not even touching the tiled floor. She moved her arm and her body floated. She felt as though she were sizzling. She felt like—like a bolt of lightning.

How could she have summoned so much magic here, in this place that was under Lucifer's control?

It didn't matter. Only one thing did.

"Stop there, woman. Do not approach me."

Miranda obeyed Lucifer, and saw the slow smile of power come again to his mouth. Before her eyes, he shifted form again. He was no longer handsome Mr. Ryder, but a beast with horns and fangs.

Confident, arrogant, the devil turned his attention to the woman splashing in the pool.

Miranda leapt into the air and flew across the room, quickly enough that Lucifer did not move or defend himself. In an instant, she was before him. He jerked around to her, his eyes blazing red. But she reached out and touched his chest, over his heart.

19

Dawn

Lucifer howled in agony, his screech ringing off the tiled walls and ceiling. His nymphs—or succubi—began to scream, as though they shared his pain. Water splashed wildly, the women writhing and weeping all around Miranda.

The devil's eyes became scarlet, and his fingers morphed into sharp, curved claws. But his arms were locked straight, his body lifted off his chaise, tension evident in his rigidity.

Miranda had no idea what she was doing. Had Lucifer lost his soul? He was a fallen angel, but could her power resurrect him? And to what?

She could not pull away, and he could not break free. Her touch had bonded them, and a golden glow encompassed them both.

The embodiment of love, he had called her.

She remembered touching the young boy in the park, and the boy who had been felled by the carriage in the inn's courtyard. To return life, she had to sincerely want him to be saved. She had to yearn for it with all her heart.

She wanted Zayan and Lukos to be freed, and Lukos to escape the bargain he'd made.

The clawed hands began to soften, the fingers drooping. A red light streamed out of Lucifer's eyes, as though the power she was sending in was forcing the light to surge out.

"Cease," he croaked. "You may have your demons free. Pull your hand from my chest, you damned witch."

"I'm not a witch," she shouted with pride. "But I will spare you—" But in truth, she could not believe what was happening. How could she have the power to vanquish Lucifer? "I will spare you, if you release Zayan and Lukos, and you let them go free. You can wreak no vengeance upon them, nor harm anyone they love. You must release them from your service. Zayan must be released from the red power, the *Pravus*, if it exists."

His body was collapsing, sinking. "I will. You have my promise. You cannot destroy me. You cannot upset the balance of the human world. Stop."

Miranda, you have to stop.

"Aunt Eugenia?" Stunned, Miranda instinctively jerked her head around. But she had heard her aunt in her thoughts.

The vampire queens, along with Althea and Serena, have given me the power to speak to you. It is the truth, there must be a balance of good and evil, and Lucifer must rule the Underworld, for mortals need the threat of his realm.

But I want Lukos and Zayan to be free. I want to stop him from creating demons—

You cannot, Miranda. Good and evil will always exist. And if you destroy him, you will take his place. You will become the devil. You've done enough.

Was that true? She couldn't take the chance it was. *But what of the queens?* she shouted in her thoughts to her aunt. *Lukos believes they want me destroyed.*

They are afraid of you, Aunt Eugenia answered. *That is the truth. But they also believe you can use your power to return Zayan's and Lukos's souls. They believe it might drain your*

power completely to make them mortal again. They would have
nothing to fear from you then. You would be safe . . .

It would drain her power. She would be normal, with nothing to hide any longer.

A jolt of pain shot through her. Grimacing, she gazed down
upon the devil. He was beginning to grow smaller, as though
her power was draining his essence and shriveling him up. The
sensation of power left her heady. She could destroy Satan.

She could do whatever she wished . . .

And what she wanted to do was find happiness and love, not
rule the Underworld. She did not want to destroy. She never had.

With a scream, she ripped her hand off Lucifer's chest. His
form slumped to the white chair. Instantly, he grew larger, his
limbs straightening.

The golden glow surrounding her hand burst suddenly in a
shower of glittering sparks.

Gold swiftly turned to black and Miranda pitched forward
into a cold, fathomless void.

The black ground hurtled at him and slammed hard into his
chest. Lukos lifted his chest, blew out a mouthful of melting snow,
and rolled onto his back, feeling the cold through his bare skin.
What in blazes had happened? One moment, he'd been Lucifer's
captive. Now he was beneath the night sky, with snowflakes
peppering his face—

Miranda.

What had she done?

"Lukos? He *freed* you? Good heavens, I cannot believe he
actually kept his promise." Miranda's babbled words poured
over him and he jerked toward her. He rose to his feet as her
warm body barreled into him. Her cheek pressed tight to his
chest, and her disheveled hair tickled him. At once her arms
wrapped tight around him. "I thought he would cheat me—"

He pulled her back, clutching her arms. "What did you do? What did you promise him for my freedom?"

Snow melted on her lovely pink lips. Gold waves of hair fell in tangles around her face—the most beautiful face he knew he'd ever seen, because it was hers.

"I didn't promise him anything. I made him promise me to let you go."

"How did you force the devil to make a promise?"

"I touched his heart."

"I told you not to—" he began. Then stopped. She had done it and survived.

"I assumed he'd lost his soul and I wanted to return it. But instead of giving him life, I was sucking his out of him. So I stopped—in return for our safety and your freedom."

"You must be one of the most powerful beings in existence."

Adamantly, she shook her head. "When you and Zayan said you both loved me, I felt my power grow. It is the three of us together who are powerful." She stared over his shoulder, and a smile curved her lips. "Zayan!" Then to Lukos, she cried, "I have you both safe. I could not ask for more."

Zayan, who was stumbling in the field rubbing his head, looked up and saw them. A broad grin spread on his face, and he ran toward them.

"Thank heaven," she breathed. Lukos cradled her as she pressed tight to his chest again. "When I found I was out in this field, I feared I was alone here at first. I feared I'd lost you both." Then she stepped back. "Are you not cold? Since you are naked?"

He had to laugh. She'd literally gone through hell for him and now worried a bit of snow would hurt him. To satisfy her, he created a cloak to cover his body. And when he summoned it, he let it fall around her too.

Zayan had reached them. Lukos willingly let her go into Zayan's embrace. At the general's questioning look, he nodded.

"I can share her. She loves us both, and I think it would be impossible to make her choose. I want her to be happy."

"As do I." Zayan hugged her and kissed the top of her head. His brow furrowed. "Over there—on the field. I see movement and sense a heartbeat."

A heartbeat . . . Barely daring to hope, Lukos jerked around. A woman was hugging her body as she stumbled across the field. The glimmer of reflected light on the snow revealed she was naked, and her long golden hair fell to her hips.

"*Ara*. Christ Jesus, that is my sister."

A wave of Zayan's hand and a cloak appeared around Ara's slender form. She stopped in her tracks and stared down at it in amazement.

Miranda clasped his arm, and Lukos met her gaze—he saw the faint tremble of her lips, the gentle smile. "Go to her," she urged. "But bring her back to us. We must go back to the slayers. Zayan's children are there. They are helping us, and I know they will help your sister too."

"Dawn's close," Zayan added.

But Lukos stared at Miranda. "Slayers? You left Zayan's children with vampire slayers?"

She nodded. "Althea, Serena, my aunt, and the men of course."

He looked to Zayan, who quirked a brow. "It is true. It appears we've struck a truce."

What astounded Lukos was not the fact that Zayan and Miranda had trusted vampire slayers. It was the reality of freedom. It struck him suddenly. He had escaped servitude to Lucifer and had rescued Ara. He had gone to this Underworld knowing he would have to sacrifice his life, believing he would not survive to have Miranda.

But he had. And after one thousand years, he was finally free.

All because of Miranda. His amazing, magical woman—

who was staring at him in shock. "Your hair!" she gasped. "The color has changed. It's golden blond."

The color it had been when he had been a mortal. He grasped a lock to see for himself. Sure enough, it was the color of autumn grass waving in a field. "I think its proof, angel, that you've freed me."

"Well, my dear, you are the only person I've known who has seen the Underworld, and who has done combat with Lucifer and won!"

Aunt Eugenia grasped Miranda's hand and drew her away from Lukos and Zayan, leading her down the hall of Blackthorne Castle. She looked back, but Eugenia insisted, "They will be fine. Zayan should go to his children, and Lukos's sister Ara needs him right now. She must heal from a horrific ordeal. And there is someone I wish to see."

Miranda found herself at the door to a bedchamber. A man lay within, swaddled beneath the heavy counterpane. Stealing forward, Miranda recognized Lord Blackthorne. "What happened to him?"

"He was found by the grooms, wandering naked near his stables, confused and weak. He was babbling about a red mist, and of a siren's voice calling to him."

"The red mist? Did it possess him as it did Mr. Ryder?"

Aunt Eugenia crossed her arms. "I believe so, but when the mist vanished, he was freed. He also spoke of you."

"Me?"

She remembered that moment in the village inn, when she'd had her romantic dreams dashed. She had found true love, though, and it was much deeper and richer than the infatuation she'd built up for Blackthorne.

Her aunt nodded. "He said he had fallen in love with Miranda Bond, a woman he could never have, because the siren told him she was the lover of two powerful demons."

Miranda flushed.

"I know it is the truth, my dear. I can also see that they are deeply in love with you."

"Will he recover?"

"I believe so."

"What of James Ryder? Has he been found?"

Adjusting the lace fichu at her neck, Eugenia said, "Yes, he was found on the castle grounds just before he died. He confessed to what he had done—he had been paid by rogue members of the Royal Society to destroy you. With the money, he intended to destroy his titled father and make the man pay for ignoring him."

"And he died?"

"Yes, his life force had been tied to that of the *Pravus*. When that was destroyed, his life force gave out. He managed to survive a few hours, to try to escape, but that was all. He was a vicious man. An evil one."

Miranda had to agree with that. "So the *Pravus* was destroyed? It is gone?"

"For now," Aunt Eugenia said. "The vampire queens believe a new one will eventually be born. Evil always exists in the world. It is our mission to combat it, to control it, and to help people turn it away."

There was something Miranda had to ask. She caught her aunt's sleeve. "When I was trying to return Lucifer's soul, you spoke in my mind. That is true, isn't it? It was really you."

Eugenia nodded.

"You told me that I could return Zayan's and Lukos's souls. Why? Do you believe they would want me to?"

"Elizabeth told me the vampire queens want you to. For them, it ensures the vampires cannot use their power to overthrow the queens. And for Zayan and Lukos—"

"They would lose their immortality."

"You are not immortal, my dear."

Miranda turned away from Blackthorne's chamber and her aunt closed the door. "Zayan tried to change me in the Underworld, when one of the succubi cut my throat. He could not make me into a vampire, though I did heal myself—with his help."

Eugenia embraced her. "For Zayan and Lukos to be at peace, I believe they should become mortal once more. Otherwise, the queens will never rest easy, and may prosecute Zayan and Lukos for past crimes. They do have the power to banish both men again."

"Are you implying that I should try to return their souls for their own protection, whether they want it or not?"

Her aunt drew back to face her. "No, love. I am advising you to ask them what they want."

But Miranda did not have the chance to be alone with Lukos and Zayan for another day. After they left Blackthorne's bedchamber, Eugenia took her to one of the drawing rooms, in which the vampire slayers had gathered, along with Lukos, Zayan, and Zayan's children. Ara was resting in her own bedchamber.

Miranda caught her breath as she recognized a man who sat in the corner of the room—Lord Denby, the man she had encountered on the mountain road, the gentleman of the Royal Society who had been betrayed by his compatriot. Lord Denby rose, crossed quickly to her, and bowed over her hand. "I must take my leave of you, Miss Bond. It is urgent I return to London. It appears there is much rot in the Royal Society that needs to be rooted out, and I am making it my task to do so." He inclined his head toward Eugenia. "It will be the mandate of the Royal Society to understand the world of magic, demons, vampires, and the like, not destroy it."

Eugenia nodded with satisfaction.

Deciding to trust Denby, who appeared to have the support of everyone in the room, from the smiles and nods that traveled around the group, Miranda clasped his hand. "I think that is wise, Lord Denby."

She noticed then a handsome, silver-haired bespectacled man who had moved to stand at her aunt's side. Althea introduced him as her father, Sir Edmund Yates. He also bowed over Miranda's hand. "I have heard much of your unique abilities from Miss Bond."

Her unmarried aunt, of course, had the same name as she did. She caught the looks of admiration—and smoldering interest—passing between Sir Edmund and Eugenia. She looked to Zayan and Lukos. Zayan was bouncing Marc on his knee, and Lukos was teasingly tugging Lina's braids. Both men sensed her gaze, and each one winked at her.

It could have been a scene in any English drawing room. The children scuttled down to the floor before the fire and played on the carpet. Althea and Serena gracefully perched on their seats, their men standing at their sides. Sir Edmund Yates was excitedly recounting stories of researching vampire lore in the Carpathians to Eugenia. But after an hour, Miranda almost fell asleep on her chair—in the midst of telling her own story of the labyrinth to the Underworld yet again.

Laughing, Lukos scooped her up to take her to bed, but Aunt Eugenia stopped him to clasp Miranda's hands. She whispered, "What you have, my dear, is a gift. The gift to heal and to give love. And whether you possess magic powers or not, you will always have that gift."

Whether she possessed magic powers or not.

Would Lukos and Zayan want to be moral—as she was? But her head felt too wooly to worry then. Her thought began to fade . . .

Lukos carried her to her bedroom, and she fell asleep in his arms.

* * *

Billows of steam and an exotic, flowery fragrance met Miranda as, smiling, Althea pushed open the door to the bathing chamber. The women had told her that she'd slept for a day and half!

Serena nudged her. "Go inside. They planned this like excited schoolboys. I never imagined I would see Lukos—who always seemed so frightening to me—look so vulnerable."

"I believe love does that to every man," Althea added. Then they both propelled Miranda into the room and backed out, shutting the door behind them.

An enormous bathtub stood in the middle of the chamber. Lukos lounged in the water, a glass of brandy in his right hand. His wet hair was slicked back, darkened to rich amber, and droplets clung to his lashes and full lips. She was not quite used to his blond hair, though it was beautiful.

Silver reflections glinted in his eyes, rippling like water. "Come here, Miranda. I want to taste you on my lips more than wine."

She knew what he meant, her heart making a merry dance of arousal in her chest. Zayan stepped out of the shadows, naked, and he stripped her bare with a wave of his hand. She should have expected it, but it still astonished her when her buttons opened themselves and her gown slithered off her body of its own accord. Winking, Zayan set her petticoats whirling up around her, a froth of white lace.

Then he came up behind her. He nuzzled her neck while her corset magically unlaced itself. As her shift leapt over her head and pirouetted by itself to the floor, he cradled her breasts. Her hard nipples tightened even more as he whispered, "I want to taste every inch of you, myself. I love you."

Lukos crooked his finger to urge her to come to him, then flicked out his tongue. She knew exactly what he intended to do.

She stood still, her hair loose and falling to the small of her back. Zayan's breath gently brushed her shoulder blades. She knew she should ask them now. She had to offer to make them mortal—

To protect them all.

Lukos reached out, water sloshing around him, clamped his hand over her bottom, and dragged her cunny to his mouth. And she knew it was not the time to talk of serious things. But she was so tense, his tongue slicking her clit made her almost melt to the floor.

She had to grip the edge of the tub. From her view, she could see his golden head at her quim, his big shoulders, the beautiful, muscled vee of his back. She could see his tailbone, and the curves of his arse disappearing into the water.

Just the sight of him seduced her.

And he was using magic. It felt as though his tongue was teasing her clit and her anus at the same time. But in her thoughts, he murmured, *I was betrayed by the demoness who took me into the Underworld. I believed I'd lost Ara, whom I adored, and you helped me rescue her. You've wiped away the pain of my past, Miranda, and helped me to discover love.*

You have done that for both of us, Miranda. Saved us from the wasted existence of anger and vengeance, and opened our hearts to love. Zayan tweaked her nipples, sending shock waves down to her throbbing clit. "We vowed to share you, Miranda."

Lukos stopped suckling. "And when we share, I want . . . mmm, the bottom half."

"Lukos," she gasped.

Zayan tickled his fingers down her spine, making her jump. He nuzzled the nape of her neck. "You can have the back, Lukos. I'll have the front."

Gazing down at Lukos, at the droplets of water that beaded on his lashes, lashes that swept over his eyes and revealed the vulnerability in his heart, Miranda whispered, "I want to kiss you both. I love you both. It is as simple as that."

She crouched until she was at the same height as Lukos's

face. He wrapped his wet, muscular arm around her. Miranda gave herself to the magic of his slow, sensual kiss. Her blood burned with the heat of it.

Then Lukos broke the kiss and took her hand. Clasping his fingers, she hoisted her leg over the side of the enormous tub. He gave a teasing tug and she fell in with a splash. And surfaced with an indignant splutter. But she climbed on him and licked the water along the edge of his hard jaw.

In a hearbeat, Zayan had joined them. "Tonight," he said, "we are at your command."

"Hell," Lukos chuckled. "The truth is, we are always at your command."

"What is your most illicit fantasy, my love?" Zayan asked, water sloshing around him. "What would you love to do with us that you would be too afraid to ask for?"

"If I am too afraid to ask, I couldn't put it into words, could I?" Miranda felt a blush sweep over her, from the tips of her nipples up to her hairline.

Lukos held her hips and guided her to float over his long, naked body. His cock nudged between the cheeks of her rump. Slicked with the warm water, he eased inside her. He pulled her down on top of him.

Oh, it felt delicious to be floating in the relaxing, hot water, and rocking up and down on Lukos's thick cock. He was huge, filling her rump, and she bit back a sob of intense pleasure.

Bracing his right hand on the tub, Zayan wrapped his left around his cock and stroked her nether lips. She hooked her arms around his neck. Then he surged inside her. The tub rocked as Zayan and Lukos thrust into her with long, powerful strokes.

To be filled by two men . . . It was spectacular. To be loved by two men was heavenly.

She could float between them forever, loving each thrust, each long stroke of their shafts. Pleasure sapped her strength and she lay back against Lukos.

His mouth kissing her neck. Zayan's mouth at her breasts. Two enormous cocks filling her. It was so much. Too much.

On a slow, agonized, cry she climaxed.

Instead of taking her to another, as they usually did, they suddenly bucked into her. They'd lost control so quickly. She closed her eyes, savoring the sensations as their hips harshly pounded against her, as they groaned fiercely, as their hot come filled her.

Both slid out of her, kissed her tenderly, and she knew it was time. "Have you thought of . . . of having your souls back?"

Zayan straightened. He moved to the side, and Lukos turned her face so he could see her eyes. "What do you mean, angel?"

"If you could choose, would you want to be mortal men again, or would you still want to be . . . vampires?"

Zayan stroked her cheek. "Elizabeth told me that despite your magic, you are mortal."

She caught his hand. "That is not why I am asking you. It's just—I have the power to do it. But I do not want either of you to do it for me. It must be what you want. And I—I don't care which way you choose. I love you either way."

"You tried before, Miranda," Zayan reminded her gently. "It didn't work."

"The queens believe it will, so I suspect that love could make the difference."

Lukos eased her off his body, and set the water lapping at her naked shoulders. "I want to be mortal again. I want to be— be human. Change me, Miranda."

Zayan's eyes narrowed. "Elizabeth also told me it would drain your powers. Are you doing this to protect us—and you— from the vampire queens? Because I promise I would never allow one of those women to hurt you."

"No, truly, I just want you both to know you have the choice."

"Try me, angel," Lukos said suddenly.

She took a calming breath. Then reached out as she had done with the devil, but this time, her heart was filled with love as she pressed her hand to Lukos's chest.

I do not feel any different. . . .

Miranda blinked as she opened her eyes. She had woken up remembering Lukos's words. He had spoken them as he and Zayan had toweled her dry after their bath. They had gone to bed with the dawn, and both men had dropped into sleep. Was that a sign she had failed?

True, Zayan had grinned as he had vigorously rubbed her rump. "I've thought of blood and my fangs did not come out. I have no urge to hunt or to feed." He had planted a quick kiss to her nose. "I think, angel, you've done it."

But she hadn't been sure.

She'd realized even if her power had not returned their souls, their capacity to love, their passion, loyalty, and devotion to family had always been there, a part of them. Zayan and Lukos had not embraced evil because they were demons, but because of anger, loss, grief, and the hunger for vengeance.

She loved them, demons or not. And she always would . . .

Sunlight. Shafts of sunlight were playing across the blankets. That must have woken her.

Then she saw what her power—her gift—had done. The drapes had been opened and she was certain her men had ensured they had been carefully closed. Someone had come in and opened them. Or had appeared in the room to do it. Miranda suspected one of the vampire queens.

There must have been clouds in front of the sun, clouds that had now rolled on. Rays of light slanted across Zayan's and Lukos's slumbering bodies. Both men stirred, grunting and grumbling as the light brought them out of sleep.

Miranda's heart soared. The light was not burning their skin. It wasn't going to destroy them. She had returned their souls and made them mortal again. She'd done it . . .

It would mean they could play with the children in the daylight. They would know again the beauty of a clear blue sky. They would see flowers bloom.

Lukos opened his eyes. Slowly, he lifted his arms. In the brilliant light, the soft hairs sprinkling his arms were gold. "You did it." His eyes sparkled at her. A beautiful blend of violet and blue. They did not reflect the light like vampire eyes. "Do you know what I want?" he asked.

"What do you want?" she asked, her heart soaring. She suspected she was being led into naughty banter.

"Ham and eggs. I can smell them cooking."

Laughter bubbled up from her chest.

"And then do you know what I would like to do?"

At his wicked grin, she lifted a brow. "No."

"I have heard of English picnics. A blanket spread on the grass. Bottles of good wine, delicious food, a blue sky above. And the blanket . . . a place for making love beneath the brilliant sun. What I want to do is go on a picnic."

Miranda laughed. "That is the first thing you want to do in the daylight?"

"Not the first."

"Indeed," Zayan said. He tossed back the covers, revealing his wide, sculpted chest. His brow lifted, and he gave a lusty chuckle. His dark eyes glowed at her with happiness. "Not the first."

Hours later, sated and exhausted, Miranda stood at the window, gazing out at the perfect spring day. Lukos and Zayan stood at her side.

"We are now just ordinary men," Zayan observed. His hand rested lightly on her hip.

"Mmm, no," she answered, "I do not think you will ever be that."

"We are fortunate enough to have an extraordinary woman."

Zayan dropped to one knee, and as she stared in shock at him, Lukos did the same thing. "Would you marry us both, Miranda?" Zayan asked.

Marry them both. "Yes," she answered delightedly.

This was a fantasy she would never have dared voice, and now it was coming true. Then the full import of it hit her. "How are we to do this? I have a family—my brother and his wife. And scads of cousins and aunts and uncles. How can I live as a normal Englishwoman married to two men?"

Zayan bent and gave the swell of her left breast a gentle kiss. "Very carefully, love."

The tension inside her broke and she laughed. "I supposed Althea and Serena have done it, so it must be possible. But what of our future, married all together? Where shall we live? What—"

Zayan put his fingers to her lips. "After existing for what seems like eternity, I've learned that all questions do not need to be answered in one day."

Lukos nodded. "We have the future to plan, angel. And for me, that is a remarkably precious thing. The sunlight is a great gift, Miranda, but you are the most wonderful gift of all."

"A treasure worth waiting centuries for," Zayan agreed.

"I am not the treasure." She held up her hand to silence the protest. Beyond the window, blooming flowers bobbed in a gentle breeze. "This is the treasure, as you said. Our love. Joy. The future."

Zayan nodded. "All I had was future and I felt I was damned because of it. Now the thought of *this* future—with you, with children, with love—fills me with joy."

"Thank you, my love—our love," Lukos whispered, "for banishing the darkness and giving us light."

There was truly nothing more precious, more intense, more delicious than love shared between three. Her heart bursting with happiness, and with dreams of the future, Miranda clasped the hands of the two men she adored. And she smiled as she saw Zayan and Lukos tip back their faces, close their eyes, and savor the sun.

Epilogue

Lord Denby cleared his throat and lifted his glass. "To the newlyweds."

Eleven glasses rose to join his. Crystal clinked and laughter followed. Out of the corner of her eye, Miranda caught the inviting smile Aunt Eugenia bestowed upon her new husband, Sir Edmund. He removed his spectacles, raised her hand to his lips, and gave Eugenia's palm a sizzling kiss. Devotion and delight shone in his eyes.

Miranda smiled herself. How wonderful to see Aunt Eugenia happy. What a perfect match she and Sir Edmund made. They planned to hunt through tombs, research moldering old libraries, and search for vampires together.

A year had passed since she had impetuously rushed from her home in a carriage, seeking escape. Now she had a home of her own. Several, actually. A sprawling house built on a breathtaking estate in Hartfordshire, which her two husbands had named Merryworth as a play on her name and to celebrate the happiness they'd all found. As well, they had an elegant townhome in London.

It was not the houses, of course, which made a home, but the people within.

And tonight Merryworth was filled with her loved ones.

As Miranda sipped her watered-down champagne, she looked around the large, round table, an enormous polished oak monstrosity large enough for their nine guests. They were twelve in all—like the Knights of the Round Table. Once it would have seemed impossible that they could all dine together—vampires and mortals, friends who had once been enemies, who had taken a long journey to come together in such a trusting way. But they were all her family now, Miranda realized.

She was married to two wealthy men: Zayan had amassed fabulous wealth over two thousand years, and Lukos was already building a fortune of his own with astute investments. They had ensured her brother, Simon, and her sister-in-law, Caroline, were safe and taken care of, as Simon had vowed to stop gaming. Tonight, Simon and Caroline had retired early to one of the bedchambers, for her sister-in-law was increasing.

Children filled her house today. They were all upstairs in the nursery—Marc and Lina, Serry, and Serena's twin boys, David and Jeremy.

And two tiny bassinets waited for more . . .

Miranda rested her hand on her large, pregnant belly. She knew Althea and Serena yearned to return to the Carpathian Mountains and learn more about the beginnings of vampires. Returning souls to Zayan and Lukos had drained away her strength, and while her men had been happy to become mortal again, the others had been content to remain vampires.

Serena still hoped to find Vlad Dracul's journal, which Denby believed had been returned to the Carpthians by one of the rogue members of the Royal Society. But it would be many months before Serena and her two husbands traveled, with their twins not quite a year old. And even though the twin boys said not much more than "da-da" and "ma-ma," and tried to toddle on their unsteady legs, Jonathon was already teaching them about science through the world around them. Drake loved to wrestle and play with his children. Eve had revealed the identity of Serena's father. Not his name, as she'd never known his true one, but he had been an angel cast out of heaven for the sin of falling in love with God's first creation of Eve, just as the Grigori were said to have been punished for desiring the daughters of man. Serena hoped to discover more about him someday, but Eve insisted he had been destroyed by his own anger at his dismissal from the heavens. His rage had become a blaze that had consumed him.

Althea's daughter, Serry, had grown into a strong, healthy child. And appeared to be a blend of both mortal and vampire. She could be awake at night or in the day, and loved to eat food, especially sweets. Miranda had helped Althea create a schedule where she could spend time with Serry before the day sleep claimed her. Yannick, the Earl of Brookshire, and Bastien were devoted to the two ladies in their lives—Althea and Serry.

Althea had taken on the task of sorting the Royal Society's books and reports, letters and diaries—a safe duty while her daughter was young. She wanted to hunt with her handsome husbands, but they had just discovered Althea was enceinte again. So there would be no pursuit of rogue vampires for her. Not with such protective men worried about her.

Miranda knew what it was to be cared for by protective men.

There was no precedence in the seating at this table. Jonathon and Drake sat on either side of Serena, as did Yannick and Bastien with Althea. Zayan and Lukos flanked Miranda, determined not to be too far from her side.

And both men were doing naughty things to her beneath the table with their free hands. Yet looked utterly innocent while doing it.

"Oh!" she squeaked as Zayan squeezed her bottom.

Lord Denby paused in the midst of his toast, which included humorous stories of his friend, Sir Edmund. He looked to her.

"Nothing," she mumbled. "Please go on, my lord." But Lukos, the demon, was sliding up her skirt beneath the table.

Denby gave a smile—a far too knowing smile.

Then Sir Edmund held up his hand during a tale about a vampiress who insisted she was Queen Cleopatra, a sultry, raven-haired siren. "Enough of that, Denby. No need to tell that one."

"You are blushing, Father," Althea teased.

Eugenia flashed a gentle, indulgent smile, as her new husband continued, "What of the Royal Society, Denby? I believe it is stronger now that you have cleaned ship."

Denby inclined his head. "It could not be abandoned because there were pockets of corruption. There is too much learning to be achieved, too much good to be done. Perhaps we will not save the world, but if we are open-minded and fortunate, we will learn to understand it better."

"Open-minded. That is very true, Denby," Drake said. "But this is a celebration of love, tonight. No more talk of the Royal Society." He raised his glass to Sir Edmund and Eugenia.

Althea and Serena urged Eugenia to her feet. "I think perhaps it is time to excuse the bride," Althea said, with a wink.

"I should like to make a toast before we go." Holding her glass, Eugenia lifted her glass. With her face aglow, her silvery hair arranged in stylish curls, she looked lovely.

Miranda's belly went rock hard. She gasped at the sudden sensation, then wetness flooded her thighs and her skirts. She jerked to her feet.

"Oh, I think I shall have to leave, I'm afraid. I'm so sorry, Aunt. Please carry on without me." She looked to Zayan's and Lukos's handsome faces. "I think it's time."

Zayan frowned, his black brows drawn together. Lukos cocked his head, surprised. Miranda realized that her husbands did not yet understand. Her gown was wet from the sudden rush of her waters, but now, when she was standing, the flow stopped.

She gave a teasing sigh at the obtuseness of men and saw an answering gleam in Althea's silvery green eyes and Serena's silvery gray ones. The women knew exactly what had happened. Aunt Eugenia wore a smile of delight and a look of busy determination. "There will be time for toasts later. We must go upstairs now."

Miranda clasped the broad shoulders of her two husbands, Lukos and Zayan. "*Our* twins are about to come into the world."

Twelve long hours later, Miranda rested in her bed. Her two baby boys were tucked into the bassinets that had been hastily brought down from the nursery. Lukos slumbered at her side, and Zayan dozed on a chair opposite her.

Miranda knew she should sleep—she would not get much rest for a very long time. Twins. She'd been carrying two boys: One was blond, one dark, and they were both absolutely perfect.

Twinkling lights of claret red swirled in the center of her bedchamber. The lights cleared, to reveal Elizabeth seated on the end of her bed.

The vampire queen bestowed a smile on the newborns. "Congratulations. Eugenia has told me, though, that you have been greatly worried. What could be troubling you, with such happiness in your life?"

Miranda swallowed hard. "I've been thinking about the Prophesy of Lukos—the one that stated his son will kill him. Will it come true? Or is that now null and void, now that he is no longer a vampire, just as he and Ara escaped the warning they would die?"

Elizabeth waved her hand. "Do not worry, gel. Prophesies

are entertaining but completely irrelevant. What did you learn, my dear, as you fell in love with Zayan and Lukos? As you faced the *Pravus* and Lucifer?"

She'd learned so many things. She'd learned about the power of love. She'd learned that her power was not a curse—it had saved the people who meant the most to her. And she'd discovered joy was the most precious treasure of all.

"You learned that you are a powerful woman, whether you have magic powers or not. For you, nothing is written in stone. There is nothing you cannot do and nothing you cannot change. I know that both your sons will grow up to know love. Those predictions written so many years ago will prove to be worthless."

The conviction in Elizabeth's voice made Miranda believe it too. Lukos had escaped his pact with Lucifer, his destiny had been changed. And so had Zayan's.

"You see, don't you?"

Miranda nodded. "Yes, I do see. We've changed the futures."

"Of course you have." Wearing a radiant smile, Elizabeth patted Miranda's knee. "For strong women—those who know the power of love—carve out their own futures, my dear."

Then a little squawk rose up from one of the bassinets. Elizabeth vanished into a cloud of sparkling light, as Zayan and Lukos instantly awoke. Miranda's heart ached with joy as both men devotedly cradled their two newborn sons.

She now had five men of her own to manage, along with a lovely stepdaughter.

Miranda brushed at a tear of happiness. There was work to do now—and she bared her full, heavy, milk-filled breasts in preparation for feeding her beautiful sons.

How she looked forward to the future—for it stretched before them all, golden and bright.